LETTER TO A DUCHESS

ALSO BY NELLIE H. STEELE

Cate Kensie Mysteries
Shadow Slayers Stories
Lily & Cassie by the Sea Mysteries
Pearl Party Mysteries
Middle Age is Murder Cozy Mysteries
Duchess of Blackmoore Mysteries
Maggie Edwards Adventures
Clif & Ri on the Sea Adventures

LETTER TO A DUCHESS
A DUCHESS OF BLACKMOORE MYSTERY

NELLIE H. STEELE

This is a work of fiction. Names, characters, places, and incidents either are the product of the author's imagination or are used fictitiously. Any resemblance to actual persons, living or dead, events, or locales is entirely coincidental.

Copyright © 2022 by Nellie H. Steele

All rights reserved.

No part of this book may be reproduced in any form or by any electronic or mechanical means, including information storage and retrieval systems, without written permission from the author, except for the use of brief quotations in a book review.

Cover design by Stephanie A. Sovak.

❦ Created with Vellum

In loving memory of Mary Sovak

ACKNOWLEDGMENTS

A HUGE thank you to everyone who helped get this book published! Special shout outs to: Stephanie Sovak, Paul Sovak, Michelle Cheplic, Mark D'Angelo and Lori D'Angelo.

Finally, a HUGE thank you to you, the reader!

CHAPTER 1

*B*lackmoore Castle rose high in front of me as I pushed the pram through the gardens below on the last day of October. Samuel, now past seven months of age, gurgled at the cloudy sky above him. Nanny fussed with his coverings, complaining the air to be too chilly and damp for a child to be paraded about the gardens this late in the autumn season.

My eyebrow arched high as I ceased my ambling again and allowed her to adjust and readjust his blankets. I suspected the real issue behind the endless fussing was not the weather but rather my pushing of the pram. Nanny took offense to any "pushing in" on my part with Samuel. She'd told my ladies' maid, Sinclair, she detested a hovering parent as it made her feel we doubted her ability to complete her job. An unfortunate circumstance given my insistence on providing a hands-on approach to my mothering. As the child's mother, I insisted on spending time in the nursery and manning the pram on our garden walks.

Soon, the weather would turn too cold for our daily walks, so I demanded we continue until flakes of snow graced the gardens. As we rounded the corner nearest the path leading to the castle, I heard Nanny harrumph as she gazed upward at the hill.

"Perhaps we should end our walk early," I suggested as she shrugged her cape closer around her.

"If you wish, Your Grace," she answered. "I would like to take the child in and settle him before his meal."

I offered her a smile and a nod. Poor Nanny, I reflected. I did test her limits.

"Please, Your Grace, perhaps I should push," Nanny said as we started up the steep climb to the castle.

"I am perfectly capable of pushing," I assured her. Though today was my nineteenth birthday, I still remained younger than Nanny.

"Of course, Your Grace, though a lady really shouldn't strain herself with such things," Nanny argued. "It is unnecessary. This is what servants are for!"

I suppressed a giggle at Nanny's objections to my unladylike behavior.

"I shall allow you to take the pram the moment we reach the drive," I told her. "I will not even accompany you to the nursery."

"I am capable of transporting the child to the nursery alone, I assure you. I shouldn't like to rob a lady of your stature of valuable time. I am certain you have many more pressing matters in a home of this size."

I hadn't many, to be honest. A lady of my stature in the usual circumstances may have more pressing matters, though, in the course of my first year of marriage, I had received little in the way of invitations and offers. Of course, my humble beginnings as an orphan meant some shied away from me, though I suspected the larger issue stemmed from the revelation throughout society of my odd ability. My reputation preceded me in many instances. My ability to communicate with the dead shocked some and frightened others. Though Robert hemmed and hawed about people's treatment of me, I had grown accustomed to it. It did not bother me. I was content to remain a homebody.

"Thank you, Nanny," I answered. "I appreciate your consideration of my interests."

The gravel crunched under our feet as we crossed the drive and entered the warmth of the castle foyer. Buchanan awaited us, a tray topped with an envelope in his hand.

"Your Grace," he greeted me.

I pulled my gloves from my hands as Nanny lifted Samuel from the pram and scurried away to the nursery. I glanced after her disappearing form, sad I hadn't been able to give Samuel one last goodbye kiss.

Buchanan stood sentinel, awaiting the return of my attention. As Nanny vanished beyond my sight, I returned my gaze to Buchanan.

"For me?" I questioned. Correspondence for me was rare. Despite my position as mistress of Blackmoore Castle, I entertained few friends and received only sporadic invitations.

"Yes, Your Grace," Buchanan answered.

I smiled at him as I grasped the letter from the silver tray. He collected my cape and gloves and left me to ponder my curious missive. I stared at the writing scrawled across the envelope. I did not recognize the handwriting, though I did not expect to.

With a deep inhale, I mounted the stairs and navigated through the halls, climbing another set of circular stairs to my tower room. A blazing fire awaited me. A smile crossed my face as I realized how fortunate I was in my new life.

I sliced open the envelope as I passed by my writing desk on my way to my window seat. I curled under a thick fur blanket and set the opened envelope on my lap next to the book retrieved from my window seat.

After taking in the view, I stared down at the two objects in my lap. On the left, a copy of *The Notting Hill Mystery*. Published earlier this year, having a mystery so new to read thrilled me.

My fingers caressed the book's binding. I smiled down at it, recalling earlier this morning when I'd found it wrapped in a ribbon on my empty breakfast plate. I remembered the slight half-smile on my husband, Robert's, face when I picked up the book, a confused expression on my face.

"'Tis a new type of novel," he exclaimed.

I cocked my head in a questioning manner.

"It is a detective novel!" he said, his grin broadening.

"Detective novel?" I questioned.

"Yes, yes," he said with a nod. "It is a murder mystery. Oh, I hope you do not find it too unsettling given the subject matter."

"How interesting," I replied. "I am sure I will enjoy it."

"It was originally published as a serial in eight parts. Though earlier this year, the parts were collated and put together in one book."

"I am very pleased. Thank you, Robert."

"Of course, dear," he said as our breakfast was served.

Admittedly, the idea intrigued me the moment I received it.

Though I was eager to delve into the mystery, the book would prove to be only the first of the birthday gifts Robert showered upon me. After breakfast, Robert ushered me into the sitting room.

"Here on the eve of the new year, I presented you with the first gift as your husband. Do you remember?" he inquired, an amused grin on his face.

I answered his question with a question. "How could I

forget?" The yellow and blue sapphire necklace framed with diamonds was so ostentatious I'd never seen anything like it in my life.

Robert spun to face me, concern crossing his face. "You do fancy it, do you not?"

A chuckle escaped me. "Fancy it? Robert, there is not a woman alive who would not fancy it! Its beauty is astounding!"

Robert narrowed his eyes at me. "You are not just any woman, Lenora."

"Yes," I assured him. "I adore the necklace." He grinned. "BUT," I added, "not because of its value, but because it was the first gift you gave to me."

Robert crossed the large room and tugged open the drawer on the table near his favorite wing-backed chair. He brandished a small velvet box. I raised my eyebrows at the thin rectangular box he presented to me, then glanced up at Robert, cocking my head to the side.

Robert's devilish grin returned as he popped open the box.

"Robert!" I exclaimed as my eyes fell upon the object inside. Limned against the black velvet lay a yellow and blue sapphire bracelet.

"A match for your necklace," he exclaimed.

"You spoil me too much," I said.

"Impossible. I hope you fancy it as much as the necklace."

"I adore it," I said as he fastened it on my wrist.

"I wavered between this and a ruby, but the sapphires remind me so of your eyes, I could not resist it."

"I simply love it," I assured him. "Though I would love any gift you give me, dear."

He raised his eyebrows at me as he slid the velvet box onto the table. "I hope that holds true."

"Why would it not?" I questioned.

He raised a finger in the air. "I have one additional gift for you. I hope to achieve your approval on the triumvirate!"

I drew in a deep breath. "Another?" I exclaimed. "Robert, it is too much."

"You are a duchess, Lenora! You must learn to enjoy the finer things! A book and bracelet are hardly spoiling!"

I glanced around the room in search of the other trinket he may have produced. As my gaze settled upon Robert and his coy expression again, he offered a half-smile and his hand.

"Come, Lenora."

I accepted his hand and he led me to the foyer. Buchanan awaited with our cloaks. Robert settled mine around my shoulders before donning his.

We stepped out into the cool October air. Gray clouds rolled across the sky at a fast clip. I glanced around our front drive. What could Robert possibly be gifting me outside? Perhaps a new flowering bush or tree.

"Close your eyes," he prompted.

I furrowed my brow at him. "Close them!" he repeated.

I humored him, squeezing my eyes shut. I experienced the sensation of being swept off my feet. A yelp escaped from me as I clutched at Robert's shoulders.

"Keep your eyes closed," he instructed as he carried me to a location unbeknownst to me.

"Where are we going?" I inquired.

"Patience, Lenora. No peeking."

"I am not peeking."

We ceased forward motion. "Keep your eyes closed," he said as he set my feet on the ground. "Are they closed?"

A smile spread across my features. "Yes!" I insisted. I felt Robert's hands cover my eyes.

"Ready?"

I nodded. "Yes," I said.

He removed his hands and my eyelids fluttered open. I glanced around, my gaze settling on the large object in front of me. A glorious all-white horse stood grandly in front of me. Its front leg cocked as it stood in a pose, tail flicking and head held high. Blue ribbons were braided into its white mane and threaded through her expertly groomed tail.

I twisted to face Robert. He strode to the horse, patting its neck and beckoned for me to join him. "Lenora, meet your new horse."

I approached the beautiful creature and caressed its nose. "What is the name?" I inquired.

"That is for you to determine. She will be your mare."

"She is beautiful," I answered. "Though I will miss Lady. She hasn't..." I began as I turned my head sharply to Robert.

"No, dear," he answered. "Lady is happily in her stall. And you are welcome to ride her at any time. But I thought you may like a more spirited ride now that your riding skills have progressed."

"I do not mind Lady's meandering," I answered. I turned my eyes back to the white horse. "Though I will not object to riding this beauty."

Robert grinned at me. "Perhaps you have stumbled upon a name for her," he suggested. "Beauty."

"A very fitting name," I agreed. "Though..."

"You have another?" he inquired.

I smiled at her. "Yes. Snow White."

"Named after a literary character. Very appropriate for you, Lenora."

* * *

My eyes fell to my first birthday gift. Very appropriate, indeed, my mind concluded. My reminiscence almost caused me to forget the letter I'd received entirely. I found myself eager to continue the novel I'd begun earlier after meeting my new steed. Though my eagerness was tempered by my curiosity. My gaze shifted to the envelope addressed to Mrs. Robert Fletcher, Duchess of Blackmoore.

My brow crinkled as I considered the sender. As Robert's second wife, I'd received little correspondence over my first year as mistress of Blackmoore Castle. As I settled in to my life here, I assumed my humble beginnings would facilitate few invitations. Still, there had been some. Though most of those came addressed to Robert rather than me.

I shoved my book aside and pulled the correspondence from inside.

As I unfurled the paper, I noted the shaky scrawl of the handwriting. I pondered who the writer may be as I began my perusal of the note.

My dearest sister-in-law Lenora,

I write you in the hopes you will take pity on me and offer your unique assistance. I have found myself in a spot of terrible trouble and have no one else to which I can turn.

I realize we are not close, but please know I require your help more than you can imagine.

I am ashamed to recount my tale of woe to you, Lenora. I can imagine you will shake your head in disgust. You may even refuse to help me, finding my circumstances a result of my own poor choices. If you choose that, I shall accept the outcome. Though I beg you to take pity on me, your wayward brother-in-law.

On the night of 15 October, I imbibed a fair amount of alcohol. Later that evening, a drinking companion of mine, Gerard Boyle, was reported for drunken behavior near the docks. When the police arrived, they found him face down. Assuming him passed out from the drink, the lawmen attempted to revive him. Unfortunately, for both me and my companion, they realized he was no longer of this earth.

A knife stuck from his chest and blood pooled under him. I apologize for the vulgar details, but it is important for you to understand what you may involve yourself in. And I pray you do, for my sake.

You see, Lenora, following Gerard's murder, I was taken into custody by Glasgow police officers. I have spent my time since in a small cell. While I have been accused of this terrible crime, I did not kill Gerard.

Lenora, you must believe me! Even in my drunken state, I did not kill the man. I swear on my life, Lenora, and beg of you to believe me.

I also beg for your help. I have no one else to which I can seek assistance. I have no funds by which to seek legal counsel. I have no way to prove my innocence. And I swear to you, I am innocent. Please, Lenora, can you help me?

You realize the relationship or lack thereof between Robert and me following the fallout of the revelation of my involvement in his first wife's demise. I am certain he would disapprove of this correspondence.

While I am reluctant to ask you to keep this information from your husband, I fear I may risk any assistance if he becomes aware of my writing to you. Please use your discretion.

I await your response, though understand if I should receive none.

Yours in hope,
　Edwin

CHAPTER 2

I swallowed hard as I read the letter. Edwin, accused of murder? Edwin's list of transgressions may be long, but murder? I could not fathom it. He'd been complicit in Annie's death, yes. But not guilty of it himself. He hadn't shoved her from the tower room. He'd merely known and allowed those around him to believe Robert's first wife had thrown herself rather than implicate his business associate, Sir Richard Prescott.

I pondered it again. Perhaps I was being naive and short-sighted. Edwin had saved my life when I ran from Richard Prescott's deadly grip. Perhaps this colored my judgement.

Still, I considered as my eyes scanned the words on the page again, he had requested my help.

His letter mentioned Robert. My thoughts turned to my husband, Edwin's older brother. I imagined Robert's reaction to the request. My mind failed to concoct any scenarios in which the conversation did not turn ugly.

With a sigh, I allowed the pages of Edwin's letter to fall from my fingers to my lap. I would give the matter consideration and hope an acceptable solution presented itself.

I'd kept mum about the letter during our dinner. We spent our meal conversing about Samuel's development. At seven months old already, he'd grown leaps and bounds and had even begun to babble. I'd kept my receipt of the letter secret. It felt disingenuous though I had not yet determined the best course to take with the discussion.

I climbed to my bedroom after our meal and, with Sinclair's help, changed into my nightclothes. I'd settled on my chaise near the cozy fire and forced my mind to focus on my book.

I found the task impossible. My mind returned to Edwin's plea for help. I pulled his letter from the pocket of my dressing gown where I had concealed it earlier. I read the words scrawled across the page again.

My mind clouded. The fallout between Robert and Edwin had been colossal. Their relationship, tenuous even in the best of times, fell to pieces when Edwin's involvement in Annie Fletcher's death was revealed. I bit my lower lip. I could not request this of my husband. I stood and approached the fireplace. Flames leapt and danced inside. I held the letter toward them, intending to toss it away and remove it from my mind.

I did not wish to upset the balance of my household, nor my husband. I was grateful for the life Robert provided me and did not wish to be a thorn in his side. Reminding him of and forcing a discussion about his brother, Edwin, may achieve just that.

The edges of the paper blackened and curled. As the flames threatened to obliterate the papers clutched in my hand, a sudden misgiving struck me. I snatched them back before they could burn completely. Snuffing out any smoldering embers, I folded the papers and placed them in the envelope, hiding them within the pocket of my dressing gown.

I would give it a night's sleep before making my final decision. With the matter settled for now, I returned my attention to my detective novel.

* * *

I tossed and turned in my bed for the first part of the evening. Indecision weighed heavily on my mind. I fretted over the appropriate course of action. I had no desire to quarrel with my husband over his estranged brother. Yet I had difficulty accepting the concept of refusing help to Edwin.

Silly, perhaps, given his previous indiscretions. But the man had saved my life. And perhaps Robert's on the fateful day when he'd been shot. Prior mistakes aside, I was indebted to him. Wasn't I?

My mind continued to wrestle with the decision as my eyelids became heavy enough to close. I drifted off to sleep with Edwin's letter swimming through my thoughts.

* * *

My eyelids fluttered open and I glanced around the room. I lay on my back. Dying embers glowed in the fireplace, casting long shadows in the room. An icy chill passed over me and I drew the covers up further. What had awakened me, I wondered?

The cold subsided as I snuggled under my bed coverings and closed my eyes. The frigid air tickled my cheek again and a whispering noise filled the room. I snapped my eyes open and glanced around the dimly lit space.

I squinted into the darkness that was my sitting room. My brows knit and I pushed myself to sitting. A figure huddled in my armchair.

"Who is it?" I called out. "Who is there?"

Sobbing reached my ears. I frowned, assuming the sound to be coming from a disturbed member of the dearly departed. The poor soul must need some assistance. As loathe as I was to climb from the warmth of my bed, I decided the spirit needed my attention.

I shoved the bedcovers aside and slipped into my slippers. With a yawn, I plodded across the room as I pulled on my dressing gown.

I slowed as I approached the doorway leading to the sitting room. Unable to identify the figure, I stepped over the threshold. As I closed the distance between us, I recognized the form was a man. He buried his face in his hands as sobs wracked his shoulders.

"Hello?" I called, forming my single spoken word as a question.

I received no response beyond the wretched crying. The man hunched over further as I reached for him.

"Hello? Sir?" I inquired again. I reached out toward him again. My fingers found purchase, wrapping around his broad shoulder. I felt the tweed fabric scratch against my fingertips as I closed my grip.

The man lifted his head and turned toward me. I released my grasp on his shoulder, stumbling backward several steps. My jaw fell agape and my eyes went wide. It took me several breaths to recover my senses and speak again.

I stared into his gray eyes and spoke another single word, my voice filled with disbelief. "Edwin?" I gasped.

He stared at me but offered no response. His tear-stained cheeks gleamed in the dim red light of the dying fire.

I swallowed hard, shoving aside my shock. I straightened and pulled my dressing gown tighter around me. "Edwin, how have you come to be here? Were you released from jail?"

Edwin still did not answer. Another sob escaped him and he twisted away from me.

"Edwin…" I began before the whispering noise returned.

Cool air rustled my loose hair. I rubbed the back of my neck as I searched for the source of the whispering. It did not come from Edwin's direction. Who else had entered my bedchambers in the wee hours of the morning?

I searched the darkness. The noise sounded again. This time, I could identify it as a quiet voice.

"Lenora," I made out as the hushed voice called to me again.

"Who is it? Who is there?"

"Lenora," the voice hissed again. Female, I noted. Had Edwin brought a woman with him?

Movement caught my eye. Light pink fabric floated from within the confines of my bedroom. The color stood out against the darkness as it moved toward me.

A figure appeared in the doorway, eliciting another gasp from me. I clutched at my robe as I recognized the soul standing in my doorway.

"Tilly!" I cried.

Her blonde hair framed her rosy complexion. Her golden locks flowed down her back. In her death, my friend remained as beautiful as she had in life.

Tilly offered me a weak smile before a tear fell to her cheek. I rushed toward her.

"Tilly, what is it? Samuel is fine!" I assured her. My mind worried he may not be. Had Tilly arrived to warn me of some harm to my child? "Isn't he?"

I began to fret over his condition when she touched my arm. "He is fine, Lenora," she said.

I breathed a sigh of relief. "Oh, thank heavens. I have tried my best to provide him with all the love and care he deserves. All the love and care you cannot give him."

Another sad smile from Tilly. The child she had died giving birth to now lived within Blackmoore Castle's walls. Robert and I had taken the orphan in when Tilly, visiting me after her death, begged me to provide for him. I could not refuse her this final request.

Or what I considered at the time her final request. It appeared, though, she had another.

"What is it, then, Tilly?" I inquired of her again.

She glanced at me before her green eyes flitted across the room. I followed her gaze. She stared at Edwin's huddled form.

My forehead crinkled. "Edwin?" I questioned. "What of him?"

I struggled to see the connection between my friend from my orphanage days and Robert's ne'er-do-well brother.

"Help him, Lenora," she said.

I cocked my head at her request.

"Please," she begged, tears forming in her emerald eyes. "Help him, Lenora."

For a moment, I remained stunned by the request. Tears glistened on Tilly's cheeks as she grasped my hand and squeezed.

I opened my mouth to respond, when she squeezed my hand tighter. "Please," she choked.

She pulled something from within the pocket of her dress. Her brow wrinkled as she stared at it, then raised her eyes to meet mine. She handed me the letter from Edwin. How had she gotten the letter, my mind pondered. I had placed it within the pocket of my dressing gown.

My brow furrowed, but I found myself nodding in response to her question. As I opened my mouth to question her further, wind whipped through the room. The leaded window pane in my bedroom blew open and banged against the wall.

I shoved Tilly behind me as another gust tore through the room. I fought my way through the gales and grasped the handle. With all my might, I struggled to push the window shut and latch it.

Out of breath, I spun and pressed my back against the wall as I sucked in air. Only then did I notice I was now alone in the room. I took two steps toward the sitting room, though it was obviously empty. Before I could enter the other space for a full search, the window unlatched and blew in a second time. Thunder boomed overhead and another rush of cold autumn air blasted me. It knocked me to my knees.

Then another howling swept through the air. The unearthly sound frightened me and I scrambled on hands and knees around the corner of the bed, putting as much distance between myself and the open window as possible.

I huddled on the floor with the bed sheltering me. The winds picked up and the bed began to move. It inched across the floor with a sickening scraping noise that made the hairs on the back of my neck stand up. I attempted to climb to my feet, but the floor had become slick with rain that poured in from the open window. I slipped and slid, unable to gain my footing.

The bed continued to push at me, and I found myself unable to move from its path. I searched for anything to grasp and hang on to. The bed frame began to move faster, gliding on the water covering the slick floor. As the wall rushed toward me, I opened my mouth wide in a scream.

CHAPTER 3

I bolted upright to sitting as I gasped for breath. My own shrieking had awoken me from the nightmare I suffered. I glanced around the space of my bedroom suite. I was alone. Not even the remnants of a spirit stalked the space. The windows, thankfully, remained closed.

Despite the lack of cool air blowing in, a chill crept over me, and I tugged the covers higher. My mind considered the odd dream I'd experienced.

Before I could give it much more thought, the doors to my suite burst open. In the dim light, I made out the form of Robert in his dressing gown. He raced toward me, his eyes scanning the darkened room.

"Lenora?" he called to me.

"Oh, Robert," I answered as he reached the bed.

"Are you quite all right? I heard a terrible shriek. It sounded as though it came from your room."

I sighed and grasped his hand. "Yes. Yes, I'm quite all right."

He glanced around again. "No… spirits?"

"No," I assured him with a shake of my head. "I'm afraid I've suffered from an ordinary nightmare."

He eased onto the bed next to me, taking both of my hands. "Nightmare?"

"Yes, a nightmare. I am sorry to have woken you."

"You needn't apologize, Lenora. I am sorry you suffered the nightmare. Was it quite terrible? Oh, forgive my inquiry if you prefer not to speak of it."

"It wasn't very terrible," I admitted as the shock of the dream wore off. "Just odd."

He nodded in understanding. "Would you prefer I stay?"

"It isn't necessary," I answered. "I would have preferred not to interrupt your rest."

"It is not an interruption, Lenora. I shall stay. Will you be able to sleep? Should I ring for Buchanan to fetch a toddy?"

"That is not necessary. I am not fragile. I do not need a hot toddy shoved into my hands at every turn, Robert."

"Mother always found it a suitable solution," Robert answered.

"Perhaps your mother was not as willful as I," I answered as Robert adjusted the covers around me.

He chuckled at my remark. "I dare say she was not."

"There you have it, then," I remarked.

"I suppose so. Well, toddy or not, I hope you are able to return to your slumber." He kissed my forehead and caressed my cheek.

I grasped his hand and squeezed. "Thank you," I murmured. I kissed his fingers before closing my eyes and drifting off to a dreamless sleep.

* * *

When I awoke the next morning, I found myself alone. The shelf clock across the room ticked the time away. I squinted at it, sure the time was incorrect. I'd slept later than I'd intended. Likely Robert had informed Sinclair, my ladies' maid, not to disturb me.

As I hurried from my bed, I spotted a note on my night table. I recognized Robert's handwriting as I flipped open the missive.

Lenora - Do not be cross with me if you sleep late. When I awoke, you remained asleep and looked so peaceful, almost angelic, I did not wish to disturb you. I have instructed Sinclair to attend to other duties until you arise and call for her. While you are not fragile, you still need your rest. I insist upon it as your husband. You would do well to heed my instructions, lest you break your wedding vows.

Robert

I imagined the coy expression on his face as he scrawled the final line. Robert played the husband card when he hoped to convince me of something he felt I disagreed with. I had grown accustomed to Robert's fussing over me during our first year of marriage. As inexperienced as I was with being cared for, I must admit, I had grown fond of it.

I smiled at the note as I slid my feet into my slippers and padded across the room to pull the wall bell. I slid Robert's note into the pocket of my dressing gown. As I did, my fingertips touched another piece of paper hidden there.

Details of my nightmare rushed into my mind, along with the particulars of Edwin's request. It elicited another sigh from me as I realized I must make a decision. Tilly's plea echoed in my mind. I recalled her tear-stained cheeks as she begged me to assist Edwin. Why had she insisted, I wondered as I sank onto my chaise?

The door opened, interrupting my thoughts. Sinclair rushed into the room. "Oh, Your Grace," she said, puffing with exertion. "You poor dear. Have you managed to get some rest?"

"Yes," I answered. "Have you run here, Sinclair?"

She gulped another breath as she nodded. "Yes, I came as quickly as I could. I imagine you are starved. Oh," she fretted, "I should have had a tray sent up as soon as I heard the bell."

I shook my head. "It isn't necessary, Sinclair. I am not famished enough to prefer eating in my dressing gown."

"We shall get you dressed at once, Your Grace," she said. Sinclair flitted about the room, preparing my clothes for the day. I returned to my introspection as I shambled to my vanity and plopped onto the seat.

The brushing of my hair roused me from my own thoughts. My eyes met Sinclair's in the mirror and I smiled.

"Are you quite sure you're all right, Your Grace? His Grace said you had a terrible night and were not to be disturbed."

My smile broadened. "Of course he did," I murmured. "I had a nightmare. Not quite as terrible as His Grace imagines, but perhaps once he learns the true reason behind it, he may find it worse than he expected."

Sinclair lowered her eyes to my hair and raised her eyebrows. In the months we'd spent together, Sinclair and I had developed our own language. This was her silent signal for me to continue should I like to discuss it, though she would not press the matter in the event I preferred not to speak of it.

"May I confide in you?" I questioned.

"Of course, Your Grace," she answered. "You know you may and I shall never betray your confidence. Not even to His Grace."

Sinclair understood my meaning perfectly. Though I detested forcing her to keep secrets on my behalf, I imagined she would not have to hold on to this one for long.

"I received a letter from Lord Edwin, His Grace's brother."

Sinclair's eyebrows rose higher on her forehead as she motioned for me to stand and begin dressing. "Gotten himself into some trouble, I imagine?"

"Trouble is putting it mildly," I answered. I paused for a moment as I slipped into my dress and Sinclair began fastening it. "He has been accused of murder."

I felt the fastening of my dress go slack before Sinclair resumed her work.

"I had the same reaction," I said.

"Why did he contact you, Your Grace?"

"He has asked for my assistance. He swears he is innocent."

"Do you believe him?"

I pursed my lips as I considered it. My momentary silence seemed to answer the question for Sinclair.

"What will you do?"

I shook my head. "I'm afraid the answer to that remains unclear to me." I sauntered to the vanity again as Sinclair finished fastening my dress and seated myself in front of the mirror. Sinclair began to sweep my hair into its usual style.

"What options have you?"

"If I plan to offer my assistance, Robert must be informed. A conversation I am loathe to have with him."

Sinclair nodded, understanding well the obvious reasons for my reluctance.

"The other option is to ignore it."

"That option provides no disturbances for His Grace. The household's balance would not be upset."

I nodded.

"But that option does not please you," she continued, her eyes meeting mine in the mirror. How well she could read me.

I shook my head. "It does not."

"Then you suspect he may be being truthful with you."

"I find the prospect of Lord Edwin as a murderer surprising, even given his rather wanton predilections."

She stopped and stared at me through the mirror. "Is there more?"

"I suffered from a nightmare last night," I answered as Sinclair returned to my hairstyle. "Lord Edwin sat in that chair, weeping."

"It is unsurprising you'd dream of him. No doubt the situation has weighed on your mind heavily."

"There's more. And it is the reason my indecisiveness has been lessened. After identifying Lord Edwin, I noted the presence of another." Sinclair finished with my hair and I twisted to face her. "Tilly visited me."

"Your friend from the orphanage? The one who gave birth to Samuel."

"Samuel's mother, yes," I confirmed.

Sinclair offered me a slight smile. "You are Samuel's mother, Your Grace."

I understood her meaning and appreciated her support. "So was she. Anyway," I pressed on, "tears filled her eyes. I thought perhaps something was amiss with Samuel. But Tilly said no. Instead, she pleaded with me to help Lord Edwin."

Sinclair's brow furrowed. "Why?"

I shook my head and shrugged my shoulders. "I haven't the slightest clue. Though it seemed very important to her."

"Perhaps your mind is playing tricks on you, Your Grace. Tilly has not visited you during your waking hours, has she?"

"No," I admitted. "No, she hasn't. And you make a valid point. Perhaps my dream was nothing more than my wavering mind attempting to piece together a solution. Perhaps I am searching for any way to justify the impending conflict between Robert and myself."

Sinclair remained silent on the matter, unwilling to offer her opinion on whether or not I should choose to quarrel with my husband.

She finished her duties within my chambers and stood in front of me with a dress draped over her arm. "I am taking this for mending," she announced.

I nodded to her as I sank my chin into my hand, my elbow balanced against my vanity. Sinclair curtsied and strode to the door. As she pulled it open, she spun to face me.

"Whatever you decide, Your Grace, I am sure it will be the best decision you can make in the situation." With a nod, she stepped out and pulled the door shut behind her.

I returned to my introspection. My fingers found the letter from Edwin. I opened it and scanned the words again. My heart twisted in a knot as I explored my options. I weighed the odds of his guilt, considered the uproar it may cause within the household, and struggled to wrap my mind around my dream.

With a sigh, I stood, intent on visiting with Samuel before reading in my tower room. My mystery novel held little sway over me, an odd sensation as reading usually served as my refuge.

After my morning visit with my ever-growing son, who I swear had sprouted even taller than when I'd seen him only hours ago, I climbed to my tower room. I sat with my book in my lap and pondered the situation again.

As I dissected the conversation with Sinclair, I considered a poignant point she'd made. Tilly had come to me in a dream, not during my waking hours. My usual communication with the dead occurred when I was awake and conscious. Though dreams involving them were not out of the ordinary for me, why had Tilly not chosen to consult with me directly?

Perhaps, I conjectured, it was because Tilly was not the source of the message. Perhaps the source was my own mind.

There may be a simple way to test the theory. I set my book aside and swung my legs over the side of my window seat. I scanned the space, then cleared my throat.

"Tilly?" I called into the empty room.

I scoured the room again, searching for any sign of her. My little cherrywood writing desk sat on the adjacent wall. Near it, my chaise lounge stretched into the room. I shifted my eyes toward the fireplace. Flames roared inside it, leaping and dancing toward the chimney. I continued my examination, ending at the bookshelf across the room, filled with many of my treasured tomes.

Nothing belied Tilly's presence.

"Tilly!" I called again. "Are you there? Can you speak to me?"

I waited a few more moments, holding every muscle in my body taut. After a time, my shoulders slumped and I released my tense posture with a sigh.

Nothing. Tilly did not appear. She did not want to speak. Or she could not. Either way, I would receive no information from Tilly. I could not confirm if she had been the true source of the emotional plea to assist Edwin or if my own mind had been.

I sucked in a deep breath and shoved my blanket aside. I could not concentrate on reading any further. Perhaps a walk would clear my mind.

I rose and crossed the room to the circular staircase leading to the floors below. After one last glance into the room, I placed my foot on the first stair leading down.

As I stepped forward, a burst of frosty air rushed past me. With it, a whisper tickled my ears. "Help him, Lenora."

I halted mid-step and clamored back up into the tower.

"Tilly!" I gasped. My eyes shot around the room as I searched for her. "Tilly?"

Breathless, I waited for some sign of her. None existed. No flutter of fabric, whiff of perfume, or glint of her golden hair.

"Tilly?" I tried again in a weak croak. "Was it really you?" I added in a whisper as my heart sank.

"Really who?" Another voice answered my query.

Startled, I leapt in surprise, spinning to face the room's other occupant. Robert stood, his hands clasped behind his back in his usual manner.

"Oh," I said, my voice faltering as I sought to explain. "I swore I heard a voice. I assumed it a visiting spirit."

Robert's face expressed discomfort and his eyes flitted around the room. He remained uncomfortable with the idea of spirits roaming about the earth, unseen by most, including him.

"There is no one here," I assured him.

His shoulders relaxed and he breathed a sigh of relief. His gaze met mine again. His brows knit and he inquired, "The voice?"

I lifted one shoulder in response and shook my head. "Unidentified."

"Perhaps the spirit is shy," he suggested.

The comment made me chuckle. "It is good to hear you joke about such things. I realize how my situation disturbs you."

"It is becoming normal to me." His posture betrayed the untruth of the statement, but the fact that he made it at all suggested he was making strides toward accepting it. "Anyway, I sought you out to determine if you would like to ride with me." He glanced to the large window overlooking the estate and motioned toward it.

I glanced at the gray November sky. No precipitation fell from the clouds, but no sign of the sun presented itself.

"The weather is not very terrible. Though you may want your cape," he continued.

"I would love to," I answered.

The response brought a surprised smile to his face. He held out his arm to escort me. I accepted it, feeling somewhat disingenuous about withholding my secret from him. I did not wish to ruin our ride, so I remained mum on the situation. My new steed proved more spirited than Lady, though my newly acquired riding skills allowed me to control her without much trouble.

"I am so pleased you were not put off riding when Lady spirited you across the estate at breakneck speeds."

I chuckled. "That was not Lady's fault," I reminded him. "And it did help us solve the mystery."

He nodded with a closed-mouth smile. Speaking of his late first wife still disturbed him, I realized. Though he did so more easily than he had in the past. I hoped the closure to her death aided in this. Perhaps he would not be so closed-minded as I assumed regarding Edwin. Perhaps time did heal wounds.

As we parted ways after the ride, I spent time with Samuel. Robert had a lunch engagement in town, leaving the two of us to spend the afternoon alone in the castle. Even my son could not pry my thoughts from my situation.

I pulled the child into my arms as I sat on the floor with him. He waved a wooden block around in his chubby fingers.

"Did your mum visit me earlier?" I whispered as I kissed the dark hair on his head.

He babbled incoherently in response.

"I wish she'd have been more forthcoming if she, indeed, visited."

Samuel leaned forward and reached for another toy. I

released him from my arms and allowed him to lay on the thick rug on the floor. He kicked his legs and squirmed as he reached for the teddy bear Robert bought him. Before I could retrieve it for him, he surged forward, pulling with his arms. He reached the item and giggled as he grasped it.

I clapped my hands in utter delight. He had begun to crawl!

"What a fantastic job, Sam!" I exclaimed. He swiveled his small head to face me, his eyes dancing with glee. The smile on my face faltered and my brows knit together. His once blue eyes appeared different to me, grayer.

Before I could study them further, Nanny West swept into the room.

"Nanny!" I exclaimed. "Samuel has begun to take the initiative to crawl!"

She grunted as she bustled about the room, tidying his toys.

"It marks a milestone in his development," I continued.

"He'll be walking soon enough," she answered. "And then we shall have our hands full!"

"I am certain!" I said as I climbed to my feet. "I daresay the moment he takes his first steps, Robert will be purchasing a horse for him to begin riding."

This comment earned a chuckle from Nanny West. "His Grace has requested I place him on the rocking horse once per day to ready him for the experience of riding."

Her admission brought a giggle to my lips. "His Grace was so pleased with that purchase. He spoke of Sam's first pony the day he was born."

"I am not surprised, Your Grace," Nanny West answered. "May I take the little sir for his nap?"

"Yes." I scooped Samuel from the floor and pressed my lips against his forehead. "Rest well, little one."

Nanny West relieved me of the child, and I watched as

she disappeared from the room with him in her arms. She cooed at him as he gurgled and kicked his small legs. Though she may disapprove of my parenting, Nanny West genuinely cared for Sam and provided competent supervision. It had been the entire reason I chose her.

As they disappeared from my sight, I let out a long breath and picked up Sam's stuffed bear from the floor. I set it on the shelf. My eyes wandered to the object displayed prominently over the room's fireplace.

The large model ship sat atop its stand, its sails starched to appear as though they billowed in the wind. My fingers caressed the object as Edwin invaded my mind's eye again. The ship, a gift for Samuel from Edwin, brought my dilemma flooding back to me.

I could not continue to waffle, I told myself. I must make a decision. I decided to take what remained of the afternoon in contemplation. I nodded as if to affirm the decision in my mind before I sauntered across the nursery's playroom.

As I reached the door, I glanced back at the proud ship on the mantel. A chill ran down my spine as a whisper tickled my ear. "Help him, Lenora."

CHAPTER 4

I recognized Tilly's voice. I whipped toward the sound but found no one. "Tilly!" I called but to no avail. She would not show herself.

Regardless, I now realized my decision was made. I could no longer question Tilly's presence. She was here, if not wholly, a piece of her. And this marked the third occasion she had requested my help.

I could not deny her this. I would not. Not even if it meant personal strife. I would help Edwin. And I would start this evening.

* * *

I pushed the carrots around in the stew's juice as we dined that evening. We'd made it to the main course without my mentioning Edwin's letter. My reluctance to face the matter head on frustrated me. Yet I could not bring myself to say the words.

Why prolong it, my mind questioned? I bit into a tender

carrot and chewed as I allowed the words to form in my mind before they left my lips.

I swallowed the carrot and lifted my eyes to Robert. He glanced at me and offered a closed-mouth smile as he chewed his beef.

"Did you enjoy the ride today?" he asked.

"Quite," I replied.

"And how did you find the horse? You did not say."

"Snow White is very lovely. Much more spirited than Lady, but I appreciate the challenge."

Robert smiled again. "I am so glad to hear it. I worried you may have been disappointed."

"Not at all."

Silence fell between us for a moment. "Nanny West informed me you have encouraged her to place Samuel on his rocking horse daily."

"Ah, yes. It is my hope that it acclimates him to the horse at a young age."

"So she said. He made his first strides at crawling today."

"It will not be long before we're buying his first pony."

Robert's love for horses made me chuckle. He looked eagerly toward teaching our son to ride. The light conversation had dampened my verve to bring up the next subject. I returned to pushing my food around on my plate.

I swallowed hard and summoned all my courage. "I received a letter from Edwin," I announced, my eyes never leaving the plate.

I shut them as the sounds of Robert's fork clattering to his plate resounded in our dining space. He cleared his throat, glancing around the room as though someone else had spoken. After a moment, he said, "What?"

I set my fork down and wiped at my mouth with my napkin before returning it to my lap. I licked my lips and raised my eyes to meet Robert's gaze. "I had a letter from Edwin," I repeated.

His eyes went wide and his jaw tightened. His hands curled into fists. "What the devil does he mean contacting my wife?"

"He has requested my help."

"Your help?" he shouted. "Good Lord, what has he gotten himself into now?"

I saw no reason not to approach the conversation bluntly. "He has been accused of murder."

Robert's jaw gaped open and his eyebrows shot skyward. "What?"

I pulled the missive from within the folds of my dress. "He maintains his innocence," I began.

Robert's bellowing interrupted me. "Of course he bloody does! The man can take no responsibility for his own actions. The coward!"

I remained silent, allowing the initial expected bout of anger to blow over. Robert ceased his tirade and glanced at me. His shoulders dropped and he lowered his voice. "Oh, I am sorry, Lenora. I did not mean to shout at you."

I offered a slight smile. "Edwin's antics disturb me so," he added.

"I realized this would be a difficult conversation. Perhaps I should have waited until after our meal."

He waved away my concern. "No, of course not. I apologize in earnest, Lenora. You attempted to be honest with me, only to be met with my temper. It was not directed at you, I assure you. And again, my sincerest apologies for my outburst."

I remained silent, bracing myself as I realized the worst was yet to come. Robert continued, "You may discard the letter. I have no desire to see it."

He retrieved his abandoned fork and stabbed at a piece of beef.

"The truth is," I began before pausing to swallow the lump building in my throat. I glanced up at him. "I considered discarding it but found myself unable."

"Unable?" he questioned.

I hesitated a few breaths before answering. "Yes," I said. I gripped the letter tightly. "I almost burned it. Yet…"

"Go on," Robert encouraged, though I was certain he would regret this statement.

"I could not. I feel drawn to help him." There, I had said it. Let the fireworks begin.

"Drawn to help him? Lenora, have you gone mad?"

"No," I said, keeping my voice calm and measured. "I… I believe him."

His eyes searched above him as though he hoped for some divine intervention to assist him in making sense of the conversation. He shook his head and uttered a single word in response. "No."

I furrowed my brow, unsure of his meaning.

"What?" I questioned.

He squared his jaw and set his gaze upon me. "No," he repeated. "I will not allow it."

I raised my eyebrows and he repeated his statement. "I simply will not allow it, Lenora."

"Robert," I began, motioning toward the parchment clutched in my hand.

"I said no!" he bellowed, slamming his fists on the table with such force that the dishes clattered. The noise gave me a start. "I will not allow my wife to become involved in this sordid business. Whatever scandal Edwin has brought upon himself will not invade our household."

I set my face, unimpressed with the conversation. Perhaps it was unladylike of me, but Robert's behavior raised my ire.

Independence may not be a virtue prized in women, but I valued mine.

He noted my expression and continued to defend his position. "I will not have it, Lenora! I am your husband! I am responsible for you and your well-being. I shall not have you exposed to this vulgarity."

With a sigh, I readied my defense. "This could cost Edwin his life."

Robert waved his hand dismissively. "Given the Fletcher name, he should incur no severely adverse punishments."

"That is untrue," I argued. "Judges are becoming increasingly harsh on the gentry."

"This is not a trend I am aware of."

"Really?" I said with a raise of my eyebrows. "Then allow me to inform you of it. Less than a decade ago, the police arrested Randolph MacKenzie, Earl of Dunhavenshire, for murder. They planned to seek the death penalty for the crime. Had it not been for his clever cousin and his cousin's wife, he may not be with us today."

Robert played coy. The edges of his mouth turned down as he raised his eyebrows. "I had not heard of it."

"Now you have."

"Are you certain you have all the facts correct?"

"Yes," I said, doing all I could to restrain my temper, "and I have them straight from Lord MacKenzie himself. He informed me of the wild tale at the Williams' house party."

"How dreadful for him," Robert said.

"Edwin could suffer a similar fate. Are you willing to allow your brother to undergo this torture when he may be innocent?"

"And what if he is not? Make no mistake, Lenora, Edwin is excellent at swaying people to his cause."

"There is something else," I said.

"Oh?"

"I am not as naive as you imagine me. I suspected Edwin's tale may be false, too."

"And what changed your mind?"

"Tilly."

Robert screwed up his face. "Your friend from the orphanage?"

"Yes, she implored me to help Edwin."

"Why would she care?"

"I know not, but I cannot deny her. She was my friend and Samuel's mother…"

"You are Samuel's mother."

I sighed.

"She has not told you why the matter concerns her?"

"No," I said as I traced the edge of the tablecloth.

"There is something you are not telling me."

"I have not spoken with Tilly directly."

"So it may not be her requesting your help."

"It is," I insisted before I turned introspective. "I do not understand why she has not spoken directly with me, but three times she has requested my help."

Robert leaned back in his chair, pondering the matter. After a time, he spoke.

"Where has Edwin encountered his trouble?"

I held back a grin, but my heart lifted. I may win this battle. "Glasgow."

"I know not how the spirit world works. I am not certain I would like to know. But I trust your judgment. We shall make plans to travel to Glasgow. I have business I must conduct there, and you may visit Edwin to discuss the matter." I could no longer hold back the smile creeping across my face. "But *only* when I am available to accompany you. I shall not have you traipsing about to a jail cell alone."

"Of course, dear," I said. "Whatever you judge is best."

"I wish not to know the details of the case. I prefer to

remain ignorant of my brother's difficulties. But I shall not abandon my wife."

"I shall hold back any information I find."

Robert nodded but did not respond. I could not tell if he approved of my statement or not. Either way, it appeared the matter was settled. I would pursue assisting Edwin.

We finished our meal and evening without speaking of Edwin again. In truth, I preferred it. As I read near the roaring fire in the sitting room, my mind wandered. I did not know what to expect in Glasgow, but I could not help but wonder. My overzealous imagination concocted all sorts of scenarios.

After a time, I gave up on my reading, finding myself too distracted to continue. I excused myself for the evening and retired to my room. I closed my eyes and collapsed against the door as I entered. With a deep sigh, I processed the evening again, though I found myself satisfied with the outcome.

I stepped into the room and glanced around. "Tilly? Tilly!" I called.

I waited for a response or sign of some kind. I received none, so I continued. "I have done what you asked. I have spoken to Robert. We shall travel to Glasgow day after tomorrow. I will speak with Edwin."

I stalked a few more steps into the room. "Tilly? Are you pleased?"

My eyes scanned the room in a desperate search for any sign of Tilly. I inhaled deeply, hoping for a scent of her perfume. I strained my ears for that ghostly whisper of her voice.

Nothing responded to me. No sights, no smells, no sounds. I sank onto the chaise, suddenly exhausted. I eyed the pull cord across the room, resigning myself to the walk I'd need to take to pull it. As I pondered the matter, the door to my room creaked open. I snapped my head to stare at it, assuming Tilly arrived.

My shoulders sagged as I realized a living being stood in the doorway. "Oh, Sinclair," I said with a sigh. "I was about to ring for you."

"Buchanan said you'd gone up. I figured I'd save you the trouble."

"Thank you," I said with a weak smile as I pulled myself from the chaise to undress.

As I slipped into my nightclothes, Sinclair inquired after my decision.

"I spoke with Robert this evening. He was not pleased, though he agreed to allow me to pursue the matter with Edwin."

Sinclair's eyebrows raised in response.

"We travel day after tomorrow," I continued. "I will need your assistance to pack for the trip tomorrow."

"Of course, Your Grace."

"And if it is not too much, I should like you to travel with us. Perhaps you might visit your mother," I suggested.

"That's very kind of you, Your Grace," Sinclair said as she brushed my hair.

"No, it isn't, Sinclair. You are being dragged into the situation regardless of your thoughts. The least I can do is make the trip worth your while."

Sinclair chuckled. "Worth my while? The trip alone is worth my while, Your Grace. A lovely change of scenery before winter descends upon us. I am quite lucky compared to most."

"What a wonderful viewpoint," I answered, finding it refreshing. "And speaking of the weather, I will see to it that you ride inside the carriage. It will be far too cold to ride outside."

"Thank you, Your Grace."

"Perhaps select a few books from the library for the trip. I know you love reading."

"And this will provide many quiet moments by which I can enjoy a book, perhaps two!"

I smiled at her. "Yes!"

We finished our nightly routine and Sinclair left me to climb into my bed. My mind swam with a variety of thoughts. We had much to prepare for the upcoming trip. What would I find when I arrived in Glasgow? What would I say to Edwin? How would he respond?

I groaned as I turned onto my side. Perhaps Robert would be proved correct. Perhaps I had a blind spot when it came to Edwin. Or Tilly. Had it actually been her who contacted me? I had not seen her in my waking hours.

I had heard her, my mind posed. Hadn't I? I thought it was her voice. I assumed it was. What if it was not?

I rolled onto my back and stared at the bed's canopy. With a sigh, I willed my mind to stop its rumblings. "Go to sleep, Lenora," I scolded myself. "Nothing can be solved tonight."

I closed my eyes and exhaustion overcame me. I drifted off to sleep.

* * *

The carriage trundled down the hill from the castle. I twisted to survey the castle as it slipped from my view. The familiar sense of melancholy washed over me as I left behind the first home I'd ever found acceptance in. Every trip away from Blackmoore Castle unsettled me. Perhaps I worried I would never return to the one place I'd found happiness.

In any case, this trip was of my making. I spun to face forward and settled in for the trip. Sinclair sat next to me, already engrossed in her book. My own sat in my lap, though

I could not bring myself to read it. Too many questions crowded my mind.

I'd planned to visit the jail as soon as we'd arrived in Glasgow. Robert, of course, did not approve, telling me it could keep one more day until tomorrow morning. I had objected, informing him I did not wish to lose another night's sleep over it. We'd had a minor spat in which Robert informed me I should not lose sleep over a louse like Edwin, and I'd shot back that I hadn't a choice in the matter. He'd pursed his lips and conceded after a moment.

I already detested the strife this situation caused. I hoped to bring it to a swift end. Perhaps with details from Edwin, I could locate the spirit of the deceased, learn the identity of the true murderer, and put the matter to rest. At least that is what I sincerely hoped.

I settled in for the long ride, determined to settle the matter as quickly as possible.

I spent most of the ride in nervous anticipation of our arrival. As we wound through the city toward our hotel, my anticipation turned to agitation. My stomach somersaulted and fluttered as the carriage slowed. I wondered if my lunch may make a reappearance as we climbed from the carriage to enter the hotel.

Odd, I mused. I had witnessed so many strange things in life, I wondered why this would bother me. Though dealings with the living often were more difficult for me than matters of the dead.

I convinced myself it was this, coupled with Robert's agitation over the matter, that caused my upset as I collapsed in an armchair in our suite's sitting room.

"Your Grace, are you quite all right?" Sinclair asked.

I swallowed hard as I willed my stomach to settle. "Yes," I breathed. I closed my eyes and swallowed hard again. "Yes, only tired from the journey."

I rubbed my forehead with the back of my hand.

"Lenora, are you ill?" Robert's voice asked.

I snapped my eyes open. "No!" I insisted. "Merely tired."

"Perhaps you should rest," he suggested.

"His Grace may be correct, Your Grace," Sinclair said. "You are terribly pale."

Despite the rolling of my stomach, I pushed myself to stand. I drew on all my strength and shoved my shoulders back. "A lack of fair weather," I said in excuse. "I am ready to proceed to the jail."

CHAPTER 5

"*L*enora…" Robert began.

"Please, Robert, I wish to have the visit over with. I am certain once it is finished, I shall feel much better."

Robert considered it for a moment. Had he changed his mind, I pondered?

After a breath, he nodded. "All right, Lenora," he said. "We shall proceed as planned. But if you take a turn for the worse, I shall cut the call short."

"Understood," I answered.

Sinclair squeezed my arm. "Good luck, Your Grace," she whispered with a slight smile.

I thanked her, donned my cape, and accepted Robert's arm to return to the carriage. My thoughts were numerous and varied as the buildings swept by us. When the carriage lurched to a halt, I felt no more prepared for the visit than I had earlier. With a hard swallow and a deep breath, I climbed to the sidewalk. Robert stared up at the building. "Lenora, are you certain?" he questioned again.

"Yes," I managed to squeak out. I felt anything but, though

LETTER TO A DUCHESS

my promise to Tilly motivated me to step forward and enter the edifice.

A large desk met us as we strode through the door. A uniformed officer stood behind it. Robert approached him.

"May I help you, sir? Do you wish to report a crime?" the man asked.

"No," Robert answered. He paused a moment. With a grimace, he continued. "I am Robert Fletcher, Duke of Blackmoore. We have traveled from Blackmoore today. My wife wishes to visit a prisoner."

The man shuffled his feet behind the desk and raised an eyebrow. "Your Grace," he said. "Yes, of course." He glanced around Robert and eyed me. "Just a moment, I shall have you both escorted down."

"Only my wife will go. I shall wait here."

The man wiggled his eyebrows at the statement but nodded before disappearing through a doorway. We waited in uncomfortable silence. I gleaned from Robert's posture, expression and mannerisms that he remained uncomfortable with the entire episode. My heart sank as I understood the embarrassment he must be suffering, though perhaps the entire situation could be rectified easily.

The officer returned with another uniformed man. "Right this way, Your Grace," he said.

"Ah, no," the first officer said. "Only Her Grace will go."

The man's eyebrows shot skyward, but he nodded and plastered a pleasant expression across his features. "Right this way, Your Grace," he said.

He motioned for me to follow him through a doorway. I stepped forward and Robert caught my arm. I paused and searched his eyes.

"Lenora," he said. His lips moved, but he found no other words.

I nodded, understanding what he expressed without needing to hear the words. "I will not be long," I promised.

As Robert released my arms, I followed the officer. We ambled down a long hallway and approached a door. He unlocked it and swung it open. A dark stairway lay beyond it. With a lantern in hand, he led me down it.

A cold dampness greeted me as we descended further down. As we ceased our descent, an overpowering sour stench assaulted my nostrils. I held my handkerchief to my nose as I followed the officer deeper into the dank prison.

We drew up to a series of cells. The officer guided me past the first and slowed as he approached the second. He dragged the key across the bars. Clanking noises echoed throughout the chamber.

"Lord Edwin, you have a visitor," he announced.

I approached the bars. A huddled form sat on a cot across the cell. His shoulders rounded as his head hung low.

"Edwin?" I croaked.

His head snapped up sharply. His gray eyes focused on me in the dim light. His forehead wrinkled as he studied my face. His hair was disheveled, his clothes rumpled, and a thick beard covered his face.

"Lenora?" he gasped. He leapt to his feet, racing toward the bars. He grasped hold of them and stared into my eyes.

He reached through the bars and grasped my hand as tears formed in his eyes.

"Back off, Lord Edwin," the officer shouted as his clammy hand clutched mine.

"It is all right," I assured the man.

He nodded and retreated several steps away. His eyes remained upon us, but we could speak freely. I turned my attention back to Edwin.

"I received your letter," I began, unsure where to start.

"Truth be told, I was not certain you would come. Though I am overjoyed you have. You believe me, don't you?"

I hesitated in my response. "You believe me, don't you, Lenora?" he repeated, squeezing my hand and shaking it.

I licked my lips as I considered my response. Did I? "Tell me what happened, Edwin," I settled on.

He released my hand and stalked away from the cell door. He raked his fingers through his mussed hair. Then he flung his arms to his sides. "I don't... I don't know," he gasped, sobs wracking his voice.

"Edwin, please, you must get hold of yourself," I said. "You must tell me from the start."

He bit his lower lip and nodded. He sniffled and drew in a deep breath.

"I had been drinking heavily of late," he admitted. "On one of my nightly binges, I imbibed several drinks with a friend, Gerard Boyle." I nodded, recognizing the name from his letter. "I am afraid my memory of what follows is hazy."

"You said police found him on the docks."

"Yes, near the tavern we frequented, The Black Horse."

"And you have no recollection of how he got there?"

"No," Edwin said with the shake of his hand.

"I see." I squashed my eyebrows together as my eyes fell to the floor.

He rushed toward me and clutched the cell's bars. "I did not kill him, Lenora."

I studied him. How did he know? If he had no recollection of the night, could he be certain he did not murder the man in a drunken stupor?

"I realize you may not believe me, particularly given my lack of memory of the evening, but I did not kill him. Please, Lenora, believe me. I know in the depths of my soul, I am innocent."

His eyes pleaded with me. I pursed my lips and creased

my brow as I parsed through my many thoughts. "I..." I began. Robert's warning rang in my mind as did Edwin's plea.

As I considered the matter, a breeze swept across my cheek. I glanced around the dimly lit space. A flicker of color caught my eye. In the far, darkened corner of Edwin's cell, a flash of pink glowed. Golden locks flowed around a small, rosy-cheeked face and fell onto a pink dress. Tilly.

I heard her breathy words reach my ears. "Help him, Lenora. Please."

I hoped to speak with her, to learn her reasoning, but as I leaned, Edwin followed my movement. He stepped between me and Tilly. "Please, Lenora," he said again. "You must believe me."

My focus snapped back to Edwin. "I do," I spouted.

His shoulders relaxed, and he uttered a thank you to a higher power under his breath.

"Edwin, you must try to tell me more," I insisted.

"I don't remember any more," he lamented.

"Try."

"But..."

"Did you leave the pub together?"

His forehead wrinkled. He shifted his eyes sideways as he considered it. "No," he answered after a while.

"Who departed first?"

"Uh," he mumbled. "I did."

"And where did you go?"

He shrugged. "I do not recall. A brothel. An alley."

I drew my lips into a thin line, frustrated with his atrocious behavior. "Where did you awaken?"

"Two streets over from The Black Horse. In an alleyway near a butcher."

He continued, "The barkeeper informed the police

Gerard and I kept company. My whereabouts could not be accounted for and I was arrested, but I did not kill him!"

I shook my head. "Oh, Edwin, why must you persist in this behavior?"

His arms fell to his sides and his shoulders slumped. He strode away from the cell bars. "I have nothing."

I glanced toward the back corner where Tilly had stood moments ago. No hints of color reflected the light. She was gone.

"That is far from the truth," I said. "Despite the quarrel between you, Robert still cares. He needs time, but your behavior does little to alleviate his anger."

Edwin dropped onto the cot. "You do not understand," he muttered.

I raised my eyebrows. "Then explain."

He shook his head and wrapped his arms around himself. "I have nothing. She is gone."

"Annie?" I questioned, understanding him to mean Robert's late wife.

Tilly reappeared in the corner. She reached her hand toward Edwin. I opened my mouth to call out to her when a new voice spoke.

"Stop blaming your problems on others, Edwin, and grow up," Robert grumbled.

I twisted to face him as he drew up to the cell bars next to me. When I returned my gaze to the cell, Tilly had disappeared again. What drew her here?

"Robert!" Edwin exclaimed.

Robert threaded his arms through the bars and leaned against them. "I cannot say I am surprised by your surroundings."

Edwin leapt to his feet, his hands balled into fists. "I did not kill him!" he shouted.

"No, you are never to blame," Robert taunted.

"She believes me!" Edwin argued, pointing at me.

"Yes, of course, you planned on that, didn't you? You louse! How dare you drag my wife into this, you horrible excuse for a man!"

"I needed help, Robert," Edwin answered, his voice cracking. "I could not come to you, big brother. You've disowned me."

"No, so instead, you secreted a letter to my wife and allowed her to do your dirty work. You knew I would not deny her any request. You used her!"

Tempers flared as the brothers argued back and forth. "I did what I must! I am innocent!"

"You took the selfish action. You are not innocent. The fact that you stand accused of this crime… that it is even plausible to make a case against you suggests your guilt."

"I AM NOT GUILTY!" he screamed.

"You are guilty of living the life of a rat, a scoundrel. You deserve nothing…"

"Stop it! Both of you!" I shrieked, my gaze flitting between the two brothers.

The bickering between the two men ceased as they stared in my direction. Robert recovered first.

"Lenora, I am sorry but…"

I held up my hand to stop him. "The fact is, regardless of his prior actions and our thoughts on them, Edwin stands accused of murder. A murder he swears he did not commit. He has asked for my help, and you have agreed to allow me to assist him."

Robert's jaw tensed, but he did not speak. Edwin rushed toward the bars and reached for my hand. He grasped it and squeezed. "Thank you, Lenora. Perhaps you can visit the scene, speak with Gerard. Perhaps he can clear up the matter and we can find some evidence to exonerate me."

Robert's eyes fell to Edwin's hand gripping mine. He sneered at it and shook his head, averting his gaze.

I nodded. "I shall try. I shall return with any news." I closed the conversation with a squeeze of Edwin's hand. Robert's patience was wearing thin. I could read it on his face. While I hoped to gain more information, I would need to do so at another time.

"Thank you, Lenora," Edwin repeated. I nodded to him. Robert gestured for me to precede him to the stairway. As I passed, I did not miss the glare he offered Edwin.

Robert remained silent as the carriage bounced through the streets of Glasgow. Exhaustion coursed through me. The emotional distress on all sides of the issue plagued me. Matters of the living always troubled me more than communication with the dead.

As the carriage trundled along, Robert shifted in his seat. After a deep inhale, he cleared his throat. "I do not like this, Lenora."

I pursed my lips at his statement. I had no response prepared. I could not blame him for this, though I had agreed to give Edwin my assistance.

"I do not like your involvement with this sordid business," he added.

"I haven't much choice," I answered. "I offered Edwin my help. I cannot go back on my word."

"You have offered your support. Leave the other business to the police."

"I have abilities the police do not," I reminded him.

He grimaced as he shifted his gaze out the carriage's side window. "A fact Edwin has capitalized on to use."

"You cannot blame him for it," I countered. "He feels trapped."

"Edwin always has an excuse to use the talents of others for his own gain."

"That isn't fair, Robert."

"Isn't it?" he inquired, turning his eyes to me. "The man is a cad, a louse. He doesn't deserve your help or your pity."

"Still, I have already offered it, deserved or not."

Robert shut his eyes and shook his head. "I wish I had never agreed to allow you to."

"Robert…"

"Lenora," he interrupted, "I have no desire to see you involved in this vile matter. Besides, what plan have you to help? Have you communicated with the deceased?"

"No," I answered. "I suppose the easiest way to facilitate a meeting with him is to go to the location where he died." I allowed myself to muse aloud about my next steps.

"Absolutely not!" Robert snapped. "I shall not have you traveling around to God-knows-where to meet with a disgruntled spirit on Edwin's behalf!"

My eyes widened, and my jaw slackened at his response. "First, we have no knowledge of the deceased state. He may not be disgruntled."

Robert waved away my explanation. "Either way, Lenora, I do not wish to see you traveling about into the most unsavory areas in Glasgow."

"Then what do you propose?" I questioned. "I cannot summon him. I am not a medium."

"I propose you abandon the gambit. It is far too dangerous."

"No," I answered.

"Damn it, Lenora! This is not a matter for debate."

"Do you wish to see your brother rotting in prison, or worse?"

"I'd prefer it to seeing you harmed in any way."

"Robert," I tried again but found myself interrupted.

"I realize your desire to help. And I am in no position to judge, given that I used your abilities in a similar way. But if you recall, the moment your life was endangered by your pursuit of Annie's truth, I demanded you stop your investigation."

"Yet I did not."

"Quite to my chagrin, dear, I remind you."

A half-smile crossed my lips as I was reminded of Robert's many attempts to circumvent Annie's communication with me. The spirit proved insistent, though. The dead can be like that.

"I recall," I admitted. "But you will also recall the dead do not work with our desires in mind."

"But this man hasn't even contacted you. If you leave well enough alone, the matter should trouble us no further. And Edwin certainly does not deserve your help."

I raised my eyebrows. "Perhaps it won't, and perhaps he doesn't, though he did save my life from Sir Richard. Though you are forgetting a vital element."

Robert raised his eyebrows at me. I continued, "My promise extends beyond Edwin. I promised Tilly."

His lips formed a frown and his forehead wrinkled. "Tilly," he repeated.

"Yes. She appeared in the cell."

"What has she to do with this?"

"I am not certain," I admitted. "Though I intend to find out. And I cannot deny her the request. She was my friend in life, Robert, and she has sought my help in death."

Robert shifted in his seat, a frown still etched into his features. He directed his gaze out the window at the passing buildings. After a moment, he sighed. "Fine. Against my better judgment, I shall give my blessing for you to continue with this... madness. Though you mustn't go anywhere alone."

"I'd hate to drag Sinclair..." I began.

"No," Robert corrected me. "Either Henry or I shall

accompany you. Henry arrives tomorrow morning. I will not be party to two women running about Glasgow alone."

I held back a chuckle, the edges of my lips curling despite my best attempt.

Robert raised his eyebrows at me. "Are we agreed?"

"Yes," I admitted. "We are."

"What do you find so humorous?"

I shrugged. "As a younger woman, you realize I have traversed the streets of Glasgow freely at my own will."

Robert cocked his head at me. "That was before you were my wife. Now, you have me to worry about you!"

"And you seem determined to do so."

He grinned at me with a coy expression flitting over his features. "I am, indeed."

We discussed a plan for visiting the scene of the murder tomorrow morning before the carriage ground to a halt outside our hotel. As I shambled through the door to our suite, I realized how tired the journey and confrontation with Edwin made me. I stifled a yawn as Sinclair removed my cape.

After a light dinner, I retired for the night, hoping sleep did not escape me.

* * *

The following day brought dreary weather to the city. Rain poured down as day broke and continued through most of the morning. I stared at the gray clouds as they rolled north. The weather matched my mood. Already missing both Blackmoore Castle and Samuel, I wondered if Robert had been correct in his request of me to abandon the matter.

I wrapped my arms around myself as Tilly's request rushed through my mind again. No, I reflected, I could not abandon the matter. Not for my homesickness. Not even for my selfish desire to wrap my arms around my child and fade away from the world. I must see it through.

Robert entered the room, noting my pensiveness. He offered me a fleeting smile before his expression turned to concern. "Is everything all right, Lenora?"

I nodded and offered a weak smile. "Yes. Though I am lamenting a trip outside in this dismal weather."

He raised his eyebrows at me and for a moment, I expected him to attempt to convince me to leave well enough alone. "We shall make the trip quickly and I shall return you to the warmth of the fire and your novel. Have you found it interesting?"

I smiled at him, proud of the strides he'd made in accepting the situation. "I must admit to having been distracted, but I have found it enjoyable. I hope to focus on it more soon."

"Then shall we proceed?" Robert inquired.

I nodded and, after retrieving our outerwear, we set off. As the carriage wound through the city streets, I found myself calm. Odd, I ruminated. I felt less disconcerted about the prospect of visiting the spirit of a murder victim than I had yesterday visiting the living. I supposed I had grown more accustomed to the dead in my nineteen years than I had to the living. Until recently, after all, I had found little acceptance. The only person who accepted me, including my odd ability, prior to Robert, was Tilly.

My heart broke for her. She died without ever holding her son. My thoughts turned to her most recent appearance. She seemed despondent over the entire matter. Why, I wondered? Was it because of my apprehension over it? Did she sense my uncertainty in how to proceed and was attempting to encourage me?

The halting of the carriage near a street leading to the docks interrupted any further thoughts. The coachmen leapt from his perch and swung the door open for Robert, unfurling the stairs. He stepped into the chilly November air. His eyes darted around and a frown formed on his face. With a raise of his eyebrows, he offered his hand, and I climbed from the carriage.

The rain had ceased for the moment but left a dampness in the air. The cool chill blew off the water and I shrugged my cape closer around me. A dense fog rolled across the river, threatening to move ashore.

"This way," Robert said as he pointed toward the water.

We strode toward it. I gazed out at the ships in the harbor as we approached the water's edge. Several men worked unloading ships, others milled about. A sign hung from the building on the corner. A black horse reared on its hind legs, surrounded by the establishment's name. The Black Horse pub stood near where Gerard met his demise.

"There's the infernal pub where the trouble started," Robert noted as we passed it. He grimaced at it before continuing on. "The officer said the incident occurred several yards to the left."

Robert motioned past a few crates and barrels and we strolled toward the location. A few men ceased their work as we paraded past. One raised his eyebrows at me as we walked, causing Robert to clutch my hand as he frowned at the man. We passed several large buildings before Robert slowed. He glanced between the building and the water. His brow creased. "Somewhere in here, I believe," he muttered.

"I do not need the exact location. This should do." I released my grip on Robert's arm and gazed around the area. My mind's eye attempted to recreate the scene on that October eve. I imagined the darkened docks, moonlight reflecting on the water, and creating shadows on the docks. I twisted to identify hiding spots. With the shifting cargo, I found it an impossible task. The crates and barrels piled in the area were not likely the same ones from the night Gerard met his unfortunate demise.

I stalked around the area, searching for a sign of the deceased. Robert's watchful eye followed my movements. I waited for several moments, my eyes scanning for a soul only I could see.

CHAPTER 6

I shook my head when no one appeared.

"Gerard?" I tried. "Gerard Boyle?"

One of the dockworker's eyes slid sideways at me. He furrowed his brow before shuffling away.

I flung my arms out. "It's no use," I said to Robert. "He is not here."

"Perhaps we should depart." As he uttered the suggestion, a large raindrop pelted me. Then another and another. Robert ducked as the skies began to spit rain. "Come, Lenora." He waved me ahead of him toward the carriage. We made it no further than the corner when the rain began to pick up. Large droplets of cold water splashed on the cobblestone.

"Hurry," Robert shouted over the rumbling thunder. "Get inside."

We ducked into the doorway of The Black Horse pub as clouds unleashed a deluge.

"Par for the course," Robert grumbled under his breath. A giggle escaped me. Robert screwed up his face as he glanced at me.

I waved away his scowl as I attempted to control my

laughter. "It has been a rather terrible trip, hasn't it? From the smell last evening to the rain today."

My laughter proved infectious and Robert began to chuckle along with me. "It has not been my best trip to Glasgow."

My eyebrows shot up. "Oh? Have you had worse?"

A grin crossed his face. "It may not be a tale for your ears."

I arched an eyebrow at him. "'Tis a long story," he added.

I cocked my head at him, a coy expression on my face. A glance out the window next to the door showed a steady stream of rain. "We may have the time."

We retreated further into the pub and slipped into a booth. Robert spent the time regaling me with stories from his youth as we enjoyed an early dinner. His final story ended with a tale of a brawl he and Edwin engaged in at a pub much like this one. My laughter faded as the troubled expression returned to Robert's features. The mention of Edwin's name brought back the stark reality of the reason for our visit to the city.

I drew in a deep breath as I sobered. I slid my hand across the wooden table and offered Robert a reassuring squeeze on his forearm. The situation with Edwin disturbed him further than he preferred to admit, perhaps even to himself.

As Robert settled our bill, the barkeeper offered him a long stare. He dried a glass stein as he narrowed his eyes at Robert.

"You a Fletcher?" he questioned after a moment.

Robert raised his eyebrows at the man. "Yes, Robert Fletcher, Duke of Blackmoore."

"Any relation to Lord Edwin?" the barkeep inquired.

Robert jutted his chin out as his jaw flexed. He swallowed hard. "I am his brother."

The man nodded as though agreeing. "You look alike. Haven't seen Lord Edwin in for a bit. He well?"

Robert set his mouth in a firm line.

"He has been otherwise engaged," I chimed in.

The man raised an eyebrow at me but nodded. "I see." He eyed me up and down before he added, "Your Grace, I presume."

"Yes. Are you well-acquainted with my brother-in-law?"

"Aye, he's in here often," the man answered. "A bit of trouble sometimes but mostly innocuous."

"Do you happen to recall the last time you saw him here?" I inquired.

The man puckered his lips, his eyes sliding upward in thought. "Been a few weeks," he said. "Dinnae think I saw him since the night his mate Gerard was murdered."

"Do you recall that evening?" I inquired.

The barman gave me a hard stare before his eyes flitted to Robert. "Please, any information you may give," he said as he gestured for the man to continue, "we would appreciate."

The man wiggled his eyebrows as he returned his attention to drying another stein. "I recall it, yes," he admitted. He licked his lips before he continued. "Busy night. Then, of course, there was the trouble."

"Trouble?" I repeated.

He nodded and turned his attention to wiping the polished wooden bar. "Aye. Your brother-in-law consumed quite a bit of whiskey that eve."

I waited for him to continue. After a moment, he offered more. "Gerard accused him of something, what I do not know. Lord Edwin began to shout and poke his finger at the man. He leapt to his feet, topping the table and several drinks. He was obviously drunk, his words were slurred and he staggered about."

"What was he shouting?" I asked.

"He said Gerard didn't know what he was talking about and should shut his mouth."

"About what?" Robert chimed in.

The man shrugged. "I dinnae know. I dinnae overhear their conversation, only the argument. I asked Gerard after, but he kept a tight lip."

"And Lord Edwin left before Mr. Boyle?" I asked.

The man nodded. "Yes, I escorted him out myself. Told him not to come back until he'd cooled off."

"The argument was that heated?" Robert questioned.

The man looked Robert square in the eyes. "Lord Edwin slammed Mr. Boyle against the wall and held a knife to his neck. So help me, I'll slice you open, he said."

My eyes closed for a moment as my stomach turned at the admission. Edwin had threatened the deceased in a crowded bar. The incident had been witnessed by dozens if the barkeeper's assessment of the crowd's size was correct. Later, the man had been found with a knife in his chest.

I glanced at Robert. He pulled a bill from his pocket and laid it on the bar. "Thank you," he muttered. "Come, Lenora, we should be going."

I smiled at the man behind the bar as Robert guided me through the door and into the chilly, damp air. We walked to the waiting carriage in silence. The carriage swayed as the coachmen climbed aboard then lurched as we set off. I eyed Robert, studying his face as we wove through the city streets.

He stared out the window, avoiding eye contact. His features formed a pensive mask with his brows knit and the corners of his mouth turning down. The admission from the pub's barman disturbed Robert. Already assuming the worst of Edwin, the story further convinced him of Edwin's guilt.

"A threat is a far cry from murder," I ventured.

Only a grunt answered me. I pondered my next move carefully.

"I should discuss the matter with Edwin..."

Robert's eyes pinched closed and he gave a slight shake of his head at my statement. After a moment, he reversed his course and nodded. "Perhaps Henry can accompany you. You should not venture to the jail alone."

"Of course, dear," I answered. "Have you business to attend to tomorrow?"

"I shall find some," he muttered before returning his gaze outside.

I realized what he meant. He did not wish to involve himself given the latest revelation, though he had no intention of going back on his promise to allow me to investigate. I admired him for it. Despite the personal tension between the brothers, Robert remained a man of his word. I hoped settling the matter in Edwin's favor may ease the strain between them. At the very least, it could not add to it, I surmised.

"Lenora," Robert said at long last, "I do wish you would not involve yourself in this. I fear you may be harmed."

"With your and Henry's watchful eye, I am certain I will not be."

He shook his head. "I do not mean physically, though, I worry about that as well. I mean your heart."

I furrowed my brow at his words. He continued, "You trust too much, Lenora. Your heart is too open. I do not wish to see you hurt if Edwin is lying."

I considered his statement. Was I too trusting? I disagreed. I'd long since come to recognize people for what they were. My difficult childhood meant I expected little from others. I found it odd to think of myself as too trusting. I considered myself a pragmatist.

My silence prompted Robert to continue. "Oh, Lenora," he said with a gentle shake of his head. "You do not agree, I know, and you may even be insulted. But you are too kind."

"I'm not," I said with a pout.

"You agreed to help me, did you not?"

My eyes widened at the statement. "Surely, Robert, you jest."

He grinned a sly smile. "I do not. I spirited you away from your life and offered a wild proposition. And you accepted without a moment's hesitation."

"I beg to differ," I retorted. "I hesitated far longer than a moment. In fact, I dithered so much you accused me of being odd!"

"I did not say odd," he rebuked playfully.

"You asked me if I was in my right mind!"

"After you asked me if I was mad."

"You had just fallen from your horse," I defended myself as our playful argument continued. "It was a valid question."

"Still," Robert contended, bringing the bantering back to its point, "you trusted me when you had no reason to."

"So did you," I countered. "And I had no reason not to trust you. It was quite obvious your account the night we met was no fable. I could read it in your face."

"And what do you read in Edwin's?"

I paused and considered his question. "Desperation," I said. "And truth."

He glanced out the window again. "Perhaps I misjudge my brother because of our difficult relationship."

"I do not mean to upset you further by offering my aid to Edwin. Really, I hoped the opposite, that it would alleviate some of the stress between you."

Robert nodded. "Yes, I realize your intentions are pure. As always. I sometimes wonder how I came to be so lucky as to have married such an extraordinary woman."

I smiled to myself at the statement as I reached for his hand. "And I wonder how luck brought such an accepting man into my life as my husband."

He squeezed my hand and leaned forward to brush my lips. "I love you, Lenora."

I smiled and began to respond in like manner when he added, "Which is why I worry."

"I shall be careful, I promise," I said. "And I love you, too."

* * *

I paced the floor of the hotel's bedroom later that night. Moonlight shone through the window, casting long shadows on the floor. The encounter and conversation with The Black Horse's barkeep replayed in my mind.

Perhaps Robert's apprehension was not unfounded. The argument between Edwin and Gerard, culminating in a knife-wielding Edwin issuing an ominous threat, painted a grim picture. Edwin's guilt seemed all but assured. He'd argued with the deceased, threatened him and later, the man had been murdered. All signs pointed to Edwin's guilt. Yet, I could not deny my initial reaction to his innocence.

I'd felt it when I read the letter and later when I'd spoken with him. And then there was Tilly and her odd fixation on the matter.

I spun and marched across the room in the opposite direction. I settled at the window and stared up at the waxing crescent moon. My lips pursed as I rubbed the back of my neck. I missed my home and my son.

My home, my son. The words echoed in my mind. I still found myself astounded at times at what my life had become. Only eighteen months ago, I had assumed my eighteenth birthday would bring me the prospect of shifting from student to teacher at St. Mary's Orphanage. At least, that had been my hope. Even that prospect seemed slim. Headmistress Williamson did not approve of me. My ability frightened her. I questioned whether I would simply be turned out on the street rather than offered a position at the orphanage.

"She'd not turn you out, Lenora," Tilly had told me.

I recalled her lounging across her tiny cot, her flaxen hair hanging in tendrils down her back. Her green eyes sparkled and her rosy cheeks glowed. She had been so beautiful in life.

When I did not respond, Tilly continued, "She is a miserable old biddy. But she realizes you are an asset."

"She does need someone to sweep the cobwebs from the attic," I agreed.

Tilly offered me a sly grin. "There's the spirit!"

I flopped onto her bed and lay on my stomach. "Do you imagine I will have my own bedroom?"

"She can't very well make you sleep with the students," Tilly answered.

I raised my eyebrows, excited at the prospect of having my own room. "I had my own room twice before," I told her. "Once with my mother and father. And then at the convent."

Tilly offered me a consoling glance. "Do you miss your parents terribly?"

I considered the statement. "Yes and no," I answered. I collected my thoughts before continuing. "I miss having a normal home. Though, after my father left, my home was not really very normal. And I've grown accustomed to this life now."

"Accustomed or resigned?" Tilly prodded.

My brow wrinkled as I contemplated the difference. "Both, perhaps."

"Oh, Lenora," Tilly chided. "Do not become resigned to this existence. We can break free! We can have better lives."

"You are the more optimistic of the two of us."

"It's true," she insisted. "You do not know what the future holds!"

How true her words were, I thought as the memory

flitted through my mind. Tears formed in my eyes as her words rattled through my brain. They faded as I recalled the rest of our evening.

Tilly rambled on about love and marriage, babies and family. She assured me we'd both find happiness. As we giggled over our prospects, ignoring the obvious lack of them, our conversation ended abruptly. Millicent Brown, another student close in age to us at St. Mary's, entered the room.

Her turned-up nose shot higher in the air and her lips pinched. She narrowed her eyes at us. "What are you two cackling about? Haven't you anything better to do?"

"No, Millie," Tilly answered her. "We haven't. We have finished all our lessons."

"It's Millicent," she said with a glare. Millicent always hated Tilly's shortening of her name. "Then you haven't been given enough to do in your classes if you are able to loaf. I shall mention it to Headmistress Williamson. It's likely Miss Gray is being too soft. I certainly believe she is."

I bit my tongue and held back, rolling my eyes. As a pet of Headmistress Williamson, Millicent felt she could speak to anyone in any way she chose. I usually avoided her and her disdainful attitude. Tilly, on the other hand, relished sparring with her.

"Do you still have work to complete on your lessons?" Tilly questioned.

"Certainly," Millicent said with a curt nod, her mousy brown curls jiggling with the sharp movement. "I am still working on my composition and my maths." She plopped into a chair at one of the room's small desks and set her papers on top.

Tilly raised her eyebrows. "You shouldn't complain to Headmistress Williamson about the workload," Tilly answered. "We should not be punished because you are not as bright as us."

Millicent whipped her head around to glare at us. "I am smarter than either of you, Matilda Anderson. And I do not need to cheat either."

"We do not cheat."

Millicent poked her finger in my direction. "She does."

My jaw fell open. "I do not!" I exclaimed.

"You do, too!" she shouted back. "You and your foul talents."

Tilly leapt from the bed. "Now you listen here!" she shouted, but the appearance of Headmistress Williamson in the doorway quieted all of us.

I shot from the bed and stood, my hands clasped in front of me. Millicent leapt from her chair, taking a similar stance.

Headmistress Williamson eyed each of us, a sneer on her face as she settled on me. "What is the meaning of this shouting?" she inquired.

"Tilly and Lenora are frittering away their time. They claim they have finished their work. They are a distraction and a nuisance with their silly giggling while I am attempting to further my education."

"Is this true, girls?" Headmistress Williamson's eyes fell upon me.

Tilly spoke up. "Lenora and I have finished our work, yes. We were discussing our future when Millicent came in and insulted us. She accused us of cheating and we most certainly do not!"

Headmistress Williamson's eyes slid to Millicent. "Is this true?"

"No," Millicent said, her eyes wide and her head shaking. "It is not! I did not accuse Matilda of cheating. I accused Lenora of cheating, yes. But she does! Her disgusting ability offers her an advantage!"

"It does not," I cried. "I do not cheat!"

"That's enough, girls!" Headmistress Williamson eyed each of us. "I will not tolerate these outbursts or this petty fighting." She stepped toward me and yanked me by the arm. "Come, Lenora. You shall spend the night in the attic as punishment."

"What? Me?" I shouted.

"Headmistress Williams," Tilly interjected. "Wait, it was not Lenora's fault. She did not do the arguing, Millicent and I did! I should be punished, not her."

"While that may be, Matilda, the fact is the argument occurred as a direct result of Lenora's... nasty ability. And for that, she should be punished."

"No!" Tilly cried. She shot me a fretful and apologetic glance. "The argument was over our lessons. I provoked Millie and I should not have. For that, I apologize, but Lenora is not the one who should be punished."

"While you should not have provoked her, at least you admitted your fault. Tomorrow, you shall write one hundred times 'I should not provoke others' as your punishment."

Headmistress Williamson pulled me toward the door.

"Wait!" Tilly shouted again. "Why are you still taking Lenora?"

Headmistress Williamson closed her eyes and set her jaw. When her eyelids fluttered open again, she said, "Your punishment does not offset Lenora's, though I do not need to explain my actions to you, Matilda. Now go busy yourself with something productive until your bedtime."

"It's all right, Tilly," I assured her. Cold nights in the attic with no bed were something I'd grown accustomed to since my first night in the orphanage. I could endure another.

A tear rolled down Tilly's cheek. "I'm sorry, Lenora."

"Save your apologies for Millicent," Headmistress Williamson snapped. She whipped me into the hall and pulled the bedroom door closed. More tears fell onto Tilly's cheeks. The last glimpse I got before the door shut was of Millicent's smirk. I held back, rolling my eyes lest I be punished further.

The next day Tilly would apologize to me again and offer to complete some of my chores for me, though I refused. The fault did not lie with her, but with Headmistress Williamson.

The memory slipped from my mind as I stared up at the moon. How I missed Tilly.

With a sigh, I trudged back to my bed before my emotions overwhelmed me. I slipped beneath the sheets and nestled into the pillow behind me. My eyes remained open, searching the darkness for answers.

I found none as my eyelids grew heavy and slid closed. Sleep finally embraced me.

Though I managed to sleep for several hours, the word rest could not be used to describe my experience. I suffered through several disjointed nightmares, which mixed a variety of my scrambled thoughts together. Edwin appeared bloodied and weeping, a knife clutched in his hands. Tilly hovered in the corner, staring at the sad scene. She reached first toward Edwin, then toward me. "I'm sorry, Lenora," she croaked.

I stared at the form of my friend, wondering what she meant by this.

CHAPTER 7

I stared at the form of Tilly in my dream, my brow furrowing as I wondered for what reason she apologized.

"Whatever for?" I questioned her.

"I'm sorry, Lenora," she repeated.

I attempted to walk to her, to reach for her outstretched hand, but I found myself unable to move. Tilly's tears formed a flood across the wooden floor and I struggled to walk through the raging floodwaters.

"Millicent," Tilly answered as I slipped and slid on the slippery floor.

I froze, my mind processing the odd comment. "Tilly, that was ages ago," I chided. "Whatever are you saying?"

"Millicent," she repeated as her voice faded away. She vaporized before my eyes and I stood alone in the room. Edwin had departed, too.

When I awoke, still exhausted, I tried to make sense of the nonsensical information. After an hour of contemplation, I came to no answers. I concluded my mind must have combined random information from my reminiscing with my current situation. It could shed no light on my current mystery.

***

After breakfast, I saw Sinclair off to visit her mother. Mr. Langford arrived at quarter after ten in the morning to escort me to the jail. Robert had busied himself with other matters, allowing him to slip away earlier in the morning. Before he'd left, he kissed my forehead and implored me to keep my wits about me. I'd reminded him Henry would be with me. The fact seemed to provide him little comfort. Before he'd stepped through the door, he'd knit his brows and hesitated. For a moment, I believed he might change his plans and accompany me to the jail, but after a breath, he offered a curt smile, a nod and a "good luck."

"Good morning, Your Grace," Henry greeted me as he strolled into our suite. "Is His Grace still here?"

"No, he left earlier this morning," I informed him.

"Ah," he said, patting his attache case. "I had a matter I'd like him to review. I hoped to leave it with him. I did not realize he had other business." His brow furrowed. "I do not recall any meetings scheduled."

I offered a slight smile. "I am not certain there are any."

Henry raised an eyebrow at me and I continued. "Truthfully, I believe the matter with Lord Edwin disturbs His Grace greatly. I believe he busied himself to avoid visiting the jail."

Henry gave a knowing nod. "Well, shall we?" he asked, motioning toward the door.

"Yes, please."

We traveled by carriage to the jail, where Henry secured a visit with Edwin for me. After verifying that I did not require his presence for the conversation, I left him upstairs as the officer led me down to the cells.

The smell penetrated through the handkerchief pressed to my nose. After a few moments, I removed it as it failed to alleviate any odor. We approached the cell Edwin occupied. The officer announced my arrival. Edwin rushed to the bars, gripping them as he pressed his face into them.

"Lenora!" He reached out for my hand. His fingers wrapped around mine and squeezed. "Have you been to the location of the murder? Did you speak with Gerard? Did he identify the real killer?"

I swallowed hard as I composed my thoughts. "Y-Yes," I stuttered.

His eyes grew wide and he nodded at me. "And?" he prompted.

"I traveled to the site where Gerard met his end. But I did not speak with him."

Edwin's shoulders fell and he blew out a long breath. "So, he did not speak to you. Is he like Annie? Still in shock? Will he speak?"

"I did not see him at all, Edwin," I explained. "I went to the location. I called to him. But he did not appear."

"Oh," Edwin said with disappointment filling his voice. His eyebrows lifted and he stared at me. "Will you try again? Please say you will."

"Yes," I promised. "Yes, I will try again."

Edwin breathed a sigh of relief. "Thank you, Lenora. I do hope he appears next time. Then this entire matter can be cleared up." He ran his fingers through his hair. "When will you return?"

"Perhaps this afternoon or tomorrow morning. Yes, I will try again, but…"

"But?" Edwin questioned.

I paused for a moment before I continued with the tale. "When Robert and I visited…"

"Robert?" Edwin interrupted me. "Robert went with you?"

"Yes," I answered. "Why?"

"I assumed you'd go alone. Perhaps Gerard did not appear because of Robert."

I wrung my hands as I explained. "Robert insisted I not travel through the city alone."

The frown settling on Edwin's lips assured me he hoped Robert had as little to do with my investigation as possible. I continued, "We were caught in a rainstorm after we attempted to contact Gerard. We sought shelter in The Black Horse."

Edwin's eyebrows raised. "Shocking that Robert set foot in the establishment," he mumbled.

"Edwin," I said, "the barkeeper was the same man who worked the night Gerard was murdered. He told a tale. I must know from you if it is true."

Edwin faced me, his eyes boring into me, silently urging me to continue. "The man claims you had a row with Gerard. Quite a serious one, in fact. You threatened him."

Edwin shrugged and shook his head. "I… we…" He paused and hung his head. His fingers clenched the bars until his knuckles were white. He roared in frustration before he paced the floor for a few moments. "Yes, we argued. I was drunk. Drunk men argue."

I raised an eyebrow. "He told us you threatened to…" My voice trailed off and I swallowed hard. "To slice him open whilst you held a knife to his neck."

Edwin chewed his lower lip. "I was drunk," he explained. "I didn't know what I was saying. Idle threats between two drunken men. Nothing more. We argued that like frequently."

I considered the statement. Edwin was known to hurl threats when drunk, which he often was. I'd witnessed his brash behavior on a myriad of occasions. "Why did you not tell me?"

"I…" His brows knit together and he frowned. "I did not want you to refuse my request. I thought telling you might taint you against me."

"Edwin, if this is to work, you must be honest with me. Completely."

"For this to work? Cannot Gerard simply give the name of his murderer once you speak with him?"

"That may not be as easy as you assume! It took months with Annie. She could not speak."

"But eventually, she did. I trust you can do it, Lenora."

"Edwin," I implored, "you cannot withhold information. The story nearly put Robert off the entire matter. I feared he may stop me from continuing my investigation."

Edwin raced toward the bars, clutching at them again. "But you won't stop, will you?"

"No," I assured him. "I will not. But is there anything else I should know?"

"No," Edwin said. "No. We argued, I threatened him, I departed."

"How drunk were you? Could you have done something you do not remember?"

"I did not kill him!" Edwin shouted.

"All right," I soothed. "What did you quarrel over?"

Edwin turned away from me and stalked to the back of his cell. "A woman," he mumbled.

My brows knit as I processed his statement. Before I could speak, he spun to face me. He rushed to the bars and reached through them toward me. "Lenora, please," he begged, raw emotion in his voice as he gripped my hand, "it was a foolish argument over nothing between two inebriated parties. I did not kill him. Please."

I nodded and squeezed his hand, letting the matter go. "I will attempt to locate Gerard's spirit," I promised. "Do you know where else he may be drawn to?"

Edwin frowned in thought. I prompted him by saying, "Perhaps he had a home in the city or a friend. Perhaps a favorite spot he enjoyed."

"We spent a good deal of time at The Black Horse. And he enjoyed watching the ships come in, particularly since he had some… dealings there."

"Dealings? Was he a merchant?"

"No," Edwin said, drawing the word out.

"Edwin, you must be honest with me."

Edwin screwed up his face and bit his lower lip. After a moment, he shrugged. "His dealings weren't quite above board you understand."

"Oh," I said, with my brows raised high. "Yes, I understand."

Edwin cleared his throat and continued. "He did not have a home here. He sometimes stayed at his brother's home. But only if his brother was not in town."

"Do you know the location?"

"Yes," Edwin said and passed along the street and number. I recognized it as a well-to-do area within the city limits. Edwin's next comment confirmed my surmising. "Gerard's brother is Lord Pennington."

I nodded in response and Edwin pursed his lips, rubbing his chin in thought. He shrugged after a moment. "Beyond a few brothels, I cannot imagine another place Gerard would be drawn to."

"I shall start with the other location you mentioned. Should you recall anything else, hold it in your mind until we speak again."

Edwin offered a weak smile and a nod. "Thank you, Lenora."

I departed from the cell and the officer led me back to Henry. He waited on a small wooden bench. With his spectacles affixed to his nose, he had paperwork spread across his lap. Henry made efficient use of his time, I noted.

He glanced up as we approached. "Ah, all finished?" he inquired.

"Yes," I answered with a nod. "For now."

Henry collected his papers and stuffed them into his attache case along with his glasses. He stood, clutching the bag, and smiled at me. "Shall we lunch?"

I began to object, preferring to finish all my business, but Henry spoke before I could form the words. "I will never hear the end of it if His Grace catches wind that I allowed you to skip a meal."

I chuckled along with him, realizing he was correct. Since I preferred Henry not incur the wrath of my husband, I agreed. As we climbed into the carriage and set off toward a cafe, my mind turned pensive.

Edwin freely admitted his argument and maintained his innocence. I should not be surprised by this, though I did feel an ounce of disappointment at the omission on Edwin's behalf. He had withheld information from me. Robert's word rang in my head and I set my mouth in a firm line as I realized he had a point.

I shoved the remark from my mind and concentrated on what I'd learned. Gerard Boyle was the brother of Lord Pennington. He, too, came from a family of wealth. He, like Edwin, was likely the product of a spoiled upbringing without a large inheritance. Instead of assuming the role of lord, he frittered away his time and money with vices.

This added a new wrinkle. One of his vices included illicit dealings in the shipyard. Outside of Edwin, one of his shipyard associates could have murdered him in a business deal gone wrong. While this widened the list of suspects, it also made it harder to track. Without speaking to Gerard, this crime could go unsolved.

Though, this did little to help Edwin. His blatant and public threat against the deceased meant whether or not another solution was plausible, it was unlikely to cast enough doubt to deflect suspicion from him as the primary suspect.

We arrived at the bistro and were settled at a table in a corner. I stared out the window, my chin cupped in my hand.

Henry's voice broke into my ruminating. "I take it your meeting with Lord Edwin was not what you hoped?"

I sighed and tore my eyes from the landscape outside. "It was not," I admitted.

He raised his eyebrows and offered a slight smile. I understood this to mean he preferred not to pry if I did not wish to share information but was willing to provide an ear. "Has Robert told you much about the situation?"

"No," he answered. "Though I have not inquired. The matter seems to distress His Grace."

I nodded. "Yes, it does. To be honest, the situation is quite vexing for everyone involved."

"Lord Edwin's consternation is obvious. The disgrace on the family name agitates His Grace." He raised an eyebrow and studied me a moment. "Are you also distressed by the situation?"

"Very," I answered. "Perhaps Lord Edwin is being dishonest, though my intuition says otherwise. Yet with each new fact revealed, I find myself further perplexed. I fear answers may not be forthcoming."

"What have you learned?"

I explained to him I had not reached Gerard Boyle's spirit, but relayed the story from The Black Horse's barman.

"And Lord Edwin maintains his innocence?"

I nodded.

"Did he admit to the argument?"

"Yes, he did," I answered. "His claim is that it was merely the result of too much drinking on both their parts."

"And what you do believe?"

"I believe a heated argument is a far cry from murder."

"So, you are inclined to believe his story?"

"I am."

"Will you try to reach the spirit of Gerard Boyle again?"

"Yes. Though this afternoon I have another spirit I hope to reach."

His eyebrows raised as our food was set in front of us.

* * *

I stepped from the carriage at the entrance to St. Agnes Cemetery. Henry squinted against the bright sun that emerged from the previously cloudy day. He twisted to face me, confusion apparent on his features.

"Tilly is buried here," I informed him.

"Ah! Your friend from St. Mary's?"

"Yes. And Sam's mother."

"Oh, had I realized we could have brought a flower or token for her."

"Quite all right," I answered. "The visit is rather for a different purpose."

Henry's jaw dropped as he drew in a sharp breath. A smile faltered on his lips and he followed it with a nod. "I see." He cleared his throat and motioned for me to lead the way to Tilly's grave.

I hoped I could find it. I had been distraught when we'd laid her to rest. As I gazed through the sea of gravestones, I began to question my ability to navigate to her resting place.

After a few moments of wandering, I found the correct

spot. I stared down at the gravestone marked with her name. I reached out to touch the cold, gray marker. Tears pricked my eyes and I blinked them away.

When I straightened, I noticed Henry had retreated several steps away, offering me a private moment. I glanced around the graveyard.

"Tilly?" I whispered, my voice wavering.

I swallowed the lump in my throat, cleared it, and tried again. "Tilly!" I called in a louder tone. I spun in a circle, searching for her.

"Tilly? Have you been trying to contact me? I have come to you." I spotted no one as I finished my circle. With a sigh and a shake of my head, I returned my gaze to the headstone. I had dealt with spirits for the entirety of my life. When I needed them the most, it seems they had abandoned me.

I waited several more moments before I gave up. For the first time in my life, the lack of spirit sightings disappointed me. With a sigh, I turned to leave the grave.

The leaves rustled across the ground as a chilly wind gust swept past me. Over the stirring of the shriveled fronds, a whisper floated. "Help him, Lenora."

I spun to face Tilly's gravestone again. "Tilly?!" I shouted. "Tilly? Is that you?"

My eyes darted around in a frantic search for her. I saw nothing. Why would she not appear to me? "Tilly, please…" I began when I was interrupted. A cold hand fell on the crook of my arm.

CHAPTER 8

*E*xpecting the hand clamped on me to be Tilly's, I turned toward the touch. I stumbled back a step when I found a wrinkled face peering up at me. It took me a moment to recognize if she was of this world or not. I gazed at Henry, who paid no mind to the elderly lady standing before me and concluded she was deceased.

"Hello," I said.

Her lower lip trembled as she stared up at me, realizing I could see her. Her grip on my arm tightened and tears formed in her eyes. "Help me," she whispered.

My mind questioned whether she was the voice I'd heard moments ago and not Tilly's. She spoke again before I could decide. "Help me," she repeated in a hoarse voice.

"What is it you want?" I asked her.

"My daughter."

"You would like me to bring her here? Or perhaps to send her a message?"

"Danger." The woman began to shiver with fear.

I attempted to soothe her. "It's all right. I will make my best effort to help. Is your daughter in danger?"

"Danger," she repeated. I lamented that conversations with the dead were not more straightforward.

"Can you tell me her name?"

The woman's eyes brimmed with tears. "Grace," she breathed.

"Grace," I repeated. "What is her last name? Where does she live? Is there anything else you can tell me?"

"Grace," she said again. "Danger." Her voice turned shrill and her face clouded with worry.

"All right, madam," I said, "I will help however I can but you must tell me more. What is the danger? What is it you wish me to do for Grace?"

Her eyebrows raised high, and she stared at something in the distance. "Can you tell me your name?" I inquired.

Her eyes flitted to mine for a moment and she breathed, "Esme," before she faded away from my sight.

"No, wait!" I called. My shoulders sagged as I realized the tiny amount of information imparted. I pressed my hand to my forehead as I considered the woman's desperate plea but lack of information to accompany it.

Henry approached me. "Are you all right?" he questioned, gripping my arm as though I may collapse at any moment.

I composed myself and sighed, offering an affirmative response.

"Were you able to speak with Tilly?"

"No," I admitted, "she has not appeared to me."

His face showed surprise. "O-oh," he stammered. "I thought…"

"I spoke with someone, not Tilly," I explained, realizing the line of his inquiry. "She begged me to help her by finding her daughter but gave precious few other details. Perhaps I can glean a few from the gravestones nearby. Her name was Esme. Will you help me search for a grave marker with that name?"

"Of course," Henry offered. "Is it often this way with the dead?" We spread out to search the nearby tombstones.

"Yes," I called as I studied a cross-shaped marker. "Many of them are confused."

"How frustrating." We spent another few moments searching before Henry called to me. "Here!" I hurried to his location. He pointed at a simple gravestone. It read:

ESME MURDOCH
1792-1865

"Oh, she has died recently."

"Yes, within the last few months," Henry agreed.

"That may explain her confusion. Murdoch," I read from the stone. "I wonder if I can use this information to find her daughter."

"Have you a name?"

"Grace," I replied.

"No surname? She may be married."

"Yes, she may be, though the woman did not tell me this."

"I suppose the best way to begin is to inquire at the church about a Grace Murdoch."

I nodded and looked to the gray stone building to the west of us. A small steeple rose from its rear with a large bell housed inside. "Do you have the time now?" I asked, eyeing the long shadows cast by the low-hanging sun.

"Of course, Your Grace," Henry replied.

We strolled through the graveyard and toward the small church building. A man with a slight build and graying hair bustled about, pulling the remains of plants from a small garden outside an equally small home hidden behind the church building.

He straightened as Henry called to him, his ankle-length cassock falling to his feet.

"Hello," he greeted us with a warm smile. "I am Father Robert. May I help you?"

Henry took the lead in introducing me. "Hello, I am Henry Langford, I manage the Blackmoore estate. This is Lenora Fletcher, Duchess of Blackmoore. We were hoping you could help us in locating someone."

"Oh? One of our parishioners, perhaps?"

"I am not certain," I said. "She is the daughter of Esme Murdoch. Grace is her name. I do not know if she has married and perhaps has a different last name. I wished to pass along my condolences about her mother's passing earlier this year. I have only just learned of it."

His brow furrowed for a moment as he considered my words. I felt suddenly wicked lying to a priest, but I did not feel explaining my true reason a wise decision.

"Yes, Esme died in June," he answered. "That was when I last saw her daughter, Grace. For the services. A simple affair. Grace and her brother, Gavin, both work for Lord MacMahon."

"Oh," Henry answered. "I recognize the name. His estate is outside of Melrose if I am not mistaken."

"Correct," Father Robert answered. "I would imagine you can find Grace there." He paused a moment and studied me with a wrinkled forehead. "How is it that you are acquainted?"

"I met her while doing some charity work," I answered.

"Ah, yes. I understand. How kind of you to pass along your condolences, Your Grace."

"Thank you for the information and your time, Father."

Henry offered his thanks and we departed, climbing into the carriage to return to the hotel. Henry escorted me to our suite where I found Robert pacing the floor of the sitting room with Sinclair wringing her hands.

"There you are!" he exclaimed as we entered. "Where the devil have you been, Langford? I've been terribly worried."

"Do not take your frustration out on poor Henry," I said. "He only did what I asked of him."

Robert frowned and clasped his hands behind his back. With a penitent glance to Henry, he offered a nod and a murmured apology.

Henry insisted no amends needed to be made before excusing himself to his own room. Sinclair, too, scurried from the room.

"Well?" Robert demanded the moment we were alone.

"There isn't much news, I'm afraid, Robert," I said.

Robert's eyes shot wide at the admission. "No news? Where have you been all day? 'Tis late afternoon! I returned to an empty suite and feared the worst!"

I poured Robert a scotch for his nerves and settled him with it in a chair. He grumbled but relented. "We made two stops and Henry insisted I not skip a mid-day meal. He was certain you'd agree."

"Quite right," Robert said with a nod. "At least he got something right."

I held in a chuckle at Robert's sudden disagreeable nature. "Don't laugh, Lenora, this is no joking matter!"

The statement caused a giggle to escape my lips. "Oh, Robert. I have never known you to be this ill-tempered. Even when I turned up with a newborn babe in my arms!"

Robert narrowed his eyes at me and took another sip of the bronze liquid. "'Tis Edwin's fault. He brings out the worst in me." He offered a grumble as he swallowed another sip before refilling his glass.

"Is there no redeeming your relationship?" I questioned.

He raised an eyebrow as he settled into his chair across from me. "That remains to be seen."

I cocked my head. "Is the man a murderer or not?!" Robert exclaimed.

With a sigh, I said, "Unfortunately, I've made little progress in determining that."

"What did he have to say for himself about the quarrel in the pub?"

"He admitted it, though added he did not kill the man over it. He maintained they were both far into the drink and both of them speaking out of turn. Nothing more."

"He held a knife to a man's throat. In the very least, it is bad taste!"

"I agree, it casts a negative light, though Edwin's behavior tends to run to the dramatic."

Robert grunted in what I understood to be agreement. After a moment, he added, "How quickly you orient yourself, Lenora. You see things others do not."

"Rather an understatement, dear," I answered.

This elicited a tiny chuckle from my sour spouse. "I suppose you believe Edwin's statement of innocence still?"

"I do," I answered.

"What did he and Gerard argue over? Did he say?"

"A woman."

Robert rolled his eyes and stared into the fire blazing in our fireplace. "A tart, no doubt." He pulled his gaze away from the dancing flames and stared at me. "Have you any luck in contacting the deceased?"

"I did not try," I admitted.

A befuddled look crossed Robert's features. "I visited Tilly's grave this afternoon. I hoped to determine why she insisted I help Edwin."

"And?"

"Nothing," I admitted with a sigh. "I did not speak with her or even see her."

"Is that not odd?"

"I found it so," I said. "I believed I heard her whisper to me but…"

"But?" Robert prodded.

"I am uncertain. Another spirit approached me and I concluded it may have been her I heard, not Tilly. After the other soul approached, I was rather sidetracked. She requested my help in finding her daughter. Henry and I discussed it with the priest and he told us her daughter, Grace, worked for Lord MacMahon."

Robert's eyebrows raised. "Cameron?" I offered a shrug. "Did Henry recognize the name?"

"Yes. He said his estate was near Melrose."

"Yes, yes, I know the estate quite well. Cameron and I went to school together."

"Oh!" I exclaimed. "Might it be possible to arrange a visit? I would very much like to find Esme's daughter for her."

"What is the reason for finding her?"

"I do not know. She was not very clear. But if we are able to arrange it, I will return to the gravesite and inquire from the woman."

"I shall write to him, yes. We should attempt the visit before returning home, perhaps."

I nodded but offered no other response.

"Do you disagree?"

"No, I do not. Though I have already grown homesick. And I miss Sam."

Robert smiled at me. "I would lecture you that this is Edwin's fault, but instead, I shall take satisfaction in the knowledge that you pine for Blackmoore Castle."

"At least I have you to curb my terrible longing."

"Wonderful to know I am useful in that respect. If you'll excuse me now, though, I will write the missive to Cameron so it may be sent posthaste."

I nodded as Robert departed, leaving me alone with my thoughts. I sighed as I stared into the fireplace. Thoughts tumbled through my mind. One notion after another vied for my attention. What I'd hoped to be a simple matter had confounded itself multiple times. And no solutions presented themselves on either front.

In fact, rather than answer any questions, I'd only found more. And now a new mystery on top of it. What did the elderly spirit at the graveyard want? What danger did her daughter face? It must be substantial in order for the woman to appear to me with such concern.

My mind turned to memories of the encounter. My lips formed a pout as my mind returned to the original problem that brought me to Glasgow. Why did Tilly continue to appeal to me on Edwin's behalf, yet when I sought her, she refused to appear?

I began to question if I had truly seen Tilly's ghost or if my mind concocted the entire scenario. My eyebrows raised high as I wondered if I was capable of tricking myself into helping Edwin. In other words, was it my own guilt concocting the visions of Tilly to assuage any misgivings I had about diving into the situation.

My chest lifted as I heaved a sigh. I had begun to question even my own motives. Perhaps it was the lack of rest I'd received of late. I felt drained. My head fell onto the chair behind me. I could fall asleep here, I reflected, I felt so exhausted. I was certain I would rue it if I did, but perhaps I could close my eyes for a few moments.

***

A knock startled me and I jumped in my armchair. My heart thudded in my chest. The knock sounded again. Outside of my racing heart, I felt groggy. I must have fallen asleep, I surmised as I stood.

I glanced around, surprised Robert had not swept in to tend to the door. He must still be finishing his correspondence.

I ambled over and pulled the door open, finding the hallway empty. I took a step through the doorway, glancing up and down the hall. I saw no one.

A chill shook me to my core, and I wrapped my arms across my chest as I stepped back inside, craving the warmth of the fire.

As I shut the door, I considered retreating to my bed to continue my nap. I decided first to check the time. As I spun to face the mantel clock, I leapt back, crashing into the closed door. A man faced me, his hard features cast in unforgiving shadows from the fire.

With his chin tucked to his chest, he eyed me with nearly black eyes. As I approached, I noticed a large red stain on his vest.

"Hello," I said, shoving my alarm aside as I realized he must be a spirit. Dark, stringy hair topped his head, and his deep-set eyes were made even more menacing by the scowl on his lips and the flickering firelight. His crooked nose appeared to have been the result of multiple scuffles of a violent nature.

He sneered at my greeting. I narrowed my eyes at him. Did he mean to frighten me? I hated to inform him, I have witnessed much worse.

"Do you need assistance?" I asked.

His teeth showed as he lifted his upper lip in a derisive display.

"Are you merely here to threaten me?"

His eyes shifted to the armchair I had occupied moments

before. A figure sat in it. My forehead wrinkled as I tilted my head to identify the room's newest occupant.

The figure leapt from his seat. I recognized Edwin. "Edwin! Have you been released? Has there been some break in the case?"

He ignored me, lunging forward at the man. It was then that I noticed a knife clutched in his hand. He shoved the man against the wall. "Never speak of her again," he shouted.

The man stared at him, unflinching. "I will slice you open if you utter such nonsense."

"Edwin, no!" I shouted. "Stop this at once!"

I raced to the doorway leading to the small office area of our suite. "Robert!" I called. "Come, quickly!"

I received no response. "Robert!" I shouted again.

With no assistance forthcoming, I hurried across the room and grasped Edwin's arm. He shook me off and I tumbled backward, crashing into a chair behind me. Pain shot through my back as it clipped my spine with its pointed edge.

"Edwin, please!" I shouted again and lunged forward toward him.

He stumbled back a step as I latched onto his arm. He twisted to face me, wildly swinging to maintain his balance. The knife remained clutched in his hand as his arms flailed, searching for balance.

I screamed as a sharp pain shot through my shoulder. Instinctively, I clutched at my arm. When I pulled my hand away, red blood covered it. I glanced at my shoulder. Blood poured from a slice, soaking my dress.

With widened eyes, I glanced at Edwin. Blood dripped from his knife. It clattered to the ground as he released it, panic showing on his face. "Lenora, I did not mean to. I did not mean to."

I stumbled backward away from him, pressing my hand

to my wound. Wooziness overcame me. Had I already lost that much blood? I inched away. My heel caught the edge of the area rug and I tumbled back, unable to right myself as my vision closed to a pinpoint.

As I fell and blackness surrounded me, I heard one thing over the blood rushing into my ears. "Help him, Lenora."

CHAPTER 9

I awoke screaming. I thrashed violently as my body shook all over.

"Lenora! Lenora!" I recognized Robert's voice calling to me.

Thoughts raced through my mind. Had he called for a doctor already? How much blood had I lost, I wondered? Was the shaking from some complication from my wound?

I snapped my eyes open, searching for him. "Robert?" I cried.

It took me a moment to acclimate to my surroundings. I sat in the armchair near the fireplace. Robert's hands grasped my shoulders firmly, his face inches from mine. My jaw gaped open and I glanced to my left shoulder. Not a drop of blood. I pulled at the fabric. It was intact, no slices had ripped it open.

I let out a breath I did not realize I had been holding.

"Lenora, are you quite all right?"

"Yes," I nodded as I squeezed my eyes shut. "Another nightmare."

Robert's jaw tightened. "I see." His hands remained around my shoulders.

I wrapped my fingers around his forearm and squeezed. "I am fine."

"Are you certain? You seem disturbed. And you are quite pale."

I nodded. "I am certain. Thank you. I am sorry to have disturbed you with my outburst."

"Do you care to talk about it?"

I shrugged. "Another haunting encounter with Edwin and a man whom I assume to be Gerard."

Robert's eyes widened. "You saw him?"

"I assume it was him. Or a version of him concocted by my mind. He and Edwin quarreled. Edwin had a knife. I attempted to stop him from pursuing the argument, and as he turned, the knife slashed my shoulder."

Robert retreated a few steps and collapsed into the armchair opposite me. He shook his head. "I do not like this, Lenora."

"It was only a nightmare."

"Or a warning."

I shook my head and began to respond when Robert interrupted. "The other man, describe him."

I offered a description of the man I'd seen in my dream. "Hmm," Robert murmured. "I have only had the displeasure of making Gerard's acquaintance on two occasions. Your description fits his."

"Perhaps it was Gerard, then," I answered. "What sort of man was he? Your comment makes me wonder."

Robert wiggled his eyebrows and a frown formed on his face. "The dastardly sort," he answered. "Calculating, underhanded. Always scheming."

"He sounds quite rotten as you describe him."

"He is… well, was. I confess it is one of the reasons I

worry about you investigating this, though, it is also the reason the shred of doubt over Edwin's guilt lives on in my mind."

I raised my eyebrows at his statement. He, too, had an inkling of Edwin's innocence. Strides were being made. Robert set his gaze on me. "He is the sort of man who assuredly had many enemies."

"Many of the sort who would stab him?"

Robert answered with a nod. "Lenora, we should take this seriously. You may not realize the extent of your gifts. How did your mind concoct the image of a man you've never met? Perhaps your injury in your dream is a warning of something to come. I do not wish you harmed in this pursuit."

"My dream ended with another plea from Tilly."

Robert shook his head. "I cannot understand this."

"Neither can I. And her refusal to visit with me beyond these equivocal appearances confounds me."

"Why do you think that may be? She seemed to have no trouble appearing to you before."

"I am not certain. This is why I am so perplexed. She readily appeared to me after her death on multiple occasions. Why be bashful now?"

Robert's brow furrowed. "Could it not be Tilly?"

"What do you mean?"

"Could some other spirit be appearing in her form? Have there been any instances in the past where you've experienced something like this?"

I searched my memory. "Not to my knowledge. The spirits I've encountered seem to be genuine. Though I admit, my mind has jumped to a similar conclusion."

He raised his eyebrows at me. "Lenora, if this spirit is not Tilly…"

I held up my hand to stop him. "We have no confirmation that is the case."

"We should exercise caution. We do not know what is afoot here."

"As always, I will remain cautious."

Robert eyed me for a moment before he nodded and said, "All right. Forgive me, I sometimes forget you have dealt with these matters long before I and have much more experience."

I offered a weak smile. "For all my experience, it seems I cannot figure them out any more easily than you can."

A knock sounded at the door. My heart leapt into my throat at the sound. Robert rose from his chair and crossed to the door, pulling it open. "Ah, Henry," he greeted Mr. Langford, "come in."

"Good evening, Your Graces." He nodded to me.

Robert slid two envelopes from the round table near the door and handed them to Henry. "I shall see that these are posted at once," Henry said.

"Please have the one messengered to Blackmoore Castle posthaste."

Henry nodded. "I will arrange it immediately."

"Thank you."

A missive to Blackmoore Castle, my mind pondered, whatever for? I did not have time to question it as Sinclair entered, signaling my need to ready myself for dinner. I did not revisit the topic over our meal. Robert attempted to keep conversation light, though my mind continued to weigh on the mystery at hand. It also feared my upcoming slumber.

As I lay in my bed, I found myself reluctant to close my eyes. My nightmares had become so frequent of late, I feared another cropping up. Had they provided me with meaningful information, I would have minded less, but they seemed nonsensical, at least to my brain.

Perhaps as the case progressed, I could glean some helpful detail from them. I considered the mystery. If I could not sleep, I would spend my nighttime hours forming a plan.

Should I try to visit Tilly again? Perhaps I should try to make contact with the late Mr. Boyle first. I could return to the scene of the crime. I could also try the Pennington's Glasgow home. Yes, I resolved, I would spend the next day in pursuit of my first elusive spirit. I would leave Tilly until I'd made some sort of progress.

* * *

Bright sunshine greeted me the next morning as I slogged from my bed. After another sleepless night, I pondered if I had the energy to traipse about Glasgow in search of the wayward Mr. Boyle. Sinclair entered the bedroom after a knock, and I determined I would sleep better only if I pushed forward with my investigation.

"Did you sleep well, Your Grace?"

"No," I admitted as she brushed my hair.

"Oh, what a shame. Perhaps you should remain abed and rest."

"No, I do not wish to keep Mr. Langford waiting."

She caught my gaze in the mirror of the dressing table. "Mr. Langford has gone for the day."

I sat straighter, the wrinkle between my brows deepening. "What? He was to accompany me on my travels today."

"His Grace said he will accompany you."

"He told you this?"

Sinclair shook her head. "Nay, I overheard his conversation with Mr. Langford. His Grace insisted he accompany you so he can ensure you are properly looked after."

"Properly looked after? Mr. Langford is more than capable!"

"Your Grace did not seem to believe so. Said the latest developments were worrisome and he preferred to monitor the situation himself."

I allowed my gaze to focus on nothing in particular as I parsed the statement. "What developments, Your Grace?" Sinclair continued. "Have you made some progress toward finding the murderer?"

"No," I admitted. "No, though I had a disturbing nightmare. I fear it has spooked Robert."

Sinclair gave me a knowing glance. "His Grace wishes to be certain of your safety."

I nodded as she put the final touches on my hairstyle. "What plans have you today, Your Grace?" she asked as she tended to my nightclothes.

"I plan to seek out Mr. Boyle's spirit. With any luck, he can clear up the matter easily."

"Do you believe it will be that simple?"

With a shake of my head, I answered, "No, no, I do not."

After breakfast, Robert and I climbed into the carriage. I passed the address from Edwin along to our driver prior to boarding. I gazed at Robert as the carriage lurched forward. "Thank you for accompanying me, Robert. I did not expect Henry's departure."

"Yes, I sent him on some business. Though the truth of the matter is, I prefer to accompany you."

"Oh? I thought the matter put you off."

"It does. Though given the nature of your dream, I should like to take no chances. It is wrong of me to shirk my duty to you onto Henry merely because I am uncomfortable with the subject."

I smiled. What strides we were making! "Well, in any case, I do appreciate it. And I am certain Edwin will, too."

"I care not what Edwin feels," he muttered. "Though your faith in him is admirable and certainly one of the reasons I question his guilt."

"You mentioned Mr. Boyle being rather a vile man. Do

you know of anyone specifically with whom he could have had issue?"

"Specifically, no," Robert said after pondering it for a moment. "Undoubtedly, the list is long and varied."

"Edwin mentioned his dishonest dealings but did not delve any deeper. Have you any details?"

Robert widened his eyes, an expression of shock on his face. "What details would you imagine I have?"

"None as a participant!" I assured him. "Though surely one hears rumors."

He sighed. "Rumors are difficult to parse through. And why the devil didn't Edwin tell you. He begs for your help, then blindfolds you at every turn!"

"I think Edwin fears losing my support by mentioning too many coarse details."

"Does he imagine you will not stumble upon them?"

I shrugged and shook my head, silently suggesting I did not know. Robert sighed. "Mr. Boyle was well known for making available a variety of goods that he received by less-than-legal means."

"So he would have dealings with sailors?"

Robert nodded. "Any one of whom could have murdered him in a deal gone wrong," I suggested.

"A plausible theory, yes."

"Or a client," I mused aloud. "Someone he attempted to sell an item to, perhaps for a higher price than the person preferred."

"Another likely scenario."

"Two possible alternatives to Edwin being the murderer. Both of which may prove impossible to track down. At least without Mr. Boyle's help."

The carriage slowed to a stop outside a stately row of townhomes. I gazed at them through the wrought-iron fence designed to keep less-than-desirable visitors away from the properties.

Robert stepped from the carriage and reached for my hand to assist me in stepping to the sidewalk.

"Which is it?" I inquired as I searched for the number.

Robert scanned the homes. "This one, no, just a moment," he put his finger to his chin as he studied them. "There, that one."

"Oh, yes, there is the number."

He offered his arm, and we strode down the sidewalk toward it. "I wonder if old Penny might be in," he said as he slowed to a stop outside the gate.

"Penny?" I asked.

"Lord Pennington. Or Penny as he is oft known to his friends."

"Are you acquainted?"

"More or less. We've had a few business dealings, though not many. Do you mind if we pay him a call, assuming he is in?"

"Not at all. It would give me the chance to determine if I can find Mr. Boyle. I do not see him outside."

"A word of warning. If we do gain entry, do not mention the late Mr. Boyle to Penny. His relationship with his younger brother is even more tumultuous than mine with Edwin."

I nodded in understanding as we mounted the stairs and Robert used the brass knocker to announce us. We waited for several moments. I scanned the area but found no one, alive or dead. Apparently, the late Mr. Boyle did not have a penchant for the exterior of his brother's Glasgow home.

The door opened and a petite girl with flaming red hair peeked from it. "Good day, sir. May I help you?"

"Yes," Robert answered. "I am Robert Fletcher, Duke of

Blackmoore, and this is my wife. By chance is Lord Pennington at home? I hoped to call upon him."

I glanced past the girl into the home's interior. If we could gain admittance, would I find Mr. Boyle inside, I wondered?

"I am sorry, Your Grace. He is not at home right now."

"Oh, what a terrible shame to have missed him," Robert said.

A shadow passed behind the maid. I wondered if it might be my elusive spirit. I squashed my lips together in frustration as the conversation continued between Robert and the maid.

"Do you know when he may return?" Robert inquired.

"He has only gone out for his morning stroll. He should return within the hour."

Robert glanced at his pocket watch. "Oh, well..."

"Would it be possible if we waited?" I inquired.

The maid bobbed her head in agreement and motioned for us to enter. We stepped through the doorway into the dark foyer, decorated in rich woods. She guided us to the front sitting room and inquired if we would like tea.

Robert declined and she left us to wait for Lord Pennington's return.

As she left, pulling the doors closed behind her, I leapt to my feet.

"Any sign of him?" Robert inquired.

"No, none so far. Though I saw a shadow before we entered and wondered if it may be Mr. Boyle." I eased the door open and peeked into the foyer. Empty.

"Where did you spot the shadow?" Robert whispered.

"Just there," I hissed, pointing out the spot. I opened the door wider. "Wait here. I shall explore."

"Lenora!" I heard him utter in a low tone as I tiptoed into the foyer and further into the house. I scanned the area, finding no trace of a spirit. A doorway on the left led to a small parlor with a pianoforte, a bookcase, and a chaise lounge. I peered inside. Nothing.

I spun and searched the area, my eyes lifting to the second floor. I could not make it there undetected, I determined, and gave up on my search. I retreated toward the sitting room. Before re-entering it, I spun to face the foyer from the vantage point of the door. I narrowed my eyes as I waited for some sign.

Moments later, the shadow crossed again. I hurried toward it and glanced into the parlor, finding the source. A large tree's branches bent in the breeze, hiding the sun from view. The effect caused a darkening in the foyer. The source of my shadow was not a spirit but the scenery.

My shoulder sagged in disappointment, and I glanced into the parlor a final time before retreating. I ceased my retreat as something caught my eye. Portraits hung on the wall across from the doorway. Likenesses of two men and a woman hung in a grouping.

I approached the wall, staring at them. Arranged in a triangle, the top portrait was of a stately looking gentleman with a handlebar mustache and graying hair. Under him, the woman was depicted with her chestnut hair pulled back and her green dress a match to her eyes. Next to her, a dark-haired man with an angular face and dark eyes stared from the painting. I recognized the man who had visited my dreams. I recognized Gerard Boyle.

CHAPTER 10

I spun in a circle, searching the room. "Gerard?" I whispered. "Gerard Boyle, are you here?"

Silence responded. I waited a few more moments before I decided the spirit would not appear. Disappointment filled me as I hurried back to the sitting room and slipped inside, easing the door shut behind me.

Robert stared at me with crossed arms. "Have you finished parading around Lord Pennington's townhome?"

"Quite," I said.

"Lenora, you mustn't take such chances. Did you find anything?"

A coy smile crossed my face at the question. As adverse as Robert was to my roaming, his curiosity outweighed his crossness. "I did."

His eyebrows shot up.

I sank onto the loveseat across the room. "A portrait of Gerard Boyle. A match to the man of whom I dreamt."

Robert narrowed his eyes at the statement as we overheard the front door open and close. Voices sounded in the foyer and I heard our names mentioned. Moments later, the door to the sitting room swung open. The man depicted in the top portrait in the parlor entered.

"Penny!" Robert exclaimed, a broad smile on his face.

"Robert!" The man grasped Robert's hand and gave it a hard shake. "This is an unexpected surprise. What brings you by? Some business?"

"No, just in the area. I pointed out your home to my wife and the whim struck me to pay a call." Robert motioned toward me and I smiled as the man's eyes focused on me.

"Oh, yes. I had heard you remarried. Well, my congratulations, old boy," he said with a clap on Robert's shoulder. He ambled over and took my hand in his as a greeting. "And good day to you, Your Grace."

"It is a pleasure to meet you, Lord Pennington."

"The pleasure is mine. Are you on your honeymoon?" he inquired of Robert.

"No, but Lenora accompanies me from time to time on business trips."

"What a good sport of you, dear," he said to me.

The conversation lulled for a moment. I overheard the knocker pounding against the door. The maid scurried past the doorway and pulled open the front door. The large wooden object blocked any view I had of the visitor.

Robert and Lord Pennington conversed about some business as I struggled to overhear the conversation from the foyer. I caught bits and pieces. The maid, still visible to me, shook her head and murmured something about Lord Pennington being busy. A moment later, a regretful expression crossed her face and she expressed something else to the party outside. She shrugged her shoulders. I heard a woman's voice answer. It grew louder, almost frantic. From what I gathered, the woman demanded to see Lord Pennington.

The voice grew loud enough that Lord Pennington swung his head in the direction of the foyer. He offered a brief smile to Robert before saying, "Will you excuse me for just a moment?"

"Of course!" Robert answered.

Lord Pennington exited, pulling the doors closed behind him. Voices continued in what sounded like a heated argument. I strained to hear the conversation, but the door muffled their voices. After a few moments of back and forth, I heard Lord Pennington shout, "Good day, madam!" The door slammed just after, causing me to jolt in my seat.

I shot Robert a glance, but Lord Pennington's return foiled any other communication. "My apologies," the man said as he re-entered the room.

"No trouble at all!" Robert assured him with a smile.

"Now, where were we?"

I glanced out the window as the two continued their discussion. A woman hurried away from the townhouse. She wore a large, rather worn coat and hat. Odd, I thought. Not just her attire, but my mind pondered what she and Lord Pennington could have to discuss. She did not look to be on the same social footing. Was it the woman in the portrait, perhaps? No, I corrected myself, she had rich chestnut hair while this woman's bouncing brown curls were several shades lighter.

I did not have the opportunity to ponder it further. Robert's conversation with Lord Pennington wound down. As they shook hands, I readied myself to depart. Within moments, we strolled toward the carriage in the bright November sunshine.

We climbed inside with a cafe as our destination. Robert gazed out of the window, watching the scenery as we wound through the streets. I found myself surprised by his silence. Had he not overheard the argument? Perhaps he was too well-mannered to gossip about it.

I considered not bringing the matter up for fear my

husband may find my interest vulgar. Though the close connection with the deceased and lack of other clues as to his murderer drove me to do it.

"Robert," I said, pulling his gaze from the window, "did you overhear the rather intense argument between Lord Pennington and his caller?"

"I overheard voices from the foyer, yes. Though I could not make out what it was about."

His statement dashed my hopes that he'd heard more than I did. "Neither could I. I wonder what it was all about."

Robert shrugged. "I couldn't say, though Penny seemed quite determined to offer an air of finality."

I reflected on the memory, attempting to piece together any additional information. "She did not appear to be his sort," I murmured.

"Oh?" Robert inquired.

"Yes, her clothes were quite tattered. She did not give the appearance that would make one think they were acquainted."

Robert raised his eyebrows but did not comment. His upbringing taught him to avoid the more salacious details. I defended my statement to him. "I only mention it because of his connection to Mr. Boyle."

Robert nodded, pressing his finger to his lips in thought. "I shouldn't imagine Penny to have many dealings in common with his brother. They were rather estranged. You'll notice he did not even wear a mourning band."

I nodded. "Yes, I did notice that. Well, I suppose, then, that was a pointless journey. Mr. Boyle would likely not return to his brother's home if they were estranged. At least you were able to visit with your friend. And I learned that the man who appeared in my dream was, in fact, the deceased."

"Do you suppose he will ever appear to you?"

I shook my head and my shoulders rose to my ears. "I do not know, but without his assistance, I fear the worst." With a sigh, I focused my gaze on the passing scenery.

Robert leaned forward and took my hand in his. "Lenora, you are doing your best. Do not let the matter trouble you so."

The carriage ground to a halt and shimmied as our driver dismounted. I offered a weak smile and a squeeze of Robert's hand, though his consolation did little to settle my nerves. Without progress, Edwin would likely find himself convicted of a crime he swore he did not commit.

We lunched, and Robert strove to keep the conversation light, preferring not to focus on my investigation, though I found my mind returning to it on several occasions. Following the meal, I requested that we return to the docks. Despite his vexation, Robert obliged.

I stood in the chilly afternoon air near the spot where the murder occurred. A myriad of thoughts crowded into my mind as I stared out over the water, littered with ships. No one but the living stood before me.

Frustration grew inside me. Though I realized the timetables of the dead were not the same as the living. It had taken me months to solve Annie's murder. In this instance, though, Edwin may not be so lucky to have that long.

I bit my lower lip as I searched again for Mr. Boyle's spirit. After a moment, I turned and shook my head at Robert. I could not even bring myself to call out to him.

We returned to the hotel. I remained quiet for most of the ride, interjecting comments to answer Robert's conversation but not offering much more. Tiredness crept through me. I collapsed into the armchair near the roaring fire. Robert suggested a nap, but I thoroughly disagreed. I feared ruining my night's sleep with the few moments of peace I may find now.

Instead, I fought to stay awake, trying to focus on my novel and finding the task impossible. My mind flitted from subject to subject. I'd been foiled at every turn in seeking Mr. Boyle. While the case could be made that another had killed him, we had little evidence to prove it.

My mind turned to the odd encounter at Lord Pennington's townhome. I could not shake the feeling it was somehow related, but my mind struggled to make any connection. Perhaps Mr. Boyle's brother had as many questionable dealings as he, though Robert did not believe so.

My shoulders heaved in a sigh as I focused on the other piece of the puzzle: Tilly. I could not even manage a conversation with her and she had been my best friend in life. Melancholy swept over me and I rested my head against the wing of the chair.

I was failing on every front and I felt it most deeply when I considered I may not be able to honor Tilly's request. She'd always stuck by me, even in my worst moments.

Memories flooded back to me, some of them bringing tears to sting my eyes. I recalled an instance in which we'd been assigned a composition on our lives. A difficult subject for me, I'd struggled to put words to paper.

Tilly had breezed through the assignment, happily detailing her hopes and desires on the page. In her version of her life, she'd married well, had a family with six children, and enjoyed life to the fullest. Her optimism astounded me at times.

I sat staring at a blank page.

"It is due tomorrow, Lenora," Tilly reminded me.

My shoulders slouched and I thunked my head against the desk in front of me. "I know," I groaned. "And I have yet to write a word."

"With all your reading, I'd think your imagination far better than mine," Tilly teased.

"I am not writing fiction, Tilly. And detailing my life is… Well, I do not wish to include any of the untoward details which have filled my days for fear they may come under fire from Headmistress Williamson."

"Perhaps you could use this essay as a chance to explain it better," Tilly suggested.

I shot her a glance and she raised her hands in surrender. Millicent sauntered into the room. "Gabbing, as usual, I see," she said in her bubbly voice.

Tilly rolled her eyes. "We are discussing an assignment. You wouldn't understand, as you have no friends to discuss anything with."

Her face scrunched and reddened, and she shot back, "Take it back. That is not true!"

Tilly rolled her eyes. "Oh, Millie, don't get your knickers in a twist, I was only joking."

"Perhaps Lenora is finding the assignment troublesome because of the subject matter. I cannot imagine it to be easy to write about one's life when the details of one's life are so vulgar."

"Her life is not vulgar," Tilly contended.

"I disagree." She twisted to face me. "If I were you, Lenora, I should hand in a blank paper. You CANNOT write about your life, and you CANNOT write a lie. Both are amoral. You'll simply have to take a zero on the assignment." She stuck her pointed nose in the air after offering her suggestion.

With a sigh, I stared at the blank page in front of me, worried her advice was exactly what I would end up doing. By the end of the evening, I'd written the words "My name is Lenora Hastings."

I climbed into bed with no more written. I hoped an idea struck me overnight and I could scribble the remainder of the essay before classes the next day.

When I awoke the following morning, the sun already lit the room, casting long shadows on the floor. I hurried from my bed and rushed to the writing desk. As I plopped in the chair, still in my dressing gown, I found a stack of papers sitting where I'd left my composition.

I shoved them aside when the words caught my eye. I snatched the papers back and read the first few lines.

My name is Lenora Hastings. I am a unique and uncommon individual. My talents are varied and rare, and it is these talents that will lead me through life. A life that I will strive to make as unique as I am.

I continued to scan the words that flowed over several pages. The handwriting was not my own, but close enough to mine that it could be accepted. The essay detailed how I planned to spend my life in the service of others, a tradition that I'd already begun and excelled at. It finished suggesting I would find happiness with a man who recognized my true value.

I sat back in the chair, stunned. Tilly ambled into the room, still in her dressing gown. A cheery smile graced her delicate features. "Good morning, Lenora!" she said.

"Good morning, Tilly," I murmured as I continued to stare at the papers.

"All finished with your essay?" she inquired, a mischievous glint in her eye.

I opened my mouth but found no words escaped it. She smiled at me and winked. "I reviewed it this morning and thought it was quite good! I think you'll receive an excellent mark on it."

"Tilly!" I whispered. "I did not write this!"

"Of course you did. I watched you write it last night. In the middle of the night, inspiration struck you and you rose from your bed and wrote and wrote."

I tilted my head at her, in both admiration and admonishment. "Tilly, this is cheating," I suggested.

She sank onto the edge of the bed nearest the desk. "It is not. You could have written that exact essay, but you lacked the confidence to do so. You've detailed it one hundred times to me before. I merely was the conduit to put pen to paper."

Before I could respond, Millicent wandered in. She scrunched her nose at us. "What are you two doing?"

"I was assuring Lenora her essay is perfect."

Millicent's brows knit and a frown formed on her lips. "What essay? It is unfinished!"

"She finished it overnight," Tilly said.

"She did not!" Millicent shot back. She reached for the papers. Tilly snatched them from my hand and dodged away from her.

"She did." She waved the papers in the air. "Here they are. How did they come to be here without her writing them?" She flashed her the first page. "Look, it is in her handwriting."

Millicent's mouth scrunched into a tight ball. She searched for a response but, finding none, she spun on her heel and stormed from the room.

I raised my eyebrows at her, still feeling a measure of guilt over the situation. Tilly, on the other hand, offered a smug smile as Millicent departed. My eyes met hers. "Thank you," I answered.

She handed me the papers back. "Though…" I began.

"Turn it in, Lenora. Do not risk the wrath of Headmistress Williamson for missing a deadline."

She had a point, I reflected. Missing an assignment would be punished, particularly if it was me who missed it. The Headmistress and I did not see eye to eye on most things. I did not wish to give her an excuse to inflict any punishment on me.

As I stared at the papers, I memorized the moment and my feelings in it. I should never forget such a kindness and hoped to repay it one day.

A tear rolled down my cheek as the feelings rushed back to me. "I will find a way, Tilly," I promised in a whisper.

As I climbed into bed for the night, my mind spun, searching for a solution. I tossed and turned, unable to sleep. The few moments of dozing that I managed did little to settle my mind.

As I stared upward, studying the moonlit ceiling, the image of Gerard Boyle formed in my mind's eye. I turned onto my side and squeezed my eyes shut. Still, I could not shake the man from my head. I spun onto the opposite side. I rose from my bed to pace the floor.

Try as I might, I could not rid my mind of the man's image. I shook my head and marched across the room in the opposite direction. I pursed my lips and pulled off my dressing gown, flinging it onto the bed. I changed into my day dress, awkwardly fastening it behind my back, unwilling to awaken Sinclair for the task.

I strode to Robert's sleeping form. I hovered over him as I decided if I should wake him. I hated to, though I was certain he would not prefer me to traipse about the town alone. But perhaps the elusive Mr. Boyle did not take kindly to Robert. This was a theory I could test in the daylight, I reasoned. Though, my mind countered, Robert would be awake in the daylight and put a stop to it.

I shook my head at my own indecision before I backed away from the bed. As a younger woman, I wandered the streets of Glasgow in less than desirable areas. I could do it again.

I slipped from the hotel room and out into the cool night air. I pulled my cape closer around me as the cool air turned colder nearer to the docks.

I hurried past The Black Horse, still wild with activity even in these wee hours, and rushed toward the murder scene. A few sailors gawked at me as I passed them. I ignored their stares and hurried to the spot. Using the buildings as a reference, I came to a stop near where we assumed the crime had been committed.

My heart sank as I found it empty. I spun in a circle, searching. Perhaps we were off on the location. I chewed my lower lip as I scanned the area. "Where are you, Gerard Boyle?" I breathed.

My heart skipped a beat as I turned toward the sea, finding a man standing in front of me. His gray skin appeared damp with perspiration. His features formed a mask of confusion. A red splotch covered his chest.

CHAPTER 11

"Gerard?" I questioned, staring at the man in front of me.

He stared ahead, his eyes wide as though shocked I had spoken to him. I wondered if he was still in shock from his experience.

I spoke slowly and gently to him. "Gerard Boyle. I can see you. I know it may come as a shock, but I am able to speak with those who have passed. Like you. Do you realize you have passed?"

He glanced around as though surveying his surroundings. I followed his gaze before shifting my head into his line of vision. This was progress, but I needed more.

"Mr. Boyle?" I queried. "Mr. Boyle, do you realize you are dead? You were, in fact, murdered."

He focused his gaze upon me. I offered a brief and half-hearted smile. "I am sorry to deliver the news if you did not realize it, but I am desperately seeking your help."

His brow furrowed as I spoke. "Mr. Boyle, do you recall your murder? Can you tell me who murdered you?"

His lip began to tremble and then they moved up and

down as though he was attempting to speak but could not. I strained to hear him.

"I cannot hear you. Please, Mr. Boyle, can you tell me who murdered you?"

His chest heaved up and down. His features twisted and contorted into a pained expression. He croaked out one word. "Edwin."

My eyes widened. I shook my head. "What?"

He repeated the statement. "Edwin."

I gulped as I realized I had heard him correctly. "Edwin," I repeated. "Did Edwin Fletcher murder you? Please, Mr. Boyle, it is very important."

"Edwin," he repeated. "Edwin. Edwin! EDWIN!"

On the last iteration, he shouted his name so forcefully it drove me back a step. My lower lip quivered at the revelation. I turned and fled from the docks. I only ceased running once I was a few minutes from the hotel. I slowed and gasped for breath. I shivered, though I was certain not from the cold.

I pushed into the hotel and into our suite. I collapsed against the door as tears flowed down my cheeks. I dragged myself to the chair near the fireplace and collapsed into it. Sobs shook my shoulders and I sunk my head into my hands. How foolish I had been.

My tears ran dry after a time and I blew out a long breath. I settled back in the chair. My mind clouded. I pondered what I would say to Edwin. What would he respond? Would he admit to the murder? Had he forgotten? I tried to concoct scenarios that alleviated Edwin's hand in lying.

The sun crept over the horizon, and I shivered as another chill passed over me. I could not face Robert when he awoke. I needed to speak with Edwin. I rose from my chair and forced myself to exit into the chilly morning air.

I strode along the streets until the jail building came into view. I stared at it for a moment, summoning the courage to enter. The conversation must be had, I told myself. With a steadying breath, I pushed into the lobby. The man behind the half-wall gave me a long look before he rushed around it.

"Madam, may I help you? Are you injured? Do you need to report a crime?" He held his hands out as though to catch me in the event that I suddenly collapsed.

I realized in an instant how awful I must appear. I attempted to smooth back my wayward hair. I straightened my shoulders and shook my head. "No. I must speak with a prisoner. Edwin Fletcher."

The man's brow furrowed. "Please, it is urgent," I added, realizing the early hour likely added to the man's confusion.

"Just a moment," he said. I nodded as he disappeared into the rear of the building. He returned with another officer.

"Your Grace," the man greeted me. He forced a smile on his face. "Please, follow me."

He led me down the now-familiar halls and into the dreaded basement. Edwin lay on his cot as I approached the cell. The officer banged against the bars and he jolted awake. "Got a visitor, Lord Edwin." The officer eyed me sideways before stepping away.

"Lenora?!" Edwin questioned as he bolted from the bed. His eyes traveled the length of me. "Are you quite all right?"

I fluttered my eyelashes as I composed myself. "No," I said. "No, I am not."

"What is it? What's happened?"

I swallowed hard and forced the words out. "I saw Gerard."

"You did?! Did he identify the murderer?" Edwin gasped out, grasping the bars and pressing his face between them.

I could not force my eyes to meet his. "I asked him," I said as my brow crinkled.

"And what did he say?"

I finally let my eyes slide upward to meet his gaze. "He said only one thing."

Edwin's eyebrows lifted toward his hairline. My lower lip trembled as I forced out the word. "Edwin. He said Edwin."

Edwin let go of the bars as shock crossed his features. He shook his head and his eyes traveled his cell in search of an answer. "No," he murmured.

"It was his only answer."

"No!" he repeated, grasping hold of the bars again. He reached toward me, but I retreated a step. "No, Lenora, please. There must be some mistake."

"What mistake, Edwin?" I questioned. "I asked about his murderer. He answered your name."

"Clearly there is one! I did not kill him!"

I stared at the man standing in front of me. Even faced with this, he maintained his story. Was he this skilled at lying? Or could he be telling the truth?

He eyed me. With a tilt of his head, he said, "Lenora, please. Do not give up on me now."

I did not respond. My thoughts jumbled. "Could there be another explanation?" Edwin inquired.

"What?" I choked out.

Edwin shrugged. "Perhaps he was confused. Did you not say the dead are often mixed up? Unable to give clear answers?"

"Yes," I admitted. "Yes, that is true, though... this answer seemed quite clear."

"I did not do this, Lenora."

I remained silent for a moment before I said, "I shall continue to seek answers. I must go now."

"Lenora, wait!" he called as I darted past the officer and climbed the stairs. As I exited the building into the fresh morning air, I gulped several breaths. My conversation with Edwin had done little to settle my nerves. I would need to relay the developments to Robert. It was a conversation I did not relish. Though it was a conversation that was unavoidable.

I wandered my way back to the hotel and entered our suite. I slumped into the armchair near the fireplace. Robert emerged into the sitting room. He stopped in his tracks when he spotted me.

I was certain I made quite a sight. My eyes, likely red and puffy from crying, my tear-stained cheeks, my hair askew, and my frown gave away any indication that I was all right.

"Lenora?!" he cried, both as a question and an exclamation. He hurried toward me. His eyes were wide as he surveyed me. "Are you … has something happened? Have you slept at all?"

I shook my head and swallowed hard before I began to explain. No words came, but another tear slid down my cheek.

Robert knelt in front of me and clasped my hands. I chewed my lower lip as I squeezed his hands, drawing support from him.

Before I could speak, Sinclair emerged in the sitting room. Her eyes widened and she hurried toward me. "Your Grace!"

"Something has happened, Sinclair. Help me get Her Grace to bed."

I should explain, I thought, but I could not bring myself to speak the words. Robert had been correct. His brother was a murderer. I had been had. Perhaps I was too naive.

"Of course, Your Grace," Sinclair said. Robert scooped me into his arms. I laid my head on his shoulder. He set me on the bed and Sinclair retrieved my discarded dressing gown and nightclothes.

Robert kissed my forehead. "I shall step out for a moment while you assist Her Grace."

I grasped Robert's hand before he stepped away. I offered a weak smile. "I am so sorry for having dragged you into this."

Robert shook his head and shushed me. "Get some rest, Lenora. We shall discuss it later."

I nodded and swallowed the lump in my throat as he departed.

Sinclair cocked her head at me. "What happened, Your Grace?" Sinclair questioned after we were alone.

I shook my head and sighed. "I may have made a terrible mistake, Sinclair."

She raised her eyebrows as I spun my back to her. "I should say so. This is not even fastened close to properly!"

I breathed out a weak chuckle at her humor. "I meant in a different respect."

"Oh?" she questioned.

"I believe Edwin may not be as innocent as I expected," I choked out.

I felt her cease her motions for an instant. She resumed within seconds and I continued. "I found myself unable to sleep last night. I could not remove Mr. Boyle from my mind. I rose from my bed and hastily dressed…"

"I should say so," Sinclair said as she finished untangling the mess of dress ties I'd created in my haste last night.

"I traversed the streets to the docks." She raised her eyebrows higher. "I know, I know. Please do not share this with His Grace until I might have the chance." She nodded and I continued. "I arrived at the docks. At first, I found no one, but then, Mr. Boyle appeared."

"Did he speak to you?"

I bit my lower lip and nodded. "Yes," I whispered.

"What did he say, Your Grace?"

I hung my head as tears threatened again. "I asked him if

he could name his murderer. He appeared dazed, but I continued to badger him."

Sinclair leaned forward and nodded, her eyes wide and her eyebrows arched.

"He said…" My voice cracked. "He said Edwin's name."

Sinclair's mouth gaped open. A sympathetic expression crossed her features and she eased me onto the bed. "Oh, Your Grace," she cooed at me.

"I feel so stupid," I admitted. "I insisted we pursue this. I believed Edwin." I gasped in a breath.

Sinclair tutted at me. "You need rest, Your Grace."

I shook my head. "I must apologize to Robert."

I tried to stand, but Sinclair barred me. "You must rest, Your Grace. Even His Grace would agree."

I heaved a breath as I sought the words to disagree, but weariness overcame me.

"Do not be too hard on yourself, Your Grace," Sinclair insisted as she pulled the covers over me. "I don't believe you are as foolish as you insist you are."

"I was wrong, plain and simple, Sinclair. When asked about his murderer, Gerard Boyle named Edwin. Though…" My voice trailed off as my brow furrowed.

"What is it?" Sinclair questioned as she adjusted my pillow.

My tired mind struggled to connect thoughts. "Something seemed off."

"Such as?"

My stinging, puffy eyes struggled to stay open. I yawned before I answered. "I am not certain. Just some odd thing my mind cannot place."

"It's all right, Your Grace," Sinclair whispered. "Go to sleep."

Exhaustion overcame me and I drifted off to sleep. Another nightmare tainted my rest. I wandered the docks, cold and alone. Each time I sought an alley to return to the hotel, I found my way blocked. The streets and buildings seemed to close in around me. I backed toward the river until I crashed into something behind me. I spun to find a stack of shipping crates.

As I inched away from them, I bumped into another object. This did not feel like shipping crates, I reflected. I bit my lower lip as I slowly twirled to determine what obstructed my retreat.

Gerard Boyle stood in my path. His chest oozed red blood. Sweat beaded on his pasty skin. I shrunk away from him.

"Murdered!" he shouted. "Murdered!"

I could find no exit, so I attempted to calm him. "Yes, I realize you were murdered. I am trying to help you."

"Murdered," he groaned again.

"Tell me by whom!"

He fell silent. He touched his bloody chest and his fingers tinged red. He reached toward me with his bloodied digits.

"No!" I shouted, "no!"

I squeezed my eyes shut as I pressed against the shipping crates that had suddenly appeared behind me.

I thrashed blindly as I searched for an exit. Warmth surrounded me suddenly, and I felt linen touch my fingertips. I snapped my eyes open, finding myself in my hotel bedroom. Moonlight streamed through the window, casting long shadows on the floor.

I breathed a sigh of relief at my surroundings. A rustling alerted me to a presence in the room. I rose to sitting and stared into the darkened corners of the room.

A glimpse of pink contrasted against the blackness. "Who is there?" I called.

I received no answer. I squinted into the darkness at the color. "Tilly?" I tried.

She stepped into the moonlight, her skin appearing almost translucent in the white light.

"Tilly!" I exclaimed as I tossed my bedcovers aside. A smile crossed my lips and I hurried to her. She reached to me, clasping my hands in hers.

"He did not lie, Lenora," she said.

The smile faded from my face as I considered the statement. I opened my mouth to ask her another question, but she dropped my hands and backed away from me.

"No, Tilly, wait!" She continued her backward retreat. "Tilly, I cannot piece this together, please!"

Tilly reached the corner and backed into the blackness, vanishing. "Tilly!" I cried again.

I thrashed in my bed. "Tilly!" I murmured. "Tilly!"

My eyes fluttered open and I found Sinclair reading in the armchair across the room. She snapped the book shut as I stirred and pushed myself up to sitting.

With a smile, she greeted me. "Good afternoon, Your Grace. How do you feel?"

"Afternoon?!" I exclaimed. "Oh, good heavens, I have slept too long!"

"You needed it," Sinclair assured me. "Do you feel any better?"

I considered the question. While extreme tiredness no longer coursed through every fiber of my being, the heartache I'd felt earlier had come rushing back the moment I recalled the details of my last encounter with the dead.

My shoulders slumped at the query. "I suppose I do," I hedged.

"That is good news. And even if you do not feel completely up to snuff, His Grace has arranged a surprise that I am sure will have your heart soaring."

I offered a questioning glance in her direction. She gave a coy smile in return as she rose from her chair. "I shall arrange a tray for you, Your Grace. I am certain you are famished."

She disappeared through the doorway before I could answer. My stomach did not feel in the slightest bit hungry. I dreaded the task ahead of me. I must share what I had learned with Robert. How disappointed he would be. Both with Edwin and me, I surmised.

The door swung open again. I expected Sinclair with a tray of food. Instead, Robert strode in. My heart broke at the sight of him. More tragic news to share.

He smiled at me and his eyes twinkled as though they held a secret. His mood seemed joyous. "How are you feeling, dear? Sinclair says you have managed a bit of sleep."

"I have," I admitted. I climbed from the bed and pulled on my dressing gown. "Robert, there is something we must discuss."

"Now, now, Lenora, there will be time for that," he insisted. "There is a more pressing matter at hand."

"Oh?" I questioned. I wondered what might demand our immediate attention. And, in truth, I was relieved at the proposition of delaying our conversation. Though the conversation with Edwin did little to resolve my angst over the latest occurrence, my dream of Tilly confounded me.

"Yes!" Robert answered with a grin. He held a finger in the air. He appeared to be holding in a chuckle. "There is something that you must see!"

Robert pulled the bedroom door open and motioned to someone outside. "Or rather some*one*." He emphasized the last syllable.

I swallowed hard, wondering who this might be.

A wide smile crossed Robert's face as Nanny West paraded into the room carrying Samuel. My heart leapt at the sight of him.

"Sam!" I cried as I hurried toward them. I scooped the child from Nanny's arms and pressed him to my chest.

Robert's smile broadened. "Are you pleased?"

"Pleased? Robert, surely you jest! I am ecstatic. Thank you." I offered him a peck on the cheek. "However did you manage it?"

"When you expressed your melancholy over being separated from Blackmoore Castle and Samuel, I messengered a request to Buchanan for Nanny to bring the boy to Glasgow."

"How did he take to the travel?" I asked Nanny.

"I kept him settled with several things, including the books you suggested."

I smiled at the response. "I am so glad he was not too fussy."

"I thought it best to bring him to Glasgow in the event we travel to Walford House."

"Walford House?" I questioned.

"Yes, Cameron's estate."

"Oh, yes," I answered as Esme Murdoch's request leapt to the forefront of my mind. "Yes, I would quite prefer he travel with us."

Samuel cooed at me and I spoke to him, assuring him I did, in fact, prefer him to travel with us. Robert dismissed Nanny from the room and I wandered to the bed and plopped on it. Sam sat on my lap as I continued to shower him with affection.

The afternoon sun shone through the windows, lighting his little face. How I adored that face. I rubbed his rosy pink cheeks with my forefinger. His mouth reminded me so of Tilly's lips, along with his fair skin. He was in every way a reflection of his mother.

He reached his chubby fingers toward my hand and grasped hold of one finger. "What a strong grip you have, my little one!" I said.

He studied the finger he'd captured with great interest. A chuckle escaped me as his eyes crossed to focus on it.

The smile faded from my face and a pensive expression replaced it. I stared at those upturned, almond-shaped eyes.

"Lenora, what is it?" Robert questioned, noting my sobering expression.

I glanced to him, the wrinkles in my forehead deepening as I pieced things together. I gathered Samuel into my arms and approached Robert. Memories flooded into my mind in disjointed segments. Tilly begging me to help Edwin, Tilly appearing in Edwin's cell, Edwin uttering, "She is gone."

Realization struck me harder than a kick from a horse. A porcelain hand reached toward Sam's forehead and stroked it. I snapped my head to my side. Tilly stared at her son.

"Tilly," I breathed. She offered me a contrite glance.

"Where?" Robert asked, his eyes darting around the room. His muscles tensed as they often did when he realized a spirit was present.

"Tilly, I…" I began when she vanished. My shoulders slumped. "She is gone."

"Did she come to see Samuel?" Robert questioned.

"Yes," I answered. I studied the boy in my arms. How could I have missed it?

"Lenora, is something the matter?" Robert inquired again.

I tore my eyes away from the infant and stared into Robert's gray eyes. "I must see Edwin."

CHAPTER 12

"What? Now?" Robert's exasperated voice answered.

I hurried to the door and called for Nanny, handing the child off to her. "Sinclair! Sinclair!" I called.

"Yes, Your Grace, I am here with your food."

"Thank you," I answered, "though there is no time for that."

"But, Your Grace, you must eat!" Sinclair chided.

Robert chimed in with support for the idea. "Lenora, what is the meaning of this? Why the sudden urgency?"

"Please, Robert, I cannot explain just yet, but I must see him."

Robert wiggled his eyebrows. "All right, I shall call for the carriage."

"Please, Sinclair, help me dress."

"Eat at least some of your meal, Lenora," Robert pleaded.

"All right," I agreed and took a bite of a biscuit from the plate.

Satisfied, Robert left the room to arrange our transport. Sinclair readied my dress, only assisting me into it after I'd finished two biscuits. I felt like an errant child. But I did what I must as my mind raced ahead of me.

After dressing, I hurried to the sitting room and found a waiting Robert. "Shall we go?" I inquired, my voice almost breathless with anticipation.

Robert eyed me warily. "If you insist, yes," he said.

I nodded and dashed to the door. We climbed into the waiting carriage outside and it lurched forward. I tapped my foot on the floor as my fingers drummed against my leg.

"You seem perturbed, dear."

I offered a weak smile and returned to my agitated behavior. I did not wish to share my inference with Robert on the off chance my suspicions were incorrect. I preferred only to share what I assumed would be vexing news if I must.

Seconds seemed like hours as we wound through the streets. I wondered if I could have walked faster but dismissed the notion, certain I was merely being impatient.

When the carriage halted outside of the jail, I flew from its door without waiting for the coachman or Robert's assistance.

"Lenora!" Robert shouted as he hurried to catch up to me.

I burst through the doors and approached the waiting officer. "Your Grace!" he greeted me with a wide-eyed expression. He fumbled for a moment before he added, "What a pleasure to see you again today."

I closed my eyes for a moment as I saw the surprise register on Robert's face.

"I must see Lord Edwin."

He nodded. "Just a moment." He retrieved another officer to escort me to the cells below.

I squeezed Robert's hand before I descended to the cells.

Edwin leapt to his feet as we approached and rushed to the bars. "Lenora," he said with a relieved sigh. "You've returned. Thank heavens."

I stared up at him. I studied his eyes. His gray eyes, a near-perfect match to Robert's, also matched another's.

"Lenora, please tell me you believe me," Edwin continued.

"I am trying, Edwin, but now there is another matter we must discuss."

Edwin cocked his head at me. "In an earlier visit," I began, "when I asked you why you insist on pursuing such crude behavior, you said, 'She is gone.' Who is gone, Edwin?"

Edwin pursed his lips, turning away from me. "At first I assumed Annie, but now..."

"Now?" he questioned, still refusing to hold my gaze.

I remained silent for a breath and so did Edwin. I licked my lips before speaking. "It is not Annie, is it?"

Edwin staggered to his cot and collapsed onto it. "No," he breathed as he studied his hands.

My eyes rested on him, urging him to continue. "I loved her, Lenora," he choked out. His lower lip quivered, and tears brimmed in his eyes. "Truly, I did. The promises I made her..."

"She died in that horrid place, Edwin, because you failed to make good on those promises!!" I shouted, surprised by the indignation in my own voice.

"I know," he cried. "Because I did not take her away. It is my fault she is dead. Tilly's loss is my fault."

Emotion bubbled up through me, and a tear escaped my eye. "Why did you not take her away?" I sobbed.

"I was weak," he answered. "Too weak to do what I promised. And it cost me Tilly."

We fell silent for a moment, each of us grieving Tilly's death. "I do not deserve to ask you a question, but why did you not mention this earlier?"

My forehead pinched at the statement. "I did not know," I answered.

Edwin offered a puzzled expression. "But Tilly..."

"Never mentioned you by name," I finished. "In fact, I convinced myself she had invented you to help her endure the lifestyle she had fallen into."

He hung his head. "No, I was quite real. Promises and all."

"Why did you not take her, Edwin? Why did you not remove her from that place when you learned of the baby?"

Edwin's face became a mask of pain, sorrow, and regret. "I did not learn of the child until after. In fact, I did not realize until the day I brought the ship. You had her scarf... I bought her that scarf as a promise."

I rubbed my forehead at the admission. "She died alone, believing you would rescue her."

"Do you think I do not know this? That it does not pain me every day? Why do you imagine I drink myself into a stupor?"

"Stop being a coward, Edwin!" I shouted. "Your cowardice landed you in this situation. Your cowardice killed Tilly!"

Tears streamed freely down my cheeks as my temper got the better of me. I bit my thumbnail as I struggled to keep my emotions in check.

"Yes," he said after a moment. "Yes, I am. I freely admit it. Tilly's death crushed me to the depths of my soul. I could not bring myself to function."

I shook my head at him. "Do not dare to use Tilly as an excuse for your poor behavior."

"It is not an excuse but an explanation."

"You cannot explain away poor decisions with grief. I grieved her. I did not sink to filling myself with drink."

"You are stronger than I am," Edwin answered.

I opened my mouth to reply when movement caught my eye. A pink dress fluttered in the corner of the cell. Blonde hair shone in the meager light. She stepped forward, her eyes glassy and brimming with tears. "Please, Lenora," she said, "do not hate him."

I closed my eyes and more tears fell to my cheeks.

"Please, Lenora," Edwin said a moment later. "Please know I did not mean harm to come to her."

I reached forward to steady myself against the bars and Edwin grasped my hand. "Please forgive me for what I've done."

I wanted to spit back at him that he did not deserve forgiveness, but Tilly approached us. She stared at Edwin, her eyes filled with love.

My heart broke for her. My poor, sweet, innocent friend. I swallowed the lump in my throat as she glanced at me. "Please, forgive him, Lenora," she begged of me.

My gaze flitted between the two of them. I offered a slow nod and wiped at my tears. "All right, Edwin," I murmured.

"Thank you," he whispered through tears. "Your forgiveness means so much, particularly since I remain unable to forgive myself." Another sob shook his shoulders.

Tilly placed her hand on his shaking shoulder. I wiped away more tears and said with a sniffle, "Do you feel the sensation of gooseflesh?"

Edwin furrowed his brow. "Yes, why?"

I gazed at Tilly. "She is here," I said.

Edwin's eyes widened and his posture stiffened. His face showed a mix of emotions. "She is touching your shoulder."

"Can she hear me?"

I nodded and whispered, "Yes."

Edwin choked out another sob. Words poured from Tilly as he struggled to compose himself. I passed them along to him.

"She loved you. She still loves you."

Edwin trembled all over from the situation. "She does not wish to see you in such pain. She wants you to live no matter how difficult it is to accept that she is gone."

He shook his head, clutching my hand in one of his and

the metal bars with the other, and I continued. "She wants you to know your child. Her child. Hers and yours."

"I love you, Tilly," he choked out.

The admission brought a smile to my friend's face. I wiped a tear away as I watched the heart-breaking yet also heart-warming scene unfold.

"She wants you to remember her each time you see Samuel."

"He is all I have left of you," Edwin said.

With her hand still on Edwin's shoulder, Tilly turned to me. "Please, Lenora. He did not murder that man. I know not why he spoke Edwin's name, but please. You must believe me and help him. For Sam."

I nodded and smiled at my friend. "I do and I will."

Edwin raised his eyebrows and followed my gaze.

"I must go," Tilly said. "Please do not give up."

"I will not give up. Goodbye, dear friend," I said.

"Is she leaving?" Edwin asked.

I nodded as Tilly retreated away from us. "No, please, do not leave," Edwin cried out.

I took his hand in mine and squeezed. "She is gone. I am sorry, Edwin."

He shook his head and pursed his lips. "I am certain she is not gone forever."

Edwin took several deep breaths and uttered a groan as he wiped at his face with the back of his hands. I waited until he had composed himself.

"'Tis a good thing my brother is not here to witness this rather embarrassing behavior," he said, making his best attempt to joke.

I smiled at the attempted humor. "Will you tell him?"

"About Samuel?"

Edwin nodded.

"I feel I must," I answered.

Edwin shook his head. "Please reconsider."

"He should know, Edwin. He should know the son he raises is his nephew, his brother's child."

"He may reject the idea."

It was my turn to shake my head. "He loves Sam. He will not reject him."

"Does he love him more than he detests me?"

"He does not detest you, only wishes better for your life than you have achieved so far."

Edwin offered a sniffle at the statement. "I could have achieved better had I had the guts."

"You cannot continue to lament the past, Edwin," I counseled. "We both wish we could change it, but neither of us can. You must move forward on a better foot."

"I should like to move a foot out of this cell." He offered me a sheepish glance. "Though I understand if I can no longer count on your assistance."

"Tilly has assured me of your innocence. I trust and believe my friend. I shall continue to investigate."

"Oh, thank you, Lenora," Edwin said as relief coursed through his voice.

"You should thank Tilly."

He firmed his lower lip. "I do."

I smiled and nodded at him. "Good night, Edwin."

He reached through the bars and squeezed my hands. "Good night, Lenora."

I strode away from the cell, my emotions still raw from the encounter. I paused before I mounted the stairs, swallowing down another round of tears that threatened. Inhaling deeply, I did my best to dry my cheeks and correct my appearance before climbing to the entrance.

Robert paced the floor in front of the door as I approached. As he spun to retreat across the space, he caught sight of me. His movements ground to a halt and he stared. I sniffled and stepped toward him.

"Lenora!" he breathed as he slipped his arm around my waist. "Are you all right? Have you been crying?"

I nodded. "Yes," I admitted as I continued toward the door.

Robert stiffened, a frown forming on his face. "What? What has Edwin done now to upset you? So help me if he has said something to disturb you, I shall throttle him myself!"

I grasped Robert's forearm. "Please, dear, let us discuss the matter at the hotel."

Robert's forehead wrinkled and he pushed out his lips but agreed with a nod, escorting me outside to our carriage.

I climbed aboard, blowing out a long breath as the carriage trundled away from the jail. I felt Robert's eyes upon me. I preferred not to discuss the matter outside of the privacy of our suite, so I avoided eye contact with him.

The thumb of my left hand rubbed at my wedding ring, and I chewed my lower lip as we wound through the streets. Thankfully, Robert did not press the matter until we returned to our hotel suite. I sought out Nanny and retrieved Sam, preferring him the be close to me. I stared into those gray eyes, now seeing so clearly his relationship to my husband and brother-in-law.

I held the child close to me, kissing the top of his head where his dark hair already began to show the curls his father had when his hair was longer.

I withdrew into the bedroom where Robert awaited me. He flung his arms out as I entered. "Now may we discuss what the devil is going on?"

I inhaled a long breath and offered Samuel another kiss. I nodded.

"What in the world did that louse do to make you cry?

And why did the officer mention seeing you again? Lenora, what is going on?"

"There are several things we must discuss, Robert. Please sit."

He raised his eyebrows at me, his fists resting on his hips. He opened his mouth to respond, then shut it and sank into an armchair. He cocked his head at me and signaled for me to proceed.

I launched into my tale, afraid I may not be able to tell it otherwise. I paced the floor as a distraction while I talked. "I found myself unable to sleep last night," I began.

"Again," Robert interjected.

I offered a nod and continued, "Visions of Gerard Boyle taunted me for most of the night. I could not shake his image from my mind."

"Did he appear to you?" Robert inquired, leaning forward in his chair.

"Yes and no," I hedged.

His eyebrows shot up again. I explained, "He did not appear to me here."

The eyebrows rose further and he narrowed his eyes at me. "I... could not sleep, so I..."

"Yes?"

"I went for a walk," I said with a shrug.

"Where?" Robert questioned.

I pursed my lips, patting Sam on the back as I spiraled and crossed the room in the opposite direction. "The docks," I admitted.

"What?" Robert shouted, leaping from his chair. "You went to the docks in the middle of the night? Alone?"

I offered a shrug and an apologetic glance. "Lenora!" he chided.

"I was not thinking clearly."

"Obviously."

I frowned at him. "If you are finished with your scolding, I shall continue."

He scowled at me but held his hands up in surrender and settled back into the chair. "I encountered the deceased Mr. Boyle."

I glanced at Robert. His discomfort with the dead made the admission difficult for him to hear, particularly on the heels of my last one.

At my silence, he mustered a question. "Was he able to shed any light on his murder?"

I shook my head, my lips pressed into a thin line. Robert cocked an eyebrow at me. "What aren't you telling me?"

My husband had grown to know me too well. "He behaved as though still in shock. I asked him if he realized he had been murdered but did not receive a response. I continued to pursue the matter and questioned him about the murderer's identity."

"And?"

"He only offered one word as a response. He repeated it several times though. Again, his behavior was odd, as though he remained in shock. I am not certain we can…"

"What was the word?"

"Well, it was a name," I hedged.

"Lenora, what was the name?"

I ceased my ambling about for a moment and fixed my gaze upon my husband. "Edwin," I said in a low voice.

Robert's face conveyed all the surprise I expected. "He identified Edwin as the murderer?!" He leapt from his chair and paced the floor. "I knew it. I knew it! That louse! That infernal man! To drag you into this in an attempt to wiggle out of charges brought against him. I shall never forgive him!"

"Robert, Robert, please!" I said.

He ceased his pacing and stared at me. "This was the source of your upset this morning," Robert surmised.

"Yes. I confess to having had a similar reaction to your own."

"I assume you went to confront him over it? This is why you insisted on seeing him when you awoke."

I pulled my lower lip into a grimace. "N-no," I stammered. I lowered my face and glanced upward at Robert. "I confronted him earlier this morning. Which is why the officer mentioned seeing me earlier."

Robert's jaw dropped open and he blinked rapidly. "Do you mean to say that AFTER you traversed the darkened streets to the docks, you THEN traipsed to the jail?"

"First, I came here, and THEN I traipsed to the jail."

Robert squeezed his eyes shut. "Lenora, please do not do these things! Not only because of the danger but..." He approached me and placed his hands on my arms. "You were obviously upset. You should not have to face such things alone."

"I appreciate that, Robert; however, I did not wish to place the burden on you. I realize how tenuous your relationship with Edwin is. I do not wish to further exacerbate the situation."

"You do not further exacerbate it! Edwin does! And this latest stunt is unforgivable!"

I shook my head. "I do not believe Mr. Boyle meant to name Edwin as the murderer."

"I thought he said it clearly, several times?" Robert asked.

"He said Edwin's name several times, but that could mean anything. The deceased are often confused and disoriented."

"Do not defend him, Lenora. You yourself said you reacted similarly."

"I did, yes. When I arrived here and you found me in the armchair, even then, I questioned Edwin's innocence."

"What changed?"

"When I slept, I had a dream. At first, it seemed nonsensical. I wandered the docks, then I became trapped with the spirit of Mr. Boyle. He rambled on about being murdered before he reached toward me with bloody hands. I screamed, and then I found myself here in this room in the middle of the night. Tilly visited and told me Edwin did not lie."

Robert shook his head at the tale. "It is only a dream."

"You yourself said my dreams have meaning. How did I conjure the image of Mr. Boyle when I had never known him?"

"We cannot rely on your dream to assure us of Edwin's innocence."

"I am not," I promised. "There is more."

Robert raised his eyebrows for the umpteenth time.

"You may wish to sit down again."

Robert heaved a sigh and retreated to his armchair. "I am not certain how much more complex this could become," he murmured.

"Even before I slept, I pondered if Mr. Boyle had made some mistake. As you know, the dead do not always work in the same way we do. When I visited Edwin, he maintained his innocence. In fact, he insisted upon it. The dream hinted at it, too.

"When I awoke, I planned to discuss the matter with you, still unsure about what I believed. But then you surprised me with Sam." I jostled the baby in my arms and offered him another kiss. "And it was Sam who helped me piece together the puzzle."

"Samuel aided you in determining Edwin's innocence?"

"In a way, yes. I have noticed of late his changing eye color. Today, as I sat with him on the bed, I was struck by them and how familiar they seemed."

"No doubt a match to his mother's."

I shook my head in disagreement. "No, they are not. They are quite firmly not similar to Tilly's. And that's when it struck me."

"I am sorry, Lenora, I do not follow. What struck you?"

"Suddenly, I wondered why Tilly would be so interested in Edwin's case. It was she who begged me to help him."

"But only in a dream. Could it have been a trick of your mind?"

I waggled my head left to right. "No. Tilly also appeared in Edwin's cell. And in a previous visit, Edwin broke down and told me he had nothing because 'she was gone.' I did not understand, but suddenly it became clear."

"You are talking in circles, I cannot understand."

I tried to find a way to put it delicately so his mind could come to an understanding. "Samuel had a father."

"Of course he does. I am his father."

"No, Robert. He had a father before you. The man Tilly loved."

His brow furrowed though it seemed his mind refused to make the final connection. "What are you saying?"

"Edwin is the man Tilly spoke to me about. The man she loved. The man who fathered her child."

Robert's eyes widened and his jaw fell open. His gaze focused on the child I held.

"Are you saying…" His voice trailed off.

I nodded. "Samuel is Edwin's child."

CHAPTER 13

Robert rubbed his jaw as the surprise set in. After several moments, he said, "So, I am raising my brother's child." He followed up with, "The man managed to father a bastard and could not even do right by the girl."

"I am afraid I offered Edwin some rather harsh words over the matter."

Robert raised his eyebrows in surprise. "Well, good for you, Lenora!"

"For all the good it did," I murmured.

Robert responded, "Oh, I am sorry. I sometimes forget Tilly was your friend. Poor woman. She had the misfortune of falling in love with my cad of a brother."

"And she remains in love with him. Which is why despite scolding him, I found myself still offering my support to him."

"Have you spoken to her?"

"She appeared in his cell again. She asked me to help him. And she declared her love for him again. Given that he is Samuel's father and Tilly's request, I did not feel I could refuse."

Robert offered me a slight smile. "And she insists upon his innocence?"

I nodded. "Yes, she does. It is the sole reason I did not give into believing in his guilt."

"What could Boyle have meant by his statements then?"

"I do not understand, but the dead often do not operate as the living."

"Yes, you mentioned something being odd. But why would he name Edwin when asked about his murderer?"

"He could have been confused and in shock. He may not have even been answering my question. He barely registered my presence."

"Why mention Edwin, though," Robert mumbled as he rubbed his chin.

"That I cannot answer."

"I suppose we need to investigate further. What should we do next?"

I cocked my head at him and smiled.

He glanced at me. "What?" he questioned, noting my expression.

"I am quite enjoying you joining my investigation."

"I'd prefer you not to traipse about Glasgow alone, that's all."

"Admit it, you find it interesting!"

"I do not! I only hope to prevent harm from coming to you."

"Well, in any case," I said with a soft kiss on his lips, "at least I had the good fortune to fall in love with the better brother."

My admission brought a smile to his face and he returned my kiss. "And I have had the good fortune to fall in love with an extraordinary woman."

His gaze fell to Samuel. I also studied our beautiful child.

LETTER TO A DUCHESS

"And we could not have been more fortunate when it comes to our little Sam," I said.

"I agree." His brow crinkled and he let out a chuckle. "I never noticed how very much like Edwin he does look. His eyes are a perfect match."

"They rather gave it away to me earlier. How foolish I have been not seeing it before."

"How could you suspect, Lenora? You who assume the best of everyone would never suspect Edwin to exhibit such poor behavior."

A knock sounded at the door, interrupting our conversation. "Yes?" Robert called.

Nanny poked her head in the door. "Sorry to interrupt, however, it is time for the little master's meal."

I nodded and met Nanny halfway across the room to pass off Samuel. With one last kiss to his cheek, I watched them depart. Samuel cooed at me as he disappeared, waving his little hand. The gesture brought a smile to my face.

As the door closed behind them, my thoughts turned to the mystery. I resumed my pacing of the floor, this time in thought rather than from agitation.

"I find myself quite at a loss," I said to Robert.

"I often find myself at the same loss over Edwin's behavior."

"Oh, I meant regarding our next steps."

"Oh," Robert said, lifting his eyebrows. "Oh, yes."

I sighed. "I suppose the best action is to seek Mr. Boyle again."

"When?"

"That is an excellent question. Did I make contact with him because it was near his time of death when I visited last? Or was it coincidence?"

"Surely you do not suggest returning in the wee hours of the morning?"

"I would prefer not to," I admitted. "The day has proven exhausting and I would very much like to rest."

"I should also prefer you to rest. Shall we try again tomorrow?"

"Yes. And if we do not find him, we may discuss trying at a different time."

"Lenora," Robert began, his lips forming a frown, "I do not wish to sound… negative, but…"

"Yes?" I prompted when he stumbled for words, falling into silence.

"It took months for you to reach Annie and discover the truth."

I spun on my heel and marched across the room in the opposite direction, my hand pressed to my forehead. I understood his concern without him going any further. "I realize that." A sigh escaped me. "And Edwin may not have that kind of time."

I ceased my pacing and faced Robert. "Is there any way you can intervene on his behalf as we continue to investigate?"

"I suppose I can inquire, though, I am not certain it will do much good. The police consider it rather an open and shut case."

I nodded. "Then I shall do my best to speed the process along."

Robert raised a finger. "But you will keep me informed, correct?"

"Of course."

"No more midnight roaming?"

I nodded. "I promise."

"We shall discuss the matter with the police tomorrow during our outing."

"Thank you, Robert."

"Now, I must insist you rest."

"I will not argue with you."

He smirked at me. "I mark this as progress. You have not argued with me about resting!"

"Merely because I am exhausted. I would not grow accustomed to it."

I kissed his cheek before calling for Sinclair to help me ready for bed. I climbed into the bed and pulled the covers up to my chin. Despite the thoughts swirling through my mind about my progress, or lack thereof, I fell into a dreamless sleep and remained in it until morning.

I awoke feeling refreshed and ready to make progress. After spending an hour with my son, we set off in the carriage. Our first stop was to speak with the police. Robert asked me to wait in the carriage, though I disagreed. I would use the time to visit with Edwin. I had no doubt after our emotionally charged meetings yesterday, he may require the support.

Robert grimaced at the notion but did not disagree. We entered the police station and Robert informed the officer behind the desk of my intentions to visit Edwin. "May I also speak to whoever is in charge of Lord Edwin's case?"

The officer disappeared to retrieve others. One man escorted me down to Edwin's cell. I overheard another introduce himself to Robert though I disappeared into the stairway before hearing anything further.

"Good morning, Edwin," I said as I approached his cell.

"Lenora, hello."

"How are you feeling this morning?"

He seemed surprised at the question. He stood from his cot and approached the bars. "As well as I can be, I suppose. And you?"

"I was able to rest last night."

"That's not what I meant," Edwin said. He narrowed his

eyes at me. "Lenora, I am so sorry about what's happened. I…"

I shook my head and held up my hand. "It is over, Edwin. We both wish there had been another outcome, but there is no changing the past."

"A fact I struggle with every day."

The pain etched in his eyes assured me he told the truth. After a moment, Edwin inquired, "Is Robert aware?"

I nodded. "Yes, I told him last evening."

"Has he disowned the poor child yet?"

"No, though he was amazed at how very much you and Samuel resemble each other."

"My brother continues to surprise me."

"He loves you, Edwin. Deep down, he does. He is inquiring after your case as we speak. He hopes to help in some way."

"I do not deserve either of you."

"You are family. Deserved or not, family helps each other."

We stood for a moment in silence before I spoke again. "Edwin, is there anything else you can think of regarding Mr. Boyle? I plan to seek him out again today, but as Robert pointed out, it took months to get through to Annie. And…"

"We do not have that sort of time. I understand. I have wracked my brain, Lenora, and I cannot think of anything."

"You mentioned his criminal dealings. Is there reason to suspect one of his associates may have murdered him?"

Edwin stepped away from the bars and wandered about the small cell. With a shrug, he said, "It's certainly possible. He could have been killed over a sum of money or a disagreement over a business deal."

"Do you know any names of any individuals involved?"

"No," Edwin said with a shake of his head. "I may recognize them if they were stood in front of me, but Gerard never shared names."

"I do not mean to be indelicate, but were you involved in any way with any of these dealings?"

"No," Edwin assured me, "I came close once but backed out of the deal. As you mentioned yesterday, I am rather a coward. I feared involving myself with the type of men he dealt with regularly."

"Can you describe any of them? Or perhaps share where he may have met them?"

"Lenora, I am not certain you should pursue this."

"You sought my help, Edwin. What do you expect me to do?"

"Speak with the dead man and allow him to tell you who did it, then disclose the name to the police!"

"You are being naive," I countered. "It took months to learn the true story of Annie and she had been dead for years. Mr. Boyle has only just died. Receiving information from him may prove impossible."

"You should not question Gerard's nefarious associates."

"Robert will be with me."

Edwin shook his head as he grasped the bars. "No. I will not share any information on that front that could endanger either of you."

"Edwin!" I protested. "You endanger us more by making us unaware of who may not appreciate our prodding!"

"It would not matter."

"What do you mean?"

"Gerard's associates worked mostly on a ship called *The Pembroke*. She is not in port anyway."

"Was she when he was murdered?"

"Yes," Edwin answered. "Yes, she set sail three days after if memory serves."

I nodded as I processed the information. "All right. So,

potentially some sailor from *The Pembroke* could have murdered Mr. Boyle then sailed away. Perhaps that is helpful information with which I can confront Mr. Boyle should I encounter him again and jog his memory. Is there anything else?"

Edwin shrugged. "No, not that I can recall."

I offered him a tight-lipped smile and a curt nod. "I shall report back when I have more news."

"Thank you, Lenora."

I climbed the stairs and found Robert pacing the floor as he awaited me. His conversation ended before mine. Not a good sign, I thought.

He offered his arm to escort me from the building. "Any luck?" I inquired after we were seated inside the carriage.

"Not much," Robert admitted. "I inquired about the case and it appears they are not considering any other suspects. Given the altercation in the pub, they believe they have the correct man in custody."

I sighed. "There is one glimmer of hope, though."

"Oh?" I questioned, my heart lifting.

"There may be a chance for Edwin to be released from his cell while he awaits trial."

"Well, that is something, I suppose. Perhaps Edwin can be useful in searching for the real killer."

"The hitch is I shall be responsible for him." Robert rolled his eyes. "A task which I do not relish."

"Perhaps it will not come to fruition," I replied.

"The officer is speaking with his supervisor. We must stop back after our travels today. How is my brother?"

"Well enough. His remorse eats away at him still, but he seemed improved from yesterday. I questioned him about Mr. Boyle's nefarious associates. While he preferred not to share details, he did tell me they were sailors aboard *The Pembroke*. The ship was docked at the time of Mr. Boyle's murder. So it is entirely possible for one of them to have murdered him."

"I see."

"He insisted we stay away from these men, claiming they were too dangerous, even with your support in the matter. However, I hoped I could tease more information from Mr. Boyle if we are able to locate him. Perhaps with some prodding, he can identify the culprit."

Robert nodded in understanding as the carriage wheels slowed. I recognized the now-familiar spot near the docks.

With a sigh, I followed Robert outside. Gray clouds raced across the sky, blotting out the sun. I shivered as the river air brushed past me. Robert wrapped an arm around me. "I do hate this so," he murmured.

"Let us hope it is soon put to rest."

We ambled to the docks. "Where did you see him?" Robert questioned.

"There," I said, motioning toward the spot where the deceased had appeared. "Slightly away from where we guessed the murder occurred but close."

We approached the spot and I scanned the area. "Do you see him?"

"No," I answered. "Mr. Boyle? Gerard Boyle. Are you there?"

A sailor meandered along the docks, shooting me an odd glance as I called into thin air. "Would you mind stepping back a few steps, dear?" I asked of Robert.

"Whatever for?"

"In the event Mr. Boyle has grown shy in his death. Beside the time, the only other difference between my previous meeting with him and this one is that I was alone."

"And that will not happen again!" Robert assured me as he backed several steps away.

I nodded as he stood under the eave of a nearby building.

"Mr. Boyle?" I called again. "Mr. Boyle, please. I would like to discuss your murder. I would like to help set your soul at peace."

I turned to Robert and shook my head. He hurried back to me. "Nothing," I admitted.

"Perhaps some lunch," Robert suggested as I frowned at my lack of progress, kicking a stone around on the ground.

I nodded. "I shall try again later. And could we visit the graveyard? I would like to try to speak with Tilly again. Or perhaps that elderly woman. I shall tell her we are seeking her daughter."

"Of course, dear," Robert said, patting my hand.

"Oh! Perhaps we should find where Mr. Boyle is laid to rest. It could provide another place we may seek him."

"I shall look into it when I speak with the police again," Robert promised.

I smiled at him. I should make progress one way or another. I stared out over the ships in the harbor as we strode toward our carriage. I stopped walking suddenly.

"Lenora?" Robert questioned as my hand slipped from his arm.

I stared ahead, my eyes lighting up. A large ship floated in the water nearby, a gangplank leading to it. Men bustled to and fro near it, unloading its contents.

"What is it?" Robert questioned, his eyes searching the horizon where I gazed.

"The Pembroke!" I exclaimed.

Robert eyed the ship bearing the name of *The Pembroke*. "So it is."

"That means the murderer may be back in port!" I grinned.

"I have never seen someone so excited about a murderer's return," Robert quipped.

I shook my head. "If the murderer has returned, perhaps

Mr. Boyle will be more forthcoming," I explained. "Or if we manage to free Edwin, perhaps he can identify the man or men involved in his dealings and we can elicit a name."

Robert shook his head. "I shall be pleased when this matter is concluded. How I detest this."

"I am sorry, Robert," I began when he interrupted me.

"No, Lenora, there is nothing for which you must apologize. The blame rests on Edwin."

"And the murderer," I reminded him. "And Mr. Boyle for his nefarious deeds."

"In any case, none of the blame rests on you."

We passed The Black Horse pub and I peeked inside. At this time of the day, only a few stragglers graced the interior. I supposed it was not worth a stop to determine if any of them were from *The Pembroke*. Not only could I not identify them, but asking the barkeep may be rather obvious given the lack of crowd.

I allowed Robert to lead me to the carriage and take me to lunch. He checked his pocket watch as we finished our meal. "Hmm, rather early to return to the jail, I'd wager. Perhaps a walk in the park? Or would you prefer to return to the hotel to rest?"

"I would not mind the walk, but could we first stop at the cemetery where Tilly is buried?"

"Of course, dear," Robert agreed.

The coachman drove us to the cemetery. I hated to step into the chilly air, but my desire to see Tilly for longer than a moment outweighed my discomfort. I wandered to her gravesite, leaving Robert to wait by the carriage.

As I stared at her grave marker, emotions shot through me faster than I was prepared for. Overwhelming sadness at her death welled up inside me. If only she had mentioned his name to me, perhaps I could have intervened. Perhaps I could have spoken to Robert about the situation. Perhaps Tilly could have been removed from that wretched place before her tragic death.

I berated myself for not doing more for her and for being blind to what was happening right under my nose. I assumed her tales to be a fantasy. How could I fail to believe my dear sweet friend? I failed her.

My mind regressed to another moment where I'd failed her. I recalled the moonlit night in the orphanage when Tilly proposed she would run away.

"Tilly," I chided, "that is ridiculous."

She shook her head. "No, it isn't. Staying here is ridiculous."

"It is not!" I countered. "Staying here is safe."

"We cannot stay here forever, Lenora."

"I should expect I will. I am nearly eighteen and have no prospects. Headmistress Williamson dashes my chances of any placement at every opportunity."

"All the more reason to make your own prospects!" Tilly said, her eyes aglow with excitement.

I offered her an unimpressed glance.

She shrugged it away. "It is what I plan to do."

"You have excellent prospects if you remain here. You will be selected as a governess, Tilly."

She shook her head. "First, I will not be. My marks are not very good."

"Still..." I began when she interrupted me.

"Second, I do not care to be a governess."

"Why? It is an excellent position. Quite enviable in fact."

"I do not wish to see to someone else's children, Lenora. I prefer to raise my own. Besides, with my marks, I would likely only achieve a maid's position and I have NO desire to be a maid."

"If you leave and begin a family of your own, you will

tend children and be your own maid," I contented. "Unless you marry very well!"

"Perhaps I will. And even if I do not, there is a difference between rearing one's own children and cleaning one's own dirt and doing that for others."

"Where will you go?" I questioned.

She shrugged again. "Anywhere but here."

"Why leave? Surely you can find a husband while enjoying the comforts of St. Mary's."

She laughed. "There are no such things as the comforts of St. Mary's. And I shall NEVER find a husband here. There is no mechanism for it. How often are we exposed to men?"

"Where do you plan to be exposed to men, Tilly?"

"I shall take a job and meet them as other women do who are not orphans."

"It is a dangerous plan."

"It is not. Come with me, Lenora," she begged.

"No. And I do not think you should go either."

"Too bad. I am going. As soon as the weather improves, I shall go. I hope by then you will change your mind. We could go on an adventure together."

I considered continuing the argument though I did not see the point. When Tilly made up her mind, there was often no changing it. I only hoped she would see the error of her ways before the weather warmed.

As I opened my mouth to reply to her, a noise startled us. Tilly's eyes grew wide. "What was that?" she whispered.

I shrugged, my eyes searching the darkness for the source. As we stood near the window, a figure emerged into the moonlight. A cloaked girl hurried from the foyer, mounted the stairs, and disappeared to the second floor.

"Come on," Tilly breathed, grabbing my hand and pulling me along with her. We raced up the stairs. Tilly glanced around, searching for the mystery woman. A rustling noise emerged from our shared bedroom. Still tugging me with her, Tilly hurried to the darkened room.

A figure moved in the darkness. In the dim moonlight spilling into the hallway, Tilly arched one eyebrow at me. Her meaning was clear. One of the girls had snuck out. The question was who and for what reason?

CHAPTER 14

We watched as the figure disrobed and pulled on her nightgown before approaching a bed and climbing in. Tilly's face wore an expression of shock as we identified the culprit based on the bed she chose.

Tilly pulled me away from the door and we descended the stairs as quietly as possible. A small squeak emerged from Tilly as we hurried away from the staircase.

"I cannot believe my eyes!" she exclaimed breathlessly.

"I must admit I am shocked, too."

"Millicent Brown? Sneaking about after hours?"

"Perhaps Headmistress Williamson sent her on an errand," I mused aloud.

"In the middle of the night? Lenora, til after midnight! What would she be doing roaming the streets of Glasgow now?"

I shrugged as my mind searched for possibilities but found none.

"Perfect little Millie, caught sneaking around in the wee hours! I'm dying to know why! And where she went!"

Tilly tapped her puckered lips with her finger.

"We may never know those answers, Tilly."

"Oh, we will," she assured me.

I raised my eyebrows at the statement.

"We will follow her next time!"

I recalled Tilly's face in that moment. Her eyes were alight with enthusiasm and her cheeks flushed with excitement. She relished the adventure we'd have spying on Millicent. Her passion for life brought tears to my eyes.

A tear rolled down my cheek and I covered my face as more threatened. A strong arm wrapped around me. The memory faded from my mind as I laid my head on Robert's shoulder.

"I am sorry for the toll this takes on you," Robert said in a soothing tone.

I offered a blunt laugh. "I did not speak with Tilly. She is not here. It is only my memory plaguing me."

He rubbed my arm as he held me close. "Shall we go so you may relax?"

I glanced around the graveyard with a sigh. "I suppose so. It does not appear she is here."

"It confounds me why she does not appear to you when you so desperately hope to see her."

"I assume she is spending her time with Edwin."

Robert's brow furrowed as he considered my statement. I explained further, "Though she cannot aid him in any way, it may make her feel better to be with him."

"Ah, interesting."

"The dead are often drawn to what they know and love after they pass."

He offered an uncertain smile, and I ended the conversation, realizing it made him uncomfortable. "Shall we?" I suggested.

At this statement, he broadened his grin and offered me his arm. I accepted, and he turned me toward the carriage. I stopped after taking only one step. The smile on Robert's face faltered as he searched my features to ascertain the reason.

"Hello, Esme," I said. The elderly woman stood yards from us. She stared at me with pleading in her eyes as she wrung her hands.

Robert's eyes darted around. I laid a hand on Robert's arm, signaling him to remain calm and to steady his nerves.

"I am searching for your daughter and hope to find her soon."

"Danger," she said.

I nodded. "Yes, you mentioned that. And I hope to find Grace soon. Can you expound on the danger?"

"Danger. Blood." Her face pinched. "Blood!" she shouted, her voice rising an octave. Her face formed a frightened grimace.

"Is the blood Grace's blood?" I asked.

"Blood. Death. Death!"

I pulled my hand from Robert's arm and held them in front of me, gesturing for Esme Murdoch to compose herself. "Esme, it is all right."

Her mouth opened in a silent cry. "Death," she repeated in a half-sob.

"Is there anything else you can tell me? Is the blood from Grace? Is she the one in danger?"

Esme wrung her hands. I took a step toward her and she vanished. A sigh escaped me at the encounter. I'd learned little more than I had during our first meeting, but this time I had felt a sense of urgency from her.

Poor Robert waited a few steps behind me. "She is gone," I reported.

"Is this the same woman you... spoke to when you were here last?"

"Yes," I said with a nod.

"Did she provide any additional information?"

"No. She said much of the same. Danger. She added blood and death but when I asked whose blood and death she disappeared."

Robert frowned as he pondered it.

"Whatever it is seems to have disturbed her. There was a sense of urgency in her words."

"Perhaps I will hear from Cameron soon."

"Let us hope. I shall do my best to reach her daughter and help in any way I can."

"You have your hands rather full already."

I shrugged. "Full or not, I must help them when I can. They have nowhere else to turn."

Robert smiled at me. "Well, let us return to the jail before our supper."

I nodded in agreement and we returned to the carriage and the jail. "Wait here," Robert said as the carriage slowed in front of it.

"I'd prefer not to," I objected.

"There is no reason for you to drag yourself inside."

"I am hardly dragging myself." Robert attempted to close the door, but I shoved my hand against it and disembarked.

With a sigh, Robert allowed his decision to be overruled, and we traipsed into the building.

"Your Graces," the officer behind the desk greeted us.

"Hello," Robert answered him. "I am here to inquire about my earlier request with Officer MacAlister."

"I shall retrieve him, Your Grace."

We waited several moments before another officer appeared. "If you'd like to step into a private room," he said, eyeing me.

"Come along, dear," Robert said, ushering me ahead of him.

We entered a small room with a wooden table and chairs.

Officer MacAlister pushed the door shut. "Your Grace, I have consulted with the judge. Given the violent nature of the crime, I preferred Lord Edwin remain in custody. Also, given his access to family money, I prefer he not be released.

"However, the judge disagreed and allowed Lord Edwin's release into your custody." He slid a paper across the table. "This outlines the terms and sum for his release."

Robert reviewed it and scrawled his signature across the page. "I have already made arrangements for the sum to be paid."

"I shall retrieve the prisoner."

"Oh, Officer MacAlister," Robert said before the man could duck from the room. "Would it be possible to gather the details of where the deceased in this case is buried?"

The man raised his eyebrows. "I do not know if we have that information, Your Grace."

"Any information you have would be appreciated."

The man nodded and disappeared from the room, stating that we should follow him through to the entrance. We stood waiting for several minutes until Officer MacAlistair appeared with Edwin in tow.

I offered him a smile as the officer reminded Robert of the terms of Edwin's release. "Yes, yes, I understand," Robert said with a wave of his hand.

"Also, I checked and our records indicate the body of Mr. Boyle was released to his brother, William Boyle."

"Lord Pennington?" Robert murmured.

The man nodded. I studied Robert's face. It conveyed surprise and confusion. Given the information he'd shared about their estrangement and the lack of outward grieving on the man's part, I could understand why. It proved an interesting development. At least we should be able to ascertain where his body was laid to rest easily.

"Well, thank you," Robert finally said.

We turned to depart from the building as Officer MacAlister offered one last warning to Edwin. "Stay out of trouble, m'lord. Otherwise, it will be my pleasure to haul you back in."

Edwin grimaced at the man's cautionary words coupled with the mild threat. We strode into the early evening air. Edwin gulped it in, filling his lungs and expanding his chest as we stepped to the pathway leading to the street.

"Thank heavens. And thank you, Lenora."

Robert pursed his lips and narrowed his eyes. "And you, brother," Edwin added.

"Come along," Robert said, his gruffness returning in an instant when faced with the prospect of a carriage ride with his brother.

We climbed inside, Robert choosing to sit next to me, leaving Edwin across from us. "A bath should be arranged immediately upon our return to the hotel," Robert stated, his nostrils flaring. The stench of the jail still clung to Edwin.

"I shall relish the opportunity," Edwin said with a grin.

Robert narrowed his eyes again. "You would do well to spend the time taking serious stock of your life, Edwin."

Edwin drew in a deep breath, his eyes rolling as he fidgeted in his seat. "Here we go," he mumbled.

Robert's tone sharpened. "Yes, here we go, brother. I have just bailed you out of a jail cell. You have been accused of murder. The evidence against you is mounting. And my wife," he said, his voice rising again as he flung his hand in my direction, "has been chasing her tail searching for answers to allow you to escape from this nightmare you have created."

Edwin slouched in his seat as Robert continued. "She has barely slept, barely eaten, and has risked her life and limb to contact this odious Mr. Boyle and settle the matter. You would do well, brother, to not be so flippant about the situation!"

Edwin frowned and lowered his eyes. I patted Robert's arm to offer him my support. The situation with Edwin disturbed him, and he had been primed for a confrontation with him. The two brothers could not have been more different. Robert approached the problem with extreme seriousness. Edwin preferred to joke about it to alleviate the stress he felt.

"I meant no harm..." Edwin began.

"No, you never do, according to you," Robert spat. "Yet here we are. Our lives are turned upside down, and all you can offer is a weak excuse about how you didn't mean to do it."

"What would you have me do, brother?" Edwin questioned, his tone turning acidic. "Shall I fall to my knees and thank you. Shall I beg your forgiveness for the inconvenience? Perhaps I could slit my wrists and bleed for you."

"A little gratitude would go a long way, Edwin," Robert snapped back. "As far as your other suggestions, I cannot imagine they would hurt."

Edwin's eyes shot wide. "Oh yes, you would agree with that. You, big brother, who is so perfect. You who has never made a mistake. You who's first wife..."

"Gentlemen, please!" I shouted before Edwin made a statement he would live to regret. "Enough!"

My statement came too late. "I would like to hear what Edwin has to say about my first wife."

"No, you would not," I contended. "He has nothing to say except making an acrimonious statement intended to wound you. It is not meant."

I shot Edwin a glance filled with a warning.

"She is right, brother," Edwin admitted. "In the heat of the argument, I only hoped to achieve a rise from you. No matter the cost."

"And this is why you should not speak out of turn," Robert grumbled.

I patted his arm and offered Edwin a prodding glance. He eyed me, his brow pinching.

"Let us not argue. I am certain Edwin apologizes for his comments."

"Oh, yes," Edwin agreed with a nod. "Yes, I do apologize."

Robert raised his eyebrows. "You ought to direct your apology to Lenora. She does not deserve what you have put her through before or now. I am sorry to have subjected you to our bickering."

Edwin's expression softened a bit and he lowered his eyes again. "Yes, you are correct, Robert. And I am truly sorry, Lenora, for what I have put you through."

I nodded to acknowledge his apology. "Thank you, Edwin."

The carriage bumped along the roads as we sat in silence for the remainder of the ride. After we arrived at the hotel and Edwin had the opportunity to clean up, we gathered in the sitting room of our suite.

I emerged from the bedroom with Samuel in my arms. Edwin stared into the fireplace, lost in thought. After his downtime, he had turned contemplative. The looming of his situation was likely catching up to him.

Robert sipped at a brandy, pacing the floor. He raised his eyebrows as I crossed the room with the infant in my arms.

"Edwin," I said gently, rousting him from his brooding, "I thought you may like to see Sam."

He snapped his eyes from the fire to me, then let them fall to the child in my arms. Robert took a few steps toward us, monitoring the situation.

"You had the child brought here?" Edwin questioned.

Robert's jaw fell open. "Yes, we had the child brought here. Why should you question it? We are his parents!" Robert shouted.

I offered Robert a cross glare and gave my head a small shake.

"I am only surprised you brought the child with you when you arrived intending to investigate a murder."

"Robert sent for him as I found myself rather lonesome without him," I explained. "And I am so pleased that he did." I offered Robert a wide smile. He returned the gesture. I hoped it alleviated the tension and snuffed out the ensuing argument. Robert was a powder keg ready to blow at any moment when his brother was involved.

"Hello, Sam," Edwin said to the child. He studied the infant's face. Sam babbled at me, waving his arms in the air. I kissed him on his forehead before I spun him to face Edwin.

Edwin offered him a weak smile and glanced at me. He'd seen the child on a few previous occasions, though he had not realized their relationship at first. I hoped to encourage one between them.

In an impulsive move, I sat the child on Edwin's knee. Robert stepped forward, then squeezed his eyes closed as though I'd set the child on top of a serpent.

"Oh!" Edwin exclaimed.

I smiled at the sight and took a seat across from them. Robert hovered nearby, shooting me a stern glance that suggested disagreement with my decision to place the child on Edwin's knee.

"He is rather a lovely child," Edwin said after a moment. "He looks so much like her." His voice turned wistful.

"He does," I commented. "He has her coloring and her mouth and eye shape. Though the hair and eye color have come from your side."

"Yes," Edwin answered. "Yes, his eyes are a perfect match to mine and Robert's. Father's were gray, too. Remember?"

He raised his eyes to Robert's, seeking an answer.

"Yes," Robert grumbled after a moment. "Yes, and mother's were green."

Edwin nodded. "And Father's hair was dark and unruly. Mother always said how like him we looked."

A small smile crept across Robert's features as memories of his childhood danced across his mind. "Yes," he murmured.

"He is the best of both of you," I said.

Samuel cooed at Robert, waving his little hand in the air at him. Robert's grin broadened as the child called to him in a series of babbles.

"He seems very fond of you," Edwin said.

"And I am very fond of him," Robert said as he approached the child and held out his hand. Samuel grasped it. Robert set his brandy down on the nearby table and lifted the child from Edwin's lap.

"He has grown so much since I last saw him."

"That's what happens when..." Robert began, then changed his mind. "Well, never mind."

"He shall be walking soon," I said. "He has already begun to crawl."

"He shall be riding soon!" Robert announced. "As soon as he is able to steady himself in the saddle, I shall have him on a horse."

I watched the interaction between the two brothers, pleased that they were no longer sniping at each other for the moment. Samuel reached for Robert's face, grasping his chin with his chubby fingers as Robert bounced it up and down. A giggle emerged from the tyke.

"I am so pleased to see him so well cared for," Edwin said.

"As am I," a voice said behind me.

I twisted my neck to find Tilly standing beside my chair. "Thank you, Lenora," she said. "It is obvious how much you and Robert love him. And thank you for allowing Edwin to know his son."

I offered a nod, unwilling to speak aloud and interrupt the conversation between my husband and brother-in-law. I would prefer to speak with Tilly but now was not the time. Her eyes glistened as she smiled at her infant son, wrapped safely in my husband's arms.

I felt her hand pat my shoulder. I tore my eyes away from the cozy scene but found her gone.

Nanny appeared, hovering in the doorway. The gesture signaled Sam's bedtime.

"Oh, Nanny," Robert said. "I suppose it is bedtime."

She nodded. "Yes, Your Grace. If you do not mind. I prefer to keep the little master on his schedule despite the travel."

"Not at all. Best to do so, yes," Robert agreed. I rose and crossed to them, relieving Robert of the child.

"Say good night to your Uncle Edwin," Robert said. "And your Mummy."

I showered him with kisses before handing him off to Nanny for the night.

Robert waited until they departed from the room before retrieving his brandy and resuming his pacing of the floor.

"We should discuss the issue," I offered.

"Can it not wait until morning?" Robert suggested.

"I would prefer to speak about it now. Perhaps with a plan in place, we will all sleep better."

Robert nodded in acquiescence and I continued. "I have had limited luck in contacting the deceased. I have only spoken with him on one prior occasion. And during that encounter, he spoke only your name. The lack of progress is frustrating."

"But you will continue to attempt to contact him?" Edwin said.

Robert huffed at him, but I spoke before he could. "Yes, though we must determine where and when we can reach him. We have asked after the location of his burial and we can try there. The other option is to go to the location of the murder around the time the murder occurred and hope he appears again."

"I prefer not to take that option," Robert said.

"It may be the only option we have," I argued. "Though I will try the gravesite as soon as we ascertain its location. Do you believe Lord Pennington may share it with you?"

"It may prove an odd request to the man, but I am willing to ask," Robert said.

"Were you surprised to learn he handled the body?" I asked, recalling Robert's expression when the officer informed him.

"Yes, I was rather," Robert answered. "Though I suppose it makes sense. Who else would deal with it?"

"I suppose you are correct," I answered as I pondered it. "Even estranged, it would fall to the family."

"Who was estranged?" Edwin chimed in.

"Penny and Gerard," Robert answered.

"I hadn't heard that. In fact, the last I knew, they were working together on several things."

"What?" Robert said, shock apparent in his voice. "What things?"

"Penny became involved in some of Gerard's more illicit dealings last I'd heard."

CHAPTER 15

Robert's jaw dropped open. "I cannot believe it," he said with a shake of his head.

"It is true. I saw them together on more than one occasion and Gerard mentioned to me of his brother's involvement."

"Why would Penny involve himself in such dealings? That makes no sense whatsoever. Are you quite sure you got it correct?"

"I told you I saw them together!" Edwin insisted, leaping from his chair and joining Robert in marching around the room.

"That is meaningless. People see us together and I am rarely involved in your convoluted schemes."

Edwin ceased his ambling and narrowed his eyes at Robert.

"Oh, stop," Robert said with a roll of his eyes as he noticed Edwin's glare. "Let's not become sensitive over it. It is the truth. They were brothers, but I cannot imagine why they would have any dealings together. I thought Penny practically disowned the man."

"Ha!" Edwin countered. "Penny needed Gerard.

"Needed him for what?" I questioned.

"Money."

Robert guffawed. "Surely you jest?"

"I do not," Edwin answered. "Penny is broke."

Robert's eyes widened at the statement. "He has been for some time as I understand it," Edwin continued. "He has been using Gerard's illicit dealings to fill his coffers and keep up appearances."

"No!" Robert gasped. "No, it cannot be."

"I assure you it is."

Robert collapsed into the armchair across from me. "I cannot believe it."

I bit my lower lip as I considered the new information. "This adds another wrinkle," I answered. "And perhaps another suspect."

An alarmed and dismayed expression crossed Robert's face. "No," he said with a shake of his head, his voice descending into a groan. "Not Penny. Surely not Penny."

I shrugged. "Perhaps in the dire circumstances, a quarrel erupted over the dealings."

"I cannot imagine Penny's temper snapping like that."

"But the potential exists," I argued. "His argument with the woman grew rather heated as we overheard."

"What argument with what woman?" Edwin asked.

"We visited Penny a few days earlier. Lenora wanted to determine if Gerard would appear there. During our visit, a woman came to the door. From the sounds of it, they squabbled over something. Though I maintain it was the woman who became tempestuous."

Edwin's forehead wrinkled.

I answered, "Still, there was an argument and Penny was involved."

"But what could it have to do with the murder of Gerard?" Robert questioned.

I shrugged. "Possibly nothing, though I am only highlighting his temper. He could have had his ire raised during an argument with his brother and lashed out."

"I suppose it is a possibility," Robert relented after a moment.

"There is, of course, the possibility of one of his associates as the culprit, too," Edwin said.

I nodded in agreement. "Yes, and on that note, we are in luck. *The Pembroke* has docked again. So, perhaps we can find the guilty party more easily now."

"I am not certain we should pursue that avenue," Robert said.

"I am afraid we must," I argued. "We mustn't question them ourselves necessarily, though knowing their identities may prove useful if I am able to speak with Mr. Boyle again."

Robert downed the last of his brandy. "It is a matter we can discuss at a later time."

I shook my head. "It is something we can discuss now," I insisted. "This is something that can be investigated now."

Robert shook his head. "No, that is unnecessary. We shall proceed with contacting Mr. Boyle at his gravesite once I ascertain the location from Penny."

"He may not appear there. I have had luck in finding him at the murder site, which is where we should try again. And while there, we should make inquiries about the sailors aboard *The Pembroke*. We do not know when they may sail again."

"Lenora, I do not care for investigating these questionable characters."

"We do not have a choice."

"In any case, can it not wait until tomorrow?"

"No. I have only reached him around the time of the murder. Which suggests this may be the only time he will appear. Which means we must try again in the wee hours of the morning."

"Must it be THIS morning?"

"I would prefer it," I said.

"Lenora, you need your rest."

"I cannot rest with this on my mind."

"I do not look forward to traipsing about in the wee hours!"

"I could escort you," Edwin said.

Robert chortled at the suggestion. "Certainly not!"

Edwin frowned at him. Robert shook his head. "I will not leave Lenora's wellbeing in your hands. Heaven knows what could happen. You aren't exactly the best judge of things, you know."

"I would never let any harm come to Lenora."

"I will not take the chance," Robert said. "Lenora, if you insist on going to the docks overnight, I shall accompany you."

"So shall I," Edwin said.

"It is not necessary," Robert retorted.

"Necessary or not, I shall accompany you. This is my doing, and I would like to see it through."

Robert raised his eyebrows and puckered his lips. "Admirable, Edwin. We should all get some rest before this excursion."

I agreed. With the details set, we laid down to attempt a few hours of sleep before wandering into the night in search of answers.

* * *

Long after the moon rose overhead, we stepped into the chilly November air. I pulled my cloak closer around me as the wind gusted past. I shivered as we turned the corner and faced the gales head on. Robert frowned and pulled me closer to him. I appreciated his warmth.

Why had Mr. Boyle died so far from our hotel, I lamented? I continued to shiver in the night air as we approached the docks. Colder winds swept in from the water. I sincerely hoped the trip was not wasted as we hurried past The Black Horse.

I glanced in, finding the pub filled. I wondered if any of the men were associates of Mr. Boyle from *The Pembroke*. We continued past and I hurried to the location where I'd spotted the deceased the last time.

The spot remained empty. I heaved a sigh of disappointment.

"Mr. Boyle," I called, my breath visible in the cold air. "Mr. Boyle?"

Robert hovered next to me. "Anything?" he inquired.

"No, though I was alone last time."

"I am not leaving you here alone, so do not even suggest it," Robert informed me.

I understood his point but was not yet ready to concede. I did not wish for the trip to be wasted. "Perhaps step back a bit," I suggested.

Robert pursed his lips and narrowed his eyes, glancing around the area. With no one in the immediate vicinity and with a frown on his lips, he agreed. He backed away several steps, pulling Edwin back with him.

I faced the spot again where Mr. Boyle appeared. "Mr. Boyle," I called again. "Mr. Boyle, it is Lenora. I have returned to help you."

No one appeared. I waited a few moments before I turned to Robert and shrugged. I hurried toward them. "Perhaps you two should go into the pub and determine if any of Mr. Boyle's associates are inside. Edwin, can you identify any of them? You could inquire after their names."

"Absolutely not, Lenora. I will not leave you out here on the streets alone."

"I am hardly being left on the streets alone. You are steps away. I will continue to seek out Mr. Boyle, but so far, no luck. We should investigate on another front."

"Steps away in a crowded pub with no way to hear you in the event you should need help. No."

"I suppose I could accompany you inside…"

"No!" Robert objected.

My shoulders drooped. "Then what you do propose?"

"We shall return you to the hotel, then we may come back here and make the inquiry."

"That is foolish," I objected. "And I do not wish to return. I prefer to continue to reach out to Mr. Boyle!"

"Lenora!" Robert chided. "It is quite cold. You'll catch your death out here. And I do not wish you to stay here alone."

"Then I shall accompany you inside the pub," I said with a curt nod.

Robert opened his mouth to object. "Please, Robert, it is rather cold and I do not wish to continue to argue."

"All right, all right," he grumbled. "Come along."

We strode to *The Black Horse,* and Robert pulled the door open, shoving Edwin forward to enter ahead of me.

"Keep close to me, Lenora," he whispered into my ear as he wrapped his hand around mine tightly.

I nodded and grasped Edwin's elbow. "If you see anyone you recognize, point them out."

A few patrons of the establishment stared at us as we wandered into the crowded place. Robert pushed past them with a nod and led us to the bar where he ordered two ales.

"And, ah, for the lady?" the barkeeper inquired as he eyed me suspiciously.

"Nothing for the lady," Robert answered.

The barkeeper raised his eyebrows as he fulfilled the order. Edwin grasped the mug and downed a good bit of the liquid before wiping his mouth with the back of his hand and scanning the room.

"For God's sake, Edwin, have some decorum," Robert murmured.

"I have been in jail for weeks on end, allow me to appreciate some of the finer things in life."

"Ale from a pub like *The Black Horse* is not one of life's finer things."

"Of course, it is," Edwin argued. "You must know how to enjoy it."

"A fact you are all too familiar with."

"Gentlemen, please," I cautioned. "Edwin, do you see any of the men you have spotted Mr. Boyle doing business with?"

Edwin sipped his ale and scanned the crowd again. He narrowed his eyes as they swept back across the room. His head ceased its swivel and he focused on someone in the back corner. A burly man with a dark beard, hair, and eyes laughed heartily before slurping his ale, some of it spilling out of his mouth and running down his chin to drip on his shirt.

"There, in the corner," Edwin said. He nodded his head toward the man. "I've spotted that man with Gerard on several occasions."

"Any others?" I questioned.

Edwin searched the faces again. He shook his head. "No, I do not see any others."

"Are you certain?"

He took one last glance around the room before he nodded. "Yes."

"All right, perhaps we can find out the man's identity."

Edwin stood still. He nodded but did not move.

"Perhaps we should ask the barkeeper," I suggested.

Edwin shook his head. "There was another man. Where is he?"

"What?" I asked.

"Another man Gerard often spoke with about business. Small, skinny with a pocked face."

"Perhaps he did not come to the pub," Robert offered.

He considered it for a moment before he answered, "He usually came here. I am surprised not to see him with the other man."

"Perhaps there is trouble between them following the murder," I suggested.

"It could point to their guilt," Robert said. "Perhaps there was a falling out amongst them."

Edwin narrowed his eyes at the dark man as he sipped his ale. "I'm going to speak with him," Edwin announced.

"What?"

"Edwin, do not be foolish," Robert chided.

"It is my issue, Robert. I shall speak with him and determine if I can ascertain any information from him."

"I shall try to solicit the name from the barkeeper," Robert offered. Robert clutched my hand and tugged me with him.

My eyes remained on Edwin as he strode across the bar and approached the table in the rear corner.

"Another?" the barman questioned.

"No," Robert said, shoving the stein back toward him. "I wonder, do you know the large man in the back there. With the dark beard and hair?"

The barman lifted his chin to peer over Robert as he leaned against the bar. He spotted the man and his gaze cut back to Robert. "Who's asking?"

Robert pulled a bill from his pocket. "No one," he said as he slid it across the bar.

The man swiped it from the top and pocketed it. "Fergus MacGuiness."

Robert glanced to me before his eyes flitted back to the barman. "He is a sailor on *The Pembroke*."

Robert nodded. "Thank you. Come, dear, let us wait outside."

I stared in Edwin's direction as Robert tugged me along toward the door. "Shouldn't we…"

"Edwin is a grown man, let him handle himself."

We exited onto the street outside. The cold shot through me after being in the warm pub. I shivered and Robert wrapped me in his arms. "Perhaps we should start back," he suggested.

I shook my head. "We must wait for Edwin."

"Edwin had no trouble navigating to and from this pub without us before."

"Robert…" I began.

"All right, all right," he said. "We shall wait. Though I detest you staying out in the cold."

"Perhaps we can revisit the crime scene while we wait."

Robert nodded and we wandered to the spot. As we approached, my pulse quickened. A figure stood staring out at the sea. "Robert," I whispered. "Can you see that man?"

"What man?" he inquired, squinting into the darkness.

The question provided all the confirmation I needed. A smile crossed my face and I approached the man. "Wait here," I breathed.

Robert ceased walking, his brow furrowed, but he nodded. I tiptoed a few steps forward. "Mr. Boyle?" I said in a low tone.

He did not budge, his back still toward me.

"Mr. Boyle," I called again, this time a bit louder.

He whipped around to face me, his face a mask of anger. I stiffened at his expression and held my hands out. "Please, Mr. Boyle, I am here to help you."

He sneered at me. "Murder," he spat out.

"Yes, you were murdered. I am very sorry about that. I hope to find out who did this to you. Might you be able to share with me who murdered you?"

His eyes narrowed at the statement. "Did you know your murderer?"

"Murder," he repeated.

"Yes, you were murdered. Did you recognize your attacker?"

He stared down at his chest. A red splotch covered it. A knife appeared, buried to the hilt in his chest. He grimaced at it and wailed.

"Mr. Boyle, no harm can come to you now. I understand it is very confusing, but…"

He clawed at the knife as he cried out. His hands passed through it as though it wasn't there. "Mr. Boyle, please," I tried again.

The situation spiraled out of my control as Gerard Boyle's apprehension increased. As he failed to grasp the knife, he held his blood-stained hands out in front of him. They trembled as he stared at them. He lifted his eyes to the night sky and cried out.

I shook my head. It was no use. He had to work through the anguish of realizing he was dead. Despite my protestations, I could do nothing but wait. I let my hands fall to my side as I waited for him to calm, hoping he did not disappear before we could speak again.

Gerard Boyle's eyes lowered to the horizon. His brow furrowed as he seemed to glance through me. His face reddened and his fists balled at his sides. He poked his finger in my direction. "You!" he growled.

"Now, Mr. Boyle," I said, keeping my voice even.

A figure approached my side. He glanced in his direction. "Is he here, Lenora?" Edwin inquired.

I snapped my gaze back to Mr. Boyle's spirit. "Yes," I said.

I kept my eyes on the deceased's face, trying to read his reaction.

"Can he hear me?"

"Yes, he can hear you."

Gerard Boyle stared at Edwin. I now realized his finger pointed at Edwin, not me.

"Gerard, old boy, please, you must help me."

"You!" the spirit shouted at him again, angrily poking his finger in Edwin's direction.

"I realize you came to a rough end. But..."

The spirit grew more and more disturbed. Anger welled in his features. I clutched Edwin's arm to stop his speech. I waved my hand at him and gave a slight shake of my head.

"What is it?" he whispered. "What is happening?"

"He seems perturbed by something," I breathed.

Edwin's brows knit and he slid his eyes sideways to stare at the emptiness in front of him before returning to studying my features.

"He is pointing at you and continues to repeat the word 'you.'" I raised my voice and spoke again. "Mr. Boyle, is there something you would like to say to Edwin?"

"You!" he said again. "How dare you! Hold a knife to my throat over some tart!"

"He is angry with you about the argument you had," I relayed.

Edwin's eyebrows lifted. "Gerard, I... I am sorry. We both had too much to drink."

"So sensitive over a little tramp," the man continued.

I did not relay that piece of the message.

"Has he responded?" Edwin inquired.

"And to hold a knife to my throat over it. Get hold of yourself man!"

"He is lecturing you on the confrontation. It is as though it is still occurring."

"Gerard! Get hold of yourself," Edwin shouted at him.

The man continued to ramble, then turned and searched the horizon. "I need another drink," he murmured.

"It is no use," I said. "He is stuck in that moment. He does not realize what has happened."

"What can we do?" Edwin questioned, desperation filling his voice.

"Nothing at the moment, I am afraid."

Edwin grasped at my hands. "Lenora, do something. You must reach him!"

"There is no use. He cannot process it at this moment."

"No, no! Gerard! Gerard, get hold of yourself, man. You have been murdered! You must identify your killer!"

"Shh," I shushed him. "You'll only make matters worse. You cannot force it."

Dismay washed over his features and his lips pinched together in frustration. "We will get through to him, Edwin," I promised, squeezing his hands.

Robert approached us as Gerard wandered away, murmuring to himself. "What's happening?" he questioned.

"Gerard appeared and told us nothing!" Edwin snapped.

"You saw him?" Robert questioned me.

"Yes," I said with a nod. "Yes, he appeared again. Though he seemed stuck in the moment of his argument with Edwin."

"He said nothing about the murder?"

"He mentioned the word 'murder' twice. However, after Edwin appeared, he was fixed on their argument and we could make no headway with him."

Robert sighed. "I told you to stay back."

"Oh, of course, it is my fault."

"It usually is," Robert retorted. "You fail to heed anyone's warnings. You plow ahead with no thought to the outcome."

Edwin's jaw tensed as he seethed at Robert's statements, his frustration building over the entire situation.

"Please," I said, "it is no one's fault. Edwin, while your timing could have used improvement and you should listen to Robert in the future as he knows more about this than you, I am not certain I would have learned much from Mr. Boyle anyway. He is still very much in a state of shock."

"I thought I could help," Edwin whined.

"Yes, I understand, and perhaps in the future, you will. However, you must let me assess the situation. If I feel presenting yourself to him would be best, I will call for you."

Robert shook his head. "Still no headway, though. Which means you must be subjected to this again to seek him out."

"I disagree. We have made headway. We now know Mr. Boyle tends to appear here around the time of his murder. It likely disturbs him and he seeks answers. So, we know we can continue to reach out to him here at this time."

Robert's lips squashed into a thin line. "This is not the answer I'd hoped for."

"I realize that, however, it does mark progress."

With a sigh, Robert said, "I suppose it does. Well, shall we return to the hotel?"

"Yes," I agreed. "I would very much like the warmth of our suite."

Edwin stood staring off at the sea. "Edwin?" I questioned.

He did not respond, his jaw still flexing as he processed his frustration. I grasped his arm and tugged. "Come along. There is nothing more to be solved tonight."

With a reluctant nod and a weak smile, he turned to accompany us. We spun to face the street housing *The Black Horse* pub. I stopped dead as I witnessed what blocked our path forward. My eyes widened and my heart began to thud in my chest.

CHAPTER 16

Robert shoved me behind him. Edwin stepped forward, further blocking me.

Fergus MacGuiness, the dark-haired man Edwin pointed out in the tavern, loomed in front of us. The blade of a large knife glinted in the moonlight as he held it out at us.

"And just where do you think you're going?" he barked at us.

"If it is money you want," Robert said, waving a few bills in front of him, "here."

The man offered a grisly smirk. "I dinnae want your money."

"All right," Robert said, stuffing the bills into his pocket. "Then what is it?"

He narrowed his eyes at us. "Why you been asking about me?"

"I do not know what you mean," Robert claimed.

"This one here come up to the table and struck up a conversation," he said, thrusting his knife in Edwin's direction. "And you asked after me with the barkeep." The knife glinted again as he waved it at Robert.

"Merely curiosity," Robert claimed.

"What's got you so curious?"

"I... I had heard you were a man who could... get things," Edwin stammered.

The man's eyes narrowed at him. "Edwin, for God's sake, be quiet," Robert breathed.

"And who'd you hear that from?"

"Gerard Boyle," Edwin answered.

The man's bushy eyebrows shot up in surprise before he scrunched them together. "And just how do you know old Gerard?"

"We had the occasion to spend some time together," Edwin answered.

The man stared for another moment. "Wait a minute," he said. "Wait a minute. You. You're Edwin Fletcher. You're the one that's killed Gerard!"

"No!" Edwin shouted. "I did not kill him."

"Oh, I ought to gut you just for that. Almost cost us a mint, you did."

"I didn't kill him!" Edwin insisted.

"Oh, no? The police and just about everyone else says otherwise."

"What did you mean when you said he almost cost you a mint?" I interjected, peeking over the shoulders of Robert and Edwin.

Mr. MacGuiness focused on me as Robert hissed, "Lenora, please!"

"I would like to know!" I insisted.

"Well, aren't you a pretty little thing," he said, grinning to show his yellowed teeth.

"Stop right there, sir. I will not tolerate you speaking in this manner to my wife."

"Your wife, is it? Well, you certainly are a lucky man."

"Yes, I consider myself very lucky. Now, please. If you would allow us to pass."

"Do you always parade your wife around the docks in the middle of the night?"

"That is none of your concern!" Robert maintained.

"Mr. MacGuiness," I said, trying to steer the conversation back to the topic at hand, "what did you mean when you said Lord Edwin nearly cost you a mint?" The answer seemed relevant to the situation. Could Fergus MacGuiness be the murderer? If large sums of money were at stake, perhaps it could drive someone to kill over it.

"What's it to you, missus?"

"I am curious, indulge me."

"Mr. Boyle and I had an... arrangement. With his passing, my business plans were nearly dashed."

"Nearly?" I questioned, picking out the one word. "But they were not?"

He narrowed his eyes at me. "You're awful nosy, missus."

"Never mind that," Robert said. "Now that the matter is cleared up, we shall leave you to your business."

"Just a moment," Mr. MacGuiness said, waving the knife at us again. "I still dinnae like you asking around about me. Especially with your involvement with Gerard."

"We shall let the matter drop," Robert promised.

He shook his head. "I dinnae like it. You're poking around for a reason."

"Listen, Fergus..." Edwin began.

"No, you listen! You're trying to pin this on me! You killed him, and you're trying to wheedle out of it by blaming me! Well, I won't stand for it!"

He slashed the knife toward Edwin. Edwin danced backward.

"Now, see here!" Edwin shouted at him.

Robert shoved me further back. "Lenora, run."

"What?" I questioned, but Robert had already spun to face Mr. MacGuiness. He sidestepped around him as the man slashed at Edwin again. Robert threw his arms around the man in a bear hug from behind.

"Run, Lenora!" he shouted.

My jaw dropped open and I hesitated a moment. Edwin landed a blow against the man's jaw.

"Run!" Robert shouted again as the man struggled to break free.

I tore past them and shot up the alley. My heart pounded in my chest and I gasped for breath. As I ran toward the main street, tears stung my eyes. I stopped and sucked in deep breaths, clutching the corner of the building nearest me.

I glanced over my shoulder in the direction I'd come from. I could not leave Robert there. I pushed off the building and stumbled a step away. I hesitated another moment before deciding to return to the docks.

I hurried several steps forward when footfalls pounded toward me. I paused and pressed myself against the building, hiding in its shadow.

As the footsteps rushed toward me, I caught sight of them in the street lantern. My heart lifted as I saw Robert and Edwin rushing up the street. I breathed a sigh of relief as I stepped away from the building.

"Oh, Robert, thank heavens!" I exclaimed.

"Lenora!" he said as he slowed. "Are you all right? Why are you still here?"

"I could not leave you!"

He grasped my hands in his. Slick, warm liquid slid across my skin. I pulled my hand away and gasped. Red blood covered it. "Robert!" I shouted in dismay.

He scowled and pulled a handkerchief from his pocket, wrapping it around his hand. "'Tis nothing," he said. "Come along. We must get you back to the hotel."

"But..." I began.

Robert finished securing the handkerchief, which had already begun to become soaked with blood. "It is fine," he assured me.

With his clean hand, Robert grasped my elbow and guided me to the street beyond. We continued the rest of our journey in silence. I nearly burst with questions as we approached the hotel. Once tucked inside the warmth of our suite, I hastened to the fire and warmed myself near it.

"Let me see your hand," I said to Robert.

"It is fine, Lenora," he said again, waving his hand in the air with a wince.

"What happened?" I questioned.

"A minor scrape as we battled with the crook." He glanced to Edwin. "I would recommend we stay away from the tavern."

I sighed. "That may be impossible. Fergus MacGuiness is the best lead we have."

"He is the only lead we have," Edwin lamented.

"He may have killed Mr. Boyle in a business transaction gone badly," I answered.

"He or his wiry associate."

"Whose name we do not yet know."

"And we will not know if I can help it," Robert interjected.

"Robert, we must!"

"This is becoming too dangerous, Lenora!"

"Dangerous or not, we must find a solution for Edwin's sake!"

"I do not wish to see harm come to either of you," Edwin chimed in. "Though he is our best suspect at the moment. Given his behavior tonight, he could have easily stabbed and killed Gerard. He nearly skewered both of us."

"What?" I gasped.

Robert drew his lips into a thin line and shook his head. "He exaggerates."

I shook my head. "The fact remains he did attack you with a knife. And Gerard Boyle was killed in the same manner."

"And we have few other suspects and no information from Gerard," Edwin added.

I paced the floor as worry consumed me. We had precious few leads and information was not forthcoming on any front.

"I propose we get some rest and plan a course forward tomorrow," Robert suggested.

As much as I hated to admit it, Robert was correct. Nothing more could be done tonight, and the situation had turned precarious. Our poking around had angered one of our prime suspects. We would need to proceed carefully.

I nodded in agreement and said my goodnights. As I closed the door to the bedroom, I collapsed against it. Worry clouded my thoughts. I attempted to clear them as I shimmied out of my dress, unwilling to awaken Sinclair to assist me given the hour.

I managed to free myself and pulled on my nightgown. As I climbed into bed, I wondered if sleep would come to me.

I tossed and turned for over an hour as sleep escaped me. I listed the suspects in my mind. Fergus MacGuiness, who proved his skill with a knife earlier. Could he have killed Gerard in a business deal gone wrong? The likelihood seemed high. How we could prove it beyond continuing to contact Mr. Boyle escaped me.

I moved to the next suspect, Mr. MacGuiness's other business partner. The man, his name still unknown to us, could have been the culprit, though I had no basis to accuse him of the crime. Given Edwin's description of him, I wondered if a wiry fellow such as himself could overpower the rather sturdy Mr. Boyle.

I searched my mind for others. Could Mr. Boyle's brother be the murderer? He seemed the least likely suspect, especially in Robert's mind. Though the rumor that he was bankrupt certainly raised the stakes. Perhaps his money woes were worse than anyone knew. Did he kill his brother in order to achieve a larger slice of the pie? Though Robert denied it, it appeared to me that the man could have a temper. His shouting at the mysterious woman proved that. Though perhaps his anger was justified.

With a sigh, I rolled onto my opposite side. The final suspect popped into my mind. Edwin. He maintained his innocence. So did Tilly, though I hoped to confirm this further with her. I believed them. But I could not deny that Edwin had quarreled with the suspect, held a knife to his neck, and threatened him. And the deceased seemed to be fixated on Edwin. That did not mean he was the guilty party, but Mr. Boyle's obsession with Edwin caused me to worry.

What were we overlooking, I wondered? And how could we make more progress? I dozed off as these two questions plagued me.

* * *

The troubles flooded back into my mind seconds after I awakened. Bright sunlight streamed through the window. I'd slept later than I'd intended. I rose from my bed and called for both Sinclair and Nanny. If anyone could bring a smile to my face this morning, it would be my precious Sam.

I spent over an hour cooing over him before finally dressing for my day. Sinclair and I discussed the events of the previous night, though, for the most part, I remained pensive.

When I emerged from the bedroom, I found a note from Robert. He'd arisen earlier and already left for the morning, intent on determining where Mr. Boyle had been laid to rest.

I eased into the armchair as thoughts continued to swirl in my head. A few moments later, Edwin entered. He looked as though he hadn't slept. Dark circles hung under his eyes, and his face was gaunt and drawn.

With his hair mussed, stubble covering the lower half of his face, and wrinkled clothes, I surmised perhaps he had slept in his clothes.

"Good morning," I offered.

He rubbed his face as he collapsed into the armchair across from me. "What is so good about it, I wonder?" he murmured. "Oh, I am sorry, Lenora. How are you? Did you sleep?"

"A little. Did you manage any rest?"

"An hour or so," he admitted. "Well, after the sun had risen."

I offered a consoling smile and Edwin continued. "Though I did not go to bed until dawn."

"Oh?" I questioned.

"I found myself unable to settle after we returned. I went out to do some investigating of my own."

I raised my eyebrows. "And where did you investigate?" My mind reeled at the thought. I conjured images of brothels or bars.

"I went back to *The Black Horse*."

"What? Edwin! Have you a death wish?"

"I did not go inside," he retorted. "I hung around in the shadows. And when Mr. MacGuiness emerged, I followed him."

"Where did he go?"

"Nowhere interesting. He spent the remainder of his night in a brothel."

"That does not help us," I lamented.

"No, it does not. And I did not see the other fellow."

"Curious," I said. "I wonder where he may be."

Edwin shrugged. Was he avoiding Glasgow for fear of being caught?

"I am still stuck on the statement he made about it almost costing him a tidy sum," I said after a momentary pause.

"I assume losing Gerard as a contact may have made moving his wares difficult."

"Yes, I understand that much. Though why did he say it almost cost him? What mechanism is in place to allow him to find a new distributor so quickly?"

"Perhaps the tale of Gerard's brother being involved is true," Edwin suggested.

"Robert seems to believe it is not."

"Robert can be blind to people's true natures," Edwin answered. "He lives in a world where politeness trumps everything. He prefers not to realize how underhanded most people are."

"Robert says I am like that."

Edwin offered a half-smile. "I am not certain you are blind to it, though you do rather prefer to see people in a positive light, Lenora."

"I prefer the term realistic. Anyway, how can we ascertain who the new contact is?"

Edwin's eyes darted around the room before resting on me. "We could follow him?" he offered, raising one shoulder in a half-shrug.

I considered the proposition. It could prove illuminating on many fronts, even those that I preferred to remain blind to. But with no other information, it seemed to be the only way we could move forward. And I preferred to actively seek out leads rather than wait and hope Mr. Boyle came around.

"All right," I said with a nod. "But how will we find him?"

"We shall go to where he was last night and wait."

"Wait? Wait for him to return?"

"No, wait for him to leave," Edwin corrected.

"Leave? 'Tis late morning, Edwin, surely..."

Edwin held up his hand to silence me. "Lenora, he is at a brothel. A man does not rise early to attend to business after a night like he experienced. And doubtless, his business is best carried out under the cover of night. Though we must follow him to determine where that business is conducted."

I bit my lower lip as I considered Edwin's statements. He rose and offered his hand. "Trust me, Lenora. I have spent many a night in a similar position." He flashed a rakish grin at me and cocked his head.

I shook my head at him. "Oh, Edwin," I murmured as he pulled me to my feet. "Just let me leave a note for Robert. He will worry himself sick if he returns to find me gone."

"Do not say anything untoward in it; otherwise, he may become angry with me."

"Undoubtedly, he will be exasperated with both of us," I mentioned as I scrawled a vague reference about investigating on the bottom of the paper Robert left for me.

"You shall get away with it. I shall not."

"Second thoughts?" I questioned as I signed my name.

"No, although..." His voice trailed off.

"What is it?"

"Robert likely took the carriage."

A confused expression crossed my face as I glanced at him.

"We will have to walk," Edwin added.

"Yes?" I said, phrasing it as a question.

Edwin shifted his weight from one foot to the other as though nervous. "Oh, for heaven's sake, Edwin, I have legs, you know. Come along."

"I shall catch hell for this," he murmured as I pulled on my cape and flung the door open.

We exited the hotel into the bright but cold day. I shielded my eyes, surprised by the brightness of the sun on a November day in Scotland. Edwin shivered against the cold. "Perhaps we should wait…" he began.

"Lead the way," I interrupted.

Edwin pursed his lips. He stood still for a moment before he motioned for me to follow him and offered his arm. We proceeded through the chilly air into a rather seedy area of Glasgow.

"He is in the building across the street," Edwin informed me as he tucked me into an alley between two buildings. The air felt warmer here without any breezes whipping past us. Edwin shoved his hands under his arms to warm them. My fur muff kept my hands from becoming too cold.

I stared at the building across the street, willing the man to emerge from it.

Twenty minutes passed and nothing of note occurred. At long last, the door opened. A woman wandered out and emptied a chamber pot into the street before returning inside.

A frown settled on my lips as we continued to wait. Edwin spoke after another ten minutes, likely hoping a conversation would pass the time more quickly.

"Did you spend some time with Samuel this morning?"

"Yes," I answered with a smile. "He is quite a happy child. He has Tilly's exuberance for life."

"It is best if he has her temperament rather than mine."

"Yours is not so terrible," I commented.

He chuckled at the response. "No? I am surprised to hear you say that, Lenora. You have been on the receiving end of some of my more boorish outbursts."

"That is the result of too much drink," I countered. "When

you are not drunk, you have quite a nice personality. I can see why Tilly was so drawn to you."

"Careful, Lenora," he said with a cheeky grin. "You'd better not fall in love with me."

"There is little chance of that. I am thoroughly in love with your brother."

We stood for another few moments, our gazes boring a hole through the brothel's door.

"Are you becoming too cold?" Edwin inquired as I shifted around.

"No," I assured him. "Merely a bit stiff."

Edwin checked his pocket watch, then rubbed his hands together to warm them. "I cannot imagine he will be much longer. Though he is rather a lazy sod, isn't he?"

"I wish he was a bit less lazy."

As if on cue, the door to the brothel opened. My muscles stiffened as we spotted Fergus MacGuiness stroll out.

CHAPTER 17

Fergus squinted against the bright light before checking his timepiece.

"Oh, finally," Edwin moaned.

I began to move toward the man as he set off down the street. Edwin held me back. He held a finger up. "Patience, Lenora. We do not wish to be spotted."

I heaved a sigh and stared after the departing form of the beastly man. When he was a good ways off, Edwin nodded and motioned for me to follow. His first stop was a public washhouse, where he spent a fair amount of time.

I cursed the cold weather as I imagined the warm water he must be submerged in inside. After his first stop, he sought out a location to eat.

Edwin studied me at the second stop. "Come on," he said as he tugged at my arm. "Let's have lunch and warm up."

"I am fine," I answered.

"Your nose is as red as a rowan berry. If I return you like this, I fear for my safety." He dragged me into a nearby restaurant. The warmth inside washed over me, and I realized how cold I had been. As we were seated, I removed my muff and wiggled my fingers.

After we ordered, I kept my eyes trained outside, watching for Mr. MacGuiness to emerge from the eatery.

"I imagine he will have a leisurely lunch," Edwin said.

I pulled my gaze from the outside and glanced at my dining companion. He studied me intently.

"Is my nose still red?" I questioned, grasping at it. I figured this was the source of his attention.

He laughed. "No, it is not. Though I have just now realized I know very little about you."

"There is little to know."

"That does not seem to be true."

I raised my eyebrows as our food arrived. "So, Lenora, tell me about yourself."

"I have already told you. There is not much to tell."

"You were an orphan before marrying my brother at St. Mary's. This is the only fact I know about you. Did your parents die at a young age?"

"No," I admitted, staring into my soup bowl as I swirled the liquid around with my spoon. "My father was a doctor. He went to India. After he left, my mother became rather despondent. She detested my ability." I shrugged as the painful memories flooded through my brain. After a deep breath, I continued, "After a time and several odd attempts to rid me of it, she took me to a convent and left me there."

Edwin stared at me for a moment. "A convent? However, did you end up at St. Mary's then?"

"After a year with the Sisters of Mercy, they, too, grew wary of my ability. Mother Superior took me to St. Mary's and left me."

"Oh my, how terrible. You poor child," Edwin said. His features showed genuine sorrow. His level of empathy astounded me.

"I suppose I knew no better. Though as a child, I felt terribly upset and missed my mother."

"You said she attempted to rid you of your... ability? Is that what you call it?"

"Rather a curse at times, though I suppose your term is fitting. And yes, she did. In a series of different ways. Feeding me white foods, performing some sort of ceremony, tying me to a tree under the full moon."

Edwin batted his eyelashes at the list. "How old were you?"

"Five," I answered.

"My God," he answered. "How terrible. Whatever happened to your parents?"

"I do not know. I have never seen them since. My father may never have returned from India. Then again, he may have. What my mother told him, assuming she was still alive, about my whereabouts remains a mystery."

"Have you any desire to find them?"

The question struck me, and I sat in a stupor for a moment. "I am sorry, Lenora," Edwin said after a moment, "I did not mean to upset you. You do not need to answer."

"No," I said, waving his concern away. "No, it is a fair question. Though I am afraid, I haven't given it much thought before."

"Fair enough."

"To be honest, I expected to spend my life at St. Mary's. I never expected I'd have the opportunity or means to find them."

"You were nearly eighteen when you went to Blackmoore, were you not? Had you no plans for after you finished your schoolwork?"

"I assumed I would stay on as a teacher at the orphanage. Or rather, I hoped so. Headmistress Williamson and I did not get along due to my... ability. She dashed every chance I had at placement in a home. I am uncertain as to whether or not she'd allow me to remain on at St. Mary's after my eighteenth birthday."

"Tilly once told me she was a horrid woman. She is one of the reasons she ran away."

My mood turned melancholy over the matter. "Tilly also maintained St. Mary's squashed any chance she had at happiness," I said, my voice taking a wistful tone.

"I regret she did not find more happiness," Edwin said. "She left St. Mary's and…"

I shook my head and reached for his hand across the table. "She was happy with you. And there is nothing to be done to change it now."

Tears shone in Edwin's eyes as he flicked his gaze outside. We sat in silence for a moment before I spoke again. "What about you?"

"Nothing interesting," Edwin claimed.

"Now it is my turn to prod."

Edwin shrugged. "I lived quite a charmed life of privilege and ease. There is not much interesting about it."

"Did you get along with Robert? Was your relationship always difficult?"

"I guess I always envied him."

"Why?"

Edwin shrugged. "He got all the attention," he said with a grin.

My brow furrowed at the statement as I tried to parse through it.

Edwin explained before I spoke again. "My parents showered us both with gifts and the like, but Robert was always pushed. Had to bring him up to be the duke, lord of the manor, all that. My parents doted on me as a way to appease me into fading into the background.

"As a result, I suppose I grew used to living a charmed life but having no responsibilities. I know, poor little rich boy, eh?"

"I see," I said. "After this is finished, I hope you will spend more time at Blackmoore Castle. You have some responsibilities now."

He smiled. "Yes, I have the responsibility to spoil my little nephew. If Robert will allow me on the grounds."

"Robert has made great strides. He cares for you, even if he doesn't always show it."

Edwin let his eyes drop and nodded. "I am not certain, though, he has forgiven me for the part I played in Annie's death."

"It will take time, but I believe you can overcome it."

Edwin's eyes remained fixed on the table and he offered a slight nod. "Edwin," I said, "I realize the situation with Sam may be awkward but..."

His eyes darted to mine and he gave a vehement head shake. "Oh no," he said. "Not at all. He is your son. Yours and Robert's. I do not wish to create any trouble on that front."

"But you are his..."

"His father?" Edwin interrupted. "No, Robert is his father. I am, however, his uncle. And if I am given the opportunity, I should like to be very close to him."

I smiled at his graciousness. He did not mean to make any trouble for us despite the child being his son.

"I should very much like you to be close to him. And I am certain Tilly would, too."

"She did right by asking you to take him, Lenora. She could not have selected better parents. I did not deserve her."

"Let's not focus on that now," I said.

"Quite right," Edwin answered, tossing his napkin onto the table. "It looks like our friend has finished his meal." He nodded toward the street.

"Oh!" I exclaimed. "We must hurry!"

My eyes went wide as I quickly dabbed my lips with the napkin. "You go outside and watch him while I settle up the bill."

I nodded and Edwin added, "Lenora, do NOT go after him without me."

"You are beginning to sound like Robert," I teased as I stood and hurried from the table.

"Wait for me, Lenora!" he called after me as I pushed through the doors to the street outside.

I searched the length of it and spotted Mr. MacGuiness strolling along the street. He turned and disappeared down a side street.

I groaned as I spun to determine how close Edwin was to finishing inside. I took a step forward, then hesitated. Weighing my odds, I considered hurrying ahead alone. Edwin had warned me not to, and with good reason. The man was dangerous. But still, if we lost him, our efforts would be for naught.

With a huff and a shake of my head, I pressed forward, hurrying down the sidewalk. As I approached the street he had disappeared down, a winded Edwin caught up with me. He puffed for breath as he slowed to my speed.

"I told you to wait," he chided.

"He disappeared down a side street. I had no choice!"

"You are quite impetuous, Lenora. You'll turn poor Robert's hair gray before long."

I shook my head and shot a wry glance in his direction. "Which street then?" he inquired.

"Just there," I said, pointing between two buildings. We reached the offshoot and I peered down it. He had disappeared.

"I do not see him," Edwin said.

After another disgruntled sigh, I pushed forward down the alley. "Lenora!" I heard Edwin shout behind me.

"We cannot locate him standing there," I argued.

"Slow down," he countered. "We should proceed with caution."

I slowed my pace a tad and we continued down the alley. We emerged at the end onto a larger street. People bustled about, tending to their daily business. My head swiveled as I searched for the man.

Tension crept into my shoulders as I did not spot him.

"There," Edwin said. I followed the direction of his gaze and spotted the man several yards away, ducking into another side street. Edwin guided me forward and we hurried to the spot where he'd disappeared.

We continued following him as he traversed the streets of Glasgow.

"Where is he going?" Edwin murmured after a few minutes.

After several more minutes of walking, we approached a park.

"All this to take in the sights?" Edwin said.

Mr. MacGuiness entered the green area and meandered among the stately trees and benches. He wandered the paths as though he had a specific destination in mind. After a few more moments, he slowed near a large tree. We continued toward him. As we approached, a bench became visible. Another man perched on it.

Edwin pulled me behind the cover of a tree as Mr. MacGuiness approached the well-dressed man. I gasped as he swung toward us.

As he stood from the bench, I recognized the man with Mr. MacGuiness to be Lord Pennington.

"Penny," Edwin said.

"Yes," I answered. "Indeed, it is."

"I told you he was involved in this."

"Do you think this is what Mr. MacGuiness meant when he said you almost cost him money?"

"That Penny was his new contact?" I nodded, and Edwin continued, "It's possible. Though I cannot imagine he has the same connections as his brother."

"But perhaps enough to pick up the pieces and carry on the business," I murmured.

"Yes," Edwin agreed.

We watched in silence as the two men across the park conversed for a few more moments. Lord Pennington poked his finger at Mr. MacGuiness. His face soured, his lips pinching into a tight pucker and his forehead wrinkling.

Fergus MacGuiness held his hands out to the sides, waving them about emphatically before he pointed a finger in Lord Pennington's direction.

CHAPTER 18

"It appears they are arguing," Edwin said.
"Yes, it does."

Lord Pennington shook his head and pounded his cane on the ground. He spoke again. "Oh, I wish we could hear what they are saying," I lamented.

"Are there any dead people around you can ask?" Edwin questioned.

I stared at him for a moment, surprised at his statement. He shifted his eyes toward me. "What?" he questioned.

"They aren't puppets, you know. I cannot order them about."

"Well, I do not understand how it all works. There, they are finished, it seems."

With an emphatic final pound of his cane, Lord Pennington spun on his heel and ambled away from Fergus MacGuiness. The man milled around a few more moments before disappearing.

I snapped my head toward Edwin. "What should we do?"
"Continue to follow Fergus?" Edwin suggested.
"Should one of us follow Lord Pennington?"

"We should not split up," Edwin answered, but pondered the question about who to follow. "What advantage have we to follow Penny?"

"Perhaps he is involved."

"In murdering his own brother?"

I shrugged. "He seems as likely a suspect as anyone."

"I cannot imagine Penny murdering his brother."

"If he is in financial trouble, he may have. Perhaps he wanted the entire pie rather than a piece of it."

"Perhaps, though I think our better bet is to follow Fergus."

"All right," I said with a nod. "We'd better hurry before we lose track of him."

The man led us through the streets of Glasgow, approaching the docks. A nauseous feeling washed over me as I recalled the incident there less than twenty-four hours ago.

Mr. MacGuiness ducked down the now familiar alley housing *The Black Horse*. Moments later, he entered the pub.

"Well, there he is for the rest of the night," Edwin said.

"Really?" I questioned. "What is the time?"

"Nearly half-past four," he said after referencing his pocket watch.

"Oh my, it has grown later than I expected."

"Shall we return to the hotel?"

I hesitated a moment before answering. "Would you mind if we stopped at the St. Agnes Cemetery first?"

"Not at all," Edwin said as he offered his arm to me.

We wound through the streets to the cemetery and entered through the front gates. I took the familiar path toward Tilly's tombstone.

Edwin glanced at me as he read the name on the marker where I stopped. "I hope you do not mind," I said.

He shook his head but remained silent. I returned my attention to Tilly's grave as Edwin wiped at his eyes.

Fingers brushed mine before closing around my hand. I glanced to my right and smiled. "Hello," I whispered.

"Hello, Lenora," Tilly said.

"I've missed you."

"What?" Edwin said with a sniffle.

I glanced at him before returning my gaze to Tilly, unwilling to let go of her hand. "It is Tilly," I answered him. I reached my other hand and wrapped it around Edwin's hand.

Edwin remained silent. I imagined the experience was overwhelming for him.

Tilly studied Edwin. "It is good to see him outside of a jail cell," she said. "Please thank Robert for me."

"I will. And we are working hard to prove Edwin's innocence."

Tilly squeezed my hand and smiled.

"I am terribly sorry to say we are not making much progress, but we are working on it."

"I wish I could help more."

"Perhaps you can."

Tilly raised her eyebrows at me. I turned to face Edwin. "Would you give me a few moments?"

Edwin nodded and turned to step away. He spun back and squeezed my hand. "Please tell her again how much I love her and miss her."

"She heard you. She knows," I relayed. "And she feels the same."

He smiled at me and squeezed my hand again before he retreated several steps. "Thank you for helping him," Tilly said.

"I would do anything for you, Tilly." My face fell and I bit my lower lip.

"What is it, Lenora?"

I pursed my lips before I blew out a long breath. My gaze flitted to her face before falling away again. I swallowed hard, debating on asking her or not. I decided I needed my mind settled, so I pushed on.

"I am sorry to ask this, Tilly," I said, my face pinching with discomfort.

"What is it?"

"How certain are you of Edwin's innocence?"

"Very, why?"

I shook my head, disappointed in myself. "I have been able to contact Mr. Boyle on two occasions only. He remains stuck on Edwin. I cannot discern why; however, my mind plagues me with the idea that Edwin may have done something he cannot recall."

Tilly shook her head. "No, Lenora," she said. "He did not."

"How can you be certain?"

"He staggered from the bar that night and dropped over in an alley. He did not move until the following morning. I stayed with him." Tears welled in Tilly's eyes. "It was a low point for him. Oh, Lenora, he is so alone. His reaction to the situation is poor, though he cannot help it."

I squeezed her hand. "I am sorry to have asked. My mind couldn't help but wander there, but now you have cleared it up. And he is alone no longer. Both Robert and I will take care of him. Now that I understand his connection to Sam, I will ensure he is close to him."

"Thank you, Lenora."

Tilly peered over my shoulder. Edwin shifted his weight from foot to foot and rubbed his hands together. "I hate to leave but…" I began.

Tilly focused on me again. "We will see each other again."

"Please try to come to the castle."

Tilly remained silent.

My lip quivered at her silence. "You can, can't you?"

She did not respond.

"Tilly?"

Tilly's jaw bounced up and down, but words did not come. "I am not certain," she admitted. "I try, but I cannot seem to get there."

"That's why you only appeared in my dreams there."

Tilly nodded. "Yes. I've tried, but I feel so weak."

"I have heard your voice."

Her face brightened. "You have? Perhaps then there is a way for me to reach you there."

"Please keep trying," I pleaded.

"I will. I promise."

I stared at her, dreading the moment we had to say goodbye. It had taken so long for me to reach her. I supposed if we cleared Edwin's name, this would free her energy and allow her to visit more freely. I made myself a silent promise to step up my efforts.

"I should go," we said at the same time. After a shared giggle, we squeezed each other's hands.

"Goodbye, Lenora," Tilly said.

"Goodbye, Tilly." I held back tears as I let go of her hand. I pressed my lips together as I blinked them away when she disappeared from my view. A lump formed in my throat and I swallowed to clear it. With a sniffle, I turned toward Edwin.

I wandered toward him. "Did she…" he could not bring himself to finish the statement.

I nodded. "Yes," I choked out.

"Shall we go?" Edwin asked.

"Yes, we had better."

We traversed the streets to the hotel, arriving as the sun began to slip behind the horizon. Edwin pushed open the door, signaling for me to precede him into the suite. I hurried inside and crossed to the fireplace.

Robert waited there, a brandy in his hand. His eyebrows shot up as we entered the room. His eyes followed me across the room, lingering on me as I rubbed my hands in front of the warm flames.

"Hello, dear," I greeted him with a smile, returning my gaze to the dancing flames.

He stood silent for another moment, his eyes still wide and his jaw hanging open. After a moment, his head swiveled between me and Edwin.

"Well, isn't someone going to explain?"

"Explain what, dear?" I questioned, finally warm enough to unfasten my cape and doff it.

"Where the devil have you two been?"

"Investigating," I said. "I explained it in the note."

His eyebrows scrunched. "That vague scrawl?"

"Yes," I answered.

"Lenora, it said nothing! You have been gone for the balance of the day. I returned to find the suite devoid of you and Edwin. I waited and waited. And as the sun began to set, I feared the worst."

"Don't worry, brother, I took excellent care of her. I even made sure she had lunch." Edwin offered a devilish grin.

Robert scowled at him. "This is not a joke, Edwin."

"Oh, Robert," I said. "Edwin took perfectly good care of me."

"Lenora, you have been out for hours. Where have you been? What have you been doing all this time?"

I shrugged, trying to convey nonchalance as I answered. "We followed a few leads."

"What leads?"

I licked my lips as I realized I would have to describe our actions in more detail. "We followed Mr. MacGuiness to determine if we could learn anything from him."

Robert's jaw unhinged and his eyes shot around the room in disbelief. "Are you mad?"

"No," I answered with a pout. "It seemed prudent to determine his activities. We have little other leads, and he is our primary suspect."

"Lenora, the man held a knife to us only last night. We had quite the scuffle with him. And you found it prudent to follow him?"

I shrugged and offered a penitent smile. "I saw no other avenues to pursue at the moment."

"How did you even find him? Or don't I want to know?"

"Edwin followed him last night and knew where to wait for him."

Robert's gaze rested on Edwin. "Which was?"

"He was at a brothel. We simply had to go there and wait for him to emerge."

"You took my wife to a brothel?"

"Do not be ridiculous, Robert. We did not go inside," Edwin said with an exasperated chuckle. "We merely waited across the street for him."

Robert's annoyance over our antics grew with each statement. I attempted to temper it by pulling the nearly empty brandy glass from his hand and refilling it. I guided him to an armchair and eased him into it, handing him the refreshed glass.

"I was in no danger, Robert. We kept our distance."

"In a dangerous part of town where there is a brothel, you were in no danger? Come, Lenora, what kind of fool do you take me for?"

"One who worries over nothing."

Robert pulled his lips into a thin line and shook his head, staring into the fire. "And you followed him from morning until night? Did you at least learn anything?"

A smile curled the corners of my lips as I realized

LETTER TO A DUCHESS

Robert's curiosity finally overcame his upset. I plopped into the chair across from him. "We did," I said, my smile broadening. "Your news first, though. Did you learn anything from Lord Pennington?"

"Precious little, I am afraid," Robert announced with a sigh.

"You were not able to ascertain the location of Gerard's grave?" Edwin inquired.

"No," Robert said, offering a sheepish glance between us.

"Why not?" Edwin demanded.

Robert launched into an explanation. "I attempted to gently work it into the conversation. I told him I'd just learned of his brother's passing through a friend and offered my condolences. I said I would like to visit the grave to pay my respects."

"And?" I prodded.

"He said it was unnecessary, but he appreciated the thought and my condolences." Robert took a swallow of brandy. "I did not let the matter rest there. I rather insisted he pass the information along. Told him Edwin and Gerard were friends and I was certain Edwin would like to visit the grave.

"But Penny told me he had no idea of its location."

"What?" I cried.

Robert shrugged, his eyebrows shooting high. "I was as flabbergasted as you are."

"Could the officer who informed us he claimed the body have been mistaken?" I asked.

"Apparently, he was."

"Who did Penny say handled it?" Edwin chimed in.

"He said he did not know nor did he care. I found it difficult to press the matter any further."

I narrowed my eyes at the statement. "How odd. Who else

would claim the body? And why would the record show it was Lord Pennington if it was not?"

"Could someone have lied to collect Gerard's body?" Robert questioned.

"To what end?" I asked.

"Perhaps he carried something valuable on him and they wished to retrieve it from the personal effects," Edwin suggested.

"Perhaps," I acquiesced. "Though…"

"What is it, Lenora?" Robert prodded.

"Perhaps Lord Pennington is not being truthful."

Robert shook his head. "I have never known Penny to act this way. It astounds me you are even suggesting he lied to me."

"You are too naive, Robert," Edwin chided.

"I am not," Robert countered.

"He may have a point," I said.

Robert's face pinched with annoyance. "How is that?"

"When we followed Fergus MacGuiness," I explained, "we saw him meet with Lord Pennington."

Robert's eyes grew wide. "What? Really?"

"Yes," Edwin answered. "It seems old Penny is up to a few tricks. So I daresay it is a very real possibility that he lied to you earlier."

"And it begs the question why," I said.

"Yes," Edwin agreed, his finger rubbing his chin, "why would Penny lie about accepting his brother's corpse and burying it?"

"To distance himself from the man, I would venture," Robert said.

"Or from some sense of guilt," I offered. "Perhaps Lord Pennington is hiding more than we know."

"You cannot possibly believe him responsible for his own brother's death," Robert said.

I sighed. "I am not certain," I admitted. "Though I would not rule him out."

Silence fell between us. "We must get more information."

"Please, not another midnight romp to the docks," Robert said.

I did not see a way to avoid it. Outside of continuing to follow our suspects, our other options were few. And even with our sleuthing skills, we may fall short of finding any evidence to suggest their guilt.

"I do not see another choice," I answered.

Robert's posture slumped, and he sipped at his brandy. "I can accompany her," Edwin offered.

"Over my dead body," Robert grumbled, leaping from his seat and stalking around the room. "We shall avoid the pub at all costs. Straight to the docks and back." He checked his pocket watch. "I recommend we have an early dinner and retire for a few hours' rest."

Robert swallowed the last of his brandy and set the glass on the table resolutely. He eyed me and Edwin. I nodded in agreement, and we readied ourselves for a light meal. After a bit of visiting with Samuel, I crawled into bed at an early hour.

I found myself unable to fall asleep and cursed the early hour, though I realized it was likely more than just that preventing me from rest. I climbed from my bed and paced the floor as the moon rose outside my window.

I stared at the blue-white object as it climbed in the night sky. My conversation with Tilly replayed in my mind. I had my confirmation of Edwin's innocence. And I had finally gotten to have more than a snippet of a conversation with my friend. As I pondered her words, wondering what prevented her from appearing at Blackmoore Castle, my mind wandered back to another moonlit night I'd spent with Tilly.

After catching Millicent sneaking around after bedtime at St. Mary's, Tilly had vowed to follow her to determine her whereabouts at the next opportunity. Five days after we'd caught Millicent on the first occasion, Tilly woke me from a sound sleep.

"Lenora," she whispered as she shook me.

"Tilly, what is it?" I asked, sleep filling my voice.

"Get up!"

"Why?" I groaned.

"Millie just sneaked from the room. Quickly!" She waved my cape in front of me.

"Tilly!" I scolded. "No! Go to sleep."

"Come on, Lenora. If you do not come with me, I shall go myself."

Even in my sleepy stupor, I realized she meant the threat. I snatched my cape from her hand and rolled out of bed. "I must change."

"There is no time. Just put your cape on."

"Tilly, I am in my bedclothes! I cannot go out."

"As am I!" She flashed her white nightgown from under her cape. "No one will see it."

I thanked the heavens it was warm enough to parade around in our nightclothes as I crept down the stairs and through the foyer.

The front door, normally locked at this hour, remained unlocked. Tilly eased it open, wincing as the hinges protested a bit. We stepped into the warm evening air. Tilly's head swiveled as she searched the deserted streets.

A figure moved in the darkness, limned in moonlight to our right. "There!" she breathed, thrusting her finger toward the woman.

Tilly grasped my hand and led me down the front stairs. We hurried to match the figure's pace. Careful to keep our distance lest we be found out, we wound through the streets, unsure of where we would end up.

As we continued our journey, I said, "Tilly, I am not at all sure this is wise."

"Shhh," she shushed me. "Don't be a spoilsport, Lenora." The giddy grin on her face made it obvious Tilly was enjoying the adventure.

After several more moments of walking, we approached an area of town where several people still milled about in the streets despite the late hour.

"Tilly," I cautioned again, "I am growing more uncomfortable."

I eyed the people surrounding us. One man stumbled about in the street before retching as he clutched the corner of a building. A scantily clad woman wearing too much rouge and thick red paint on her lips sauntered down the street, approaching any man within sight. A pair of men slung their arms around each other and belted out a tune as they spilled from the doorway of a tavern.

"Tilly, we should not be here."

"Oh, Lenora, no one even notices us. Look at all this life!"

"This is not life, Tilly. This appears to be the exact opposite, in fact," I said with a grimace.

"Do not be so sour," she said.

"What is Millicent doing in an area of town like this?" I questioned as we proceeded further.

"Indeed!" Tilly said with a squeal and a giggle. "What is perfect little Millie doing here? Perhaps she has a beau! Oh, how I envy her if she does."

"I am not certain I would envy her, Tilly. I am not certain her beau is entirely respectable if she is meeting him in the dead of the night here."

"We should soon find out, look!" Tilly called my attention

to Millicent as she ducked into a pub. "Let's follow her!" She grasped my arm and tugged.

"No!" I argued, pulling against her.

"Oh, Lenora! We've come this far!"

I wrenched my hand from her grip and folded my arms across my chest. "No. I will not enter a pub in my night things!"

"We shall leave the capes on. No one will know!"

"No, Tilly, this I absolutely refuse! We shall wait here if you'd like, but I will not enter a pub without clothes!"

"Oh, we hardly are without clothes, Lenora," Tilly chided, though I stood firm in my decision.

We argued a few more moments before the bickering was put to an end for us. As we quarreled, becoming oblivious to our surroundings, a man approached from behind us.

"And what are you two pretty things doing here all alone?" the gruff voice growled.

We spun to face him, finding his appearance matched the gruffness in his voice. Greasy, blond hair was plastered to his head. Stubble covered his face from his cheeks to his chin. He flashed a crooked grin, showing his missing teeth. A light breeze brought a smell from him that assaulted my nostrils.

"Get away, old man," Tilly shouted at him. "We are no business of yours!"

"Oh?" he spat back. "Well, I beg to differ. Now, what can you two lassies offer me?"

"Nothing," Tilly said.

He raised his eyebrows at us. "Well, that just won't do!"

Tilly rolled her eyes and shook her head at him as she turned to retrain her eyes on the pub door.

I swallowed hard and my jaw dropped open. I grasped Tilly's arm and tugged her attention back to the old man. The blade of a knife glinted in the light from the nearby pub.

"Now, like I said, what can you two lassies offer me?"

CHAPTER 19

I gulped at the sight of the knife clutched in the old man's hand. We had no money to give him. Though in this area of town, the man may expect another form of payment. I shuddered as I considered our circumstances.

My eyes searched the area. With the pub at our backs, we had nowhere to run. I bit my lower lip as my knees turned to jelly. I wondered if I would soon become one of the dearly departed that I often came into contact with during my short life.

"Please," Tilly began when a new voice entered the conversation.

"Leave them alone," Millicent's nasally tone threatened.

The man snapped his eyes in her direction. A small blade poked from within her cloak.

The man's eyes widened before he stumbled back a step and let out a harsh cackle. He clutched his belly as it shook from his laughter. His face turned serious in an instant and he thrust the knife forward again. "What do you expect you'd do with that, lassie?"

"I expect to inflict harm at the very least."

The man let out another sharp laugh. "Ha! I doubt it. A wee thing like you?"

"Leave my friends alone," Millicent threatened.

"Or what?"

She thrust the knife forward with adept skill and it sliced across the man's arm. Blood soaked his shirt as it gaped open from the cut.

"You little bitch!" he shouted as he clutched at his arm.

"I said go! Or I'll do worse."

The man grumbled but relented and backed away from us. I gulped and closed my eyes for a moment as I steadied my breath. My arm remained clutched around Tilly's, and I felt her cease her trembling.

"What are you two doing here?" Millicent barked at us.

I struggled to search for words to explain. Tilly recovered more quickly and beat me to it. With her hand stuck on her hip, she thrust her chin out and raised her eyebrows high. "What are YOU doing here?"

I stared at Millicent as we awaited a response. "None of your business. Headmistress Williamson will be quite angry when she hears about this!"

"She will not be pleased about you sneaking out several times either!"

Millicent set her face in an unimpressed stare and crossed her arms. "Fine. I will not tell if you promise not to mention it either."

"And you'll leave Lenora and me alone? No more tattling to the headmistress?"

Millicent narrowed her eyes.

Tilly shrugged, her hand still resting on her hip as she jutted it out. "Or we could explain all about this to the headmistress. I'm sure she'd love to know all about why you're in this tawdry area night after night."

"Fine," Millicent spat. "But do not follow me again."

"What are you doing here anyway, Millie?" Tilly questioned.

"None of your business!" she shrieked. "Now go back to St. Mary's!" She spun on her heel and stormed away from us, disappearing between two buildings.

"Should we follow her?" Tilly inquired.

"No!" I squealed. "Tilly! We very nearly just lost our lives or something else! We should return to St. Mary's."

"But we have not determined why Millicent is here!"

"And I do not want to. Tilly, she just stabbed a man with a knife! I have no desire to cross her. Nor any of the other characters lurking around this area."

Tilly pouted and slumped her shoulders. "Oh, Lenora," she groaned. "We've failed in our mission! And she didn't stab anyone. She only wounded him slightly."

"I have no desire for her to wound me slightly. And it appears we are at a stalemate. Which I am happy to accept, considering her antics usually win me a night in the attic or worse."

Tilly frowned. "You are correct, as always, Lenora. It is you who suffers the most in our war against each other." She sighed in disgust. "I suppose we should return to St. Mary's before we raise the ire of Millicent or Headmistress Williamson."

I nodded. "I am sorry we did not determine Millicent's reason for being here. But perhaps it is for the best. And most probably, it is none of our business."

We grasped each other's hands and hurried away from the horrid location.

* * *

I stared up at the moon as the memory faded from my mind. Tilly and I would never determine the reason for Millicent's midnight romps, though we would notice several more of them before we all departed from St. Mary's. If she'd had her way, Tilly would have had us sleuthing many more times despite the run-in we'd had. Ironic, I ruminated, that I'd wind up sleuthing at all hours of the night.

With a slight smile at the corners of my lips, I shuffled back to bed and climbed under the covers. I drifted off to a fitful sleep.

I awoke to Robert gently shaking me. "Lenora," he whispered.

"What is it?" I moaned. Suddenly, my eyes snapped open wide. "Is it Sam?"

"No, he is snug in his bed. Which is where I wish we were," Robert lamented. "Instead of traipsing about the city."

Our plan flooded back into my mind. "Oh, yes," I said with a yawn as I threw back my covers.

"If you are too tired to go, please stay in bed."

I shook my head and the sleep from my body. "No, I would never forgive myself if we missed this opportunity. We desperately need Gerard's help."

"All right," Robert said as I stood and stretched. "I'll awaken Sinclair."

"No, don't bother. I can manage. Just give me a moment."

With a dubious glance, he nodded and slipped from the room. I quickly donned a dress and clumsily fastened it. With a cape on, it would do well enough.

I exited into the sitting room. Robert slid my cape around my shoulders and I fastened it tightly. "Ready?" he inquired.

"Yes," I answered with a nod.

We met Edwin outside and hurried to the docks. I cursed the weather, not as warm as when Tilly and I traversed the streets on a sleuthing mission. My throat went dry as we turned the corner leading to the docks. We kept our distance from the pub.

Cold wind whipped from the water, fluttering my cape around me as we approached the crime scene. I scanned the spot, finding it empty. Why did Gerard Boyle insist on being so difficult, I lamented?

"Mr. Boyle?" I called. "Mr. Boyle?"

I received no response. We waited several more minutes. I swiveled to face Robert and Edwin, thrusting my arms out at my side.

I spun back toward the water and wrung my hands. I tried calling again, but still nothing. We waited until my fingers began to go numb from cold. Robert approached. "Lenora," he whispered. "Any luck?"

"No," I said with a sigh. "He has not shown up."

"It is growing quite cold," he answered.

"Yes, I know," I said. I wavered between waiting a few more moments and departing. In the end, I decided to return to the hotel. I slogged along next to Robert and Edwin, with Robert's arm wrapped tightly around me.

As we entered our suite, I fought back tears. "I am sorry, Edwin," I choked out.

"Do not be sorry, Lenora," he answered. "It is not your fault."

His lips formed a smile, but I could see the distress in his eyes. Tiredness washed over me along with worry.

"You should get some rest, dear," Robert insisted. I nodded and dragged myself to the bedroom, peeling off my dress and pulling on my nightgown. I slipped between the covers, glad for the warmth the bed offered. Within minutes, I drifted to sleep.

I spent several quiet hours in a dreamless sleep. I awoke after the sun had risen, though its rays were blocked by thick gray clouds, marking another dreich day in Scotland. As I drew in a deep breath and stretched, I sat up. I froze mid-stretch, my arms still thrust in the air. My eyes widened and my jaw gaped open as I stared ahead of me.

Robert sat in the armchair across the room. "Ah, you're awake!" he said as he closed his book.

I did not respond. "Lenora?" Robert questioned as my brows knit and my jaw remained open.

"Hello," I breathed, finally letting my arms lower to my sides.

"Hello," Robert answered.

I narrowed my eyes before I finally let them flit to Robert. I returned them to the original object of my focus. I pursed my lips and studied it.

"Lenora, are you quite all right?" Robert asked after another moment.

"Shh," I said, waving my hand to stop him. Robert rose from his chair, a concerned expression on his face.

I licked my lips and said, "Why have you come?"

Robert hurried toward the bed, giving a wide berth around where my sightline rested. He reached over and grasped my hand as he stood near the bed. He drew in uneven, ragged breaths.

"Who is it?" he whispered.

I cocked my head. Nothing that happened seemed to spook the specter. Without removing my eyes from him, I whispered to Robert, "Mr. Boyle."

Robert's eyes widened at my admission. I studied the man in front of me. He stood silent at the foot of the bed. His deep-set, dark eyes bored a hole into me from under his bushy eyebrows. He still wore the clothes I assumed he wore when he died. A bloodstain marked the front of his vest, though the knife no longer protruded from his chest. It marked progress.

"Mr. Boyle," I said, raising my voice and addressing him. "Have you come for help?"

He did not answer. "Can you speak?"

Nothing. Not a twitch. Not a nod. Not even a narrowing of his eyes. No movement of any kind that I could discern as a response came.

"All right," I said to him. "I shall be here when you are ready."

I expected him to disappear from my view, but he remained. I waited a few moments before deciding to rise from my bed. I quickly donned my dressing gown.

"Is he gone?" Robert hissed.

"No," I answered. "He is still there. Standing just at the foot of the bed."

"What does he want?"

I shrugged. "He seems unable to speak." I glanced at his statuesque form. "Or move, for that matter. He hasn't fluttered so much as an eyelid since I awoke and found him there."

"What does it mean?"

"I do not know, though he no longer sports the knife he had when I saw him at the docks."

"You mean to say you saw a knife embedded in his chest when you have encountered him before?"

"Yes," I said with a nod. "Now there is only a bloodstain."

Robert's jaw unhinged. After a moment, he swallowed hard. "I am sorry you see such things, Lenora."

I waved his concern away. "I have seen worse. The dead are often in a shocking state."

"I am not certain I could stand that," Robert murmured.

"Anyway, it marks progress. If he no longer appears with the knife, he may be getting closer to helping us and himself."

Robert cocked his head at my statement, his uncertainty as to its meaning obvious. "When I first encountered Annie, she did not appear as she did in life. But by the end, she appeared normal. Their changing appearance often connotes progress on their part toward acceptance."

"And the closer they become to acceptance..." Robert left the statement unfinished, his implied question obvious.

"The more communicative they become."

"Yet he seems less so. You said he hasn't spoken or moved."

"No, but prior to this, he wasn't very communicative either. He only babbled about his murder and Edwin. He seemed stuck."

"And he isn't now?"

"I hope not, though," I said as I glanced at the man again, "he seems rather stuck still." I sighed.

"I suppose this marks progress in that we do not need to traipse about the city in the middle of the night to contact the man."

"Unless he disappears again."

"Oh, please, Gerard, stay," Robert said, waving his handing the air.

I held in a chuckle at what I found a comedic display. "Well, I suppose I should go about my business."

"I shall arrange breakfast for you."

"Thank you, dear. Though I should like to dress before I eat. Could you send in Sinclair?"

"Of course," Robert said. He brushed my lips with his before his face reddened. "Oh..." He swallowed hard, glancing near the foot of the bed. "I suppose I should not do that with..." His voice trailed off and he tossed his head in the direction of Mr. Boyle.

I squeezed his hands and stole another peck from him. "I do not mind a kiss from my husband no matter who should see it."

Robert smiled at me, his gaze lingering for a moment.

"Well, I shall summon Sinclair!" he exclaimed, waving a finger in the air and striding to the door.

I mouthed a thank you to him as he pulled the door closed behind him, then whipped around to face Mr. Boyle. He still stood at the foot of the bed, though he had spun to stare at me.

"Well, now we are alone," I said. "Perhaps now you'd like to speak?"

CHAPTER 20

I raised my eyebrows at him. His eyes bored into me, but no words emerged from his tightly closed lips.

"Have you recovered from your shock?" I asked.

Silence met my query.

"Do you realize you were murdered?"

No response came.

I sighed and prepared to take another route when Sinclair entered. "Good day, Your Grace," she said with a bright smile.

"Good morning, Sinclair," I greeted her. "Oh, it IS still morning, is it not?"

"Yes," she said with a chuckle. "You have not slept THAT late."

She assisted me with dressing, safely tucked behind a screen. As she fashioned my hair into its usual style, I bit my lower lip. Sinclair met my gaze in the mirror. "Everything all right, Your Grace? Are you still tired? You do not seem yourself."

I sighed as I considered my response. My eyes shifted in the mirror to gaze at another. Still at the foot of the bed, the unmoving man continued to stare at me. "It is not tiredness," I admitted.

"Oh? Illness? Frustration?"

"Frustration, yes, that captures my mood," I answered. "Though we may have some progress."

"Did Mr. Boyle appear to you last night?"

"No," I answered, "though he appears to me now." I flicked my eyes to watch her reaction. She froze for a moment before continuing to situate a comb in my curls. In our time together, Sinclair had risen admirably to the challenge of a mistress who communicated with the dead regularly.

"And is he here now, Your Grace?" she questioned as she focused on my hair.

"He is. I awoke to find him by the bed. He has not moved. He only turns to stare at me wherever I go."

Sinclair finished my hair, and I thanked her. "I do not understand how you manage it, Your Grace. I would find myself quite disturbed."

"What disturbs me more is his lack of communication. He just stands and stares!"

"I imagine Lord Edwin would prefer he name his murderer outright, as well!"

"As would I." I paused for a moment. "Perhaps that is a tactic to try, though, Sinclair."

"What is?"

"Naming his murderer. Perhaps the proper name will elicit some sort of reaction from him."

Sinclair's eyes grew large. "I shall not try until you've departed, Sinclair, I promise."

She breathed a sigh of relief at the admission. "I am too faint at heart for it, Your Grace."

"You are not. Your behavior during Annie's fiasco was admirable. Though I understand your preference to not involve yourself whenever possible."

"If you need me, Your Grace, I shall gird myself. But if it's all the same, I shall leave you to your conversations with the dearly departed."

"Perfectly fine. And could you send in Sam?"

"Oh…" she hesitated.

"Never mind, you are quite right, Sinclair. Perhaps I should go to him rather than bring him here with Mr. Boyle."

"Quite right, Your Grace. I shall tell Nanny to expect you."

I offered her my thanks and dismissed her as Robert returned with a tray of breakfast. I thanked him and took a few bites before my focus rested on Mr. Boyle. I narrowed my eyes at him.

"Is he still here?" Robert inquired.

"Yes," I answered. "He stayed throughout the time Sinclair was in and remains just near the foot of the bed."

Robert eyed the space, empty for him, with a scowl.

"Sinclair led me to an interesting idea," I said.

"Oh?"

"She suggested you would prefer he name his murderer rather than remain mute. I agreed, and the idea occurred to me that, perhaps, he would react if I were to correctly name his murderer!"

"I suppose it is worth a try."

"I shall try now before I visit with Sam."

"Oh, did you wish me to have Nanny bring Sam now?"

I shook my head. "No, as Sinclair pointed out, Mr. Boyle's presence may disturb him."

Robert's brow furrowed. "But surely the child would not see him, as I do not."

"Perhaps not, but at that age, children may be sensitive enough to sense a disturbance."

Robert nodded and left the matter go. I ate a few more bites and turned my attention to Mr. Boyle. I studied his statue-like posture as I finished my breakfast.

As I shoved the tray aside, I stood and began to pace the room. "Mr. Boyle," I said, ceasing my ambling to address him, "do you realize you were murdered?"

No response.

I resumed my pacing and continued, "I am going to assume you do realize this. And I should like to determine who committed this vile crime.

"As such, I am now going to say several names. If one of them happens to be your murderer, indicate it. You do not need to speak, but some small gesture will suffice."

I received no response. I inhaled a deep breath, pondering who to begin with. Perhaps someone I knew was innocent. With a nod, I faced him.

"Edwin Fletcher," I said in a resolute tone. I studied his features. There was not a flinch. He remained steadfast.

"Well?" Robert inquired.

I shook my head. "Nothing," I reported.

"Good," Robert said with a nod and a firm chin.

I tried another. "Fergus MacGuiness."

I stared at him. Not even one muscle twitched. Was it due to the man's innocence? Or was he merely frozen?

I pondered the next suspect: the wiry associate of Fergus. I did not know his name. I figured I would try anyway. "What about Fergus MacGuiness's associate? A small, wiry fellow. I do not know his name."

I sighed when I received no response. I raised one eyebrow and tried the final name on my list. "Lord Pennington, your brother."

My eyes narrowed as I searched his features. Did he move? It appeared he gave the slightest twitch of the lips. Or had I imagined that.

I rushed a few steps toward him, turning breathless. "Is that it? Lord Pennington? Did your brother murder you?"

Robert's eyes went wide and his jaw dropped. "What is it? Has he named Penny?"

My shoulders fell and I twisted to face Robert. With a shake of my head, I said, "No. I thought he gave the slightest movement when I mentioned his name. But when I asked again, he did not move."

"Perhaps he did not move the first time," Robert ventured.

"Perhaps," I answered, returning my gaze to the ghost. "Though I could have sworn I saw just the slightest twitch of his lips."

I stared at him for another moment before I said, "Well, I am off to visit Sam. We should convene in the sitting room to discuss our next steps afterward."

"Of course, I shall collect Edwin."

With a smile at my husband, I departed from the room, leaving Mr. Boyle standing near the foot of the bed. Nanny waited for me in the sitting area. She balanced Sam on her lap as she read a book to him.

"Good morning, Nanny!" I said cheerfully. "And good morning, my little darling." I lifted the infant from her lap and showered him with kisses. A giggle escaped his chubby cheeks as I lifted him high before setting him on my hip.

"And what are we reading today?" I glanced at the book as I accepted it from Nanny. "Would you like Mummy to read to you for a bit?"

He babbled a response and I took that as a yes. I crossed to the other armchair, my step faltering for a moment before I continued. Next to the chair stood the ghastly form of Gerard Boyle. He stared at me, unmoving. At least, I figured, he was past his shy stage.

I plopped onto the chair and set Sam on my lap. Opening the book, I began to read to him. He pointed at the page as I read. We enjoyed the book for several minutes before I set it aside and crawled on the floor with him to play for a time.

After an hour, Robert entered with Edwin in tow. Nanny took the cue and stood from her chair. "Well, time for the little master to prepare for his lunch."

I scooped Sam into my arms and kissed him. The gesture brought a smile to his little face. His smile so resembled Tilly's. I stood with the child in my arms, prepared to hand him off to Nanny.

Sam caught sight of Robert across the room. His face lit in a wide grin and he clumsily clapped his hands together. "Da-da," he murmured.

My heart skipped a beat, and my jaw dropped open. "Sam!" I exclaimed, kissing his cheek. "Excellent job!"

Robert's face glowed as he approached us. He lifted the child from my arms and offered him a kiss on his forehead. "Yes, yes, wonderful job, son," he said with a grin. "You can tell he's a Fletcher! He is smart as a whip!"

"That he is, Your Grace, that he is," Nanny agreed. She pulled the child onto her hip. "Now wave goodbye to your Mummy and Daddy." Samuel fluttered his hand in the air at us. Robert and I returned the gesture.

"And your Uncle Edwin," I added.

Nanny eyed him a moment, then waved the child's hand toward Edwin. Edwin smiled and waved at him before Nanny bustled from the room.

Robert beamed as our little boy disappeared. He puffed his chest as he strutted around the room. "Smart boy," he boasted.

Edwin beamed, too. "He is, isn't he? You must be very proud."

"Well, both of us. He is our flesh and blood. A Fletcher through and through."

I crossed to the armchair and eased into it, watching the two brothers bond over their son. The edges of my lips curled into a smile as they talked civilly rather than sniping at each other. Perhaps there was hope for their relationship yet.

After they finished their discussion, Robert glanced at me. "I filled Edwin in on Mr. Boyle's odd appearance in your bedchamber this morning. Do you imagine he is still there?"

"No," I answered.

"Oh." Robert's face fell at the admission and he sighed. "Too bad. I hoped he might stay so we did not need to seek him out."

"There is no need for that either," I said.

He squashed his thick eyebrows together and eyed me.

"Has he imparted the killer's name to you?" Edwin questioned, hope filling his voice.

"No," I said with a shake of my head. "No, he has not. Though I still believe I saw him flinch when I mentioned Lord Pennington."

"I suppose we may not find out unless we can locate him again," Robert lamented.

"There will be no problem there."

Robert frowned at my statement and I continued. "He is here." I motioned over my right shoulder.

"He is here?" Edwin inquired.

"Yes," I said. "He has not left my side since this morning."

Robert studied the room. "Where is he exactly?"

"Just here," I said, gesturing to the armchair's rear. "Standing behind the armchair on my right."

"Was he here the entire time you were with Sam?"

"Yes," I answered. "He followed me from the bedroom. He still will not speak, and he barely moves, but he seems glued to my side."

Robert's eyes narrowed as he focused on the spot I'd indicated moments earlier.

"May we question him?" Edwin asked.

"We can try. Though as I said, he does not seem capable of or willing to speak at the moment."

Edwin nodded as he chewed his lower lip. "This is quite odd," he said after a moment.

"On a positive note, he does not seem to be disturbed by your presence, Edwin."

"How do you interpret that, Lenora?" Robert asked.

"I hope it means he has progressed further from dwelling on the incident between them. With any luck, he has now recalled the events on that fateful night and is processing them."

"Gerard," Edwin shouted as I finished my statement. "Gerard, old boy, can you help us? Please, you must!"

I studied the deceased man's features. He continued to stare at me. "He remains unfazed," I said.

"Please, Gerard, for your old friend! It is me! Edwin! I need your help!"

"Nothing," I reported.

"Perhaps leave it to Lenora," Robert suggested. "All you are doing is shouting at the poor man."

"We must get through to him, Robert!" Edwin argued. He spun to face me. "You said he did not flinch when you brought up the names except, perhaps, Lord Pennington's?"

"Correct."

"What names did you call out?"

"Yours," I began when Edwin's frown stopped me. "I believe you are innocent, but I needed to determine if he would react to an innocent person's name."

Edwin offered a sheepish nod and gestured for me to continue. "Fergus MacGuiness. Then I mentioned his associate, whose name I do not know. And then Lord Pennington."

"And he flinched, you said?"

"I thought I detected a small twitch of his lips. It could be nothing."

"And it could be everything."

"You are pinning your hopes on foolishness, Edwin. I cannot imagine Penny killed his own brother."

The two brothers bickered in the background as I studied the deceased's face. He stared at me, sadness etched on his features. Did he just realize he had passed over, I wondered?

"Are you all right?" I asked him.

The men ceased their conversation and glanced at me.

"It is all right, Mr. Boyle. You have crossed over. You were murdered. Do you recall this?"

His forehead wrinkled and his lips quivered. Poor man, I thought. He is coming to terms with his own death.

"Who did it?!" Edwin shouted.

Mr. Boyle clutched the back of the chair, doubling over. "Well?" Edwin demanded.

"Edwin, stop!" I said, leaping from my seat. "Stop, you are disturbing him."

"Disturbing him? He is dead!"

"I believe he may only be realizing that now."

"What?" Edwin questioned, his face a mask of confusion.

"The dead do not always realize they are dead. Particularly in situations like these. Something is disturbing him at the moment."

"So, he is now reacting or moving?" Robert questioned.

"Yes. He stared at me with quite a sad look. When I spoke to him, his features formed a pained expression. And he seems rather upset."

"My goodness," Robert murmured, unable to find any words suitable for the situation. He rubbed his lips with his forefinger.

Edwin swallowed hard, running his fingers through his hair.

I returned my attention to the spirit at my side. He'd pulled himself to stand erect, though his hand still trembled on the chair's back.

"It is all right, Mr. Boyle," I said in a soothing tone. "I am here to help you."

He stared at me, discomfort on his face. "I can see you. Though no one else can. You were murdered. I am very sorry to inform you of that if you do not remember."

"We," I said, motioning to Robert and Edwin, "have been attempting to determine who murdered you. Do you recall the incident?"

I received no indication that he did or did not. I shook my head. "Let us try another way. I shall offer you names again. If you recognize your murderer, please signal me."

I waited a moment before beginning. "Edwin Fletcher."

No movement. The man appeared to have settled back into his nearly comatose state.

"Fergus MacGuiness."

"Anything?" Edwin whispered. Robert smacked him in the chest, a warning to remain silent. I shook my head before turning my attention back to Mr. Boyle.

"Lord Pennington."

The color from the man's face drained, leaving him ashen. His jaw gaped open, and a pained groan escaped him, his face froze in an expression of agony.

CHAPTER 21

My eyebrows raised high, and my eyes widened. I cocked my head at his outburst. Hardly damning evidence, but the largest reaction I'd witnessed so far.

"What is it, Lenora?" Robert whispered.

I hesitated a moment before I spoke. "He has reacted to the name of Lord Pennington."

"Reacted?"

"Rather poorly," I explained. "He seems disturbed by the mention of his name."

Edwin's eyebrows shot up. "Perhaps Penny is the murderer!"

"It can't be!" Robert insisted, spinning away from us and stalking the length of the room.

"He has indicated as much!" Edwin argued.

"He hasn't indicated guilt, only a reaction," I corrected.

Robert shot a knowing glance at Edwin. "Though, I tend to agree with Edwin's assessment. He may now be my primary suspect. He has had no reactions to other names."

"Lenora, you can't possibly believe Penny did this."

"You give him too much credit, Robert," Edwin countered. "He is penniless. Lack of money can drive people, particularly such as Penny, to great lengths."

"But murder? I cannot fathom it!" Robert exclaimed, continuing to pace the floor.

I shrugged. "We must follow up on this, at least. There is something that disturbs Mr. Boyle about his brother. We also have other bits of evidence stacking against him."

"Such as?" Robert demanded.

"We realize he can have a temper. We witnessed his uncouth behavior with his female guest. And we do know he was involved in the misdeeds of his brother. He met with Fergus MacGuiness."

"I would venture to say he is the reason Fergus only nearly lost his money. He has stepped in for Gerard."

Robert shook his head as though we uttered nothing more than nonsense.

"We need a plan to gather evidence on Penny," Edwin said.

Robert huffed at the conversation.

"That may prove tricky," I answered. "He denied any involvement with his brother's body. I doubt he will readily admit to anything."

"No, I agree. We have our work cut out for us," Edwin said.

"While I believe this to be madness, I will assist in any way I can," Robert offered.

"You should stay out of it, brother," Edwin said, earning a scowl from Robert.

He opened his mouth to respond, but I beat him to the chase. "Edwin makes a good point." That comment earned me a scowl as well. "He has admitted nothing to you."

"Oh, and he will admit it to you? Or Edwin?"

"He is more likely to admit something to Edwin than anyone else. Or me."

"Unlikely!" Robert grumbled.

"She is correct. I was involved with Gerard. He may think I know something already and admit more to me than he would to you. With you, he attempts to hide behind his good name. He will never admit to any nefarious dealings."

"And I have the advantage of being able to use his deceased brother. He may not realize how little he has communicated with me and let something slip."

Robert puckered his lips, his unhappiness with our assessment obvious. "So, I suppose I shall be sat here like a lame duck."

"Perhaps you could take Samuel for a walk in the park?" I suggested, wringing my hands and offering an apologetic smile.

His eyebrows raised high, and his gaze flitted between Edwin and me. "Yes, quite fitting, I suppose. I am reduced to childcare while my wife and brother run about the town solving a crime."

Edwin's eyebrows edged closer to his hairline and he bit his thumbnail. He flicked his gaze toward me and offered a wide-eyed expression.

"Of course not, dear," I said to Robert. "We appreciate your help very much, though I do not see how you can help us at this moment. You have already been more than helpful, and I am certain, will prove helpful again."

Robert waved his hand to stop my babbling attempt to stroke his ego. "I understand, Lenora. My feathers are only a little ruffled that I cannot be the one to save the day. Though in either case, I hope this matter is soon ended." He kissed my cheek. "I shall enjoy the day with Sam."

He stalked across the room, waving a finger at Edwin. "Do not take her to another brothel. And for God's sake, let nothing happen to her. I wish no harm to come to her. And this time, take the carriage instead of having her traipse about the entirety of the city on foot!"

Edwin held his hands up in a silent gesture of acceptance. Robert stalked from the room, retreating further into our suite.

"I suppose I should arrange for the carriage," Edwin said after we were left alone.

"Yes, and while we ride, we should discuss a strategy to approach this with Lord Pennington."

Edwin nodded and disappeared from the room. I fastened my cape around my neck in preparation for the chilly weather. Mr. Boyle remained a fixture by my former seat.

"Anything to add?" I asked him as I retrieved my muff. Silence met my query. With a nod, I added, "I hope to have this solved for you soon. Perhaps then you can rest easier."

Edwin retrieved me and we left the hotel, climbing into the carriage for our mission. As the conveyance trundled along through the streets, we discussed our plan.

Edwin would visit first, alone. He would attempt to discuss Mr. Boyle with his brother and determine if he would be more open than he was with Robert. If that failed to offer any clues, I would follow up in the afternoon with a visit and disclose my odd affliction. I'd offer some information about Mr. Boyle and determine if guilt would play a role in retrieving some clues.

I hoped it did not come to that. I felt like a charlatan, using my skill to elicit information from an unsuspecting party. Still, without it, we may find ourselves unable to prove Edwin's innocence. Even with it, my mind plagued me. We may be unable to pin the crime on someone else.

I chewed my lower lip as my mind dwelled on that last notion.

"I did not mean to cause any trouble between you and

Robert," Edwin said with a wince as he noted my pensive expression.

I shook my head, forcing a smile onto my face. "He seemed to recover nicely before we departed."

"Are you recovered?"

I offered a quizzical glance at him. "You seem upset," he added.

"Oh," I said with another shake of my head, "not over that. I only hope we can come to some definitive information. I worry we may not."

Edwin nodded. "It is my sincere hope as well. But in any instance, I am thankful for your help."

I smiled at him as the carriage slowed to a stop outside of Lord Pennington's Glasgow home.

"Ah, here we are," Edwin said as the buggy bounced to and fro when the coachman alighted. "At least it's not a brothel." He flashed a cheeky grin at me as the door opened and he disembarked.

I shook my head at his attempted humor as I waited in the carriage. I stared out the window, watching Edwin amble up the walk and knock at the door. A maid answered and he spoke a few words. A large grin appeared on her face and her cheeks flushed. I shook my head again. Typical Edwin, I contemplated, always a flirt.

After a moment, the maid stepped aside and motioned for him to enter. He twisted his head toward me and I detected a wink before he disappeared through the doorway.

As I waited, I sent up a silent prayer that Edwin gleaned some information. My hopes that we would clear Edwin's name were quickly diminishing. Despite the breakthrough with Gerard, who now sat next to me in the carriage, I'd gathered no new information from him. I doubted my skills as a regular detective.

I faced my silent companion. "Do you realize where we are?" I questioned him.

He stared out the window at the house. "It is your brother's house. Lord Pennington."

The pained expression remained on his face. "Is there something you would like to tell me about your brother?" I prodded.

A moan escaped his lips. Perhaps I would make progress. My heart thudded in my chest as I pressed him more.

"Did he harm you? Is he involved in your death?" I became breathless as I forced the words out.

The man continued to stare at the stately home through the window. His eyes flitted around the area as though he searched for something. Or someone.

"What is it, Mr. Boyle?" I questioned as my eyes scanned the scenery. Did he perceive something I did not?

Another whimper escaped his lips, but he offered no further information. With no information forthcoming, I would need to investigate myself. "Wait here," I instructed, hoping he listened.

I pushed the conveyance's door open and exited onto the sidewalk. The coachman's eyes widened. "Your Grace!" he shouted as he scrambled from his perch. "I did not realize you were getting out. You should have knocked."

"Thank you, Jones. Though I am capable of alighting on my own. I just wanted to stretch my legs while we wait for Lord Edwin."

He nodded. "I shall accompany you."

I waved him away. "Thank you, but please remain with the carriage. I shall not be long."

His lower lip bobbed up and down as he attempted to formulate a response. I used his indecision to proceed with my plan unencumbered and darted down the street with a wave. I hurried toward Lord Pennington's home but did not enter his gate.

I glanced back at the carriage. The coachman stood staring after me. I offered another wave as I tried to ascertain where Mr. Boyle's gaze fell. It appeared he focused on a row of boxwood hedges at the edge of the property.

I studied them, noting nothing of interest. I chewed my lower lip as I glanced between the hedges and the house. I preferred not to be seen creeping onto the property, particularly if I must return this afternoon.

As my gaze flitted back and forth, I caught sight of something hidden behind the hedge. A wisp of rose pink winked from between the greenery. I stepped closer, squinting at it.

It was no use. I could not discern what it was from through the gate. With a huff and a glance at the house, I pulled the gate open and crept inside.

I delicately tiptoed onto the lawn. As I approached, the pink object moved. Was it a bird, I wondered? Though I had never seen a bird of this color. I inched closer when, suddenly, the color burst forth from behind the hedge.

The object, which I now understood to be a woman, flew past me, knocking me over in the process. She fled down the street, her rose-pink coat flying behind her as she ran. I recognized the tattered garment. It belonged to the woman who had quarreled with Lord Pennington when I'd visited with Robert.

What was she doing here again? And why was she hiding behind the hedge? Questions darted through my mind as I felt hands grasp me under my arms.

"Oh, Your Grace!" Jones exclaimed as he lifted me to my feet. "Are you quite all right? That woman knocked you clean over."

"Yes," I answered as I stood with his assistance and dusted myself off. "I am all right."

LETTER TO A DUCHESS

"Are you certain? Can you walk?"

I nodded. "Yes, I can walk." I stared at my hand, which had broken my fall somewhat. A large scrape where it caught the stone sidewalk reddened it. I scowled at the angry scratches as I squeezed my hand shut. I opened it quickly, finding the scrapes stung when touched. When I winced, Jones snapped into action.

"What is it, Your Grace? Are you hurt? Perhaps I should return you to the hotel where His Grace can consult a doctor."

"No," I answered. "No, I do not require a doctor. I shall return to the carriage and await Lord Edwin. I am perfectly fine. Though, thank you for your help."

We strolled back to the carriage with Mr. Jones keeping his hand on my elbow in case I should falter. He assisted me inside, and I waited for Edwin's return.

"That did not work out the way I'd hoped," I confided to my deceased companion. "Is it the woman you were staring at?"

He did not answer, though I noticed his attention was no longer focused on the house.

"Can you tell me her name?"

Silence filled the carriage. I drew in a deep breath. "Or anything about her?" I received no response.

Any further conversation was quieted when the front door to Lord Pennington's townhome popped open. Edwin hurried from inside. Lord Pennington appeared at the door, wagging his finger at him.

Mr. Boyle lurched toward the doorway, pressing his face almost into the window. He relaxed once the door slammed shut. Edwin rolled down the path and to the sidewalk. Voices sounded outside the carriage.

I heard Mr. Jones recounting the tale of my tragic fall. I almost popped out of the carriage to correct several details when the door flung open. Edwin stuck his head in, his features screwed up with worry.

"Lenora, are you all right? Jones said you took quite a spill! What were you doing outside the carriage? And how hard were you struck on the head?"

"I was not struck on the head," I corrected. "I left the confines of the carriage to investigate something. A woman darted from the hedges and bowled me over. I am quite all right, I assure you."

"Jones said you have a nasty scrape on your hand."

"It is fine."

"Let me see it," Edwin insisted.

I brandished my battered hand for him to study. He murmured for a moment, then said, "Perhaps we should return to the hotel."

"Is there no need for me to speak with Lord Pennington this afternoon? Have you gathered enough information?"

"No," he admitted, his brows pulled tightly together, "though…"

"Then we should keep to the plan," I insisted. "Come into the carriage so we may continue on with lunch."

Edwin hesitated a moment before he turned and spoke a few words to Jones. The man glanced inside at me, then began to climb up to his perch. Edwin ducked into the carriage and pulled the door closed.

"I am going to catch more hell for this than when I took you to the brothel," he said as he settled across from me.

"It is really quite fine," I insisted.

"Why did you disembark?" Edwin questioned.

"Mr. Boyle seemed very interested in something. I went to investigate. I saw a flash of color behind the hedge. When I approached for a closer look, a woman raced from behind it and knocked me over."

"Mr. Boyle?"

"Yes. He has made the journey with us. He became perturbed while near his brother's home."

Edwin grimaced as I spoke. I continued, "It further confirms my theory that his brother is somehow involved."

"He has not yet spoken?"

"No. What of your errand? Did you learn anything of value?"

Edwin puckered his lips into a frown. "Unfortunately, no. I tried several avenues and eventually landed myself in hot water and found myself nearly tossed onto the street."

I cocked an eyebrow at him. "Tell me the details," I instructed.

"Well," Edwin began as we bounced through the streets, "to start, I offered my condolences. He seemed less than enthusiastic about my visit when I mentioned being a friend of Gerard's. I said I hoped to pay my respects, but he claimed to have no knowledge of his burial."

"Again, he denies it."

"Yes. I told him I learned he'd claimed the body from the police. He maintained they were mistaken in passing the information along."

"Did you mention his murder at all outside of paying your respects?"

"Yes, I asked if there had been any progress on the case. I worried he'd tell me he knew of my arrest."

"And?"

"He made no mention of it."

"Perhaps he is as polite as Robert deems him," I offered.

"According to Penny, he has no interest in the matter. He has told the police to leave him out of the matter entirely."

"Really?" I inquired, raising my eyebrows.

"That is what he claimed," Edwin answered with a shrug. "I very nearly argued with him over it. I said I'd have thought he'd want his brother's murderer brought to justice.

"He stated otherwise. He again claimed no interest. He said he and Gerard were so far estranged it was as though he didn't have a brother."

My face scrunched in confusion.

"Yes, that's the same reaction I had," Edwin said as he eyed me. "Clearly, Penny was less estranged than he'd care to admit."

"Perhaps he is looking to cover any involvement in the criminal business ventures."

"Obviously."

"What else?"

"Nothing much," Edwin said.

I frowned at him. "He nearly tossed you out. What did you say to garner such a reaction?"

"Well," Edwin began, "after he refused to offer any information, I tried another tactic."

I waited with bated breath for more information. Edwin continued, "I said I hadn't realized he and Gerard were estranged since Gerard had confided in me about their joint business venture."

My eyes went wide. "What was his reaction?"

"He feigned confusion. He said he had no idea what Gerard meant. I followed up by saying I believed he had an operation involving less-than-legal goods being sold and hoped to step into Gerard's role in the business.

"And that is when he leapt to his feet and shouted 'How dare you, sir?!' at me before asking that I remove myself from the house."

"So, you have burned a bridge," I said with a sigh.

"Yes, I should say I have."

"And while we have more suspicious behavior, we have nothing that confirms he murdered his brother."

"Sadly, no," Edwin said.

I glanced to my side. Mr. Boyle sat staring ahead, unmoving. "During this entire conversation, Mr. Boyle has shown little reaction."

"Do you imagine that points to Penny's innocence?"

"No," I answered. "At least I do not believe so. He appears to be almost numb. Perhaps the conversation is too difficult for him to process. The realization that one's own family member murdered them may prove to be too much."

We rode along for another few moments in silence before we pulled to a stop outside an eatery. As we settled at a table, Edwin leaned forward and whispered, "I must admit the presence of Mr. Boyle in our carriage disturbs me."

I leaned toward him and lowered my voice. "I am sorry to say he is standing just at my elbow."

Edwin's eyes grew to the size of saucers, and he leaned away from me. He blinked his eyes several times as he studied the space next to me.

I shrugged at him with an apologetic smile. "This must be so distressing for you," Edwin settled on after a few moments.

"I have grown used to it."

"It disturbs me that he hears our conversations and wanders around with us."

"Perhaps it will be useful when I visit Lord Pennington."

"One can hope."

We chatted over our meal about lighter topics before we departed, again, heading to Lord Pennington's townhome. My mind whirled as I considered the task ahead of me. With any luck, Mr. Boyle would assist me in the conversation.

I felt my throat go dry as the carriage halted. I pursed my lips as Mr. Jones leapt from his perch and pulled the door open, offering his hand.

"Good luck," Edwin said with a tight-lipped smile.

I nodded, unable to push words out. Mr. Boyle met me on the sidewalk outside. It was as though he anticipated my plans. I studied his features, searching for any indication of what was to come.

As I walked down the sidewalk, I pondered what may come. Would there be an outburst from my deceased companion? Would I finally learn the truth? And if I did, would there be enough evidence to clear Edwin's name?

I swallowed hard as I stared up at the house. I squared my shoulders and strode forward to the door. With my resolve firmed, I used the knocker to summon someone from within.

CHAPTER 22

For the first time, I found myself alone. I spun and searched the yard. I found Mr. Boyle standing on the walk several steps behind me. He stared at the house, refusing to venture forward.

I motioned for him to follow. "Come along, Mr. Boyle. We shall speak with your brother."

He did not budge. The door swung open, and I spiraled to face it. A wiry man with bushy white eyebrows stood tall in front of me.

"May I assist you, Madam?"

"Yes, I am Lenora Fletcher, Duchess of Blackmoore. I have come to visit with Lord Pennington. Is he in, by chance?"

"Good afternoon, Your Grace," the man, who I assumed was the butler, said. "If you would care to wait in the sitting room, I shall announce your arrival to Lord Pennington."

I nodded my appreciation and entered the foyer, darting into the sitting room. I glanced out the window as I waited for Lord Pennington, finding my deceased companion still standing on the walk out front. He stared at the house but refused to move toward it.

I considered stepping toward the window to catch his attention, but Lord Pennington's arrival stopped me in my tracks.

"Your Grace," he said in greeting. "What a pleasant surprise!"

"Lord Pennington, hello," I said. I clutched my purse strings hard enough that I thought they may snap.

His face conveyed confusion at my visit. He searched around the room before he said. "Not accompanied by His Grace?"

"No," I admitted. "While I did discuss the matter with my husband, we felt it best that I visit alone as it is somewhat personal."

No sense in holding back. I have always believed honesty is the best policy. Lord Pennington's features further betrayed his surprise. "Personal?" he inquired.

"Yes," I stated, preparing myself for the anticipated angry reaction based on his previous discussions with Robert and Edwin. I licked my lips and continued. "You see, I have a unique... well, Robert calls it a gift, though I sometimes see it as a curse." A chuckle escaped my lips as I attempted to soften the situation with levity.

Lord Pennington furrowed his brow further. "Perhaps you would care to sit down."

I nodded and took a seat on the sofa while he settled into the loveseat across from me. "You see, Lord Pennington, I have an odd ability that allows me to communicate with persons who are... deceased."

"What?" he questioned, the incredulousness obvious in his voice.

I nodded and swallowed hard. "Yes, it began at a very

young age. I have grown used to it over the years, though many find it startling, even disturbing."

Silence fell between us as he considered my words, likely doubting every one of them. As I opened my mouth to broach the subject of his brother, a tapping noise drew my attention to the window. Mr. Boyle's face pressed against it, and he tapped on the glass with his index finger.

"My apologies, Your Grace, though I do not see the reason you are sharing this," Lord Pennington said when I did not continue.

I turned my attention back to him and offered a weak smile. "You see, Lord Pennington, I have been in contact with your deceased brother."

At those words, Lord Pennington leapt from this seat and stalked around the room. Clearly, the admission disturbed him. I let the words linger between us, remaining quiet in an attempt to draw out any information.

After a moment, he spoke. "My brother and I were quite estranged."

I narrowed my eyes at him. No admissions one way or the other. He hoped to ferret information from me. I had little to give, so it would not work out for him. Though it may not work out for me either, considering I had little leverage to use against him. My mind spun through the angles as I considered my next step.

"He does not give that impression to me."

His gaze snapped toward me. "Oh?" he fished, his eyebrows raised as he prodded for more information.

I crafted my next step carefully. "He is still adjusting to his death. However, any reactions I have garnered during our encounters have been when you are mentioned. It seems to me he is very much not estranged from you, at least in his death."

Lord Pennington's forehead wrinkled, and he pulled his

lips into a frown. "Odd," he said. "And has he said anything specifically about me?"

"No, he lacks the ability to speak," I admitted. "Though the mere mention of your name sends him into a fit." I worded my reaction statement carefully to try to elicit information as best I could.

Lord Pennington narrowed his eyes at me. "What is your game here, Your Grace?" he said after a moment.

"Game? I have no game. I merely hope to assist your brother's soul into a quiet repose."

"I have no idea why my brother would react to only my name. And, by the way, where have you had these… encounters, as you call them."

"They began at the site of his murder. However, now he follows me everywhere I go."

"And is he here now?"

"Yes. Well, no. Sort of," I stammered.

"What am I to make of that answer?"

"He followed me here, but he will not enter the house. Instead, he is standing just outside the window, peering in at us." I motioned toward the front window.

Lord Pennington's eyes flitted toward the window before settling back on me. He narrowed them and his jaw tensed. "So you claim my brother follows you everywhere you go but will not enter my home."

"He does follow me everywhere I go," I answered, irked at the insinuation that I told him a lie. "I am attempting to set his soul at ease."

"By coming into my home and discussing the matter with me? How does this help him?"

I shrugged. "I do not understand what disturbs him about you, but there is something. I hoped, perhaps, to trigger something on your end that might help settle him."

"What exactly did you hope to trigger, Your Grace?" he

said. I perceived a note of disharmony in his voice. He was growing perturbed with me. Why?

"You mentioned being estranged. Perhaps he feels badly about this and hopes to settle it before he can rest. I do not know, Lord Pennington. I only hope to help him as there are few others who can."

"Does your husband know of your visit?"

"Yes, I told you, I have spoken on the matter with him at great length."

"And does he approve?"

Now my jaw tensed as annoyance grew in me. "Yes," I said coldly.

"Is this the reason he visited me and inquired after Gerard's grave? And your brother-in-law, Edwin, only this morning appeared, questioning the same."

"Lord Pennington, I feel…"

My words were interrupted by Lord Pennington's rather gruff response. "Allow me to stop you, Your Grace. If we are to discuss feelings, I feel rather taken advantage of. Given the estrangement between Gerard and me, I am beginning to suspect you hope to pin his murder on me. I do realize it is your brother-in-law who stands accused."

My eyebrows shot up. "So, you have followed the case despite your denial of it earlier."

His eyes narrowed. "Get out, Your Grace."

I pursed my lips as I clutched at my purse strings and rose from the sofa. I shook my head at the man and stepped toward the door. As I passed him, I added, "I only mean to help your brother."

I stalked from the room and out the door before he could respond. Mr. Boyle met me out front, standing in my path and blocking my way.

I skirted around him and hurried toward the waiting

carriage. He appeared again in front of me on the sidewalk. I set my jaw as I sidestepped around him.

In the next instance, he stood in the gateway, barring my exit. Frustration filled me, and in an exasperated tone, I said, "Stand aside, Mr. Boyle!"

He stared at me, unwilling to move. I huffed at him. "I said stand aside!"

A slight shake of his head indicated I'd be going nowhere. My irritation grew. "Unless you have something to confide in me, there is nothing more I can do here," I said. "I have been roundly thrown out of the house. Now, stand aside!"

The man's chest rose and fell as though he was frustrated with me, but he stepped aside to allow me to pass. I sprinted toward the carriage. Edwin popped from within.

"Lenora, are you all right?"

I nodded and took his hand to climb inside. I met Mr. Boyle again as I settled into my seat.

"Did you learn anything?" Edwin inquired as he sat across from me.

"Nothing solid," I admitted as I chewed my lower lip.

"How did Gerard react? Is he here with us now, or did he stay with Penny?"

"He is here," I said, motioning to my right side. "Mr. Boyle did not even enter the house. He stood outside. When Lord Pennington arrived, he came to the window and tapped on it."

"And Penny's reaction? Did you tell him about Gerard?"

"I did. He did not take it well. He threw me out, in fact."

Edwin's eyes went wide. "He suggested I hoped to pin the murder on him and told me he realized you were currently accused."

"So, he has been following the case," Edwin murmured.

I nodded my head vehemently. "Yes!" I exclaimed, my eyes

wide. "Yes, that is what I said. Which is when he threw me out!"

"I cannot believe he threw you out!" Edwin said.

"He became extremely angry, it seemed. Which only increases my suspicion."

"Yes, what has he to hide? What exactly did you tell him?"

"That the only reactions I have received from Mr. Boyle were when his name was mentioned."

Edwin puckered his lips. "Still no obvious evidence, though," he said as he slouched in his seat.

I shook my head. "No, however, we have confirmed he has lied to both you and Robert. He denied any involvement with Mr. Boyle and claimed he did not care to follow the case, yet he has."

"Suspicious, I agree; however not enough proof to help me out of my predicament."

"No, but with any luck, Mr. Boyle will become more responsive."

We arrived at the hotel and I spent the remaining afternoon hours with Sam. Over dinner, we explained the results of our efforts to Robert. While he held to the notion Lord Pennington was innocent, his doubt was growing.

"Why would Penny lie?" he questioned.

"Because he is hiding something," Edwin said.

Robert shook his head, his forehead wrinkled. "But what?" I questioned. "Is it merely his involvement with illegal activities or more?"

"And you say Mr. Boyle would not enter the house?"

"No, and when I left, he tried to bar me from departing."

Robert raised his eyebrows. "Oh, I am sorry, dear," I said. "It seems I have cost you your friendship with Lord Pennington. I am certain he is quite angry with me."

Robert waved my concern away and shook his head. "I

care not! His dishonesty and his treatment of you make me angry with him!"

With that matter settled, we continued to discuss our minimal evidence.

"I suppose our only recourse is to continue to follow Lord Pennington and hope Mr. Boyle provides us with some information," I said at long last. My lips drew into a thin line. "Though, I am afraid the prospects look rather grim."

Edwin pushed the peas around on his plate, his eyes not lifting from it. I pitied him. For once, Edwin had not behaved poorly, and yet he faced a terrible price.

"Yes, we will do what we can," Robert agreed with a firm nod.

I rose from my seat. "If you do not mind, I am quite tired. I should like to retire for the evening."

"Of course, dear," Robert said with a smile. He rose and kissed my cheek before I departed. Sinclair assisted me in donning my bedclothes, and I crawled between the sheets. Tears stung my eyes as I squeezed them shut in the hopes of falling asleep.

I bit my lower lip as one escaped from the corner of my eye and rolled sideways to fall on the pillow below. I would not be able to free Edwin. I would let Tilly down. I frowned at the silhouette of Mr. Boyle, standing in the corner near the bed. What good was communication with the dead if they could not help, I lamented?

I squeezed my eyes shut again and wept before drifting off to sleep.

* * *

A shiver ran through me, pulling me from my sleep. With my eyes still closed, I tugged on the covers to raise them over me. I met with resistance. I yanked again but found myself unable to free the covers.

Snapping my eyes open, I searched for the impedance. My lips formed a frown as I found the impediment. Mr. Boyle loomed over me, my bedcovers clutched in his hand. I narrowed my eyes at him and tugged at the covers again.

"Let go," I insisted.

He shook his head. I yanked the blanket from his grasp and threw it over me, settling back onto my pillow. Satisfied, I closed my eyes. The covers slid down my body. I clenched my fists around them and held tight.

"Stop it!" I insisted.

He let go of the sheets. My victory proved to be temporary. Instead of grasping the covers again, he took hold of my shoulders. He shook me until I thought I may break into pieces.

I waved my arms to signal him to stop. He stood straight, staring at me. I threw back the covers and climbed from my bed, pulling my dressing gown around me.

"You've picked a fine time to want to talk," I groused. "What is it?"

He motioned toward the door. Still not talking, I lamented. "You wish me to go to the sitting room?"

He shook his head and pointed out the window. I raised my eyebrows. "You wish me to go outside?"

A head nod responded. My shoulder slumped. "In the middle of the night? Why?" I cried.

He grasped my hand and pulled me along toward the door. I pulled back against him. "Wait!" I hissed. "I am in my dressing gown! I must dress!"

"Now!" he bellowed. He yanked me by my arm toward the door. I tugged and tugged but could not free myself. The door flung open and Mr. Boyle shoved me through it. I skittered across the sitting room floor.

"At least allow me to grab my cape," I requested as he pushed at me. I grasped it and snugged it around me as Mr. Boyle waved at the doors. "Yes, yes, I am coming."

I threw the door open and exited, hurrying toward the exterior door. Mr. Boyle waited on the opposite side for me. He pointed in the direction he wished me to go. I followed the direction indicated, and he hurried along beside me.

Icy air gushed past me, and I wished I would have had the opportunity to dress as we traversed the streets. "What has you so upset, Mr. Boyle?" I queried.

"Hurry," was the response I received.

"Yes, but hurry to where?" I questioned.

"Penny," he moaned.

I ceased walking and stared at him. "Lord Pennington? Is he your murderer?"

He grasped my hand again and tugged. "Hurry," he insisted.

I hastened along the sidewalk, hoping I recalled the way to his townhome since I'd never traversed the route on foot. Mr. Boyle led me the entire way, so I had no need to worry. Though I wondered if I could make the return trip with as much ease.

We arrived outside of Lord Pennington's townhome. Lights still blazed within. Mr. Boyle dragged me to the door, which I was astounded to find propped open.

My heart beat harder in my chest as I pulled back against my deceased companion's grip. I studied the ajar door.

Mr. Boyle entered the foyer without hesitation, a marked change from his antics earlier in the afternoon. He beckoned to me.

"Lord Pennington?" I called as I tiptoed through the doorway and into the foyer.

Mr. Boyle motioned toward the sitting room. I swallowed hard and called out to the man again.

"Lord Pennington. It is Lenora Fletcher. Your brother insisted I come," I said as I wandered into the room. I caught sight of the man's head poking above the back of a high-backed armchair that faced away from the entrance.

"Lord Pennington?" I questioned again. I wondered if, perhaps, he had fallen asleep in the chair. I rounded the chair slowly, clutching my cape around me. As I faced him fully, I gasped and fell back several steps.

I nearly lost my footing as I collided with a table behind me. It screeched as it skittered across the floor. I swallowed hard, but my jaw continued to gape open. Mr. Boyle knelt next to his brother. A pained expression covered his features. "Help," he moaned.

My bottom lip quivered as I studied Lord Pennington. A large knife stuck out of his belly. Thick, red blood oozed around the wound, soaking his clothing.

CHAPTER 23

As I stared at him, I noticed the barely perceptible rise and fall of his chest.

"He is still alive!" I exclaimed. I raced to his side and felt for his pulse. Weak, but there.

I recalled an incident in my very early years of a man with a similar injury. "Do not remove the knife," my father said to his assistant. "Not until we are ready to repair the damage."

"Why?" the man inquired.

"He will bleed to death. The knife is the only thing keeping him alive."

"We must fetch a doctor right away," I said to Mr. Boyle. He nodded, a grim expression on his face.

I raced to the foyer and screamed at the top of my lungs. "Help! HELP!"

I hoped it would suffice as I hastened back into the sitting room. I retrieved a small pillow from the sofa and pressed hard against the wounded area, careful not to disturb the knife.

Moments later, the man who had answered the door

earlier this afternoon when I'd visited entered the room. His eyes widened as he spotted me.

"Quickly, fetch a doctor!" I instructed.

"Your Grace?" he breathed, his voice betraying his shock. He rounded the chair and the color drained from his face as he spotted the dying Lord Pennington.

"Quickly, he hasn't much time!" I shouted.

The man offered a weak nod and scurried from the room. Chaos erupted as he awakened other staff members. A lanky man raced away from the house as the butler returned with a maid in tow.

"We must remove the knife!" he said.

"No," I argued. "No, we mustn't. He has lost a great deal of blood. He will lose more if we remove it. We must wait for the doctor but keep firm pressure on the wound."

The maid's face blanched, and she staggered sideways into the butler. He steadied her before she fainted. "Towels. Get towels to help with the bleeding," I said.

"Quickly, Jean," the butler murmured, sending the girl on her way.

Mr. Boyle paced the floor behind me. Seconds seemed like hours as we awaited the doctor's arrival. I feared Lord Pennington may slip away at any moment.

At long last, the wiry man arrived with a doctor. He knelt beside me and I dared remove the towel, now soaked in blood for him to assess the wound.

"The wound is quite deep, the knife is buried to the hilt," I explained. "He has lost quite a bit of blood though I kept constant pressure from the time I found him. I do not know how long he bled before though."

"We must spread him out so I can work." With the help of the butler and the man called Andrew, Lord Pennington, was carried to his bed. The doctor bent over him.

"Can he be saved?" I inquired.

"He has not died yet," the doctor responded. "Though I must repair the damage. It will be tricky alone." He dug into his bag.

"I will assist you."

He shot me a stunned glance.

"My father was a doctor," I explained.

"All right," he agreed with a nod. "Position yourself there. Do you know the names of the tools?"

"Yes. It is a bit foggy, but yes, I can muddle through."

"You may wish to remove your cape, eh…" His voice faltered as he realized he did not know my name.

"Lenora," I provided.

"I shall take it, Your Grace," the butler said.

I handed it over to him, my cheeks flushing as those in the room realized I wore my dressing gown. "There is an explanation," I said. "I shall provide it after he has been stabilized."

"Quite right," the doctor agreed. "Lord Pennington should be our first priority."

The doctor worked for two hours. By the end, Lord Pennington lay repaired and alive, though still comatose. I wiped my blood-stained hands on a towel.

"Thank heavens you found him when you did. He would not have survived much longer, Your Grace," the doctor said.

"How did you come to be here at that hour?" the butler inquired.

"Well," I began when Robert's voice interrupted me.

"Lenora! My God!" His eyes lingered on my bloodied hands. He rushed to my side and wrapped me in his arms. "Are you all right?"

"Yes," I answered. "The same cannot be said for Lord Pennington. He very nearly died."

"Your wife saved his life in my estimation," the doctor said.

Robert studied my face in search of an answer. "Mr. Boyle woke me and insisted I come. I tried to retrieve you first, but he wouldn't allow me. He did not even allow me to change. I suppose time was of the essence."

Robert shook his head and held me closer. "You poor thing, you must have frozen on the walk. Thank you for retrieving me," Robert said to the butler.

"Of course, Your Grace. Though I still remain confused by your arrival."

I opened my lips to explain, but Robert spoke before me. "It is not necessary that you understand, Jennings. Only that we are all grateful to Her Grace for arriving and tending to Lord Pennington when she did."

"Quite right," Jennings stated. Though likely inadequate for him, he possessed enough training to realize he should not continue to ask questions.

"Will he awaken?" Robert inquired of the doctor.

The doctor answered with a shrug. "While I cannot say with certainty, I expect so. The timing will be unpredictable though. It may be hours or days."

Robert nodded. "Jennings, will you please keep us informed?"

"Of course, Your Grace," the man said with a nod.

"Thank you. We shall take our leave. Her Grace should rest. Oh, if the police need to speak with her about the incident, please direct them to our hotel."

Robert led me from the room and to the waiting carriage. While he'd hurried here on foot, he'd requested the carriage be brought after him to ease our journey home.

I collapsed into the seat and rubbed at my forehead as the buggy bounced to life.

"Are you certain you are all right?" Robert questioned.

With a sigh, I answered, "Yes. Merely tired."

"Too tired to provide more of an explanation?"

"No," I responded. I suppose he deserved one. He had just been awoken and summoned to someone else's home after being told his wife was there in the middle of the night. "Though there is not much more than I already relayed. Mr. Boyle woke me. He insisted I follow him. When I refused, he shoved me out the door. I barely managed to grab hold of my cape and don it. He hurried me along to Lord Pennington's townhome. When I arrived, I found the door ajar and Lord Pennington himself stabbed in his sitting room. I shouted for the staff and did my best to keep him alive until the doctor arrived."

"You did more than your best. According to the doctor, you saved his life!"

I nodded but offered no other response. "Lenora, are you certain you're fine?"

"Yes," I said with a weary sigh. "Merely tired. And confused."

"Confused?"

"Yes," I admitted. I allowed the thoughts that had plagued me since finding Lord Pennington bleeding in his chair to spill from my mouth. "If Mr. Boyle awakened me and forced me to his brother's side to save him, what are the chances he is our killer?"

"Oh," Robert said, his forehead crinkling, "I hadn't thought of that."

"I have," I answered. "More times than I can count. I am beginning to believe his reaction to Lord Pennington's name was not due to anger but because he suspected harm may come to him."

"Which lessens the chances Penny is the murderer."

"And sets us right back to nowhere," I groaned.

When we arrived at the hotel, Robert insisted I go straight to bed with no further discussion. Had there been any staff about, I am certain he would have demanded a hot toddy be made immediately.

I remained unsure if I could sleep, though exhaustion overcame me the moment the warmth of the bedcovers coursed through me.

When I awoke, sunlight streamed through the window. I arose and entered the sitting room, still in my nightclothes.

"Good morning, dear," Robert greeted me, his eyes lifting from his paper.

I plopped into the armchair across from him. "Good morning," I said with a yawn.

"Did you manage any rest?"

"I did, yes. Have the police called yet?"

As I inquired this, Edwin stepped into our suite. "Police?" he questioned as he headed straight for our drink cart to pour a brandy.

"For heaven's sake, Edwin, it is only morning," Robert groused.

Edwin rolled his eyes as he sipped the amber liquid. "And I am a fully grown man," he answered after his drink.

"Yes, the police," I said, steering the conversation back on track. "There was an incident last night. I suppose I should dress in the event they arrive earlier than expected."

"Incident?" Edwin questioned.

"Yes. Penny was stabbed last night and quite nearly killed!" Robert relayed.

Edwin choked on his brandy. "What? Where did you hear this?"

"Lenora was present?"

Edwin's eyes went wide and his jaw dropped. He set the brandy down on the table and stared at me. "Is he serious?"

"Unfortunately, yes," I admitted. I recounted my woeful tale.

Edwin leaned against the mantel near the room's fireplace. "This is incredible. Thank God you reached him in time."

"Yes," I answered, "though it does pose a problem."

"As Lenora astutely pointed out, it is unlikely he stabbed his brother given Gerard's reaction to the stabbing."

"Yes, and what are the chances both Penny and his brother were stabbed in unrelated instances?" Edwin added.

I nodded. "My thoughts exactly. Which puts us back to having little to no suspects."

Edwin shook his head. "I disagree."

"Oh?" I asked with raised eyebrows.

"It simplifies things."

"How?" Robert asked.

"Simple. I doubt they were stabbed in unrelated incidents. There must be a common denominator. On top of that, once Penny wakes, he can finger the correct suspect. And I can be cleared. I was here last night."

"Can anyone attest to that?" Robert inquired.

"You can," Edwin shot back.

"I can attest I saw you here, but in the middle of the night, I cannot. I did not share your bed. Did someone else?"

Edwin pursed his lips. "I was alone in my bed, so no one can corroborate my whereabouts, I suppose. But Penny will be able to tell."

"Assuming he awakens and remembers the incident," Robert retorted.

A knock sounded at the door. I excused myself to dress, assuming the visitors hoped to question me about the incident with Lord Pennington.

When I emerged from the bedroom, I found Robert and Edwin engaged in a discussion with the officers. Robert introduced me to them, and I recounted my story.

"And you say the door was ajar when you approached?" one of the gentlemen asked.

"Yes," I said with a nod. "Standing open. I called inside and received no answer. I found it strange that the door was open though. I proceeded into the foyer. I saw light coming from the sitting room and entered. I saw the form of Lord Pennington in the chair and wondered if he had fallen asleep, though that did not explain the ajar door. When I rounded the chair, I found him unconscious with the knife in his belly."

The man nodded and proceeded with another set of questions. "Did you see anyone departing from the estate? Someone running as you approached, perhaps?"

I shook my head. "No, I did not. I am assuming the confrontation happened at least twenty minutes prior to my arrival."

The officer jotting notes stopped for a moment, a confused expression on his face. "Based on the amount of blood lost from the wound," I clarified. "My father was a doctor. I have some cursory knowledge of medicine."

"And you did not remove the knife when you spotted it?"

"No. As I explained, given my father's occupation, I knew enough not to disturb it until a doctor arrived. Despite being a gruesome sight, the knife stopped him from bleeding to death."

"Along with your heroic actions, I understand. You tended his wound then assisted the doctor."

I nodded. "Yes, I did. Though I would not call them heroic by any means."

"You do not give yourself enough credit, Lenora," Robert said, wrapping his arm around my shoulder. "Gentlemen, have you gathered the information you needed? My wife is quite tired from all the commotion."

"Actually, we have a bit more," one of the officers said.

The two officers shot each other a glance before the taller one proceeded. He pressed his lips together and swallowed hard before he said, "Your Grace, forgive this question…" His voice trailed off and his eyes darted around the room, settling on Robert. He squeezed his lips together and then refocused his attention on me. "What were you doing at Lord Pennington's townhome at that time of night?"

I understood the implication and why he'd eyed Robert nervously before speaking. He assumed something untoward given the hour. I attempted to explain without giving away all of the details and hoped it would suffice.

"I had visited with him earlier in the day to discuss his deceased brother. The conversation had not gone well. I…" I hesitated as I searched for the right words. "When I awoke in the middle of the night, I had a terrible feeling about him. I rose and went to his house, hoping to resolve our earlier conversation more fully."

The officer's eyebrows shot up and he offered a nod and a smile. His eyes flitted to Robert then back to me. Robert remained unflinching, so I suppose my story convinced the officer since no outbursts from my husband occurred. "Right," he said as he jotted something in his notebook. "And you had seen him earlier in the day?"

"Yes, in the afternoon. I paid him a call regarding his deceased brother, Gerard."

"Why?"

"To offer my condolences."

"And it went badly?"

"Yes. It seems he was estranged from his brother and did not wish to speak of him."

"I see. This is Gerard Boyle, the man recently stabbed to death on the docks, correct?"

"Yes, it is."

The man's eyes flitted to Edwin. "A man you stand accused of murdering," he said as he poked his finger toward Edwin.

"I did not kill him," Edwin maintained.

"And here we are with a second victim while you roam the streets. A victim who is related to the first decedent. And with whom you also shared a visit with just prior to his stabbing."

"Gerard and I were friends. I visited to express my condolences to his next of kin."

"And perhaps during the course of that conversation, things became heated as they did with his brother."

"And what?" Edwin retorted. "I waited until the dead of night to sneak back and stab him?"

The man cocked his head. "Interesting theory."

Edwin narrowed his eyes. "I was here the entire night."

"Can anyone corroborate that?"

Edwin stared at him. "Both my brother and sister-in-law can confirm I returned home last evening and that they saw me again this morning."

"But in the wee hours of the morning, you could have slipped out, stabbed Lord Pennington, and returned."

"In that course of events, I likely would have unwittingly passed my sister-in-law in her mad dash to Penny's home. Lenora, did you see me last night on your way to Penny's?"

"No," I admitted.

"You may have taken another route home. It's easy enough to remain unseen."

"You're reaching," Edwin claimed.

"Gentlemen, please. I did see Edwin enter his bedroom last night, and we saw him again this morning. When I departed to retrieve my wife in the wee hours, I did not see him along my way. Can we please keep the questioning on track? Again, I am certain my wife is tired."

The officer offered a half-grunt, half-laugh. "I'm certain she is, too."

"That's quite enough," Robert said, grasping the man by the collar. "I will not have you impugn my wife's morality."

"Easy, Your Grace," the man said, holding his hands up in front of him. "I meant no harm in it."

"May wish to tone it down," his partner said, "before you are accused of murder."

Robert unhanded the man and straightened his jacket. "I had no reason to harm Penny; the man was an old friend."

"An old friend whose brother was recently murdered and whose life currently hangs by a thread from a similar attack. And one who may have been involved with your wife. Perhaps you stabbed him in a fit of rage over your wife's late-night visits."

"How dare you, sir!" Robert shouted, lunging at him again. Edwin held him back. "I did nothing of the sort because there was no reason to! How dare you impugn my wife's virtue."

"Could be that your wife inflicted the wound then regretted it," the officer suggested.

Robert's face flushed red. He wagged his finger in the air at the man before I grasped his arm and tugged it down.

"I did nothing of the sort," I said. "I had no reason to harm him either."

"Perhaps a lovers' quarrel turned nasty," the officer said.

"That's it," Robert growled, fighting at Edwin to throttle the man.

Edwin held firm to his shoulders. "Leave it, Robert," he suggested.

"Get out!" Robert shouted.

"Lord Pennington and I were barely acquainted. His staff can confirm that I have not been to the house but for three occasions. Once with my husband. Once alone yesterday afternoon, then last night. With the exception of the hurried trip last night, my husband has been aware of both prior visits."

The man narrowed his eyes at us. Robert shrugged off Edwin's grip and straightened his jacket again. "I hope that explanation, which is more than you deserve, suffices. Now, if you are quite finished, gentlemen…"

The man offered a fleeting smile. He flipped his notebook shut. "I think that's all for now. Though we may need to question both you and the Lord Edwin again."

The officers filed from the room, leaving us alone inside.

Robert stalked around the room. "The cheek of that fellow to suggest Lenora and Penny were… And that she… " His voice trailed off as he refused to voice the idea of Lord Pennington and I engaged in a torrid love affair or that I had stabbed the man. He shook his head.

"He accused me, too."

"Not of that!" Robert shouted. "And besides, your reputation makes the accusations a bit easier to hurl. But to accuse Lenora! He must be quite out of his mind."

"I imagine they are quite at a loss right now and willing to hurl many accusations."

"It is ridiculous! I sincerely hope Penny awakens soon and straightens this matter out."

"Who would gain by stabbing him?" Edwin questioned.

"The only common denominator I have come to is Fergus MacGuiness," I chimed in.

CHAPTER 24

"Yes," Edwin agreed. "Yes, perhaps Gerard quarreled with him. And then it appeared from the conversation we witnessed, so did Penny. Yes, I am beginning to suspect Fergus."

"Though, according to Fergus," I said, "Gerard's death nearly cost him. So, why chance it?"

Edwin shrugged. "And," I continued, "even if he killed Mr. Boyle and stabbed Lord Pennington, how can we prove it?"

I sank to the armchair and bit my lower lip. Robert strode to the door. "Where are you going?" Edwin questioned.

"I am going to check on Penny's status. With any luck, he will awaken and clear the entire matter up."

Robert disappeared from the room, leaving Edwin and me alone. We shared a glance before Edwin collapsed into the armchair across from me. "Have I mentioned how sorry I am about all this?" he said after a few moments.

"There is no need to apologize," I answered.

"I feel there is," Edwin countered. "Because of me, you have now been accused of several vulgar things. You would not be in this position had I not required your help."

I remained silent for a few moments before I sighed. "Unfortunately, answers do not seem forthcoming, either."

"Is Gerard still with you?"

I shook my head. "No, he did not return with me after taking me to Lord Pennington. I imagine he remains at his side."

Edwin widened his eyes. "Perhaps you should have gone with Robert! Perhaps he will be more forthcoming now."

"I am not certain. He was not forthcoming last night. And, in truth, I thought it may be a poor choice to visit with a man I've just been accused of stabbing."

"Good point. Though Robert did."

"I fear we could not have stopped him."

"I cannot imagine another culprit outside of Fergus," Edwin said. "Perhaps we should follow him again."

"Or ascertain his whereabouts. Perhaps he was unaccounted for last evening."

I stood from my chair. "What? Now?" Edwin inquired.

"It is better than sitting here and doing nothing."

We pulled our cloaks around us. As we stepped out the door, Edwin murmured, "I sincerely hope we do not need to visit a brothel. Robert will have my head given his current mood."

Even with the dire circumstances, the comment earned a chuckle from me. "I would suggest we begin with *The Black Horse*. Perhaps someone can point us in the right direction."

"Good thinking, Lenora."

We made our way on foot to the pub near the docks and pushed inside. At this hour, only a few men graced the interior. Edwin made his way to the barkeeper and inquired after Fergus.

The man trained his eyes on the glass he dried. "Gone," he answered. "*The Pembroke* shipped out this morning."

"And Fergus was on it?"

The man nodded. "Aye. Fergus was on her."

Edwin thanked him and guided me outside. I sighed as we exited onto the street outside.

"So much for following Fergus," Edwin lamented.

"Yes," I said, matching his expression of frustration. "Though given the timing, I suppose it is possible that he stabbed Lord Pennington then boarded the ship and sailed."

"Yes, I suppose so. But now we have no way of proving it with Fergus gone!"

"Unless Lord Pennington awakens and names him as the attacker. With any luck, he has. Perhaps we should return to the hotel and determine if Robert has any news."

With a dejected nod, Edwin offered his arm to me and we strolled back to the hotel. We returned before Robert, settling in the sitting room to await his return. Within minutes, he stalked through the door and straight to the drink cart.

As he poured a brandy, Edwin commented, "That doesn't appear to be good news."

"It is not," Robert admitted.

"Has Penny taken a turn for the worse?"

Robert shook his head as he sipped the amber liquid. "No," he answered. "But he has not improved either. The doctor remains uncertain of when he will awaken. Now he supposed it may be days!" He took another sip before slamming his hand against the mantel. "Damn it!"

I placed my hand on his shoulder. He grasped it and squeezed.

"We also have news of a not-so-good nature," Edwin reported. He recounted the tale of Fergus sailing on *The Pembroke* early this morning.

Robert huffed. "So, there goes our culprit. He slips right through our fingers."

"Our alleged culprit," I reminded my companions. "Perhaps we should use the time to search for other suspects."

"But who?" Edwin questioned. "We've no leads! Lenora, please, go to Penny's and speak with Gerard again. He is our only hope!"

Before I could respond, a knock sounded at the door.

"Oh, what the bloody hell is it now?" Robert groused.

Edwin headed for the door as I refilled Robert's brandy. "Try to relax, dear," I suggested. He shot me a glance that suggested he did not appreciate the comment but understood my point.

Edwin returned from the doorway with an envelope in hand. "For you, brother," he said, handing it off.

Robert accepted it and retrieved the letter opener from the drawer in the table near the doorway. He sliced it open and perused it, his brows knitting.

"What is it?" I inquired.

"An invitation."

"To what?"

"To spend time at Walford House, Cameron's country estate outside of Melrose. In all the confusion, I'd forgotten I'd sent the request. He writes that we should come out at our convenience and stay for as long as we'd like."

Memories of the old woman flooded into my mind. "Yes, of course. I'd nearly forgotten my promise to Esme, too!" I exclaimed.

Robert glanced at me, the letter still clutched in his hands. He raised his eyebrows. "Given the circumstances, perhaps I should decline."

I pondered it, inclined to agree with him, but something held me back. I shook my head after a few breaths. "No. No, we should not decline it. I do wish to see it through for Esme."

"But when shall we go?"

"Perhaps now is the best time," I suggested. "We have little to do here but wait for Penny's recovery and no other avenues to investigate."

Robert considered my suggestion. "I suppose if you'd like, we could. I should send Cameron a note and tell him our expected arrival date so they can prepare. Would you feel up to traveling tomorrow?"

"Yes," I agreed.

"What about me?" Edwin questioned.

"Oh, for pity's sake, Edwin, stand on your own two feet once."

"Perhaps it is best if he comes with us," I suggested. "In the event of any more trouble, he is accounted for."

Edwin wagged his finger at me. "Yes, yes, Lenora is correct. I should travel with you."

Robert sighed. "Well, I suppose I am responsible for you, so I should take as much care as possible to ensure my investment is protected."

We settled on the plan and informed everyone that we would travel tomorrow, leaving mid-morning for Lord MacMahon's estate. I requested one last trip to the cemetery in the afternoon to attempt to gain any additional details from Esme.

Robert agreed to escort me, and we set off for the cemetery following our lunch. I marched to the gravestone near Tilly's. "Esme?" I called into the air. I searched around the grave markers for her. "Esme. It is Lenora. I am going to find your daughter."

I waited a few moments to determine if that would elicit a response. "Esme?" I called one final time. With no one in sight, I spun to return to Robert and the carriage.

Rosy cheeks, porcelain skin, and a pink-lipped grin met my gaze. Her flaxen hair framed her face. "Hello, Lenora," Tilly said.

"Hello, Tilly," I greeted her with a smile.

"You look tired."

"I am," I admitted with a deep sigh.

She placed her hand on my forearm, concern written on her pretty features. "I visited Edwin. By the worry creasing his face, I gathered there has been no luck?"

I shook my head, emotions bubbling to the surface. I fought back the urge to weep. "In fact, it has gotten worse. Gerard's brother has been stabbed."

Tilly raised her eyebrows. "He was our prime suspect at the moment," I added. "But with the attack on him, that casts our suspicions in a rather doubtful light."

My lower lip quivered as I grasped Tilly's hand. "Oh, Tilly, I fear we may fail!"

She firmed her mouth and squeezed my arm. "Do not lose faith, Lenora," Tilly urged.

I nodded and swatted away the tears that had fallen to my cheeks. I stood silent for a moment before I said, "I should tell you we are traveling to an estate outside of Melrose tomorrow for a short while. Another resident of this graveyard insisted I find her daughter. I know not why, but it seemed so very important to her. With our progress stalled, I felt it wise to take care of the matter now."

"You needn't explain, but thank you. Safe travels, Lenora."

We said our goodbyes, and after one final look around the graveyard for Esme, I returned to the carriage.

"Did you speak with her?" he inquired after I'd settled into my seat.

"No. I could not locate her. The dead can be so frustrating at times."

His brow wrinkled at my response. "I spoke with Tilly," I added, realizing he must have seen me conversing with the air.

"Ah," he said with a nod. "I hope she is… never mind."

"You hope she is what?"

"I was about to foolishly say I hoped she was well, but obviously, that is not the case."

I chuckled. "She is well enough, I suppose, given her condition. She urged me not to lose hope in finding the solution."

"And I do the same. Let us hope the jaunt to Cameron's estate clears our minds and allows new developments to surface."

I smiled and nodded at him. A thought occurred to me, and I leaned forward with my eyes wide. "Robert, would you mind terribly another stop?"

"No, where?"

"Lord Pennington's townhouse. I feel I must speak with Gerard."

"Of course." Robert knocked at the window and the carriage slowed. After a brief word with our coachman about the changed plans, we set off again. "What changed your mind? You thought it best not to go earlier."

"I should like one last visit with him before we depart. Just in case. I feel I've left a stone unturned if I do not try. Police be damned."

The statement brought a smirk to Robert's face as we trundled along. In short order, we arrived at the house and were admitted by the butler. A chill passed over me as I recalled my previous experience here.

"Lord Pennington has not yet awoken," he informed us as we stood in the foyer. "There has been no change."

"Might we visit with him? So the old chap knows he has friends about," Robert said.

"Of course, Your Grace." The man showed us to the bedroom where a pale Lord Pennington lay. Memories of the delicate work with the doctor flooded into my mind.

Robert said a thank you, dismissing the butler from the

room. "Well?" he whispered to me as his eyes darted around the room.

I nodded. "He is here. Just there." I motioned toward the corner near the head of the bed. "He is watching over his brother."

Robert nodded, and I detected the trace of a frown on his lips that typically existed when he realized the dead were present. I approached Mr. Boyle.

"Hello again, Mr. Boyle." His eyes remained fixed on his brother's body. "I am pleased we were able to save Lord Pennington."

No answer. "I am only sorry we were not able to do the same for you," I prodded.

Met with silence, I continued on. "Do you know if you shared an attacker?"

"Do you know who attacked your brother? Was he the same man who attacked you?"

My questions did little in the way of gaining information, though I noticed Mr. Boyle's hands ball into fists as I spoke.

He stalked the few steps toward the bed and leaned over his brother. "He is all right," I assured him. "We were able to save him. Though if we could identify the attacker, perhaps you would be more at ease."

His face reddened and his fists remained tightly clenched. He muttered something under his breath.

CHAPTER 25

"What? Please, Mr. Boyle, speak up."

A noise emanated from him again, so soft I could not identify it.

"Mr. Boyle, please, you will need to speak up if I am to help you in this."

He murmured again, and I strained to hear him. After that, he went mute again. I prodded him three more times but to no avail. He simply stood and stared at Lord Pennington, unmoving.

I shook my head and indicated to Robert that we should depart. We returned to our hotel in relative silence.

When we entered, we found Edwin in the sitting room. He slouched in the chair, an almost empty brandy glass clutched in his hand. His eyelids drooped half-closed. By the low level of amber liquid in the decanter, I would guess he was three sheets to the wind.

"Ah!" he slurred as we entered. He staggered from the chair in a clumsy show. "My favorite brother and sister-in-law." He raised the glass as though to toast us.

Robert's eyes burned with fury. "You are drunk," he growled, shoving Edwin back onto his rear in the armchair.

Edwin chuckled at the statement. "Oh, dear, I have upset big brother."

"Pull yourself together," Robert spat at him. He attempted to wrench the glass from Edwin's grasp but was unsuccessful.

Edwin pulled the glass closer to his chest, an expression of triumph on his features. "I am quite together," he slurred, his lips forming an amused grin.

I realized the reason for Edwin's drinking. Though disappointing that he'd returned to his old ways before even escaping the trouble he was in, I understood his reaction. Tilly had been with him earlier. Perhaps he sensed her or she pervaded his thoughts. That coupled with our lack of progress and impending departure, caused him strife. To escape, he had drowned his sorrows in a bottle. It was an easy and familiar route to ease his pain.

Robert's attitude, while correct, only proved to exacerbate the matter, rather than resolve it.

"Robert," I said quietly, "might you check on Sam?"

Robert set his face in a scowl and shook his head at Edwin. "Well..." he began before his gaze flitted to me. I offered him a pleading glance which I hoped he read correctly. He stammered for a moment, then agreed. "Yes, yes, I think I will do that. Excuse me."

He strode from the room and, left alone, I turned my attention to Edwin. He brooded in his chair, staring into the roaring fire nearby.

I eased into the chair across from him. "I spoke with Tilly earlier."

He did not answer, though the pained expression on his face suggested he'd comprehended my words.

"She worries for you, Edwin. And now I can see why."

"There is no need for concern on your part. I am perfectly fine." He rose from his chair and stumbled toward the drink cart. "You see?" He offered a wry grin and a mock bow that nearly caused him to lose his footing.

I crossed the room to him and slammed the lid of the decanter down before he lifted it off. "No," I said in a firm tone.

He attempted to wrestle the bottle from me, but I kept hold of it. "Stop this nonsense at once, Edwin," I said.

We battled for several seconds over the decanter. "I can manage myself without your help, MOTHER," he spat at me.

"I am not your mother. Had I been, I would have given you a crisp smack on the mouth. Now stop it. Robert is correct. You are drunk. And it solves nothing."

"There is nothing to be solved. I shall soon be spending my days behind bars. Or worse. I may as well enjoy life while I can."

He made another swipe for the decanter. I clamped both hands down onto it to keep it from him. "Give it to me," he growled.

"No!" I exclaimed. He attempted to pull my hands from the glass bottle. A scuffle ensued, and I ended up toppling to my backside. I landed with an "oof" on the thick carpet. My head smacked off the padded arm of the chair.

Edwin's eyes widened and he hurried to kneel by my side. "Lenora! Are you quite all right? Where does it hurt?" He clutched at my hand as the air returned to my lungs.

I opened my mouth to respond when Robert rushed in. "My God, Lenora! What happened?" He turned the conversation to Edwin, his voice becoming heated. "What the devil did you do to her?"

"I did not mean to…" Edwin began.

My heart sank at his words as I realized what Robert's reaction would be. With only five words spoken, Robert's face turned to a mask of fury. He grasped Edwin by the collar and dragged him up to standing.

"Robert, please!" I shouted.

Robert continued his assault against his brother. He shook him, shouting, "You sorry excuse for a man! It isn't enough that you ruined your own life, and now you must harm Lenora?"

I rolled onto my hands and knees and pulled myself upright with the assistance of the armchair.

"Robert, stop," I said as I got to my feet.

As he saw me standing, Robert released his grip on Edwin, returning to my side. He eased me into the armchair. "Are you all right, Lenora? Are you hurt?"

"No, I am not hurt. Please, Robert. Leave him be. He is drunk."

"That is no excuse," Robert said, shooting a scowl in Edwin's direction.

"I am sorry," Edwin said. "We... I just wanted the brandy."

"Take it, then. And get the hell out."

Edwin's hands shook and his lower lip quivered. He stood for a moment, looking like a lost child. This cycle could not continue, I realized. It must stop. Edwin swallowed hard and stalked to the drink cart.

"No," I said, feeling as though it was the word of the day. I leapt from the chair and put my hand over the decanter again.

"Lenora!" Robert chided.

"No, you will not take the brandy and slink away to drink yourself into oblivion."

Tears filled his eyes. "I need it," he whispered.

"No, you do not," I insisted. He began to balk when I continued, "I understand your loss. I share it. You must learn to deal with it without turning to drink, Edwin." I placed my hand on his arm and gave it a gentle squeeze. "She is with you in spirit still," I whispered.

A blubbering cry escaped him before he wiped at his face and sniffled. "Go sit down. I will fetch some coffee."

"I shall fetch the coffee," Robert offered. "Then I will not have to witness you blubbering like a fool." He strode from the room in search of the sobering agent.

Edwin scrubbed his face. I took what remained of the brandy and emptied it into the fire. It produced a burst of flames. Edwin stared at me as though I'd just chopped off a limb.

"Robert will not be pleased," he murmured.

"Robert will understand. If you cannot stay away from the drink, then I shall ensure there is none to tempt you."

Edwin bit his lower lip. The scene earlier had already gone a long way at sobering him. He shook his head. "I do not deserve your concern."

"You are Sam's father, you were Tilly's love, and you are my brother-in-law. All of these qualify you for my concern. Now, stop indulging in your sorrows and realize you still have people who care. There have been several developments that should be discussed."

Edwin nodded, his face set in seriousness. "You said… you spoke with… " he stammered.

"Yes," I answered. "I went to the cemetery to try to wrangle additional information from Esme. I spoke with Tilly. She was with you earlier this afternoon. She worries for you."

Edwin's forehead wrinkled and he refused to meet my gaze. "Suddenly, memories of her flooded into my mind as I visited with Sam. I…I couldn't stand the silence here. I poured myself a drink. Then another. And another." He flicked his eyes to my face. "Lenora, I am sorry about earlier. I meant you no harm."

"It was an accident. It is over now," I said. "Let us move forward."

He nodded. "Did you speak with the old woman?"

"No. She was not there. The dead can be so frustrating at times."

"So you have gathered no additional information about the danger her daughter faces?"

"None," I said, turning my palms upward and shrugging. "I am making as much progress on that front as on any other." I sighed.

"Well, there isn't much progress to be made on the other front," Edwin said as Robert returned with a pot of coffee and a cup and saucer.

He poured the dark liquid into the cup and handed it to Edwin with a gruff, "Here."

Edwin accepted it and took a sip, grimacing at the bitter taste. "Sugar?" he inquired.

Robert's expression alone answered Edwin's question. He slouched in his seat and sipped at the coffee.

"Did you tell him?"

"Tell me what?"

"That while you were here drowning your sorrows like a petulant child, we visited Penny, and Lenora spoke with Gerard. He offered precious little information but still," Robert lectured, "while you selfishly indulged yourself, we were attempting to resolve the situation."

"I am grateful for that," Edwin said, shooting a glance at me.

"Try showing it next time," Robert retorted. He wandered to the drink cart. "Where the bloody hell did the brandy go?"

"I am sorry, dear," I answered. "I've tossed it into the fire. It provides too much temptation for Edwin at this moment."

"So we must all be made to suffer," Robert grumbled

under his breath. He shook his head as I opened my mouth to reply. "No, no, you are quite right as always Lenora."

"You said you visited Penny and spoke with Gerard?" Edwin asked.

"Yes. He was of little help. Most of his energy is focused on fretting over his brother's condition."

"So he said nothing?"

"Very little. I asked him several times about his attacker and Lord Pennington's. He was only able to murmur something that was nearly incomprehensible."

"Any hint of what he was saying?" Edwin inquired.

"It sounded as though he was murmuring 'her.'"

Edwin pursed his lips in thought. "Could it have been 'Fer?'" he suggested.

I crinkled my brow, attempting to recall every detail of the low rumble I'd heard from Mr. Boyle. "Perhaps," I said with a shrug.

"Well, you see, I am thinking he is referring to Fergus MacGuiness. Perhaps all he can speak is that much. Or perhaps he called Fergus Fer as a nickname."

"Oh, clever," I said to Edwin. "Yes, though…"

"What is it?" Robert asked.

"I do not recall an "f" sound, but I suppose they are similar enough."

Edwin's arm dropped onto the chair's bolstered arm. "It does us little good unless Penny awakens and confirms Fergus to be the attacker."

"Perhaps by the time we return from Cameron's, there will be some word," Robert said.

With nothing more to discuss, I retreated for a visit with Sam and to ready for the journey to Melrose tomorrow.

Dreary weather greeted us for our trip to the country. We climbed aboard our carriage to depart. I shook off the rain that had fallen onto my cape as I darted from the hotel.

Sinclair, Nanny, and the other servants would follow us in a separate conveyance. After a brief but spirited discussion, I won the right to take Sam with me. Odd, considering he is my own child, but Nanny felt firmly that he should stay with her for the ride in case he became too fussy for my taste. She insisted I should not be bogged down with the child when I had other matters to attend to.

I situated him on my lap, nestled in the folds of my cape for warmth. Sam cooed and called to Robert as he entered the carriage. After the fuss we made, he had taken to repeating his charming nickname for his father at every chance. He waved, calling "Dada" and causing my heart to melt.

We trundled along on our journey, which took half a day. We planned to arrive in the early afternoon. We would lunch in Melrose, then continue on to Lord MacMahon's estate.

As we traveled, the skies turned less gray, and when we arrived in the small town of Melrose, I was pleased to see the sun peek through fluffy white clouds.

Nanny was pleased to see her charge, rushing toward me to alleviate my so-called burden and asking if he'd caused much trouble.

"None at all," Robert informed her with a proud grin. "Such a pleasant little chap."

As we emerged from the small cafe to continue our journey, I studied our surroundings. I had never been to Melrose before. I found it interesting how different it was from Blackmoore, yet how much the same.

People bustled about on the town's streets, completing their afternoon errands. They hurried through the cold to and fro. I glanced in the direction of the MacMahon estate. "Is it very far from the town?" I inquired of Robert.

"No, not very. Closer to town than Blackmoore Castle is to Blackmoore."

As we climbed back into our carriage, I scanned the horizon for any hint of the estate. With the flatter lands here, I found none. Though my brow furrowed as I caught sight of something else. A woman in a tattered rose-colored coat disappeared down an alley. Odd, I thought as I sank into my seat, that was the same color coat my attacker had worn.

CHAPTER 26

*O*ur carriage lurched forward and picked up speed as we trundled down the Main Street of the town. As we passed the alley, I peered from the window down its length. Not a soul graced it. Perhaps my mind had been playing tricks on me, I thought as I settled back in my seat.

Within minutes, we bounced along the path on the rather flat estate, and I was struck at how different it was from Blackmoore. Brown stone covered the exterior of the rather boxy structure. It was devoid of the turrets and towers jutting skyward from Blackmoore Castle's rambling halls.

Still, I found it lovely and pointed out several of the more ostentatious things to the child on my lap, like the banners that waved in the air.

The carriage slowed to a stop, and I noticed the staff lined on one side of the door. A well-dressed man and woman stood on the other with two boys around the ages of eight and six. I took the handsome couple to be Lord and Lady MacMahon. Lord MacMahon's light-brown, curly hair rustled in the wind, topping a kindly face that still seemed to sport baby fat, though his broad shoulders and burly body suggested him well into adulthood.

Lady MacMahon's mahogany hair had been pinned up in a style similar to mine though soft tendrils framed her face. I always found dangling hair too fussy. Her slight lips were set in a pleasant and welcoming expression.

One of their footmen stepped forward as the carriage stopped and pulled open the door. Robert departed first, reaching in to relieve me of Sam and assist me to the ground below. Edwin followed me, and introductions were made.

"Cameron," Robert said with a large grin, slapping the man on the back.

"How excellent you were able to come, Your Grace," Lord MacMahon answered. "You remember Cora, my wife, and our two boys, Amos and Levi."

"Your Grace," Lady MacMahon greeted him with a curtsy.

Robert waved away the formality. "Robert, please. This is my wife, Lenora." I received the customary bow and curtsy, of which I was still unaccustomed to receiving.

With a smile, I indicated they may skip the formalities on my part, as well. "And, of course, you remember my brother, Edwin."

"Of course," Lord MacMahon said, "though I daresay the last time I saw you, you were still in the nursery."

"Yes, he's come a long way from the nursery," Robert commented dryly. His tone changed immediately when he patted Sam on the chest and said, "And this is my son, Samuel."

"Oh!" Lord MacMahon exclaimed. "How very out of it I must seem. I had not even heard the news."

"Well, it came as rather a surprise," Robert said. "But he is already seven months."

"What a darling child," Lady MacMahon cooed.

Samuel studied the two strangers in front of him, then

the small children below. His head swiveled, and he studied Robert. "Dada," he said.

"And smart, too!" Robert said with a chuckle.

"And I daresay he has your eyes, Robby," Lord MacMahon commented.

"A Fletcher through and through," Robert agreed.

I noticed the pride shining in both his and Edwin's faces. In short order, we paraded into the foyer. A grand staircase trimmed in heavy decorative wood led up to the second floor. Before entering, Robert handed Sam off to Nanny to situate in the nursery with the other children. I wondered for a brief moment how the other nanny may fare with Nanny West.

We all spoke briefly for a few moments in the sitting room before Lady MacMahon suggested we might view our rooms and rest before the dressing gong. Relief coursed through me as I found myself more tired than expected from the journey.

I retired to my room and used the time to fret and pace the floor rather than rest. Robert and Edwin had gone riding with Lord MacMahon, leaving me alone in my room. I wrung my hands as I considered the task that lay ahead of me. What would I say to Grace when I found her here? I had no idea what type of danger she was in. I couldn't even hint at it.

Perhaps once the woman revealed herself, Esme would appear and be more forthcoming with the details. I could only hope.

Sinclair appeared shortly after the dressing gong. "Have you recovered from the journey, Your Grace?" she asked as I readied for dinner.

"I suppose I have. And you? Was the journey very taxing for you? How are your accommodations here?"

"Oh, they are quite nice, Your Grace. No need to worry

about that. I have recovered from the journey. It was not too much, and I've had a light afternoon."

"I wonder, Sinclair, if I may ask for your assistance in the matter that brought us here."

"Of course, Your Grace!"

"Might you ask around to determine which of the staff is Grace?"

Sinclair nodded. "I plan to scout her out at our dinner. Only a few of the servants were below stairs when we arrived, but everyone should be there this evening. Do not worry, Your Grace, I shall find her."

"Good, thank you," I said with a sharp nod. At least, perhaps, the finding of Grace would be a matter easily settled.

Robert returned and, after changing for dinner, escorted me downstairs to join the others for pre-dinner cocktails. Lady MacMahon had arranged for several other guests who had not yet arrived. While we awaited their arrival, she suggested she and I may sneak away for a few moments to check on the children in the nursery.

"Oh, how relieved I was when you suggested this," I said as she led me through the halls.

She offered a kind smile. "I thought you may want to ensure Samuel has settled in."

"Quite," I said. "I tend to be rather a hands-on mother," I added.

"Yes, I gathered as much when you elected to have the child ride in your own carriage and not left with the nanny or even at home!"

"I realize the sentiment may seem coarse, but I am simply thrilled with the prospect of motherhood and cannot seem to tear myself away."

She smiled again, this time looking quite coy. "Wait until

he is walking and racing about the estate. Then you may tire of it more easily," she said with a wink.

I chuckled, understanding her meaning about the overzealousness of a child, particularly of the male gender. "I have no doubt he will tire us all in the course of a day soon."

We arrived at the nursery and I found Samuel enjoying playing with a model train along with the other two boys. He clapped his hands with delight as Levi pushed the small model along the floor, making a chugging sound followed by a woo-ing noise like a train whistle.

I smiled at the scene as Nanny approached. "How has he settled in, Nanny?" I asked. "Any trouble?"

"Not a lick," she assured me. "He is quite well-adjusted even with the travel and enjoying his new companions."

"I see that." To Lady MacMahon I said, "Your nursery is quite lovely."

"Oh, thank you. Cameron and his siblings all used this same nursery. I insisted on a few changes when Amos was born. You would have thought I'd asked for the house to be torn down and rebuilt."

"I am certain Lord MacMahon can now appreciate your modifications."

"To be certain."

I spent a few more moments observing Sam before I tore myself away, not wishing to extend my stay and keep my hostess from her other guests. We discussed the nursery at Blackmoore Castle on our return trip.

The rest of the evening was spent in pleasant conversation. Robert and Lord MacMahon seemed to get on swimmingly as they sparred playfully during our dinner conversation. Lord MacMahon regaled us with several comical tales of Robert's youth.

After our meal and nightcap, I opted to return to the bedroom for the night while Robert, after inquiring if I minded, chose to engage in a card game with the other men of the party.

Happy to leave him to his time with his old friend, I kissed him goodnight and returned to the bedroom. Sinclair arrived shortly after, a triumphant expression on her features.

"Ask me if I have found her, Your Grace," she said with a jubilant smile.

"You have!" I said, clapping my hands together.

She nodded. "I have!" She grinned. "She's a housemaid for the family. Oh, just a little mouse of a girl. She's got red hair and chubby cheeks. I don't think I heard her mutter a word during our supper."

"Hmm," I murmured as I considered the information.

"And I thought," Sinclair continued, "now what has a girl like that gotten into that's so dangerous? I tell you, Your Grace, I cannot fathom what it could be. She seemed perfectly pleasant. Didn't seem like she'd harm a flea. I cannot imagine why she'd be in danger."

I pursed my lips before blowing out a long breath. "I cannot say either. Though I hope the answer presents itself before any harm may come to her."

"You are not responsible if anything happens to her. You realize that, don't you, Your Grace?"

"Yes, I do. Though at the same time, I feel oddly responsible. To have come all this way and failed to prevent whatever tragedy Esme believes is coming would be rather disheartening."

We fell into silence, both pondering the matter. After a few moments, I said, "Sinclair, do you think you could arrange a meeting between us?"

"I am certain I could, yes."

"Good. Perhaps if I am to meet the girl I may be able to come to some conclusion or prompt a visit from her mother."

"Leave it to me, Your Grace. I shall arrange it."

As we parted ways for the evening, I climbed into bed. My mind wandered through what I should say during the meeting with Grace. In the past, I had always found honesty to be the best policy; however, I imagined the conversation unfolding with the poor girl and wondered if there was a more tactful method by which I could deliver the news.

I fell asleep worrying over the details. My slumber was haunted by the specter of Esme. I ran through darkened halls in search of the chubby-cheeked redhead, Grace. Several times I caught sight of her. I called out to her, but she'd disappear before I ever reached her. "Danger," Esme called from behind me. "Danger!"

Breathless, I continued to race through endless halls and confusing corridors until finally, with a stabbing pain in my right side, I halted and doubled over to ease the pain.

"Hurry! Danger!" Esme shouted at me.

"Yes, I know!" I acknowledged. "But what is the danger?"

"Danger," the old woman growled at me, her eyes narrowing and her wrinkles deepening.

"But from what?" I asked, my voice thick with pleading.

"Death," she breathed. "Death."

I swallowed hard at the admission. "Death?" I questioned. "Grace's death?"

The woman's shoulders straightened, and she raised her chin. "Her," she said before she vanished.

"No, wait!" I called. I spun in circles, searching for her, but she did not reappear. The stone walls that surrounded me seemed unyielding. I pressed against them as I searched for an exit. I found none. Hadn't there been a hallway here only a moment ago?

Panic began to confuse my thoughts. I clawed at the walls but could not find an egress. The space in which I was trapped seemed to shrink with every second. As the walls closed in on me, I screamed for help.

* * *

I vaulted upright to sitting, gasping for air. I glanced around, temporarily confused by my surroundings. Slowly, I began to recall where I slept. As my confusion subsided, details of my dream flooded back to me.

I climbed from bed and pulled on my dressing gown. I paced the floor as my heart rate slowed. The old woman had told me "danger" multiple times. That was no surprise. It had been what she'd told me from the start.

But she'd added that the danger was related to death. Whose death, I pondered? Grace's death? Esme's death? The death of another?

I pivoted and retraced my steps. My foot faltered and my brow crinkled as I recalled the last word Esme spoke to me in the dream. "Her," I repeated aloud.

"Her," I said again as I resumed my aimless ambling. It was the same word I'd thought Mr. Boyle had said to me. Odd that it should pop up again.

With a sigh, I sank onto the bed. Perhaps not, I concluded. Perhaps my tired mind had combined the two situations, melding them together into one.

I huffed and climbed under the covers again after doffing my dressing gown. After some tossing and turning, I managed to drift off to a dreamless sleep.

When I rose the following morning, my mind dwelled on my upcoming encounter with Grace. I hoped to find the right words when the time came.

The dream played on my mind, and I felt more unsettled over the matter than I had yesterday. I drummed my fingers on the dressing table as I waited for Sinclair to appear.

"Good morning, Your Grace," she said as she flitted into the room.

"Good morning, Sinclair."

She lifted her eyebrows as she readied my clothing for the day. "That does not sound good, Your Grace. Did you have a bad night? Perhaps you did not sleep well in the new location."

"I slept," I admitted. "Though I had a nightmare at the start of the night. And I confess it disturbed me. I am a bit worried about meeting with Grace today. Were you able to arrange it?"

"Yes, Your Grace. I was able to arrange it. Was your nightmare very terrible?"

"No, though it disturbed me. Esme visited as I attempted to search for Grace in the halls. After she reminded me of the danger she'd spoken of before, she added a new and ominous warning."

"Warning?"

"Yes. Death, she said."

Sinclair's eyes widened. "Whose death? Grace?"

I shrugged. "I do not know! I asked her for the information, but she would give none. And then she disappeared. Though before that, she uttered one other word."

"What was the word?"

"Her," I repeated.

"Her? As in Grace?"

With a sigh, I sank onto the chair at the dressing table. "Again, I do not know. Though I suppose she could be referring to Grace. Why she would say her instead of Grace, I cannot say."

Sinclair shivered. "Oh, Your Grace, how awful this is! Poor Grace! I have not known her long, but she seems a sweet girl. Very accommodating when I spoke with her last night and again this morning. If she turns up dead…"

"I realize how taxing this knowledge is, Sinclair. If she turns up dead, I will feel quite responsible."

"Oh, I do not mean to say that, Your Grace! You are no more responsible than the Queen of England! But to know ahead of time and then see it come to fruition... Well, that's downright eerie!"

"I do not know what I will say to her," I said as I studied my hands, refusing to make eye contact with Sinclair.

"I am certain you will find the words, Your Grace. You always seem to put those around you at ease."

"I am not certain the news I need to impart is synonymous with ease, Sinclair," I said, my eyes darting to hers.

"I suppose not, but you always manage to give this type of information with grace and poise."

"The problem is how do I approach it? I cannot very well say 'Hello, Grace, I have spoken with your dead mother, and you are in danger, possibly from death. Though I know no more than this.'" My shoulder slumped as the ridiculous statements tumbled from my lips.

"No, I believe I'd try a different approach, Your Grace."

For whatever reason, the statement made me chuckle. Sinclair also gave in to the laughter, and we found our spirits lifted for just a moment.

"When did you set the meeting?" I inquired.

"At ten. I learned she will be tidying in the sitting room at that time. We can slip in and speak with her then."

I nodded. "Fine. I would be ever so grateful if you went with me. At least for the introduction. I imagine she may be quite overwhelmed if I entered and struck up a conversation."

"I would venture to say so. She is rather backward."

"I am certain she would be less awestruck if she realized my origins."

"Your Grace, most would not believe that tale! I'd wager

those you rub elbows with assume you were born to the station."

I arched an eyebrow at the statement. I remained awestruck even at that moment at how easily one becomes accustomed to their roles in life, for better or worse. "Born to a station or not, we all have common bonds, Sinclair. We are all people just the same."

"No, Your Grace, that is where you are wrong. Title or not, you are a special woman."

She finished with my hair and I climbed from my chair. "Well, let us hope I am able to find the right words. Shall we meet in the foyer at five minutes to ten?"

Sinclair nodded. "Yes, Your Grace. I shall see you then."

With a wrap in my hand, since I did not know how warm or cold the house may be, I left the confines of my bedroom and traversed the halls to the dining room. Breakfast had been set on the sideboard, and the butler assisted me with serving. I settled into my seat as Robert and Lord MacMahon appeared.

"Ah, good morning, Lenora!" Robert said with a large grin.

"Good morning, dear. Out and about already?"

"Yes," he said as he filled a plate with the breakfast foods. "Cam and I were out for an early morning ride. It is so flat here compared to Blackmoore. Quite easy to take in the sights."

"I hope the uncomplicated ride did not bore you," Lord MacMahon said.

"Not at all!" Robert said with a carefree laugh. "Still quite invigorating without the horse climbing here and there."

Lord MacMahon sat at the head of the table and set his gaze on me. "Do you enjoy riding, Your Grace?"

"I do, yes."

"I shall tell the staff to remain alert in the event you'd like to take in the estate on horseback. Simply go to the stables and they can see to a horse for you."

"I have just purchased Lenora a new horse for her birthday," Robert chimed in. "A beautiful white mare."

The men descended into talk about riding, horses, and the best horse breeders. After a few minutes, Lord MacMahon addressed me again. "Please forgive our overzealous discussion. Robby and I both enjoyed riding while at school."

"Yes, I gather Robert has always enjoyed riding. He aims to make certain Sam enjoys it as well."

"I have Nanny place the child on his rocking horse every day to prepare him for the saddle."

"With you as a teacher, I imagine he'll take it like a fish to water."

"From your lips," Robert said with a smile.

I'd seldom seen Robert grin so much. Regardless of the outcome with Grace, I was pleased we'd made the trip to the MacMahons seeing how much Robert enjoyed himself. I supposed going forward I would need to extend more invitations for house parties and the like. Visiting with friends seemed to bring Robert much joy.

After breakfast, I took in the estate on foot with Robert. We discussed the situation with Grace, and I informed him of my plan to speak with her. As the hour approached ten, Robert wished me luck and left me in the foyer. Sinclair approached moments later.

"Ready, Your Grace?"

With a deep breath, I nodded. "Ready," I answered.

Sinclair pushed the doors open to the sitting room. Inside, a short redhead waved a duster over several items on an end table.

"Oh!" she exclaimed as I paraded into the room, my hands

clasped tightly in front of my waist. "Terribly sorry, Your Grace. I'll only be a moment."

"No, please," I said. "I was hoping to speak with you."

Her eyes went wide and she swallowed hard. She bit her lower lip and her chubby cheeks flushed. "With me, Your Grace?"

"Yes," I answered. "I hope you do not mind, but Sinclair told me you would be here, and it is quite urgent."

"Of course, Your Grace. Is there something amiss in your room?"

"No," I answered with a shake of my head. "It is a personal matter. Perhaps you should sit down."

Another hard swallow preceded her next statement. "If you do not mind, Your Grace, I should prefer to keep to my feet."

She clutched her duster tightly in front of her. I offered a slight smile and proceeded. "I have a message for you…" I paused for a moment, not sure it would help temper the news. "From your mother."

CHAPTER 27

Her forehead wrinkled as she attempted to look anywhere but at me. "My mother, Your Grace?" she questioned.

"Yes," I said with a nod.

"Begging your pardon, Your Grace, but might you have me confused with someone else? My mother passed six months ago."

I offered her a consoling smile and another nod. "Yes, I realize that. Again, you may wish to sit." I motioned toward the sofa.

I felt pity toward her as she struggled to maintain her decorum in front of a duchess. "Please, Grace," I said, and Sinclair put her arms around the girl's shoulders and guided her to the couch.

"There, there. It's all right, dear. Her Grace would not ask you to sit if she did not mean it."

The girl allowed herself to be eased onto it. She teetered near the edge, ready to leap up at any moment. I joined her, perching next to her.

"I realize your mother has passed, however," I began as

my eyes flitted to Sinclair, who offered an encouraging nod. "I suffer from a peculiar oddity which allows me to see and sometimes communicate with those who have passed."

Grace's jaw gaped open and she quickly covered it with her hand before she clamped it shut. She did not respond, though I did not expect she would. Most did not after I imparted such news.

"While visiting the St. Agnes cemetery, your mother appeared to me. She implored me to seek you out. She seemed to think you were in some kind of danger. I am sorry, I do not know much more than that. I hope to learn more, though I did want to pass the message along in the event you may understand its meaning better than I."

Grace licked her lips and the color drained from her face. She stammered for a few moments, her lower lip quivering. Eventually, she forced out a few words. "I... I do not know what it may mean, Your Grace."

My shoulders fell, and I shook my head. "Unfortunately, neither do I. Though your mother was quite insistent." I reached out and grasped her hand in mine, giving it a squeeze. "Please be careful, Grace. I know not the meaning, but she was terribly, terribly upset."

Grace's wide eyes stared down at my hand as though a sea urchin had clamped onto her. Sinclair put an arm around her shoulders and patted them. "'Tis all right, Grace. Her Grace is a kindly soul. She is genuinely worried about your well-being."

I imagined such behavior likely did not exist within the MacMahon household in general. Though kind people, both MacMahons had grown up in society's upper crust. Sentimentality toward servants was not often encouraged. Poor Grace likely found my behavior most coarse, though I felt the need to impart the importance of the mind-boggling message to her in some way.

She forced a weak smile on her face and wrangled her hand from my grasp. "I shall do so, Your Grace." She stood awkwardly, nearly pitching into Sinclair. "If you'll excuse me…"

With that, the pale girl hurried from the room on unsteady feet. I followed her departure before turning my attention back to Sinclair. She offered a shrug and a half-smile. "You tried your best, Your Grace."

I heaved a sigh. "No appearances by Esme," I responded. "I had hoped contact with Grace would have elicited another appearance."

Sinclair frowned. "You passed the message along. Perhaps that is all she wanted."

I considered the statement. "I doubt that, though this may be my own guilt speaking. Poor girl. Though her reaction is not unexpected."

We spent another few moments in silence before I climbed to my feet. "Well, I suppose that is that. Perhaps I will go for a ride after lunch to clear my mind."

"Sounds lovely, Your Grace. And do not worry about Grace. I will check in on her later."

"Thank you, Sinclair." I grasped her hands in mine and squeezed. "You are such a joy to work with! Please report back to me if you learn anything. Or even if not, how she is taking the news."

Sinclair nodded and smiled, and we parted ways. I pushed through the front door into the chilly air as I adjusted my cape around me.

I glanced around before choosing a path leading to my right. As luck would have it, Robert approached as I neared the corner.

"Ah, Lenora! Enjoying the day?"

"Yes, I thought I might go riding," I said.

His eyes lit up at the words. "Would you mind if I join

you, or would you prefer to ride alone?"

"I would very much enjoy your company," I assured him and grasped his elbow as he led me to the stables.

"Have you made any progress on speaking with Grace?" he inquired.

"Yes," I said with a sigh.

Robert's eyebrows wiggled at my response and he slid his eyes sideways. "That sounds... less than favorable."

"She did not react well. Though that is to be expected given the news."

We reached the stables, and Robert requested our horses to be saddled. After a few moments, the staff had us situated. Robert rode a large chestnut steed while my gray mare stood a foot smaller than his. He postulated that I would enjoy the ride on the rather flat terrain.

As we left the stables behind and cantered across the large field, Robert inquired, "Did she have any ideas about what the warning could mean?"

"No, she did not. At least not that she shared with Sinclair and me. Though I am uncertain as to whether or not she believed my story to begin with."

"Well, you have done your part and passed along the message. Perhaps that was all that was needed to avoid any tragedy."

I shook my head but did not respond verbally.

"You do not agree?" he asked as we slowed our horses to meander along the tree line.

"Sadly, no," I responded. After a moment, I continued, "I had a dream last night. Esme's expanded on her warning. She implied it involved death."

Robert screwed up his face in thought and I added the final detail. "There is one odd thing though."

"Oh?"

"When Esme said death, I inquired as to who the threat

applied to. Was it Grace who was in danger? And she said one word before she disappeared."

"What was it?"

"Her," I reported.

"Her?" Robert questioned, his face wrinkling further.

I nodded.

"As in Grace?" he suggested, forming it as a question.

I shrugged as the horses wandered along. I opened my mouth to reply, but my forehead wrinkled, and I squeezed my lips shut in thought.

"What is it?" Robert inquired.

"That is the same word Mr. Boyle said when I spoke with him about his and Lord Pennington's attacker."

"Yes, I recall you mentioning that. We considered that he may have been saying 'Fer' for Fergus."

"Yes, though I am certain Esme said 'her' not 'fer.' It cannot be a coincidence!"

"Is the her Grace?"

"I conjectured that, but what would Grace have to do with Mr. Boyle's death and Lord Pennington's attack?"

Robert pondered it a moment, his lips pursed. "You don't think…"

My brow furrowed as Robert's words hung in the air. "What I mean to say is…"

"Well," he finally said, "could it be that Grace is somehow involved?"

"But how?" I inquired. "Surely she was not in Glasgow days ago when Lord Pennington was attacked."

"No, I suppose you are correct."

"I postulated that perhaps the death danger Esme spoke of were not directed at Grace but rather caused by Grace."

"An interesting theory, Robert, but again," I stated, "could she have been in town to stab Lord Pennington?"

"I would doubt it, though I will make a subtle inquiry with Cameron."

"Thank you, Robert. I would appreciate that greatly."

He smiled and nodded with me. "Of course, Lenora. I am grateful to be of use!" With a broad smile, he grasped his reins and said, "And now, I propose a race back to the stables!"

"Are you joking?" I said incredulously.

"Not at all! On this easy terrain, you should be up to it."

With a less-than-certain expression, I agreed, and we set the horses to running. They thundered across the ground in full gallop. I clung to my reins, though I found the galloping quite a bit easier to take when the horse wasn't frenzied. The last time I'd raced at full speed had been when the specter of Annie had sent my horse fleeing across the property. At least this time, I had control of my horse.

Realizing that, I urged her on, pulling ahead of Robert slightly. A grin spread across my face as I spotted the stables in the distance. I aimed my steed toward it and flew across the remaining space, slowing her to stop and turning to find Robert bouncing in his saddle as he slowed behind me.

"Did you let me win?" I asked with a laugh.

"No," he assured me, "I most certainly did not!"

I raised my eyebrows at him as my horse trotted in a circle.

"I didn't!" he claimed again. "That would be the day Robert Fletcher allowed himself to be bested on horseback by a lady on purpose," he added for good measure as he dismounted.

I chuckled at him as he assisted me down from my horse while the groom held her steady. I did not believe him, though I did not care very much even if he did allow me to win.

As we strolled back to the house, Edwin approached us.

"Well, good afternoon," Robert said in greeting. "I wondered if you were ill."

Edwin narrowed his eyes at him. "No, only having a leisurely rest."

Robert pursed his lips at his brother. "Is this the new term for recovering from a drunken stupor?"

"I was not drunk!"

"To Edwin's credit," I interjected, "I did not see him imbibe anything alcoholic last night. Even his wine sat untouched at the dining table."

Robert mulled it over. "There, you see?" Edwin spat. "Now, have you found the girl, Greta, or whatever she is called?"

"Grace," I corrected. "Yes, I have, though…"

Edwin interrupted me with a wave of his hand. "Good. Should we arrange to return to Glasgow? Have you heard anything about Penny's condition? You left Henry behind to monitor it, did you not?"

"I have not heard anything as yet, but I did ask him to keep me apprised, particularly of any changes," Robert said. "And no, we will not abandon our hosts."

"But the task is complete, and we have other things to focus on."

"The task is not complete," I argued. "I have only just told Grace about the warning. We have no idea what trouble may be lurking, and I do not wish to abandon the girl or our hosts."

"But…" Edwin began when Robert cut him off.

"Henry will keep us apprised of any changes. If Penny awakens, he will send a messenger straight away. Relax, Edwin, try to enjoy the scenery."

With that, Robert tugged me away toward the house.

"I would enjoy it better if I was a free man!" Edwin shouted behind us.

"That man is insufferably selfish!" Robert grumbled.

I patted his arm. "I suppose he is quite on edge with the murder charge still looming."

"Yes, I realize that, Lenora, but can he not have any concern for anyone else?"

"With little to no information about the type of danger, I suppose Edwin finds there to be little point in staying. What can we do to help?"

"We have the information that the danger is death of some kind. We should pursue it as best we can to prevent the poor girl from coming to harm."

"That bit was imparted in a dream. It could be nothing," I reminded him.

"Your dreams never prove to be nothing, Lenora. You conjured the image of Gerard Boyle. I would not discount the additional information so easily."

"If the threat applies directly to Grace, who would kill her? And why?" I asked as we arrived at the front door.

"I do not know," Robert said with a sigh, "but if you receive any other information, please let me know at once. I do not like this, Lenora. If danger is lurking about, I do not wish you to be harmed."

"I shall inform you of any developments."

Robert nodded and checked his watch as we stepped inside. "We have some time before the dressing gong. What will you do?"

"I think I shall read. I have yet to finish the novel you gave me for my birthday. I shall make a good run on it this afternoon, I hope."

"Enjoy your reading, dear," he said with a kiss on my cheek. "There is a business proposition I would like to discuss with Cameron. And I shall discreetly inquire about Grace's whereabouts in the last several weeks. Wish me luck!"

I imparted my best wishes for his work, climbed the stairs, and meandered to my bedroom. I found the novel on my bedside table, likely placed there by Sinclair in anticipation of my desiring it over the course of our stay.

I curled on the chaise near the fireplace in the room and opened my book. I hadn't read two words when my mind drifted.

Thoughts crowded into my brain from every direction. I wondered about Lord Pennington's condition. I worried over Edwin's predicament and our lack of solution at present. And finally, my mind settled on Grace.

For a fleeting moment, I pondered Robert's earlier statements regarding Grace's involvement in the murder. Perhaps the girl was not in danger. Perhaps she *was* the danger. With a shake of my head, I snapped the book shut and used the service cord to call for someone, with any luck, Sinclair.

I paced the floor for a few moments before she arrived.

"Oh, good, I had hoped it would be you, Sinclair," I said as she entered the room.

"How can I assist you, Your Grace?"

"Sinclair, have you heard anything from the servants about recent travel?"

"Travel?" She puckered her lips and shook her head. "No, Your Grace."

I continued my ambling about. "What I am most interested in is Grace's whereabouts when Mr. Boyle was killed and when Lord Pennington was stabbed."

Sinclair's brows pinched together. "You don't mean to say..." Her voice trailed off.

"Robert mentioned it earlier, and I cannot discount it. He conjectured Esme's meaning to be that Grace herself was the danger, not that she was in danger."

"Oh, my!" Sinclair answered, her eyes widening. "How

extraordinary! My mind never would have jumped to that. Though I cannot imagine it out of that mouse of a girl!"

"I must say, I cannot either, Sinclair, but people react strangely due to all sorts of circumstances, and we have little idea why at times."

Silence consumed the room for a few moments before Sinclair said, "I will work to find out what I can. Though I am still astounded if Grace is involved in any of the Glasgow trouble."

I lifted my shoulders. "The odd thing of it is in my dream, Esme's last word to me was 'her.'"

"Her? As in Grace?"

"I do not know, but after Lord Pennington's attack, when I returned to visit him the following day, Mr. Boyle said the same word. He repeated it several times, almost inaudibly. When I could make out what he was saying, I thought it was the word 'her.' It cannot be coincidence."

"My goodness! I should say not, though still, I cannot imagine Grace as a murderer!"

"We shall see, Sinclair," I answered.

She nodded. "I shall see what progress I can make and report back as you dress for dinner."

I agreed to the plan and thanked her before she slipped from the room with a wry smile and a wink.

With a deep breath, I returned to my helpless state and waited for news. I tried several times to begin my book. I muddled through a chapter before tossing it aside. I spent the rest of the time before the dinner gone in reflective thought. I'd come to no new conclusions when Sinclair reappeared in my room.

Judging by the coy expression on her face, I guessed she had information to share. "You look rather pleased. Am I to understand you've learned something?" I said.

"Indeed, I have, Your Grace," she answered. She arched an

eyebrow at me. "It appears our little miss Grace was in Glasgow when Mr. Boyle was murdered!"

My eyebrows shot toward my hairline. "What's more," Sinclair said, leaning in and lowering her voice even though we were alone, "she was unaccounted for at the time he died."

My jaw fell open. "How did you learn this?"

"One of the footmen, Your Grace. He said she'd returned quite late. He thought perhaps she had a liaison. Of the romantic sort."

"How interesting," I said. This presented a wrinkle I had not expected. I wondered if she could have been responsible for Lord Pennington's assault, too. If she'd been in Glasgow then, we may have solved our mystery. Though something niggled in the back of my mind about the supposed solution.

"She denied it. Said she was meeting her brother and gotten mixed up or something or other." Sinclair flitted her hands in the air as though explaining away the problem.

"Could Robert be correct, then?" I murmured aloud.

"Well, possibly. Though this is where things take a turn. It seems she was not in Glasgow when Lord Pennington was stabbed. So she could not have been the culprit."

"Not for that crime, no. Though we are only assuming they are related. Perhaps someone hoped to match the details of the first crime in the hopes of having them both pinned on one person."

Sinclair nodded in agreement with my supposition. "At any rate, Sinclair, you have done wonderful work. This is most interesting and very useful."

Sinclair offered another satisfied smile and a nod. I finished dressing for dinner and Robert escorted me down. On the way, he imparted similar news to what I'd heard from Sinclair.

"Yes," I answered after he'd recounted his tale, "Sinclair heard as much from the other servants."

"Oh, please be careful, Lenora," he implored me again. "I know you believe you must rescue this girl from some danger, but I worry she is the danger."

"I shall be careful," I promised.

Our conversation ended as we entered the sitting room and greeted our hosts. The evening passed uneventfully, though I noticed Robert eyeing Edwin's full wine glass several times over the course of the meal. At the end of the dinner, he offered his brother a congratulatory nod. While Robert seemed pleased, I noted that the full wine glass likely added to Edwin's agitation.

As I dressed for bed, Sinclair imparted that she had learned nothing new since we'd last spoken. Grace, though, she said, had avoided her.

"She likely believes me mad," I murmured, my chin resting in my hand as Sinclair brushed my hair.

"I suppose she has lumped me into the same basket," Sinclair said.

I met her gaze. "I am sorry, Sinclair. I realize my oddity condemns me to the enmity of others, but now it has claimed you, too."

"Ha!" Sinclair guffawed. "I shall likely never see these people again after we depart. Even if we return, I shall barely spend much time with them overall. So, I care little what they think of me."

"You are wise, Sinclair," I said with a wistful smile.

"You know what matters to me, Your Grace?"

"Tell me."

"My family. Those people who love me matter to me. My mother was ever so proud that I was a ladies' maid to a duchess. And she remarks at what a fine lady you must be taking so much concern over your staff as to allow them to visit with their family at any chance. And I told her, Her Grace is gracious to a fault and the best lady I've met. I am proud to be your ladies' maid, and I count you as one of my own family, Your Grace, if I may be so bold. I don't give a fig about your 'oddity,' as you put it."

"I am quite glad to hear you say that, Sinclair. I worry that you would regret taking the position. I am pleased that you do not."

"Never, Your Grace."

We finished our nightly tasks and Sinclair departed. At least, I reflected, as I climbed into bed, Sinclair did not regret her position nor despise me for my peculiarity. "One thing solved," I murmured as I heaved a sigh.

With my eyes shut tight, I willed myself to sleep. The tactic did not work, though after a time, I finally drifted off. I awakened with a start and a shiver. Coldness washed over me, and I shuddered again and reached blindly for the bedcovers with my eyes still closed.

I grasped hold of the blanket and attempted to draw it up over me. Icy fingers wrapped around my hand, stopping me in my tracks. My eyes shot open. I glanced down at my hand. Gnarled, blue-tinged fingers gripped me. I followed them up to a wrist, arm, shoulder, and then a face.

The ghost of Esme Murdoch stood perched over my bed. She narrowed her almost-glowing eyes at me. "Esme!" I exclaimed.

CHAPTER 28

With her free hand, Esme motioned for me to climb from my bed and follow her. I sat rather dumbfounded, staring at her for a full minute before she motioned again.

"What is it, Esme?" I questioned, unwilling to crawl from my nest to parade about the house.

"Danger," she said in a hoarse voice.

"Now?" I questioned. "It's the middle of the night, surely everyone is..."

"Danger!" she exclaimed again.

"All right," I said with a huff. I dangled my feet over the side of the bed and shoved them into my slippers before tugging my dressing gown around me.

"Danger!" she hissed at me again.

I stood and fastened my dressing gown's tie. "Lead the way," I said.

She wandered to the door and disappeared through it. I tugged it open and my head swiveled to find my deceased friend. I spotted her a few yards ahead of me in the hall and hurried to catch up to her.

Already breathing hard, I attempted to gasp out a question to the woman. "Where are we going?"

She did not respond and merely continued to wind through the halls. We descended the main staircase and she flung the front doors open before reaching them and slipped outside. I followed her, grateful that I'd taken the time to don my slippers as I had little desire to traverse the estate in my bare feet. Esme had set a fast pace, and I struggled to keep up with her as she led me across the lawn.

The night air chilled me and I shivered against it. I snugged my dressing gown tighter around me and crossed my arms. I wished Esme was more communicative with me regarding our destination. I began to worry we would walk further than I anticipated when she made an abrupt turn.

At first, I assumed we were heading to the stables. An unsubstantiated fear came over me that she might ask me to saddle a horse and ride away. She quickly quashed that notion when she bypassed the stables, swinging around them and continuing on.

I groaned internally as I passed by the warm walls, wishing I was inside instead of out here, where the frigid wind played havoc with my light nightclothes. Even the thick robe was blown about mercilessly. My fingers were beginning to hurt, and I shoved them further into the crevices under my arms.

"Esme, where are we going?" I demanded again, my tone turning as icy as the air.

Only silence responded. We left the stables behind and continued into the open space. Pale moonlight guided our way. In the distance, I could make out a structure. I squinted at it, wondering if that was the location where Esme was leading me.

As I studied it, I saw a flicker of light from within. My heart skipped a beat. Someone was there. While their presence would not be a problem for Esme, it could very well be for me! I hesitated, uncertain if I wanted to proceed further.

Esme halted in front of me and waved me on. "Is that where we are going?" I questioned, motioning to the folly on the property. "Why are you leading me there? Who is there?"

"Danger," she repeated and continued her trek forward.

I rolled my eyes. "Danger," I mimicked. "And you wish to lead me right to it." With a huff, I followed. I scanned the horizon, searching for a hiding spot in the event I needed one. With no trees or any large foliage, I would be stuck.

We approached the stone structure. Large columns rose to the unfinished roof. Stone stairs led up to the inside. I stared up at it. The light inside bobbled around. Esme pointed toward the entrance.

"No!" I whispered.

Esme pointed again.

"I cannot go in there. I have no idea who is inside!"

Esme grasped hold of my arm and tugged. My feet slid unwillingly toward the stone stairs.

I wrenched my arm free. "All right, all right," I acquiesced. "I shall explore."

I crept up the stairs and slinked around one of the large columns, keeping my body pressed against it. Voices wafted from inside.

I inched away from the stone pillar toward the opening. A man's voice sounded then a woman's. I strained to hear them. I pressed my back against the stone wall and turned my head toward the doorway.

"... could be nothing!" the man's voice claimed.

"She knows something," the woman's voice hissed.

"You don't know that," the man responded.

"She was quite aggressive over the matter!"

"Why would she be involved? What would she gain from it?"

I struggled to understand the conversation as it continued. Who were they referring to and what was the matter at hand, I wondered?

"I do not know," the woman's voice whispered. "Though I am concerned. This comes out of the blue! It cannot be coincidence."

"No one knows but me, correct?"

"Yes," she said with a sigh. "Yes, but... I don't know. Perhaps someone else was there. Perhaps they saw something. Perhaps *she* was there!"

"Why would she be there?"

"How else would she know?"

"What did she say to you again?"

There was a pause then the woman answered, "She said Mother told her I was in danger." My eyes widened. Grace was the woman inside the folly! And I was the subject of their clandestine conversation.

"And you explained Mother passed away six months ago." Mother, I questioned? This man must be Grace's brother. The priest at St. Agnes mentioned him when I inquired after her.

"Yes."

"And she told you..."

"She said she knew that. Mother had contacted her in the afterlife to give her the message."

"You'd think she could come up with something better than that weak story," the man groused.

I puckered my lips, a frown forming. Weak story, I ruminated? I had traveled here especially to warn Grace, and they thought I was lying! With a shake of my head, I dismissed it as best I could in order to concentrate on the rest of the conversation. I'd certainly dealt with disbelievers in the past.

"Where else could she have gotten the information?"

LETTER TO A DUCHESS

"You cannot believe she got it from Mother, can you, Grace?"

"No, of course not, but she has information from somewhere! What she said has to be a threat. It has to be! Why else come and warn me of danger? She knows something."

There was silence for a moment. Then Grace's brother spoke again. "Try to avoid her as best you can and her ladies' maid, too. Perhaps they'll leave soon. I'll try to find out what I can on the sly."

"All right," Grace said.

"Now, we'd better get back," he answered.

My eyes widened as I heard the shuffling of footsteps. I hurried to the stone column and skirted behind it. Grace hastened from the folly first followed a few moments later by her brother.

My eyes followed their hurried pace across the field and to the house, their lantern lights bobbing around in the darkness. When they were a safe distance away, I began picking my way across the open space. With no lantern and little moonlight, it was slow-going as I feared turning an ankle on a divot in the grass. I had no ghostly companion to guide me, either. Esme had disappeared at some point before her children emerged from within the folly.

As I made my painfully slow crossing, shivering from the cold now, I pondered the conversation. The pair clearly referred to me. And they were obviously upset by what I'd told Grace. Neither seemed to believe I'd actually spoken with her deceased mother. That snippet did not surprise me. Plenty of people discounted my ability or disbelieved it entirely. The number of charlatans who claimed to be able to summon and speak to the dead did not aid me in this matter.

My mind continued to tumble through the conversation. Something about it struck me as odd, though. Something outside their inability to believe I'd spoken with their mother. Grace took it as a threat. Of what, I wondered? "She knows something," her voice echoed in my head.

What would I know that would be perceived as a threat to Grace? My mind centered on one thing. Was she involved in Gerard Boyle's demise? Had Robert been correct? Did Grace think I knew something about her involvement?

"Perhaps she was there," I whispered into the dark. The phrase stopped me in my tracks. The "she" was me. Where had she conjectured I had been? On the docks the night of the murder?

A sinking feeling grew in the pit of my stomach as I pushed forward toward the house. Was Grace the murderer?

The thought kept me from sleep for the rest of the night, despite my best efforts. I laid in bed, appreciating the warmth, but unable to fall asleep. When the sun crept over the horizon, I was already up and pacing the floor. I called for Sinclair early to dress for the day.

As we worked through our morning preparations, Sinclair told me she had very little extra information to share.

"It seems they are avoiding me, Your Grace," Sinclair said.

"I am not surprised," I answered. I confided to her about my midnight visit and subsequent rambling about the property.

Her eyes shot wide at the story. "Your Grace!" she exclaimed before leaning closer to whisper, "do you think she's the murderer?"

"I am not certain, but it seems to be a plausible scenario."

Sinclair's eyes narrowed. "What is it?" I questioned.

"Could it be her brother?"

"Oh!" I said, my eyebrows raising high. "Oh, perhaps!" My eyebrows scrunched down as I ran through this possibility. "In that case, is Grace part of the danger or in danger from her brother?"

Sinclair puckered her lips as she pondered it.

We came to no conclusions by the time I was presentable. "In any event, Sinclair, please be careful!" I implored, laying my hand on her forearm. "There is still much we do not understand about this situation."

She nodded. "I will, Your Grace. I will not go around them until we've solved this."

"Good," I said with a nod.

She departed and I followed her into the hallway. My stomach disagreed with any notion of eating. Instead, I hoped to find Robert and discuss the matter with him. First, though, I made a stop in the nursery to visit with Sam and the other boys. Both of them seemed pleased to have a small playmate and gushed over the games they'd engaged in with him. I found myself wondering what Sam may be like at that age. And whom he may play with.

I spent three-quarters of an hour there before I set out again to find Robert. At this time of the morning, he was likely enjoying a morning ride. I would try outside and see if I spotted him while I took a morning walk.

On my way to the front door, I came across Edwin.

"Good morning, Lenora," he said with a sigh.

"Good morning, though from your tone, I question the sentiment."

"My head is splitting. And I must confess, life is terribly boring without alcohol."

I bit my lower lip to suppress a giggle, certain it would do more harm than good.

"Oh, you find that funny, do you?" he inquired. Apparently, I'd not hidden my amused expression well enough.

"A little," I admitted. "Though I am sorry about your headache."

"I've had more headaches without the drink than with it," he lamented as we traversed the halls.

"Perhaps some breakfast," I suggested.

"May I escort you, or have you eaten?"

"I have not, though I am uncertain my stomach will bear it. It was rather upset this morning, though it has improved now."

"Perhaps you should take your own advice," he offered with a smile.

"Yes," I said, sliding my hand into the crook of his arm. "We shall muddle through the meal together."

"What has your stomach upset?" he asked as he led me to the dining room, where a buffet breakfast still awaited us.

"I had a difficult night," I answered. "If you'll accompany me on a morning walk, I shall expound." I whispered the last statement so as not to be overheard by the butler, who still manned the dining room in the event we should require something.

We made light conversation over our small meal before departing into the crisp sunshine beyond the house's walls.

"You were confessing your difficult night to me," Edwin said as we meandered along a path leading from the house.

"Yes," I answered, "and I am wondering if our trip here has not been a waste as you may feel it was."

"I didn't say that…" Edwin began when I waved my hand to stop him.

"I realize you are anxious about the murder accusation, and I understand that you believe this trip out of our way not only distracts us from our focus but also robs us of time to solve the crime."

Edwin lifted his eyebrows and pursed his lips as he shrugged. "Well…" he began again.

"I am beginning to suspect it is not, though!"

"What makes you say that?"

I took a deep breath before I launched into my explanation. "Last night, Esme Murdoch awakened me from my sleep and took me on a wild fugue across the property ending at the folly."

Edwin screwed up his face as I spoke. "You went wandering around the property in the wee hours?"

"I hadn't much choice," I responded.

"No wonder Robert worries over you."

I arched an eyebrow at him. "At least she only took me to a folly, not a brothel."

"Touché, though I contend you were perfectly capable of getting to a brothel on your own since you did so on several occasions before Tilly…" He paused for a moment before saying, "Continue."

"When I made it to the folly, I overheard two individuals discussing something. A man and a woman."

"Ooooooh," Edwin exclaimed. "A romantic liaison?"

"No," I said with a roll of my eyes at him. "A brother and sister, actually. And that brother and sister pair turned out to be Grace and her brother."

"Grace as in the woman you sought out here?"

"Yes. They were in a discussion about me."

"And your message?'

"Correct," I answered. "It seemed they found my tale of speaking with their deceased mother questionable."

"Are you very surprised?"

"No," I admitted. "That is not what stuck out to me. The pair seemed to think my message was some sort of veiled threat against them. They continued to ponder what I might know and if I was 'there.'" I framed the last word of my statement in quotes.

"There? Where?"

"I do not know," I said. "They were not clear. But it seemed a very major concern that I might be aware of something and using my knowledge to threaten them."

Edwin's features pinched in thought.

"There's more."

Edwin cocked his head and raised his eyebrows, prompting me to continue. "Do you recall our discussion after I visited Lord Pennington's bedside following his stabbing?"

"Yes," Edwin said.

"Mr. Boyle murmured something that I did not quite catch. I thought he said 'her,' and both you and Robert conjectured it was 'Fer' for Fergus."

Edwin nodded.

"Well, the night before last, I had a dream in which I followed Grace through the halls with Esme. Esme continued to give me the warning about danger. Then she added death. When I questioned her as to her meaning, she said one word. 'Her.'"

Edwin sucked in a breath and ceased walking. He faced me, his face pinched.

"Which made me question whether or not Grace was the one in danger. Or the one causing the danger."

His eyes widened at the veiled accusation. "Are you saying…"

"That Grace is the murderer, yes."

Edwin grasped my arm, threading it through his and pulling me along.

I continued, "It appears Grace was in Glasgow when Mr. Boyle was stabbed. The only issue with this is we do not believe she was there when Lord Pennington was injured."

"We also have no confirmation the incidents were related."

"You are correct. And the one that matters most is Mr. Boyle's murder since you stand accused of that."

Edwin nodded in agreement. "Plus, Penny can identify his attacker once he is awake."

"We must keep an eye on Grace. It may prove difficult to confirm her as the culprit."

"But we must. She is nervous now. Perhaps she will slip up and give away some detail."

"Yes. We shall hope for that."

"Or..."

"What?" I asked when his voice trailed off.

He shook his head. "Never mind," he said, flitting his hand in the air.

I side-eyed him, searching for more of a response but received none. After a few moments, I said, "What were you going to propose?"

"Oh, nothing," Edwin answered.

I narrowed my eyes at him. It was obvious he was lying, but I could not drag the truth from him. "Do not do anything foolish, Edwin," I cautioned.

"Me?" he said with mock innocence. "When have you ever known me to do something foolish."

I offered a wry glance and shook my head at him. We continued our walk, finding Robert along the way. He dismounted from his horse and led it along as we talked. The three of us discussed what I'd just gone over with Edwin. Robert agreed we should proceed with caution but continue to monitor Grace for any sign that she could be our murderer.

Unfortunately, most of my day was spent ambling around aimlessly. It appeared I would have no ability to monitor Grace. I caught sight of her once in the hallway and she darted to another room and disappeared before I could speak with her again. Sinclair expressed a similar sentiment. It seemed Grace was determined to avoid us.

I lamented as much to Sinclair as I dressed for dinner. Her avoidance only made me more suspicious of her. I hoped to find something in the way of evidence soon before we had worn out our welcome with the MacMahons.

As the day slipped away and, with Sinclair's help, I undressed and readied for bed, I began to worry we would not find anything to exonerate Edwin. Though the trip had not been a waste, it had not aided us in our quest either.

I found myself spending another night staring at the ceiling, a pounding in my head preventing me from falling asleep. Eventually, I drifted off as one final thought pinged in my mind. We had come so far, but would likely fall short.

A haze still clouded my mind as I slowly awakened. With a deep inhale, I glanced around, confused. Darkness still enveloped me. But my covers were gone. With bleary eyes, I searched for them.

My gaze landed on the transgressor. Esme Murdoch stood at the foot of my bed, my bed coverings clutched in her hands.

CHAPTER 29

"Not again," I groaned. I swung my legs over the side of my bed and began to don my slippers and dressing gown before she even spoke.

"Danger," she hissed at me.

"Yes, yes, I know," I said with a sigh, sounding more flippant than I intended. I stood and faced her. "Where are we off to tonight?"

She motioned for me to follow her. Her lack of other communicative skills frustrated me, but I did as she commanded and wandered out of my room and down the hall to the front door. My mind bemoaned another trip outside, but I followed her as she floated out into the cold night air.

I had not noticed the time, but I surmised it must have been closer to midnight again. I wondered if she was leading me to another clandestine meeting between brother and sister. I hoped it would bring me further clarity that could be used to confront Grace and settle this matter in Edwin's favor.

Edwin, my mind dwelled on him for some reason. I could

not cease picturing his face. Worry seemed to cloud my mind. I glanced ahead of me, finding Esme stopped and beckoning. I shook the haze from my mind and continued toward her. It appeared she led me on a similar path again this evening.

At least the moonlight this evening was brighter, unencumbered by any clouds. It bathed the field in an eerie white light. I squinted into the distance at the folly, assuming Esme would lead me to it. No light bobbled inside this time, though a small glint of light shined from within. At this distance, I thought perhaps it was moonlight peeking through the broken roof. Perhaps we had a different destination tonight.

We continued across the field and Esme positioned herself at the foot of the stairs to the folly again. I cocked my head, unsure as to why she'd brought me.

She pointed inside, her warped finger creating a crooked line toward the entrance. "Danger," she growled.

I scanned the inside, not spotting anything of note. I inched up the stone steps and peered inside. The shard of light flickered but failed to illuminate much. A groan sounded from within, echoing off the stone walls.

My features pinched and I crept closer. As I approached the door, I spotted a figure lying on the floor and a lantern in a similar state. On its side, its weak light flickered as it rolled from side to side.

As the lantern rolled closer to the figure on the floor, I caught sight of his face. "Edwin!" I exclaimed as I rushed to his side. I dropped to my knees, my eyes wide.

"Lenora," he gasped out along with a choking cough.

I righted the lantern and raised it overhead to assess the situation. My jaw quivered and my heart seized as I noted the source of Edwin's distress.

Dark liquid covered his waistcoat. His fingers pressed against his stomach, slick with red blood. He groaned again.

I set the lantern aside and turned my attention to assessing Edwin's wound. It appeared deep.

"Lenora," he choked out again. Edwin winced in pain as he spoke.

"Shh," I hushed him. "Do not try to speak."

I lifted his hands away from his abdomen. He grunted as I gently pulled at the slice in his waistcoat. His hands trembled, and his breathing became ragged.

I pressed his hands against his body.

"Edwin," I said. I snapped my eyes toward his face. He squeezed his eyes shut, his jaw tense as though he was grinding his teeth.

"Edwin!" I called to him again. I leaned forward, hovering over his face, and lightly tapped his cheeks with my hand. "Edwin!"

His eyes fluttered open and he stared at the ceiling before he shifted his gaze to me. He shivered and whimpered in pain. I pulled my dressing gown from around me and covered him with it.

"Listen to me," I said as I hurried to cover him. "I must go for help. I cannot move you alone, and I doubt you can stand."

"No," he sniveled. "Please do not leave me."

"Edwin, I must," I said as I leaned over him again. "Listen to me. Keep as much pressure on your wound as you can. Do you understand?"

He shuddered again and offered a tentative nod as a tear slid from his eye. A sob escaped him. "I will not be long, I promise." He sniffled as he pursed his lips before blowing out a shaky breath.

I grasped his cheeks between my thumb and fingers and

forced him to focus on me. "Do not die on me, Edwin," I said. "I do not want you following me about as a ghost."

The last statement earned a weak chuckle. I stood and grasped the lantern and tore out of the folly. I ran as fast as I could across the field, holding the lantern in front of me. The icy air cut through my thin nightclothes. A few tears slid down my cheeks as I worried for Edwin.

I reached the house and flung open the front door, leaving it standing open behind me as I raced up the stairs. I wound through the halls and pushed through the door into Robert's bedroom.

I nearly threw myself on him, shaking him in a frenzy to awaken him.

"Robert! Robert!" I cried as I shook him hard enough to jiggle the bed.

"Lenora?" he questioned as he awoke.

"Yes, come quickly. It is Edwin."

"Edwin? What? What is going on, Lenora?" Robert inquired, slow to rise and still confused by the mantel of his sleep.

I tugged on his arm. "There is no time for questions, Robert. A doctor must be fetched immediately. Wake Lord MacMahon, call for the doctor, and meet me at the folly."

"Lenora!" he shouted after me as I fled from the room, still only in my nightgown.

With no time to lose, I retraced my steps. I arrived back at the folly gasping for breath. Despite the cold, beads of perspiration had formed on my forehead. I wiped at them with the back of my hand as I approached the body on the floor.

Edwin lay unmoving. His eyes were closed and his head slumped to the side. His skin, pale and cold, I feared the worst. I laid my head against his chest and felt a slight rise in his chest. A faint thumping met my ears, giving me further proof that he remained alive. For now, I reminded myself.

I pulled back my dressing gown and eased away Edwin's limp hands. Blood still oozed from his wound. I balled my dressing gown and pressed down hard. A moan escaped from Edwin's lips. He shuddered to consciousness.

"It's all right, Edwin. I've sent for help. Try to lie still."

Moments later, I heard shouts from outside. I dared not lose my concentration, so I continued to keep firm pressure and monitor Edwin's life signs as best I could. Robert, Lord MacMahon, and a footman joined us shortly after.

"My God!" Robert exclaimed, bending to one knee next to me. His face blanched at the sight of his weakened and injured brother. My dressing gown sopped with blood.

"He has lost a fair amount of blood, but he is alive," I said.

Robert glanced at Edwin's pale face, then at me, then down to my hands as they worked to manage the bleeding.

"It appears to be a knife wound," I reported.

"Should we move him?" Lord MacMahon questioned.

"It would likely be for the best to allow the doctor to work; however, we must be careful to keep pressure on his wound."

"Perhaps between the two of us…" Lord MacMahon proposed to Robert.

I shook my head. "We must carry him flat. Try to keep him as still as possible so I can maintain the pressure on him to stave off more bleeding. We also do not wish to have the wound jostled and torn open further."

Lord MacMahon nodded, and for the first time, I noticed his own skin was pale and clammy. "Robert, you and I shall lift his shoulders and Tom, you carry his feet. Lenora, can you maintain the pressure if you walk beside him?"

"Yes," I said and readied myself to stand.

With some effort, a limp Edwin was lifted into the air. He

cried out as they bobbled him around before finding a suitable position for the trek across the property. Robert's eyes shot wide at the sound.

"He is likely in pain. The faster we move him, the better," I advised.

"How could this happen?" I heard Robert mutter as we made the journey across the field. The manor home loomed in the distance. I checked often to keep track of the steady progress and to keep my mind from wandering to the more grim details of our situation.

At long last, we made it, carrying Edwin up the stairs and settling him in bed. Several servants milled around, waiting for instructions.

"I shall need a clean sheet or towel to continue to keep pressure," I requested. "The doctor will likely also request water and more sheets or towels."

Lord MacMahon acknowledged my request, barking orders for the staff to disperse and attend to the matters. Within moments, a maid shoved a white linen toward me and, carefully, I switched it with my dressing gown, which she relieved me of.

Sinclair appeared moments later and assisted me in nursing Edwin until the doctor could arrive. When he did, I offered a report as he assessed the wound.

A sigh of relief escaped both mine and Robert's lips as the doctor reported, "Nothing vital hit, it appears. Though it will take a bit of work to repair. We still face the risk of blood loss and infection. It seems, Your Grace, you've done an admirable job of ensuring he did not bleed to death."

I offered a weak smile. "Now, if you'll all clear the room so I can work," he said as his young assistant bustled about the room preparing things.

"Lenora," Edwin groaned before we could depart.

"Shh, quiet now, young man," the doctor said, tapping him on the shoulder. "Do not try to speak."

"Lenora," he repeated, his voice hoarse and weak. He flailed an arm toward me.

I hurried back toward the bed and clasped his hand in mine. "I am here, Edwin. But you must rest. The doctor will repair the damage. Then we can speak." I stroked his forehead with my other hand in an attempt to soothe him.

He thrashed his head on the pillow. "No!" His breathing came in gasps and turned ragged as he struggled to impart whatever it was he felt necessary to say.

"Calm down, son," the doctor advised. "Lie still."

"Edwin," I advised, "you must rest now. It's all right."

"Grace," he choked out.

Robert joined me at Edwin's bedside, peering at him over my shoulder. "Grace?" he questioned. "Did she do this? Did she stab you?"

"No," Edwin groaned. "No. Danger."

I nearly groaned at the vague reference. "Edwin, are you trying to say Grace is in danger?"

A slight nod. "Yes," he breathed.

"All right. We shall search for her. Now lie back and allow the doctor to take care of you." I squeezed his hand, and he exhaled a sigh, seemingly in relief as he settled back into his pillow.

The doctor gave us a nod and waited for us to depart. As we stepped into the hall, I went directly to Sinclair.

"Have you seen Grace?"

"Lenora!" Robert interrupted.

"You heard Edwin," I said. "Grace is in danger! Likely from whoever did this to Edwin! It is imperative that we find her."

"I shall ask the housekeeper to check her room," the

butler offered, spinning on his heel and striding down the hall.

"Lenora, you cannot go running about the property dressed like that!" Robert groused.

"Well..." I began. For the first time, I glanced down at my clothing. I realized I wore only my nightgown at this point but had not realized how disheveled it had become. Red blood stains were smeared on the front. Rust-colored blood also stained my hands.

"Oh, dear," I murmured. "I do rather look a fright."

"Come, Your Grace," Sinclair offered, "and we shall get you more presentable before you search for Grace. With any luck, she is here in the house. I shall bring her back straight away, Your Grace." She directed the last statement to Robert.

Sinclair wrapped her arms around my shoulders and lead me to my room.

"I'm afraid both the nightgown and dressing gown are soiled beyond repair, Sinclair," I admitted as we worked feverishly to dress me.

"Do not fret over it," Sinclair replied.

"I am not. Though what I wish to say is that you should not either. Do not worry about cleaning them."

She offered a nod. "Shall I fix your hair?"

I glanced down at my hair cascading over my shoulder. It, too, had blood caked on it.

"No. There isn't time."

"At least allow me to braid it. I promise to be quick."

I agreed with a nod and she fashioned a long braid for me. I returned to Robert to inquire after Grace's whereabouts.

"Has she been located?"

"No. She had not been in her room. Her roommate said she must have slipped out in the middle of the night. Her brother is missing, too."

"What places have been checked? Has a search party been formed?"

"Yes," Robert answered. "The staff is searching for her now."

I nodded. "Come along, we can join them."

"Lenora, you have had entirely enough excitement for the night," Robert argued. "You should be in bed with a toddy. Though I will take awaiting news with me in the sitting room with brandy as a compromise."

"Robert!" I exclaimed but was waved into silence.

"I will not have you wandering about the property while a madman is on the loose! And I would very much like your support while we await news of Edwin."

I allowed myself to be led to the sitting room. Robert poured me a brandy and I sipped at it. A sigh escaped me as I pondered how helpless I was at the moment. Grace was in danger and here I sat with a nightcap awaiting word.

I leapt to my feet and paced the floor. After a few moments, I flung my hands to the sides. "I cannot sit here and do nothing!"

"Perhaps your book, dear," Robert suggested.

With a huff, I agreed. "I shall fetch it."

"I will call for Sinclair."

"No, no, the staff has enough right now. I am capable of fetching my own book."

I stepped from the room and climbed the stairs, navigating the halls to my room. I grasped hold of my book and departed.

As I stepped into the hallway, I nearly ran into someone. I stumbled back a step before I realized it was not a living soul I'd almost collided with.

CHAPTER 30

"*E*sme!" I gasped.

She clamped onto my forearm with icy fingers. "Death!" she hissed. Tears filled her eyes and fear painted her features.

My heart skipped a beat, and for a moment, I wondered if she meant Edwin. I swallowed hard, searching the corridor, expecting to see a ghostly form of Edwin, bloodied and pale, wandering toward me.

In the moment it took me to recover, she had already flitted down the hall. She beckoned for me to follow. "Hurry!" she shouted. "Death!"

The urgency in her voice prompted me to obey her. My book clattered to the floor as I picked up my skirts and sprinted toward her. She disappeared around the corner. "Esme, wait!" I gasped out.

I reached another branching in the hallways and desperately searched for her. I spotted her disappearing into a stairway and hurried to catch up. My feet pounded down the stairs, and I threw myself through the door at the bottom.

Chilly night air smacked me in the face as I tumbled onto

the grass outside. I regained my footing and scanned the horizon for Esme.

She flitted across the field in the opposite direction of the folly. With a deep inhale, I plowed forward, pushing my body to run as fast as it could to catch up.

Esme threaded along a path through the woods. The terrain here was rougher and I struggled to maintain her in my sights. After a while, she disappeared, able to move much faster than I could. I continued along the path, hoping I moved in the correct direction. When I emerged from the thick trees, I found the path led to a small body of water. I had seen it in the distance when riding with Robert.

A boathouse stood nearby. Esme hovered outside of it, scanning the tree line. When she spotted me, she waved frantically.

Light glowed from inside the small structure. I hurried toward it. Blood rushed in my ears, and my stomach turned over. My legs felt wobbly as I worried about what I might find.

I approached the dirty window, ducking to the side in an attempt to keep out of sight. Voices carried from within. I risked a glance through the filmy glass.

I spotted Grace, cowering behind the form of her brother.

"Please," he said to someone I could not quite see. I shifted to the opposite side of the window and searched the inside of the small boathouse. My eyes caught movement and I pressed my hand against my mouth to suppress a gasp. A woman in a dirty pink coat waved a knife at Grace and Gavin. My stomach turned as I realized this was likely the instrument that stabbed Edwin. I also recognized that she had left a bloody trail in her wake. Pink-coat lady, whoever she was, had likely stabbed Mr. Boyle, Lord Pennington and now poor Edwin. At least two of her three victims should survive.

"We won't bring you any trouble," Gavin said.

"You've already brought enough!" the woman, whose face I could not see, shouted. "You've been spreading stories."

"I have not been! I have not spoken of that night except to Gavin," Grace whimpered.

"Then what's brought the fair Duchess and her contingent here? She was poking around in Glasgow, too. All over that troublesome brother-in-law."

"I told her nothing," Grace assured her.

"Not likely," the woman shot back. "What prompted her trip here to begin with?"

"Her husband is friends with Lord MacMahon. They are school chums," Grace explained.

"Ha! Too large of a coincidence for my taste!"

I narrowed my eyes. The woman in the coat moved oddly. And something about her plagued me. Something was familiar.

"She said she had spoken to my dead mother," Grace confessed. "I did not believe her. I said nothing to her!"

"Please," Gavin entreated again. "Please, think of your baby."

Baby, my mind screamed. Yes, that was it. I shifted again for a different view and could now see the bump in her belly. She was pregnant! I wondered who the father may be. Could it have been the late Mr. Boyle's child? I thought him unmarried, but that did not mean he did not father a child.

"I've done nothing but think of this baby since I found out!" the woman screamed. Her voice was bordering on hysterical. "First, Gerry wanted no parts of me. And, well, you know how that turned out. And he bloody well should have stepped up. It's his bleeding baby!

"And that la-di-da brother of his turned me out, too. Would like to see his own flesh and blood raised on the streets!"

Her ringlets bounced as she continued to strafe with the knife wildly during her soliloquy. That hair, that voice. My eyes widened. Millicent! My jaw hung open. The woman standing inside threatening two lives was mousy Millicent from St. Mary's!

"And now I've got no choice," she continued, her voice breaking.

"Yes, you do," Gavin responded. "I will marry you. I'll say the baby is mine. We can raise it together. You see?"

"But your nosy little sister knows too much," Millicent said, jabbing the knife toward them. "She saw me with Gerry that night. She saw what happened. She can ruin me!"

"I would never say anything!"

"Grace understands," Gavin said soothingly. "You were upset. Shocked. You reacted badly. But she would never tell."

So, Millicent had killed Gerard Boyle in a fit of rage, likely over his denial of fathering her child. She'd likely then gone to his brother, hoping for a handout, and, having been refused, unleashed her fury on him. Why had she attacked Edwin, I wondered?

Movement drew my eye again. Millicent, after having taken a moment to consider her prospects, was apparently unhappy with the deal offered by Gavin. "Too much risk," she spat at him. "I think I'll just finish you both off and disappear."

I wondered if Gavin possessed the ability to fight her off. It did not appear he had a weapon. I could not leave it to chance.

I scurried to the door and prayed it did not creak when I inched it open. With her back toward it, Millicent did not notice me slip inside. I held a finger to my lips in silent warning to the others who could see me.

Oars were propped nearby. I grasped hold of one as Millicent ordered Gavin away from his sister.

"Millicent, wait," he pleaded. She made a quick motion with the knife, drawing blood from a slice in his forearm.

He winced as he clutched at his arm. "Now away, I said," she ordered again.

I lifted the oar, cursing its weight. With as much strength as I could muster, I swung at Millicent. A crack sounded as the oar smacked against her head. I winced as she slumped, her knife clattering across the boards of the boathouse floor.

Gavin lurched forward and caught her before she smacked against the ground. Grace snatched up the knife, her hands shaking.

"Is she breathing?" I questioned, dropping the oar. It rattled against the floorboards, causing Grace to jump.

"Yes," Gavin answered.

"Thank God. Quickly, the doctor is at the house. He should assess her, particularly with the baby."

Gavin nodded, but Grace did not move. Her eyes clouded with tears and she swallowed hard. The poor girl must be in shock, I assumed. If Gavin carried Millicent, I would help Grace back to the house. She needed a warm drink and a chair. I suddenly understood Robert's insistence on shoving toddies at me with every bad turn.

"Come along, Grace," I said, standing and reaching for her.

"Get back," she shouted, her voice laced with panic. She wielded the knife at me. I stumbled back a step.

"Grace!" Gavin shouted.

"No, Gavin. She came here. How did she know? She is in league with her!"

"I am not!" I cried.

"Then how did you know we were here?"

"I came here to give you a message from your mother. After I found Edwin, he said you were in danger. It is your mother who led me to you!"

She shook her head, fear in her eyes.

"Please," I begged, "try to understand. I have an odd ability. Esme has been appearing to me for quite some time. As I was unraveling Mr. Boyle's murder, which I assumed was unrelated, she begged me to find you. I did not realize the two were so intertwined. And I certainly did not know Millicent was the murderer."

Grace's hands shook as she waved the knife again. "How did you know her name?"

"We are acquainted," I answered. "We both attended St. Mary's School for Girls."

Grace shook her head. "No. No, you are a duchess. You…"

"I was an orphan before I married His Grace. Grace, please! I mean you no harm!"

"You sent your brother-in-law after me. You are all in league!"

My forehead wrinkled as I tried to piece her accusation together. Realization dawned on me. In a misguided attempt to corner Grace, Edwin must have attempted to charm her during a midnight meeting.

"He was waiting for me at the place Millicent summoned me to!" she continued.

"Lord Edwin has no dealings with Millicent," I answered. "He is only attempting to prove his own innocence in Mr. Boyle's death. And, as a result, he, too, has been stabbed!"

Grace's face blanched and I added, "Yes, he is being tended to by the doctor now. He very nearly died as a result of her attack."

Gavin approached Grace. Her brow furrowed as she processed the events. "Grace," he cooed, "give me the knife."

She relinquished it without much trouble. I saw her begin to sway and rushed to her side. "It's all right, Grace. It is all over now."

I nodded to Gavin, signaling him to retrieve Millicent's

limp form from the floor and, together, we proceeded back to the manor.

"Take her through the front door," I instructed.

"But…" Gavin began.

"I shall explain it to Lord MacMahon myself," I assured him.

"Yes, Your Grace," he said.

I led him to the door and shoved it open. He squeezed through with Millicent, still limp, in his arms. I followed, keeping my arms around Grace in the event she was still unsteady.

A contingent of men stood in a circle inside the foyer. Robert was among them. His eyes widened as we entered.

"Lenora! Thank God! I have been worried sick! We were just arranging another search party. Where have you been? What the devil is going on here?" His eyes scanned my curious company, falling to Millicent.

"Lay her in the sitting room," I instructed Gavin before turning to Robert to explain. I addressed the group at large. "I beg your pardon for the disruption to your household. As I retrieved my book, I…" I paused, uncertain I wanted to expose my secret to everyone. "That is to say, I suddenly realized where Grace may be. With no time to waste, I hurried to the location and found them before tragedy struck.

"The limp woman Gavin carried is Millicent Brown. I believe you will find she is the one who murdered Mr. Boyle, stabbed Lord Pennington, and Edwin. And she would have done the same to Grace and Gavin had I not struck her when I did. She is alive, but I would prefer the doctor to see her when he finishes with Edwin. As you may have noticed, she is with child."

"My God," Robert muttered. "You must sit down. Perhaps the doctor should also see you." He guided me into the sitting room. Lord MacMahon disbanded the group of servants and followed us.

"Everything she said is the truth, m'lord," Gavin confirmed. "Grace witnessed Millicent stab Mr. Boyle. Millicent threatened her and then attempted to kill us tonight. She was convinced Grace had confided something to Her Grace."

Lord MacMahon's face betrayed his confusion. "I spoke with Grace earlier this week. I did not wish to say this in front of the crowd, but I suffer from the odd ability of being able to communicate with those deceased. Her mother sought me out. I am afraid it was the reason for our visit. She wished me to warn Grace of the danger she was in."

Robert slid his arm around my shoulders in a show of support. Lord MacMahon's eyes were wide, and he glanced between us. Robert offered a slight nod.

"It is how I learned what happened to Annie."

"My goodness," Lord MacMahon exclaimed. "How extraordinary!"

His eyes fell to Millicent. "And our Millicent…"

"Is not quite so innocent," Gavin said.

"Your Millicent?" I questioned.

"Yes. Millicent was within our employ until a few months ago. When we found out about her circumstances, Lady MacMahon dismissed her. Had I realized how much trouble it would have caused, I would have offered her something. How terrible she has turned into this." He turned to Grace, who hovered in the doorway.

"Grace, are you quite all right? Please, sit down."

"Yes, m'lord," she said meekly.

"Perhaps a brandy," I suggested.

"Quite right, Lenora," Robert said. He strode across the room to pour it despite Grace's objections.

I settled her in a chair and Robert handed her the drink.

She sipped at it, fidgeting in her seat as though unsure of what to do next.

The doctor appeared in the doorway and poor Grace leapt from her seat, nearly spilling what remained of her brandy.

"Oh, doctor," Lord MacMahon said, "what news of Lord Edwin?"

"Lord Edwin is resting comfortably. I was able to repair the damage. He must be careful not to overexert himself, but he should heal nicely."

"What of travel?" Robert inquired.

"No need to ask after that, Robby," Lord MacMahon said. "He shall stay with us until such time as he is well enough to travel."

"I'd estimate he would be able to tolerate a trip in a carriage in a matter of a few days," the doctor answered. "And Tom here tells me I have another patient?"

As he asked, Millicent groaned and thrashed her head. "Yes," Lord MacMahon answered, gesturing toward Millicent. "This woman was hit on the head and lost consciousness. As you can see, she is in the family way." His face reddened with the last statement.

"Hit on the head?" the doctor inquired as he bent over her to check a few vitals.

"Yes," Lord MacMahon explained. "Millicent is... well, that is to say, she is the source of Lord Edwin's wound, along with several others, including a death, I'm afraid. She threatened Grace and Gavin. Her Grace... well..." He stammered through the last bit as though embarrassed to out my deeds.

I chimed in, "I hit her with an oar, I'm sorry to say. I hadn't much choice. I do hope she is all right. I did not mean to harm her, only stun her so we could escape unharmed."

"You did what you needed to do, Lenora," Robert said,

snaking his arm around my shoulders again and pulling me close to him.

"Indeed," Lord MacMahon agreed.

"Yes," Gavin said, standing and approaching me. He gave a bow and said, "Your Grace, my sister and I owe you a deep debt of gratitude."

"No thanks are necessary. I am pleased I could help. And I, again, apologize for any confusion." I directed my last statement to Grace.

"No, no," Gavin said, "there is no need for you to apologize, Your Grace."

Grace joined us. "Yes, and thank you for passing along the message from..." She paused and her eyes slid from side to side. "My mother," she said in a whisper.

I offered a nod and a tight-lipped smile.

"Well," the doctor said from across the room. "She will be all right."

"And the baby?" I inquired.

"I would need to perform a more thorough exam, but I suspect both baby and mother were not harmed."

"Please, doctor, if you wouldn't mind. We can move her upstairs once she awakens."

Millicent again thrashed her head and groaned. Her eyes fluttered open and she glanced around the room, disoriented. Her eyes settled on me, and her face turned into a grotesque frown. "You!" she spat.

CHAPTER 31

Robert pulled me tighter to him and turned me slightly away. "Do not speak to my wife!" he shouted at her.

I pushed back so I could face her. "It is all right," I said. "Millicent and I are acquainted."

Robert's brow furrowed in a silent question. "From St. Mary's," I explained.

Understanding dawned on him as I broke from his grasp. "Hello, Millicent," I greeted her. "I wish we could have met under better circumstances but…"

"The circumstances seem quite a bit of all right from your end," she said with a sneer. "How did you end up so lucky, especially given your freakishness."

"How dare you, woman!" Robert shouted, shoving me behind him.

"I would not speak of freakishness, Millicent," Lord MacMahon cautioned. "You are in quite a heap of trouble."

Her eyes grew wide, and she attempted to leap from the couch and run.

"No, no," Lord MacMahon said, grasping hold of her

shoulder. "The police have already been summoned. And you should allow the doctor to examine you in the meantime."

Millicent collapsed back onto the couch. The jig was up. And she realized it. Her gaze sank to her thighs, then rose to her belly. She grasped hold of it and wept.

Despite all the trouble she caused, the scene was quite pitiful and broke my heart. I removed myself from Robert's embrace and went to her side. I eased onto the couch and put my arm around her shoulders.

"Oh, get away," she sobbed.

I tightened my grip on her and she relented, sagging against me and shaking in my arms as she continued to be wracked with sobs.

"What will happen to my baby?" she choked out.

"We shall find a solution," I promised.

The police arrived, filing into the sitting room after the butler. Lord MacMahon explained the situation to them. Before they took Millicent into custody, the doctor insisted on a full examination. One officer escorted Millicent and the doctor to a private area while the other stayed behind to take our statements.

Given the information, they would contact the Glasgow police about the developments. With the situation in hand, I retreated to Edwin's bedroom to check on his condition. Robert pulled a chair over for me, and I sank into it, suddenly feeling exhaustion settle over me. I reached out and grasped Edwin's hand. A large bandage covered his abdomen. I stared at it for a moment, realizing how close he'd come to death.

He stirred after about thirty minutes. His lips formed a grimace, and he winced as he fidgeted. After a moment, his eyes fluttered open and he stared at the ceiling.

"Edwin," I said, leaning over him.

Robert, who had fallen asleep in an armchair across the room, stirred. "What is it?"

"Edwin is awake," I answered. He joined me at Edwin's bedside.

"Edwin," I said again, stroking his forehead. "How are you feeling?"

I received no response for a full moment before he moaned, "Awful."

"Yes, I imagine you are in a fair amount of pain. The doctor has left some medication. Would you like to take some now?"

He blew out a long, ragged breath and gave me a nod. "Robert, can you fetch some tea and perhaps a bit of bread and a spoon for the medicine?"

Robert nodded and disappeared to arrange the small meal. I eased back into my chair. Edwin kept a firm hold of my hand, squeezing it tight.

His eyes shot open after a moment, and he whipped his head toward me. "Grace?!" he exclaimed.

"Is fine, and Millicent has been apprehended. Grace witnessed her stab Mr. Boyle. And once Lord Pennington awakens, I am certain he will identify her as the culprit as well. And, of course, she stabbed you."

Edwin settled back into his pillow. "Good."

"Edwin," I said after a moment, "what were you doing at the folly?"

He attempted to shrug, wincing in pain. "I thought Grace was our man, so to speak. I hoped to use my considerable charms on her to solicit some information that may have helped." He offered a crooked grin.

"Your considerable charms nearly cost you your life," I said with an unimpressed glance at him.

"Yes," he said, a sheepish expression on his face. "If you hadn't found me when you did…"

"I did," I said, interrupting his statement before it turned too maudlin.

"How? What were you doing at the folly at that time of night?"

"Esme woke me and led me to you."

"Oh," he said, his brow crinkling. "Esme Murdoch? Grace's mother?"

"Yes," I answered. "She was quite insistent. Apparently, your charms still had an effect on her." I puckered my lips in an amused grin.

The statement earned a half-smile from him. "At least my charms still work on someone."

"At any rate, this whole nightmare should be over soon. I imagine you shall be cleared of any charges before we even return to Glasgow."

"Thank heavens," Edwin said as Robert returned with the meager meal.

* * *

We spent the next several days nursing Edwin back to health enough to travel to Glasgow. Word came the morning after Millicent's arrest that Lord Pennington had awoken and identified his attacker as Millicent. The investigator from Glasgow visited to take an official statement from Edwin and informed us the charges against him had been dropped.

We returned to Glasgow before continuing on to Blackmoore Castle. Robert visited with Lord Pennington and announced after the visit that the man would take in Millicent's child. Apparently his finances were slowly recovering. His argument with Fergus MacGuiness had been regarding taking their affairs to a more legitimate side of the law. He anticipated once the arrangements were made, he would be able to recover his wealth. Robert, of course, offered to back his project as long as it was above board.

I visited the cemetery. I had not spoken with Tilly since the entire matter unraveled at the MacMahon estate. I found her waiting near her gravestone.

"Lenora!" she cried.

"Hello, Tilly," I greeted her with a broad smile.

"I worried when I did not see you. I could not find you. I…"

"We traveled to Melrose to visit with friends of Robert."

"Oh," she said, sounding rather dejected. Her eyes fell to the ground below.

"And as a result, I have some wonderful news for you!"

Her eyebrows lifted, and she raised her eyes to meet mine. "We have identified the culprit in Mr. Boyle's murder. All the charges against Edwin have been dropped!"

"Lenora," she said, grasping my hands, "that's wonderful! However did you do it? And in Melrose?"

I explained the entire matter to her. She was shocked at the odd coincidence that Millicent should be the culprit. Tears fell onto her cheeks as I told her of Edwin's injury. I assured her Edwin would make a full recovery and asked her to visit the hotel before we departed the following day.

"It is odd that you cannot visit Blackmoore," I said, turning pensive as our conversation came to a close.

"I cannot understand it either. Perhaps because I never visited there in life."

My shoulders sagged. There was so much she hadn't been able to do in life. "Yes. Well, I hope to discover a way to allow you to visit there. I have not given up, Tilly!"

"Thank you, Lenora," she said, squeezing my hands.

"We will find a way," I promised.

"No, not just for that. For everything. For Edwin. For Sam."

I clasped her hands tightly. "There is no need for thanks, Tilly."

We said a tearful goodbye in which I swore to research the situation further in the hopes of allowing Tilly to appear to me at Blackmoore Castle. I returned to the carriage wiping tears from my cheeks.

Robert offered me a sympathetic smile. "Ready, darling?"

I nodded, unable to force words out. I waved out the carriage window at my friend as we pulled away from the cemetery.

* * *

When we returned to Blackmoore Castle, a surge of joy overtook me. As I spotted the castle high on the moor, surrounded by its usual mist, I could have cried with happiness. The journey, a bit hard on Edwin, had been slow-going. We arrived in the evening and settled in. I climbed to my tower room and spent an hour alone admiring the view from my window in quiet solitude.

Robert insisted the doctor visit the next day to oversee Edwin's recovery. He reported the patient continued to recover well. He would return in a few days' time to assess the progress made.

After he'd examined Edwin, I asked for a private word with him. I saw him off as we finished our discussion and wandered to the sitting room. I sank into an armchair there and bit my lower lip as I reflected on our conversation.

Robert entered moments later.

"Was that the doctor I saw leaving? What is his report on Edwin?"

"Yes. He says Edwin is making good progress, and he will check back in a few days."

"Good," Robert said as he poured himself a brandy.

"I also spoke with him," I said.

The statement caused Robert to whip around and eye me. With widened eyes, a myriad of unfounded statements spilled from his mouth. "Are you ill? Were you injured? Perhaps when you struck Millicent? No, likely all the traveling and roaming about in the cold. Have you a prognosis? Is it bronchitis? Pneumonia? Should you be out of bed? No more roaming about, Lenora!"

I held my hand up and shook my head. "I am not ill."

"Oh?" His eyebrows squashed together as he processed my statement. "Well, then why did you speak to the doctor?"

I offered him a demure smile and placed a hand against my abdomen. To further clarify, I offered, "I am with child."

Robert collapsed into the armchair across from me. His jaw hung agape, and he sat silent for several moments. I began to worry the news might be unwanted.

"Lenora," he finally managed. Then a smile spread across his face and he raised his eyes to meet mine. "This is simply wonderful!"

Pleased that the news was well-received, I smiled at him and reached for his hand. Our little family would expand soon. I wondered about my child. Would it be a boy or a girl? What would he or she be like? Would the child take after Robert or me?

While the child would bring us much joy, it would also propel me into a new and darker chapter in my life. But that, dear reader, is a story for another time.

***

Continue the series with *Asylum for a Duchess,* Book 3 in the Duchess of Blackmoore Mysteries.

A NOTE FROM THE AUTHOR

Dear Reader,

Thank you for reading this book! *Letter to a Duchess* is the second in Lenora's series. Lenora is a character I love to write. I enjoy her unique view on life and her forward thinking in an olden time.

I hope you enjoyed reading the story as much as I enjoyed writing it! If you did, please consider leaving a review and help get this book and series into the hands of other interested readers!

Keep reading for a sneak preview of *Shadows of the Past*, Book 1 in the *Shadow Slayers* series! If you enjoy supernatural suspense, you'll love the Slayers!

If you'd like to stay up to date with all my news, be the first to find out about new releases first, sales and get free offers, join the Nellie H. Steele's Mystery Readers' Group! Or sign up for my newsletter now!

All the best, Nellie

SHADOWS OF THE PAST
SYNOPSIS

If Josie doesn't confront what lurks in the shadows of her past to reclaim her life...it won't just be her own soul on the line.

Haunted by all-too-familiar bloody nightmares, Josie Benson's life is falling apart. Even the best medical professionals can't provide answers...though maybe the strange man who's stalking her every move can.

She sees him everywhere she goes, and she's drawn to him with a power she doesn't understand...until he shows up on her doorstep with an antique music box, calling her a name she almost remembers, and warns her that an old enemy has resurfaced.

An enemy she can't remember, who's coming for her and everything she loves. Including the very world she lives in.

When her nightmares seep over into visions more real than memories, Josie realizes she has to trust this mysterious stranger, recall every lost memory, and remember who she really is in order to save not only her family, but the world.

Fans of Dark Shadows and Beautiful Creatures will devour this supernatural mystery where family, fate, and desire collide.

Find out if Josie can discover the shadows lurking in her past in *Shadows of the Past*!

SHADOWS OF THE PAST EXCERPT

"Josie!" Damien called behind her. "JOSIE!" They caught up to her and Damien grabbed her elbow. "Josie, please, wait."

"D, sorry, this isn't the best time. I'm busy trying to get things figured out so we can get back to normal. Now, please, let me go. Go back to the house. Read a book or something and go home on Monday."

"No, Josie!" Damien said, "I will not accept that. No way!" Damien's insistence surprised Michael.

"D, please, I can't explain it now, I can't but I definitely want you and Michael to go. I'm pleading with you to leave."

"Why, Josie? This is beyond bizarre and I'm not leaving without you. I want you to come home with us."

"I can't come home yet, D, I can't."

"Why? Please, Josie."

"There is nothing to worry about. But I can't come home." She turned to leave.

"Josie, come on," he said, grabbing her arm again. "You can't expect us to go home and leave you here. Do you realize how bizarre this looks to ANYONE on the outside of it?"

She pondered for a moment. "I realize how bizarre it is,

yes. It's as bizarre as it was to me when Gray first approached me but it makes sense, it does, but I can't explain it. Now, please…"

"No, Josie," Damien continued, "no. I'm beyond worried about you. I'm exceptionally concerned. This bizarre story about you being someone named Celine who that kid told us lived here when his mother was a kid, these people bringing you here, you going along with it, have they brainwashed you? Are they threatening you or someone in our family?"

"No and no. I'm not brainwashed. They are not threatening me. I am here of my own free will, believe it or not. And I have other things to do. Now, please," Josie said, pulling away from Damien's grip and heading off down the path.

Damien opened his mouth to call after her but gave up, surmising it would be useless. Michael clapped a hand on his shoulder. "Well, we're right back where we started, still no information, but a terrible feeling that something is wrong."

"Something is wrong," Damien said, turning toward him. "And if Josie won't tell us, then I'll confront the guy who brought her here. One way or another we're getting some answers. Come on!"

Keep reading *Shadows of the Past* by clicking here!

OTHER SERIES BY NELLIE H. STEELE

Cozy Mystery Series

Cate Kensie Mysteries
Lily & Cassie by the Sea Mysteries
Pearl Party Mysteries
Middle Age is Murder Cozy Mysteries

Supernatural Suspense/Urban Fantasy

Shadow Slayers Stories
Duchess of Blackmoore Mysteries

Adventure

Maggie Edwards Adventures
Clif & Ri on the Sea

Made in the USA
Middletown, DE
29 February 2024